THERE IS
A SEASON

BOOKS BY GILBERT MORRIS

THE HOUSE OF WINSLOW SERIES

1. *The Honorable Imposter*
2. *The Captive Bride*
3. *The Indentured Heart*
4. *The Gentle Rebel*
5. *The Saintly Buccaneer*
6. *The Holy Warrior*
7. *The Reluctant Bridegroom*
8. *The Last Confederate*
9. *The Dixie Widow*
10. *The Wounded Yankee*
11. *The Union Belle*
12. *The Final Adversary*
13. *The Crossed Sabres*
14. *The Valiant Gunman*
15. *The Gallant Outlaw*
16. *The Jeweled Spur*
17. *The Yukon Queen*
18. *The Rough Rider*
19. *The Iron Lady*
20. *The Silver Star*
21. *The Shadow Portrait*
22. *The White Hunter*
23. *The Flying Cavalier*
24. *The Glorious Prodigal*
25. *The Amazon Quest*
26. *The Golden Angel*
27. *The Heavenly Fugitive*
28. *The Fiery Ring*
29. *The Pilgrim Song*
30. *The Beloved Enemy*
31. *The Shining Badge*
32. *The Royal Handmaid*
33. *The Silent Harp*
34. *The Virtuous Woman*
35. *The Gypsy Moon*
36. *The Unlikely Allies*

CHENEY DUVALL, M.D.[1]

1. *The Stars for a Light*
2. *Shadow of the Mountains*
3. *A City Not Forsaken*
4. *Toward the Sunrising*
5. *Secret Place of Thunder*
6. *In the Twilight, in the Evening*
7. *Island of the Innocent*
8. *Driven With the Wind*

CHENEY AND SHILOH: THE INHERITANCE[1]

1. *Where Two Seas Met*
2. *The Moon by Night*
3. *There Is a Season*

THE SPIRIT OF APPALACHIA[2]

1. *Over the Misty Mountains*
2. *Beyond the Quiet Hills*
3. *Among the King's Soldiers*
4. *Beneath the Mockingbird's Wings*
5. *Around the River's Bend*

LIONS OF JUDAH

1. *Heart of a Lion*
2. *No Woman So Fair*
3. *The Gate of Heaven*
4. *Till Shiloh Comes*
5. *By Way of the Wilderness*

[1]with Lynn Morris   [2]with Aaron McCarver

LYNN MORRIS
GILBERT MORRIS

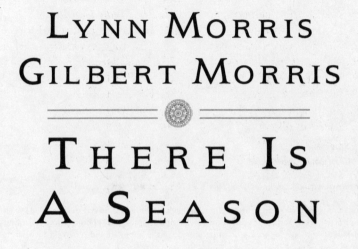

THERE IS
A SEASON

BETHANYHOUSE
MINNEAPOLIS, MINNESOTA

Published by Bethany House Publishers
11400 Hampshire Avenue South
Bloomington, Minnesota 55438
www.bethanyhouse.com

Bethany House Publishers is a division of
Baker Book House Company, Grand Rapids, Michigan.

Printed in the United States of America

ISBN 1-55661-573-6 (Paperback)
ISBN 0-7642-2798-X (Large Print)

Library of Congress Cataloging-in-Publication Data

Morris, Lynn.
    There is a season / by Lynn Morris & Gilbert Morris.
        p.   cm. — (Cheney & Shiloh : the inheritance ; bk. 3)
    Summary: "Historical novel set in 1870 St. Augustine, Florida. Cheney and Shiloh's vacation to Florida turns very mysterious and they wonder if perhaps Sangria House is not the haven they had thought it would be"—Provided by publisher.
    ISBN 1-55661-573-6 (pbk.)
    1. Duvall, Cheney (Fictitious character)—Fiction. 2. Saint Augustine (Fla.)—Fiction.
3. Women physicians—Fiction. 4. Married women—Fiction. I. Morris, Gilbert. II. Title
III. Series: Morris, Lynn. Cheney & Shiloh ; bk. 3.
    PS3563.O874439T47   2005
813'.54—dc22   2005008542

DEDICATION

To Ron, because you're not only family
but you're also a good and loyal friend.
To Stacy, because without your support
I never could have done it all.
To Andrea, because you're so sweet and you've
helped me so much more than you know.
And especially to Eric, because you always made me laugh
no matter how much I wanted to cry.
Thank you, with love.

GILBERT MORRIS & LYNN MORRIS are a father/daughter writing team who combine Gilbert's strength of great story plots and adventure with Lynn's research skills and character development. Together they form a powerful duo!

Lynn has also written a solo novel, *The Balcony,* in the PORTRAITS contemporary romance series with Bethany House. She lives in Atlanta, Georgia. Readers are invited to contact her at Lynn@morrisbooks.com.

ACKNOWLEDGMENTS

I must thank Professor Anil Aggrawal, because without his wonderful Web sites I never would have found out about thallium and many other interesting things that I imagine will show up in later books, with his kind permission.

Also, I'm very grateful to Ed Friedlander, MD, aka Ed the path guy, because his Web site taught me—and his great cartoons showed me—about autopsies. Ed, you're a true Renaissance man, because I also used some of your learned and fascinating notes on *Macbeth,* with thanks.

To every thing there is a season,
And a time to every purpose
Under the heaven. . . .

Ecclesiastes 3:1

CONTENTS

PART I

~◦►◦~

A TIME TO EMBRACE, AND A TIME TO REFRAIN FROM EMBRACING

Ecclesiastes 3:5

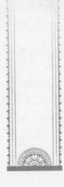

CHAPTER ONE

Siren's Song

AS LIGHT AND AIRY AS the downy feather from a swan, the snow-flake fluttered and danced coyly around Captain Geoffrey Starnes's cap, hesitated a moment, flitted lightly in a circle, and then fell slowly, slowly down to land on his shoulder. Shiloh Irons-Winslow stared hard at it and then muttered, "Looks like Calvin Lott's trick knee is a true oracle."

"It generally is," Captain Starnes agreed, "though I can hardly credit such old wives' tales. I'm not superstitious, as many seamen are."

"No, of course not," Shiloh said gravely. He had seen, many times, the captain of *Locke's Day Dream* whistle for a wind or scratch a backstay for luck.

As if some heavenly snow bowl had been overturned right above their heads, it suddenly started snowing hard with big dry flakes that zigged and zagged as they came down. The snow became so thick that it was impossible to pick out individual flakes; and all at once Shiloh and Captain Starnes could not see the dock of South Street Seaport Slip 15, where *Locke's Day Dream* was berthed.

Able Seaman Calvin Lott, a swarthy, sturdy British "tar" of the old school, limped by carrying an armload of wood. He gave them a look of grim triumph.

Captain Starnes said, "Lott, how is the new stove doing?"

Lott stopped, ducked his head in lieu of a salute since his arms were full, and answered, "Fair as fair, sir. She's drawing as pretty as you please and ne'er a whiff of neither smoke nor soot in the cabin. Dr. Cheney's sainted mother, Miss Irene, and her da' should be as warm as at their own hearth, sir."

"Good, good, Lott. Carry on."

In the viciously cold and icy winter of 1869 and 1870, Irene Duvall had suffered from influenza, and then a relapse, for months. In January and February Richard Duvall's old war wound had gone into rheumatism, and he had once again developed a limp and leaned heavily on a cane. Cheney and Dev had persuaded them to winter in Florida, and Dev and Victoria Buchanan had rented a plantation home—Sangria House—in St. Augustine. For the journey Shiloh had ordered that his cabin on *Locke's Day Dream* be outfitted with a cast-iron heating stove. Even though the trip to St. Augustine was expected to take only a few days, Shiloh knew that his mother- and father-in-law had not been feeling at all well this bleak winter, and he had determined to make the trip aboard his beloved ship as comfortable and enjoyable for them as was humanly possible.

Anxiously he looked up at the midnight sky. But all Shiloh saw were big white blobs of snowflakes falling into his eyes. "D'ya think it's gonna be all right?" he asked worriedly.

"If my forty-some-odd years of experience are worth anything," Captain Starnes replied, "I'd say we're going to be cold, but we should catch a good strong tide and make a clean break of it, Mr. Irons-Winslow. And of course, there's always Lott's knee. It twinges, says he, for snow; but there's na' the shooting searing pain of a snowstorm wi' banshee wind," he finished wryly in an excellent mimic of Lott's broad commoner's British. Captain Starnes had a cultured British accent.

Shiloh grinned and began to answer, but a small figure popped up suddenly in front of the two men.

"It will not do, sir! It simply will not do!" he said in a high squeaking voice. It was Phinehas Beddoes Jauncy, Shiloh's valet, a short excitable little man.

"Calm down, PJ. What's the trouble?" Shiloh asked.

Dramatically Jauncy answered, "I have just now discovered that in her haste Fiona packed the two alpaca lap robes!"

Shiloh waited; Jauncy stared at him with clear outrage. Finally Shiloh asked hesitantly, "And . . . this is . . . a bad thing, I guess?"

"Sir! Have you forgotten? Alpaca! Mrs. Irons-Winslow prefers the cashmere lap robes, for she finds alpaca chafes!"

"Alpaca chafes?" Shiloh repeated, mystified.

"It is entirely unacceptable," Jauncy almost shouted. "I simply must return to Gramercy Park and find the—"

"No," Shiloh asserted. "No one's leaving this ship. It was like herding a flock of cats to get you all here, and I'm not going through that again."

Shiloh had brought Jauncy, Sketes, Fiona, and the two dogs, Sean and Shannon, aboard, along with all of their luggage and supplies. Cheney and Dev were coming with Irene and Richard, while Victoria had the entire Buchanan entourage with her. There was to be a favorable tide at midnight, but Captain Starnes had wanted to wait until at least eight o'clock that evening to gauge the weather before he decided whether or not to leave.

Finally he had decided that they would be able to catch the midnight tide and have clear sailing on this night of February 22, and he had sent word of his decision to all of the parties at nine o'clock. The three families had been ready to sail since February 15, but since snow threatened every day, they had been obliged to wait until Captain Starnes judged that the weather would not be so heavy as to keep them in port.

Shiloh took out his watch and held it close under the lantern over the binnacle. "Ten thirty-eight," he announced. "You're definitely not leaving, PJ. Just run along, will you, and check the big cabin? I want to be sure that Colonel Duvall and Miss Irene have everything they need and will be as comfortable as we can make them. See if I've forgotten anything."

"Sir, I'll be glad to see to it, but there is also the matter of the missing glove case," Jauncy said, agitated. "Do you also suggest that we sail without your *glove case*?"

"I have a glove case?" Shiloh asked blankly.

"Sir!"

"All right, all right. And so it's . . . uh . . . missing? What does it look like—oh, forget it, PJ! I've got gloves on. They'll just have to do."

"But, sir, those are leather gauntlets! Your kid driving gloves, and your dress white gloves, and your black suit gloves, and—"

"PJ, I'll get new gloves if I have to," Shiloh said. "But for now, just go check on the cabin and then get below. You look like a little frozen sorbet."

Jauncy was wearing a black wool overcoat and a fashionable black wool top hat with a bright green scarf under it, tied beneath his chin. But still he was shivering and his nose was bright red. "Yes, sir, American humor," he said sourly. "Very well. But when Mrs. Irons-Winslow breaks out in hives because of the alpaca lap robes, and when you cannot find your white dress gloves, it will not be on my head."

"No, PJ, it will not be on your head," Shiloh agreed solemnly, winking at Captain Starnes, who was pretending not to hear. But he did look vastly amused.

Jauncy saw the wink, sniffed disdainfully, turned on his heel, and disappeared into the swirling snow.

"Y'know, Cap'n Starnes," Shiloh drawled, "life sure seemed a lot easier when I was a poor, homeless, unloved orphan."

"Yes, sir."

"I'm not complaining, mind you," Shiloh went on, "but sometimes it seems like bein' the head of a household just means that you got more people to boss you. Lots and lots of people, it seems like sometimes. And dogs too."

"Yes, sir," Captain Starnes said again, his dark eyes alight.

A short plump figure now materialized in front of Shiloh: Molly Sketes, wrapped up so thickly in so many layers that she looked more like a big round woolen ball than a human. Still, she managed to put two short arms akimbo and said accusingly, "Sir, there is not a drop of goat's milk, and could I find any molasses at all? No, sir, I could not!"

"Goat's milk?" Shiloh repeated, glancing guiltily at Captain Starnes. The dignified authoritative captain looked as alarmed as did Shiloh.

Sketes said to both men, speaking in a slow deliberate voice as if she addressed idiots, "Goat's milk. Milk-from-a-goat. I know Mrs. Buchanan's told you that little Dart must have it once a day for his puny digestion! And what about those two dogs? Did you forget, Mr. Shiloh, that Sean and Shannon need goat's milk? For their shiny coats?"

"Er—no, I didn't exactly forget, Sketes . . ." he began.

But just then Calvin Lott stumped up to them, put a knuckle to his forehead, and said, "That there little girl dog, what with the little red stockings and muffler, just ran down the gangplank, sir. Shall I send someone to fetch her back?"

Shiloh groaned and took off running. Lott, with a questioning glance at Captain Starnes, whirled and limped after him.

Sketes, her mittened hands still planted indignantly on her hips, turned her accusing gaze on Captain Starnes.

"Goat's milk, you said. I'll see to it," he said abruptly, then turned on his heel and hurried off.

Sketes rolled her eyes. "It'll be by the grace of the good Lord alone," she muttered to herself as she made her way back to the galley, "if we get everyone and everything on board, in one piece and not half froze to death, to catch this midnight tide. By the grace of the good Lord alone!"

And so, at ten minutes after midnight, the harbor tugs pulled the great clipper ship *Locke's Day Dream* out of port, past Sandy Hook, a great soaring shadow in the swirling snow.

She glided, dark and silent and majestic, out into the Atlantic Ocean, and by the grace of the good Lord sailed south to light and warmth and the siren's song of the southern seas.

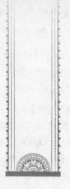

CHAPTER TWO

Dead Right

LOCKE'S DAY DREAM arrived in St. Augustine waters three days later, on the twenty-fifth, about a half hour before midnight, and the storm arrived an hour later. It wasn't a dangerous storm—to ships such as *Locke's Day Dream,* anyway—but Captain Starnes, like all true sailors, feared a shore under his lee when the sea was wild. The tide was supposed to be on the wane, but the storm brought with it tricky gusts of high winds and choppy seas and vengeful darts of lightning. The great lighthouse on Anastasia Island bravely shone out in the torrid darkness, but its light was a warning, not a comfort.

Shiloh came up on the main deck and found Captain Starnes standing on the lee rail, his hands clasped tightly behind his back, staring through the squall toward the shore. At least Shiloh assumed it was the shore that the captain was sighting. Shiloh himself couldn't see a blessed thing except a sort of watery blurry film over his eyes from single raindrops boring into them as if they were aiming. At least it was warm rain instead of ice needles, he reflected ruefully.

"So that's St. Augustine?" he asked Captain Starnes.

"No, that's St. Augustine Inlet. To port is Matanzas Island, to starboard is Conch Island, and in between the two is a small passage into Matanzas Bay. The mainland is about three miles in."

Shiloh felt a cold finger of dread trace lightly down his spine. *The Day Dream—my father's ship—wrecked trying to thread a sea needle, almost like that passage, during a hurricane in Charleston. Loss of all souls . . .*

Except me.

It gave Shiloh the oddest feeling, for he had always pictured the wreck of the *Day Dream,* and the death of his mother and father, as if he were an omniscient being, with mind and eyes only, standing far away, gazing at them dispassionately. He had never before had to worry about having flesh or blood or sorrow during these visions.

Now, for the first time, he felt a strange shift in his eyes and mind, as if he were truly his father, Rory Winslow, on his deck of the *Day Dream* trying to sight through the maelstrom to James Island, talking to his captain, worrying about his wife and son and his son's sweet nurse, Pearl, and the other seamen and servants and friends on board. It gave Shiloh a clammy, shaky, fearful feeling, and for the first time in his life he felt a link with his father, inextricably binding them together forever.

He knew now that his father would have been fearful for everyone on his ship, but there was one who would have filled his heart and thoughts and mind, the one who completed him as a person: Kallan Torbjörn Winslow. His wife. Shiloh's mother.

And though the thought of losing any of his friends or family or even his ship or crew would have hurt Shiloh terribly, the thought of losing one person—Cheney Duvall—frightened him so much that he felt sick deep in his gut.

"We're not going in tonight," he growled.

Captain Starnes looked up. Although the storm was noisy, the thunder crashing and roaring and the sea pounding like timpani against the sides of the ship, he heard the rough edge in Shiloh's voice. "Yes, sir," he finally said evenly. "I wouldn't like to attempt it in these seas."

Shiloh nodded curtly. "So what do you mean to do? Sail back out to sea, ride it out?"

Captain Starnes began to answer, but just then Devlin Buchanan appeared through the sheets of black rain. He was wearing an oilskin raincoat that he clutched tightly about the neck and was clapping a floppy oilskin hat onto his head for dear life. As always, Shiloh's well-worn knee-high cavalry boots, along with his dependable old canvas "fishskin" duster and wide-brimmed cavalry hat, had stood him in good stead through years of all kinds of weather in all sorts of climates. He sternly made himself stop laughing inwardly at Devlin Buchanan, who was, after all, only a hopeless landlubber, and gave him a quick hand to stop him from slipping down and perhaps sliding right out a scupper into Matanzas Bay. "Evenin', Buchanan," he said easily. "Quite a night, huh?"

"Yes, quite," Dev gasped. "Shiloh, the great cabin is flooding. Is the ship going down?"

"Huh? No! I mean, no, Buchanan, it's not even a remote possibility. It's just a good blow, is all," he added in a kinder voice. Captain Starnes, swaying easily with the heaving deck, looked back toward his lee shore and pursed his lips but said nothing. Shiloh went on, now with concern, "You said the cabin's flooded? Is Miss Irene upset?"

"No, no, she's . . . calmer than I am, actually," Dev said. He made a funny little bobble again and grasped Shiloh's outstretched hand like a lifeline. "But, Shiloh, I'm concerned about her. It's very chilly and clammy in the cabin, and of course we put the fires out when this . . . this . . . tempest began. And although she hasn't mentioned it, I believe she may be feeling the first symptoms of seasickness. I think she would do much better in a warm—and unmoving—bed."

"Right," Shiloh agreed. He turned to Captain Starnes. "I think I'd better go ashore and see if we could get the ladies to Sangria House tonight. I'll just take the dinghy—"

"Begging your pardon, Mr. Irons-Winslow," Captain Starnes said sternly, "but I don't think that would be wise. My crew will take you ashore in the launch." The captain's crew, with the captain's coxswain in charge, consisted of the most skillful boat crewmen on the ship. Shiloh didn't particularly feel the need for seven sailors to baby-sit him, but he had found out very early that the captain of the ship was the boss, and it didn't matter if you were the owner of the ship or the King of Siam, whatever the captain said was law.

"All right, Cap'n," Shiloh agreed.

"I'm going," Dev grumbled, turning to make his treacherous way back to the hatch leading below to the passengers' cabins.

"Wait, Buchanan," Shiloh said, grabbing his arm. "You're going to go down that hatch head first if you don't let somebody give you a hand." Shiloh started walking Dev along, holding on to his arm, pulling him and steadying him at the same time so he could remain upright. "You don't have to go ashore with me, you know," he said kindly. "It's a miserable night."

"You're not miserable. You're just fine," Dev said accusingly.

"Well . . . yeah. But I've—"

"Forget it. I'm going. If I have to be miserable and wet and cold, I'd rather at least be standing on solid earth. But I need you to tell Cheney to get Miss Irene warmed up a little. See if Sketes or someone could come up with a warming pan for her feet, or maybe some bricks or something could be heated in the galley. Colonel Duvall was looking exhausted too, so ask Cheney to give them both some warm brandy. Give me about ten minutes to wring out my clothes and to tell Victoria I'm going ashore, and then I'll be ready."

Saint Augustine, Florida, was a small, very old town. Ponce de León touched ground here in 1513 on *Pascua Florida,* which was Easter Sunday, but the phrase literally means *feast of flowers,* and so the explorer named this lovely land *Florida.*

But Shiloh and Dev and the launch's crew saw no flowers nor any feasts as they neared the mainland. Brooding above them, blocking the view and utterly commanding the small bay, was Castillo de San Marcos, the great Spanish fort built of *coquina,* a native shell stone quarried on Anastasia Island. It looked as out of place as a dinosaur in the New World.

Coxswain Billy O'Shaughnessy roared commands to the launch crew as they rowed past the giant fort into the calmer waters of Matanzas Bay. The rain still fell in semisolid sheets, but the wind had abated, and the thunder and stabbing lightning seemed farther away, less threatening. The launch pulled up neatly alongside one of the small piers so that even Dev was able to step up onto the pier without faltering. He and Shiloh stood silently surveying the town—at least what they could see of it. Shiloh and Dev knew, from detailed handmade maps, that Mr. Grider, the owner of Sangria House and Plantation, had explained in a letter to Victoria that St. Augustine was actually on a long thin spit of land that was almost an island. The Matanzas River flowed along the east side of the island and opened up into the Atlantic Ocean, and the San Sebastian River ran along the west side. St. Augustine had grown up on the fertile peninsula, and the town was only seven blocks abreast at its widest part. The pier where the launch docked was just at the foot of a wide cross street, and on the corner was, of course, a tavern.

Shiloh pointed to it. "Guess that's our best bet," he bawled in Dev's ear. The rain was pounding down harder now, though the thunder and lightning had stopped.

Dev nodded, still clutching his hat and oilskin tightly. They hurried to the saloon, which was just like a million others in the world that sprung up like toadstools in every seaport. It was a rickety shabby shanty with one dim lantern outside and one dim lantern inside. Women's raucous shrieks of laughter, men's gruff growls, and the staccato blaring of an upright piano being played badly came to their ears as they neared, along with the inevitable reek of tobacco and stench of whiskey.

Shiloh looked back before he went in and saw that Billy O'Shaughnessy and Calvin Lott had followed them.

Shiloh shook his head. "No liberty for anyone tonight, Billy-O."

The coxswain was a swaggering, handsome foretopman, while Calvin Lott was an old hand, swarthy from decades of sea, sun, and salt. They both assumed melodramatically injured expressions, and Billy-O said, "No, sir, Mr. Locke, no liberties tonight, we know. We've got to get Dr. Cheney settled in, o'course, and what about her sainted mother, Miss Irene? And Dr. Buchanan's lady? We're just here to help you get the landsmen and . . . er . . . women . . . ladies snug at home."

Shiloh narrowed his eyes suspiciously but then nodded and went inside the tavern.

Dev huddled up on the small porch, took off his hat, and turned it upside down, and a veritable river of water streamed out. His black hair was flattened to his head and soaked. Water dripped from the corners of his mustache. The two sailors, standing out in the rain unconcernedly, watched him. Dev sighed and gave them a slight nod, which they returned coolly.

To the sailors, Devlin Buchanan and Victoria and their entourage were just high-hat rich passengers who had nothing to do with *Locke's Day Dream,* and therefore nothing to do with them or their lives or their world. It was different with Cheney and Shiloh; they belonged to the ship. In a sense, they belonged to the crew. This was why they felt, and expressed, the odd familiarity with Cheney's mother and father. Most of them didn't know that Dev was the Duvalls' adopted son, and it wouldn't have made any difference if they did. It was because of Locke, her husband, that Cheney belonged to the ship, and it was because of Cheney that her parents were bound to *Locke's Day Dream.* Dev had nothing to do with these ties of blood and ship and sea. That was just the way it was.

In a short time Shiloh came back out. "No cabs or carriages tonight. The saloonkeeper knows Sangria House, and he thinks they keep a buggy and stables, but he doubts Grider would have sent the carriage and driver into town to wait for us."

"Do we know where Sangria House is?" Dev asked.

"Yeah, it's straight along this street. The saloonkeeper says this is King Street, which goes straight across town and right past the gates of Sangria Plantation, a little over a mile from here."

Dev said tentatively, "It is my understanding that the plantation has a carriage and horses that are ours to use while we're here, so I suppose we could walk to Sangria House, hitch up the buggy, and come back to fetch the others."

Shiloh frowned, crossed his arms, and stared into the far distance. He, too, like the sailors, seemed oblivious to the rain, the cold, the discomfort, the uncertainty.

Dev admired this about Shiloh and reflected ruefully that he would probably never be that rough-and-tough, devil-may-care, take-on-anyone-or-anything kind of man. What Dev didn't realize was that he did have the same confidence and natural authority when he was in his own element, which was with patients or facing risky surgeries or life-threatening traumas. *Doctor* Devlin Buchanan was every bit as tough and dauntless as Shiloh Irons-Winslow.

But right now Dev was just cold and tired and discouraged.

Shiloh finally focused again and nodded to himself, a sign that he'd made up his mind. "Buchanan, you'd do better to go back to the ship and see about Miss Irene. But I got kind of a bad feeling about this whole deal, so I'm going to go on to Sangria House." He turned to the two sailors. "Billy-O, you take the doctor back to the ship, and then in a couple of hours come on back and wait down at the pier for me. I'll either be there or I'll send word."

Billy-O and Calvin Lott both looked mutinous. "Mr. Locke, sir, the boys can row Dr. Buchanan back dry. It seems like the rain and wind's slacking a bit," Billy-O argued. "We could come with you, sir, and give you a hand with looking into that place. It might even be that you'd need to send one of us back here, rather than you coming yourself, if need be."

Shiloh considered, and then nodded. "You're right. Okay, Billy-O, go on down with Dr. Buchanan and tell Siggy that he can cox'n back and return here in two hours. We'll either have the buggy here to pick up Miss Irene or one of us will be here with word of what's going on."

While Billy-O was making his arrangements, Shiloh went back into the tavern to get more explicit directions. The saloonkeeper, a short round man with a bulbous nose and shiny bald pate, roared over the noisy din, "If you get to the gates and the gatekeeper's lodge, you've gone too far; old Grider wouldn't never pay no gatekeeper, not a penny would he. Turn back around and look for a little drive, just a path, really. It's a tradesman's entrance for carts and the like, and it goes right down to the big house."

Shiloh, Billy-O, and Lott were healthy strong men, and one of Cheney's hot poultices had, it seemed, healed Lott's trick knee. They made the walk to Sangria Plantation in no time. They found the small carriage drive that cut through the citrus groves, and as they entered the groves Shiloh saw a light off to his right flickering weakly through the torrent, and he knew that must be the north gatekeeper's lodge. Shiloh knew that his cousin Bain and Mrs. Buchanan's brothers, Carsten and Beckett Steen, were joining the party and were to stay in the two gate-keeper's lodges on the plantation. He didn't know if Bain and his servant Sweet were in this—the north lodge—or whether Beckett and Carsten had chosen that one and Bain and Sweet were in the south lodge. It didn't make much difference to the situation, at any rate. The four men had come to St. Augustine on two yachts, so they wouldn't have a carriage and horses at their disposal either.

Unless Beckett and Carsten bought an outfit, Shiloh thought wryly. *They'd be more likely to do that than to put up with some rented nag and cart. Just like Mrs. Buchanan . . .*

Shiloh was friends with both Beckett and Carsten, who had been part of the Young Jackanapes, as Polly Slopes, Cleve Batson's housekeeper, had dubbed them; or the Fine and Dandies, as the press had dubbed them when they were a rowdy bunch of young men on the town in the months leading up to Victoria and Dev's wedding. Those had been Shiloh's wild days, before he had become a Christian, but that was not the reason he hadn't been out on the town with the Fine and Dandies much in the last two years. It was, of course, because he was now a staid, solid married man. But Shiloh had noted that while in New York, his cousin Bain had been going around town with the Fine and Dandies—Beckett and Carsten Steen, Dr. Cleve Batson, Troy Bondurant, and Austin Darrow.

The rain had slackened down to a mean drizzle as they trudged down the muddy cart path that ended at the detached kitchen. They stared up at the big house. The windows were dark. The kitchen was dark. Turning, Shiloh gazed back across the lawn at the servants' cottages; they were all dark. The place had the unmistakable air of desertion, the settled stillness of an empty place. Though he knew very well that no one was in the house—Shiloh had that kind of intuition—he went up to the massive wooden door and banged on it. The blows sounded hollow and echoed back, sounding like deep laughter. The three men waited, but no warm lantern was lit, no sash thrown open for someone to call down a welcome.

Shiloh turned to consider the servants' cottages again, rejected them as a hopeless cause, and then went back up the cart path. Wordlessly Billy-O and Calvin Lott followed, exchanging knowing glances that said in their particular language, *Can't trust a landsman for naught; it's a good thing we're along to look after Mr. Locke and Dr. Cheney and her sainted mother, Miss Irene . . . .*

Cutting through the grove, Shiloh went straight to the front door of the gatekeeper's lodge, a welcoming-looking cottage, one low story with a red-tiled roof, built in a U shape to enclose a small courtyard in the Spanish manner. Through the lead-paned windows the light inside dissipated to a round soft yellow glowing ball. Shiloh knocked on the door. He heard a woman's voice, alarmed but giggling, some thumps and bumps, and his cousin Bain call out, "Sweet? What are you doing back! Just a minute, man—"

The door flew open, and Bain stood staring at Shiloh in disbelief.

Bain Winslow was not nearly as tall as his first cousin; he was five-ten and slim with glossy dark brown hair and light, almost tan, brown eyes. His complexion was smooth and full, though he had developed some crow's-feet at the corner of his eyes, mostly because he had become something of an outdoorsman since moving to the Caribbean island of Bequia. He no longer had the fleshy, doughy look of a dissipated man. He was tan and vital and strong. Now twenty-nine years old, Bain actually looked younger than he had several years ago when Shiloh had first seen him.

His shirt was unbuttoned to his waist. He held a brandy snifter in one hand and a candle in the other. When he grinned, his teeth were very white and even, and his eyes were sparkling with that certain glint of someone who had been drinking but was not drunk, only rowdy. Cocking one booted foot toe down and leaning against the doorframe he said, "Well, good evening, Locke. If I had known you were coming, I would have thrown a party."

Shiloh rolled his eyes. "Sounds like you're partying enough for the both of us, Bain. And you did know I was coming today."

He shrugged. "Didn't, old man. Sorry."

"But Mrs. Buchanan said that it was understood that Mr. Grider would have the house all ready for our arrival either yesterday or today," Shiloh said. "You and Beckett and Carsten knew that, right?"

"No, sorry," Bain said shortly and took a sip of brandy. Hearing a noise behind him, he quickly moved to stand square in the doorway and pull the door almost closed at his back.

Shiloh watched him curiously. He knew Bain was acting strangely, but he figured it was because he had a woman in the cottage and didn't want Shiloh to know. Shiloh reflected that it was none of his business. He had no intention of trying to rule his cousin's life—as long as what he was doing was legal, and Shiloh had no reason to assume that the lady giggling in the back room was there against her will.

"But didn't Mr. Grider know that we were arriving today?" Shiloh persisted. "I mean, you're here. Didn't he make arrangements for the servants to have the house ready for the rest of the party?"

Bain narrowed his eyes to slits that glittered in the orange candlelight. "I have no idea what Grider knew or didn't know. Why are you asking me all these questions, Locke?" he asked suspiciously.

With exasperation Shiloh retorted, "Bain, all I want is to get into the house, and the reason I'm asking you these questions is because I don't know how to find out how to get in!"

One of Bain's eyebrows twitched upward, a peculiarity of the Winslow men. Shiloh did it sometimes too, though at the moment his brow was dark and lowering. Bain almost grinned. "Well, Locke, whyever didn't you say so in the first place? You need to go wake up the Espys, the servants. They'll know more than I know."

"Sure hope so," Shiloh rasped. "So just where are these servants?"

"In one of the servants' cottages," Bain answered, obviously baiting him.

Shiloh glared at him.

"Oh, very well, Locke, I was just trying to have a little fun with you, but I can see you're not in the mood. They're in the second cottage in the front row."

"Well, thanks, Bain, you've been so helpful," Shiloh said, turning on his heel. Then he turned back. "By the way, Bain, is there a carriage and horse here? On the estate?"

Bain's aristocratic features went suddenly very bland, as though trying to figure out whether or not to tell the truth. His eyes glazed, and he stared off behind Shiloh's shoulder. "Yes," he finally answered. "That is—no. I don't know, Locke."

Shiloh rolled his eyes. "It's not a trick question, Bain. I just need to know if—oh, forget it. Go back to your party, Cousin. The grown-ups will handle this."

"Fine, Old Cuz, Old Stick!" Bain called, now rowdy and raucous again as he went back inside and closed the door.

Shiloh and his two silent shadows went back toward the servants' cottages. But Shiloh stopped when they came to the drive, for one outbuilding was obviously a stable and another probably a carriage house. He went into the stable and was surprised to see that it was full—or very nearly. Slowly walking down the central isle between the stalls, he noted there was one empty corner stall in which they could put Bellah, the goat they'd brought on the trip.

There was a Morgan trotting horse, sleek and smart, who tossed his head as Shiloh looked into his stall. Right next to him a shaggy, sturdy cart pony munched thoughtfully on some hay and watched Shiloh sleepily. There was a fine black, an Arabian stallion; and a sleepy chestnut, obviously a comfortable old saddle horse. In the stall next to the chestnut was a huge gray gelding, a muscular animal that looked about two years old, who eyed Shiloh suspiciously and stamped one hind foot.

In the largest corner stall at the very end of the long building, a snappy little Thoroughbred mare rolled her eyes and pranced. A lady's sidesaddle, finely tooled with ornate silver fittings, hung on the stall's saddle rest. Reaching over to stroke the lively little horse, Shiloh smiled and murmured, "So you belong to the mystery lady. She does have good taste in horses."

Behind him, standing stiffly and obviously uneasy, Calvin Lott and Billy-O rolled their eyes. They trusted nothing on the fixed earth, most especially large unpredictable beasts such as horses.

Next Shiloh looked into the barn, and sure enough, he found a brougham and a cart inside. "Right," he said with satisfaction to the sailors. "At least we're not afoot." They agreed, but both men looked as if they'd prefer being afoot.

Shiloh led Lott and Billy-O straight to the servants' cottages and knocked on the second one in the front row. "Hello!" he bawled out. "Mr. Espy? It's Shiloh Irons-Winslow, from the party that has leased Sangria House!"

They heard a man's voice calling faintly, "Just a minute. Stop that infernal noise, and I'll be along in just a minute!"

Finally they heard scratches as the door was unlocked and creaked open a tiny crack to reveal a candle and a single eye. "I have a gun!" the man growled.

"So do I," Shiloh said dryly, "but I won't shoot you if you won't shoot me. You are Mr. Espy, I presume? I am Shiloh Irons-Winslow. I'm with the Buchanan party."

The eye blinked.

Shiloh tried again. "Mrs. Victoria Buchanan's party? She has leased Sangria House for three months."

The door didn't open any further.

Despairing, Shiloh asked, "Are there any other servants of the plantation? Does Mr. Grider have an overseer, perhaps? Or a steward?"

A woman, unseen, snorted, and her waspish voice darted out from behind the man's back. "As if that old penny grubber would pay anyone when he's got us to do all his dirty work for starvation wages!"

The man turned, said something in a low voice to the woman, and then turned back. "We don't know nothing about this woman nor this lease nor anything else. And we're the only servants on the place."

The door began to close, but Shiloh was losing patience, and he stepped up, stopped the door, and then pushed it open even farther. The man stepped back, and Shiloh saw the couple clearly: a man of average height with sorrowful dark eyes and dark thin hair, gaunt hands and hollowed cheeks. A woman with an unpleasant look in her hard eyes and deep dissatisfaction lines running from her nose to the down-turned corners of her mouth.

Shiloh said firmly but not unpleasantly, "Mr. and Mrs. Espy? I am sorry to disturb you at this late hour, but there is a large party here, and I assure you that Dr. and Mrs. Buchanan have made arrangements with Mr. Grider to lease Sangria House for the next three months. Mr. Grider has told you nothing about this?"

The man gave his wife a furtive glance out of the corner of his eye. Her mouth tightened, but she said nothing. Finally Mr. Espy muttered, "We didn't know nothing about Mr. Grider and his *arrangements*."

"But someone must have known something about our party," Shiloh said with exasperation, "because my cousin Bain Winslow is already in the north gatekeeper's lodge, and I assume that Beckett and Carsten Steen are in the south lodge. Right?"

"I dunno," the man said stubbornly. "I dunno anything about Mr. Grider's goings-on."

"We are not 'goings-on'! We're perfectly respectable people who just ... well," Shiloh went on in a more good-natured tone as he reflected about his cousin, and Beckett and Carsten Steen. "Some of us are anyway. Sir, ma'am, listen to me. Our party, which includes my wife and her parents, need to move into Sangria House as soon as possible. I am here to see when, exactly, that might be. Now, are you going to let me into the house, or am I going to have to break into it?"

Once again the couple exchanged dark glances. They obviously didn't know that Shiloh was joking. Neither of them seemed the type to have a very keen sense of humor.

Finally the man said begrudgingly, "Well, I got a key to the back door, the servants' entrance. I guess I'll let you in."

"I would greatly appreciate it," Shiloh said with relief. "I really didn't intend to break in, you know."

The man's dark eyes narrowed as he slid silently back to close the door. "Uh-huh," he said with disbelief. "I'll be a minute, getting the key and getting dressed and such. And Flo, she's coming with us, to see to it." The door closed decisively.

"Oh, good," Shiloh said brightly to the door. He turned to Billy-O and Calvin Lott. "Flo's coming. To see to it, you know."

"Uh-huh," Calvin Lott said in an eerie echo of Espy's grunt. Billy-O hid a smile.

"I feel so much better now," Shiloh said, and Billy-O barked out a laugh. Calvin Lott gave him a dark glance; Lott was of the old school of sailors who thought it was an "impert-NANCE," as he pronounced it, to be too familiar with owners or officers.

But Billy-O was younger and an all-American boy, unlike the old Royal Navy Lott, and he and Shiloh exchanged quips until Espy came back out holding a lantern.

"We'll go now," Espy said, and he and his wife went straight up the drive, never looking back to see if Shiloh and the men were following.

But they were, and when Espy reached the back door, he pulled out a three-inch-long heavy iron key, fit it into the keyhole, jiggled it around with heavy dull metal scrapes until it engaged the tumblers, and with loud metal creaks, drew the bolts.

"That must be a really old lock," Shiloh commented.

With seeming reluctance, Mrs. Espy explained, "All the doors and

locks in the house are originals. Spanish, they are, from when Don Francisco Becerra built Sangria House in 1761."

"Really?" Shiloh said, impressed. "I had no idea the house was that
old."

Espy pushed open the four-inch-thick oak door. It was utter dark
inside.

"This here's the entry into the servants' workroom," Mrs. Espy said
with just slightly less ill humor. "Extry house lanterns stored in here."
She opened a cupboard door with the quick practiced movements of long
familiarity, pulled out a lantern, checked the oil, rolled up the wick, lit
it, replaced the glass chimney, and handed it to Billy-O without a word.

Shiloh stepped just inside the door, stopped, and sniffed. "Smells
close, closed up. Not musty, just not aired." He turned to Mrs. Espy,
who stiffened and looked temperamental again. "I'm not criticizing your
housekeeping, Mrs. Espy. It's just that we were expecting to have the
house cleaned, aired, fires built, stores put up."

She put her hands on her hips and tipped her head. Lott glowered at
her, but she just tilted her chin up and said, "Ain't none of those things
done because Mr. Grider never told us about no party coming here."

"That's right," Espy said, as if Shiloh were arguing.

Wearily Shiloh took off his hat and smoothed his wet hair off his
brow. "I understand that, Mr. Espy," he said, speaking slowly and deliberately. "I'm just trying to figure out what to do now."

Mrs. Espy said smartly, "Well, I don't spose there's much you can do
now, young man. There's no firewood, no stores, no cleaned linens, and
no one who'll wait on you hand and foot—"

"Now wait just a minute there," Lott finally roared, unable to take
any more. "You mind your sauce, ma'am. Don't you know who you're
talking to? That's Mr. Locke Winslow!"

She snapped, "And I don't b'lieve that's the name he give us when
he came banging on my door and hollerin' fit to raise the dead, now is
it, Mr. Smarty Pigtail! And he did confess right up that he was going to
break into the house anyways. Maybe we should have just waited and
called the sheriffs on the lot of you!"

"Go ahead, woman, I'd love to see some popinjay of a sheriff try to
arrest Colonel Richard Duvall!" Lott shouted.

"Lott! That's enough," Shiloh ordered.

"But, sir!"

"We must be polite to the ladies, Lott," Shiloh said. "Always. Mrs.

Espy, you are exactly right. There is some confusion about my names; even I'm confused by 'em all sometimes. But I assure you, we do have a lawful claim on Sangria House. Now please, just show me the rest of the house."

With a single triumphant glance at Lott, Mrs. Espy turned, grabbed the lantern from her husband, whose sole reason for being there, it seemed, was to stand dumbly by while his wife "saw to" everything, and went out into a large room on their right. "Now then. This here is the dining room, as you can see by the—What's that? Jerome! He left his food out and we didn't—"

Mrs. Espy's mouth shut with an audible click when Jerome Espy lowered his head and shook it imperceptibly.

Shiloh walked to the long dining table. In the dim lamplight the long rows of chairs—there were nine on each side—somehow looked ominous. The one chair that was out of place gave the impression that perhaps some ghostly diner had just hastily pushed the chair back and hurried off when they entered the room, leaving behind a plate with the remains of a mutton chop and hunk of bread, a crude glass tumbler, and an empty wine bottle. Shiloh noted that the bottle had no label and wondered if the people who owned the house had made it themselves.

As he neared the table there was a sudden movement and a furtive scurrying of something that the lantern light didn't quite reveal. Mrs. Espy gave a little scream, Jerome Espy grunted, startled, and even Shiloh and the doughty sailors flinched. Shiloh grabbed the lantern from Billy-O and held it up. "Just a rat," he said with disgust.

"There!" Mrs. Espy exclaimed in a high, excited voice. "He would leave his food out, and o' course there's rats! There's rats!"

She threw herself against her husband, and he put one long arm around her. "It's all right, Flo. The rat's gone." Looking up, he told Shiloh, "She don't like rats."

Shiloh sighed. "I got some ladies with me that aren't going to be too crazy 'bout 'em either. Look, Espy, why don't you take Mrs. Espy on home. I'll finish looking around by myself, and then I'll decide what to do. I don't suppose you two have any intention of working while we're here?"

"Ain't paid to be your servants," Espy said defiantly.

"Fine," Shiloh said shortly. "We won't be bothering you again. Except—wait a minute, where does that door go to?"

Espy looked up the dim hallway to the massive door at which Shiloh was pointing. "That goes down to the wine cellar," Espy answered. "We ain't never had no key to the wine cellar, you can bet." He turned again, still holding his wife close.

"Just a minute, Espy, I need to know about the keys. Do all of the rooms have doors with keyed locks?"

"Yes," he threw over his shoulder, "but the only ones Mr. Grider kept locked always was the outside doors and the wine cellar."

"But don't you have a key to the front door?" Shiloh asked, following them out through the workroom, envisioning Victoria Elizabeth Steen de Lancie Buchanan coming through the back servants' entrance.

Mrs. Espy whirled, and to Shiloh's astonishment she was crying. "No! Leave us alone! We don't know nothing about keys, and you're not welcome here!"

Shiloh stopped in his tracks and stared at her tear-ravaged, reddened face.

Jerome Espy draped his long thin arm around her again and said soothingly, "C'mon, Flo. This don't concern us. Don't worry about it. Don't worry about none of it." He turned her around and again they made their slow way toward the door. Espy looked back at Shiloh. "She don't like rats."

They finally disappeared, and Shiloh heard the heavy door bang shut behind them.

He turned, and the three men stared at one another.

"Flo's scared of rats," Shiloh finally said.

"Women!" Lott said scathingly. "Who can tell of 'em? Mr. Smarty Pigtail, indeed! Lemme tell you something, Mr. Locke, you don't need them two anyway. You just let me head on back to the barky and get my messmates. We'll have this place scrubbed clean. I tell you, them two have never seen clean before, from the looks of this place! Scairt of rats, my eye, more like she's scared of a little hard work scrubbing and airing! We'll bring the ship's stores, and Molly Sketes will have food cooked and put up fit for a king *and* for Dr. Cheney's sainted mother as soon as wink your eye!"

Shiloh hesitated, and the less excitable Billy-O said quietly, "I think ol' Lott here is right, sir. We can get enough crewmen out here cleaning and building fires and washing linens so that you could move everyone out here by noon tomorrow."

"Dead right," Lott sniffed.

Shiloh looked around the big musty room and once again caught the red eyes of the rat in the lantern light. "That does it," he muttered. "Billy-O, you head on back to town and bring back enough crewmen to get this place spanking shiny clean. Bring all the stores, and Sketes too. One dollar cash on the barrel for every volunteer and extra ration of beefsteak, bacon, and eggs for each volunteer when I replace the ship's stores. Lott, me and you are gonna take care of that rat. Right now."

Lott sniffed again, and his slitted eyes burned. "Dead right, Mr. Locke. Dead right."

CHAPTER THREE

Sangrìa

DENYING THE DISMAL storms of the night, Tuesday's dawn was picture-perfect and the day was lovely: a bright cerulean sky, a jolly yellow sun, clouds like woolly lambs, and warm breezes. However, Shiloh's face was as dark and threatening as the skies had been the night before.

He stood on the porch of Sangria House, glowering at Andrew Barentine. "You're telling me that we're all going to have to troop in and out of the servants' entrance while we're here?"

Shiloh, several of the sailors, and the servants had worked all night to get the house livable and food and stores ready. At first light the sailors had brought everyone in, for the parlor and dining rooms were cleaned and comfortable. But still the problem of the keys and the locked front door had not been solved.

Andrew Barentine was a sturdy, solid, unhurried young man of unremarkable appearance: average height and frame, with brown hair and eyes. But his voice was deep, a most pleasing baritone, and his characteristic thoughtfulness and steadiness made him a good husband, father, and employee. His official position with the Buchanan household was as stableman and coachman. But Victoria had brought him along mainly to be with his wife, Hannah, as she cared for their son, Alex, as well as Dart, Solange, and Lisette. In the past five days Shiloh had found Andrew invaluable, as he was very good with the Irish wolfhounds, Sean and Shannon. He also was a sort of jack-of-all-trades who could step into any situation and lend a hand, as he was doing now. Shiloh had asked him to see if he could trip the front door lock so they might be able to open it, and then rig it so it wouldn't lock when it was closed. There was an enormous old wooden bolt on the inside that would satisfactorily bar anyone from entering the house from the outside.

Andrew shook his head slowly. "Sorry, sir. With a good hacksaw I could cut the bolts, but that would ruin the lock."

"No, we can't do that," Shiloh said. "All right, Andrew, then would you see to it that the back entrance is at least as convenient as possible? Make sure the steps are cleaned and not slippery, and see if you can find out if there are some carpet runners to put down through the workroom."

"Yes, sir," he said and left, going down the steps, onto the lawn, and around the house in order to go back inside.

Shiloh turned to stare at the front door of Sangria House with helpless frustration. He knew from what Florence Espy had said the previous night that it must be the original door and lock from when the house was built in 1761. It was an enormous wooden door, four inches thick, made of heart of oak that, in spite of its age, was still as solid and true as Duvall steel.

The hinges were ornate black iron, as were the handle and the faceplate of the lock. On a whim Shiloh bent down to look through the keyhole. He could see a small glimmer of red in the vestibule, which he knew was one of the velvet-covered entryway chairs. Straightening again, he wondered what kind of man Louis Arthur Grider was. He sure didn't seem to know how to receive guests, even—or perhaps especially—paying guests.

Sangria House was habitable, as it turned out. All of the furnishings were there, the kitchen pots and pans and utensils were intact, the rugs were still down, and there were some accessories—decorative candelabra, paintings, urns, and the like—still in the house. The library was well stocked with books, and the fine old banker's desk had pens and plain stationery, though no personal papers at all. The drawers were locked. There was a roomy storage closet in the library that held other supplies such as paper and envelopes and pens and bottles of ink and an enormous freestanding safe with a combination lock.

Mrs. Espy had told Sketes that the owners' personal possessions had been stored in one of the servants' cottages. The only thing that seemed to have been left behind was a large locked trunk at the foot of the bed in the master bedroom, which Victoria had insisted that Richard and Irene occupy. Mr. and Mrs. Espy said they knew nothing of it, so it was decided simply to leave it. If Mr. or Mrs. Grider needed it, surely they would send for it.

But as Shiloh had discovered the night before, the house had not been cleaned or aired; no firewood had been laid up, no stores or supplies provided. Mr. and Mrs. Espy insisted that Louis Grider had said nothing to them of a party leasing Sangria House. Another problem was that, although there were comforters, quilts, and pillows supplied for all of the bedrooms, there were no bed linens left in the house at all. Mrs. Espy had said that she knew nothing about the linens, and she had no key to the other servants' cottages to see if, for some reason, the Griders had stored the linens. Finally, exasperated, Shiloh had sent for all of the linens on board *Locke's Day Dream* to be brought to the house and had sent Hannah Barentine and Fiona into town to buy all the bed linens they could find.

One good thing about Sangria House was the stables. The Morgan was a fine carriage horse, and the hardy pony pulled the cart easily. As Shiloh had speculated, the Arabian mare and the finely tooled sidesaddle had disappeared sometime during the long night, presumably along with the very merry lady who had been in Bain's cottage. The other saddle horses had been cared for well, and Shiloh knew that Mr. Espy, in spite of his denial that he was still doing any work for Louis Grider, must be taking care of the stables.

Now surveying the front gardens of Sangria House with a jaundiced eye, Shiloh realized how neglected the place was. The house itself was fine; it was a large house with big, high-ceilinged rooms to allow the tropical heat to rise, so the rooms would be cool. Built of coquina and painted a modest tan, there was evidence that it had been repainted many times, and all of the coats had mellowed over the years to a pleasing golden yellow. Black shutters faced all the windows, which were deep seated and glassed in the English tradition rather than the eighteenth-century Spanish tradition of simply having openings with sturdy shutters. Of two stories, it was raised four feet, for the wine cellar was eight feet high and countersunk four feet. On Shiloh's left, down two steps and with an arched opening framing it, was the door into the wine cellar. Shiloh had already tried to open it. It was as massive and strong as the front door and was just as securely locked.

Two small porches were on the first and second floor, shading the front door. Upstairs the door from the porch led into a passageway to the bedrooms. At least that was what Shiloh had understood the sailors to say; he hadn't been upstairs yet.

The gardens and the fountain and pool looked as if they had not been tended in years, perhaps decades. All of the flower beds, squared off by paths of coquina stone, contained only brown sticks. The fountain, which was a stone bowl with a sullen brown trickle in the center, was discolored a moldy green, as was the circular pool. The water in the pool was unhealthy looking, dark and still.

A commotion above his head interrupted his reverie. He realized it was his valet, Jauncy, and Calvin Lott shouting at each other loudly enough to be heard in Jacksonville. The shouting was accompanied by an odd series of thumps.

"Here, sir, what do you think you're doing?" Jauncy yelled. "Unhand that carpet thrasher this instant! This instant, I say!"

"You just"—*whump! whump!*—"stand back there"—*whump!*—"you little muffin! I'll thrash"—*whump! whump!*—"you"—*whump! whump!*—"if you make a swipe for it again!"

"Muffin! Just who do you think you are, you big sea-going ape! If you don't cease and desist immediately I shall—"

"What?"—*whump!*—"Scream like a girl and hope some grown man comes along to save you?"

"Certainly not! I shall strike you with my umbrella!"

"Yeah?"—*whump! whump!*—"And where might this turrible weapon be? Packed up with yer bloomers?"

Shiloh heard quick footsteps fading down the upstairs passage, and he thought it was probably Jauncy running to fetch his umbrella. Shiloh decided that he'd better sober up and take charge of this situation, so he made himself stop grinning, went down the steps, and started backing up in the front lawn so that he could see the second floor porch.

Sure enough, Calvin Lott had a long length of some heavy green material folded over the balcony railing, and he was beating the tar out of it with what Shiloh had always called a rug beater but which he was sure was Jauncy's carpet thrasher. It was an iron rod with a curlicue on the end. With satisfaction Calvin Lott stood in a cloud of fine dust that poofed up with every determined *whump!* To add richness to this vignette, behind Lott, Jauncy emerged from the cool shadows of the upstairs passage, his face as dark as death, his umbrella already raised for the killing blow.

"PJ! Lower that umbrella! Now!" Shiloh ordered.

Calvin Lott turned to look behind him and sneered in a low tone, "Aww, did the grown man come and rescue you, little muffin?"

But Shiloh's hearing was acute, and he called out sternly, "That's enough, Lott! What's the matter with you two anyway? You're worse than Dart and Alex!"

Jauncy stepped up to the balcony railing and leaned over to say earnestly, "But sir! He's *thrashing* the *draperies*!"

"He is?" Shiloh said blankly. "I mean—you're not supposed to thrash draperies?"

"Sir!"

"What? I don't know and neither does Lott. Looks to me like they're pretty dusty, so—"

"But sir, they are very fine-woven velvet draperies! One must *brush* them, not seize them up to the grating and flog them to death!" Jauncy said with the sort of elegant disdain that only the upper-class Englishman, or his "gentleman," could possibly project.

"Oh," Shiloh said in a subdued voice.

"Oh," echoed Calvin Lott, staring at Jauncy. His thrasher was stilled midblow, as it were, so Jauncy grabbed it.

"Mr. Lott, I appreciate your zeal, certainly. But just as I would defer to you on the deck of a ship, I must ask that you defer to me in the purview of my occupation," Jauncy said in a lecturing tone. "Now, I shall fetch a coarse brush and illustrate to you how to brush so as not to insult the warp and weft. . . ." His voice trailed off as he disappeared again down the passageway, his umbrella now tucked neatly beneath his arm.

Calvin Lott shook his head in wonder and called down to Shiloh in a stage whisper, "Can't he say a mouthful when he gets wound up, Mr. Locke?"

"Yes, as Sketes says, he's a fine-spoken gent, but—What? What is that?" Shiloh threw one hand up to shade his eyes, squinted, and backed up a step. He thought he saw something on the roof.

The second-story porch had a pediment that obscured most of the hipped roof from where Shiloh was standing. Quickly he backed up, squinting from the bright sun, which was just now at the noon zenith. The roof line came into his view, and there! He did see one—no, two—sailors carrying something, tripping merrily along on the roof as if they were skylarking on the ratlines of their own ship.

"Hey, you two! Is that you, Mylonas? Who is that with you? What do you think you're doing up there?" he bellowed, still backing up.

Ludicrously Lott leaned backward over the balcony railing and tried to see the roof, which was, of course, impossible. "Lott, stop before you fall and break your fool neck," Shiloh growled. "Hey! You two other fools up there on the roof! Ahoy!"

But the two fools were busy laughing foolishly, and Shiloh could see they hadn't heard him. He saw with disbelief that they had brought up a ladder and placed it against one of the high chimneys. Now one of them—Shiloh thought it must have been the crazy Frenchman, Auguste Bettencourt, who was the armorer and an able seaman on *Locke's Day Dream*—climbed to the top of the ladder and stared down into the depths of the chimney. He had something in his hand, which he hefted up against his shoulder and pointed down into the chimney.

Shiloh took another huge backward stride, shouting "No! NO! Bettencourt—"

Calvin Lott did a funny double take, looking upward and then down at Shiloh. Then he grasped the porch railing, leaned over as far as he dared, and bellowed, "Mr. Locke, *stop!*"

Several things happened simultaneously, so that later Lott could only helplessly say, "It all happened so fast, like!"

Auguste Bettencourt aimed a double-barreled shotgun down the chimney and fired. An enormous deep thunder sounded and a black cloud as thick as night shot straight up out of the chimney. Bettencourt dropped the shotgun as he grabbed his face and then tumbled off the ladder and began sliding downward.

The low wall of the pool hit Shiloh right in the back of the knees. Jarringly he bent and sat, his legs flew up, he fell backward—a huge splash—and his hat floated to the top of the water.

From inside the house came a woman's high-pitched piercing scream that went on and on.

Shiloh bounded up, leapt over the pool wall, and shook his head like a wet dog, trying to clear the water from his eyes. He looked up and shouted hoarsely, "Bettencourt! Be still!"

He was hanging from the roof, about thirty feet up. Hearing Shiloh, he stopped wiggling and just hung there by, it seemed, his fingernails. Both hands were grasping the rain gutter that encircled the roof line. His legs dangled in front of one of the upstairs windows.

Lott, who had been watching Shiloh dumbfounded, now whipped around and saw Bettencourt. But he was about ten feet away from the balcony. Helplessly the old sailor looked around in desperation.

Shiloh, too, stared around, his thoughts firing like a Roman candle's quick bursts. *No rope—have to go around back—upstairs—haven't been, don't know where that bedroom is—*

No time.

Cheney, Richard, Irene, Victoria, and Dev hurried around the corner of the house, looking for the cause of all the commotion. As if their voices had been cut with a sharp knife, they all stopped talking and pulled up short.

Shiloh noted, even as he was already on the move, that Cheney's head turned toward him, her face already watchful to see what he was going to do.

He dashed by them, shouting up to the sailor on the second-story porch, "Lott! Go inside and see if any of the drapery pulls are strong enough!"

Lott turned and disappeared into the house.

Shiloh, now at a dead run, hit the ground floor porch, used it as a spring, leapt up with all his strength, and grabbed the bottom rail of the decorative railing of the second floor porch. In a smooth swift glide, as graceful as a circus acrobat's, he swung his legs to give himself propulsion and jumped again to grab the top railing. Now he bent his legs, kicked off from the front edge of the stone balcony floor, swung up, and as neatly and surely as if he did such things every day, landed on the second-story porch. He went to the side, leaned out to the right as far as he could, and said calmly, "Bettencourt? I'm right here. I'm going to get you down. All you have to do is hang on for just a few minutes longer. You understand? Just keep your grip for another few minutes. You with me?"

Auguste Bettencourt managed to turn his head a fraction and whisper, "*Oui, Monsieur* Locke. I'll hold on."

"Good man." Shiloh reached up to feel the back corner porch upright, and to his vast relief, found it was a pillar of coquina stone, not a wooden upright that might be shaky, or even worse, rotted.

Jauncy and Lott came running out onto the balcony. Lott gasped, "Mr. Jauncy had this good stiff rope that he tied up the ladies' trunks—"

But Shiloh had already grabbed the rope. He flicked two arm's lengths out and then began tying a knot. Lott's face lightened as he realized what Shiloh was doing. Lott leaned over the balcony railing and rasped, "We've got a rope now, Bettencourt. Mr. Locke's going to get you."

"Ah, so?" the Frenchman said weakly. "What will he do? Throw me the rope so he can pull me down?"

Shiloh finished tying, and then said curtly, "Everyone clear out."

Jauncy and Lott just stood there dumbly.

Shiloh began twirling the rope. It started to make a high-pitched whine as it whirled at high speed.

"Oh," Jauncy gulped as it went past his nose like a bullet. He ducked inside, followed by Lott.

Shiloh twirled the lasso, his eyes narrowed to blazing blue slits. Twice he threw it and missed. Undaunted, he snapped the rope back and started twirling again. On the third try he got the loop positioned right under Bettencourt's dangling feet, yanked up in a whipping motion, saw the loop rise to just about waist high, and pulled it hard and fast. The noose tightened around Bettencourt's waist so hard that he grunted.

Quickly Shiloh took up the slack, looped it around the porch upright, and called, "Lott! Jauncy!" The two men popped out onto the balcony, and both of them looked, understood, and grabbed the rope out of Shiloh's hands. Shiloh turned to Bettencourt and said, "Now you've got a lifeline, Bettencourt. You see? If you fall, we'll catch you before you hit the ground. Right?"

"Um-hmm . . . right . . . Monsieur—" He started to gasp, his face reddened with strain, but his lips were white. Shiloh noticed a trickle of blood coming down from his right hand.

Quietly he said, "Auguste? Here's what I want you to do. Start sliding your hands along so that you get closer to me. No, don't look at me. Don't look down. Just concentrate on sliding along, one hand after the other, over this way. Okay? Good, that's right, that's real good, Auguste, you're a lot closer already. Just remember, if you fall, we'll catch you. But if you can just slide a little closer, I'll be able to reach you. That's it . . . that's it . . ."

Blood was running down Bettencourt's arm like a river now, turning the sleeve of his white shirt to crimson. His eyes were closed. His left hand moved, slid along the gutter, and then his right hand. Over and over. Shiloh kept talking, kept leaning out farther and farther, his hand straining to reach the young man's slim waist. He kept talking, Auguste kept inching closer.

Finally Shiloh leaned dangerously far out, his left hand looped around the porch upright, his right arm shot out, and he grabbed Bettencourt's waist. In a smooth motion he tightened his arm and leaned backward, bringing the young man with him.

They both stood on the balcony. Slowly Auguste Bettencourt opened his eyes.

He was a proud young French bantam rooster, so his chin came up and he said evenly, *"Merci, Monsieur Locke. Je m'oblige."*

Shiloh rolled his eyes. "Welcome," he grunted.

Cheney was there. He heard a soft rustle of silk, smelled her scent, and turned.

She was holding her medical bag, and she said sternly to Auguste Bettencourt, "Untie your silly self, Monsieur, and go downstairs to the servant's workroom to wash up. I'll be along in a moment to see about that hand."

He wiggled out of the lasso, shamefaced now, helped by Lott and

Jauncy. "Silly grass-combing lubber!" Lott said in a loud, slow voice usually reserved for ignorant landsmen. "Ain't I told you, Frenchie, not to do stupid landlubbers' tricks? It's dangerous out here ashore! You could get hurt doing stupid landlubbers' tricks! Ain't I told you?"

"Oui, Monsieur Lott, you have told me," Bettencourt said meekly. He leaned down, stepped out of the loop of rope, and then pulled it up to hand it over to Jauncy.

He used his right hand, which was cut fairly badly and was bleeding profusely, though Bettencourt, a tough sailor, barely paid attention to it now. His hand was covered with bright red blood, his shirt sleeve was soaked in it, and now even the rope had drops plopping from it down to the stone floor, making big messy red splotches.

Jauncy valiantly reached out his hand, fully intending to take the rope. He swallowed hard. Every bit of color drained from his face. His hand started to tremble, his eyes rolled upward . . .

Shiloh caught him as he swooned.

Lott and Bettencourt stared goggle-eyed. Lott's jaw even fell slightly open.

Shiloh grunted, "Whatsa matter with you? Never seen anybody faint before?"

They still stood like dumb statues.

Cheney giggled.

Shiloh rasped, "Excuse me? Please?"

The two men stepped aside, and Shiloh swept past them, Jauncy's head bobbling in his arms like a child's ball. Cheney followed him, barely managing to stifle her giggles. Shiloh looked into the first doorway he passed, saw a bed, and dumped Jauncy unceremoniously onto it.

Cheney knelt by the bed and pulled smelling salts out of her medical bag. "That was quite a performance. You're like a circus act all by yourself, Shiloh. Acrobatics, trapeze, rope tricks . . . I was impressed."

"Yeah?" he grunted. "Well, I sure hope Bettencourt was impressed enough not to do a fool stunt like that again. Big Frog dummy."

"Mm-hmm," Cheney said, waving the small brown bottle under Jauncy's nose. He started to gag. "I do have one question, though, Husband."

"What?"

She looked up at him, her green eyes dancing merrily and the corners of her wide mouth twitching. "I was just wondering . . . Why are you all wet?"

"All—" Shiloh looked down at himself. He'd completely forgotten about his dunk in the fountain pool. "Aw—my favorite denims! And they haven't brought my trunks yet!" He threw his arms up theatrically and rolled his eyes heavenward. "What is this place anyway? Some kinda . . . kinda . . . crazy house? Like a lunatic asylum? Only you come here to *go* crazy, not after you're *already* crazy!"

"Shiloh, you're ranting," Cheney said soothingly. "Look, Mr. Jauncy's coming around." Jauncy's sallow cheeks turned a very light shade of pink, and his eyelids started fluttering.

"You know, *sangria,* though we use it now as a name for the wine, comes from the Spanish *sangría,* which means 'bleeding,'" Cheney said in a lecturing tone as she lightly waved the salts under Jauncy's nose again. "Perhaps the house's name is unlucky."

"It will be if you explain it to PJ when he comes to," Shiloh said, turning to leave. "I'm going down to the servants' workroom to wring myself out. Then I'm going out on the lawn to try to dry up in the sun." He tramped out of the room, squishing ignobly.

Cheney looked down at her patient, who was staring up at her with woeful brown eyes.

"Did I faint again?" he moaned.

"I'm afraid so, Mr. Jauncy."

"Oh, dear! Was it because—oh, bother, I don't want to know. I don't want to remember," he said, sitting up and straightening his tie.

"That might be best," Cheney said soothingly as she corked the bottle of smelling salts and put them back in her bag.

Jauncy swung his legs over the side of the bed and stared at the door through which Shiloh had gone. "I am wondering about something, however, Mrs. Irons-Winslow."

"Yes, Mr. Jauncy?"

He looked at her in bewilderment. "Was he all wet?"

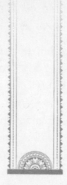

CHAPTER FOUR

Sailors and Servants

THE COURTYARD OF SANGRIA HOUSE, a small brick-paved rectangle on the east side, was very pleasant in the afternoons. The bricks were still sun warmed, but the east side of the house was shady and cool. The courtyard extended right up to the orange groves that grew on the east side of the property. On the west side were lemon and lime groves.

A lush green lawn ran from the courtyard all the way up to the servants' cottages. Even now, in February, the grass was green and thick, and smelled good—that rich smell of black dirt and healthy growing things. Cheney and Victoria had already decided that the lawn would be perfect for lawn bowling and lawn tennis, which, in some bygone day before Grider's shadow fell across this place, Spanish gentlemen and ladies probably played.

On the bricked courtyard were two small lacy wrought-iron tables, each with two chairs, but Shiloh, with foresight, had had the sailors bring the deck chaises from *Locke's Day Dream.* He drowsed in one of them now, his boots stuffed with brown paper and standing together like funny shabby sentinels out in the last rays of the afternoon sun on the green expanse of the lawn. Shiloh's shirt and socks were mostly dry, but his thick denims were still very wet. But he was warm enough to doze.

Nearby, at one of the small tables, Irene and Richard drank tea and read newspapers the seamen had bought for them in one of their trips through St. Augustine to the ship. Even in this little old village, the tobacconist had New York newspapers. True, they were three days old, but Richard and Irene didn't care. It was a ritual they had done for many, many years: read the evening papers as they drank either tea or coffee.

Victoria had gone to see Dev off. His ship, a small passenger steamer, was departing at four thirty. Andrew Barentine had driven them in the brougham, reporting to Shiloh that the Morgan horse was a fine trotter indeed. The other four horses, however, along with the cart and the brougham, had finally been confirmed by Jerome Espy as belonging to the Griders. He had said—very begrudgingly, as the Espys always seemed to be—that the "young gentlemen," which Shiloh took to be his cousin Bain and Carsten and Beckett Steen, had been using the saddle horses and had been tipping him to keep the stables. The day had been so busy that Shiloh hadn't gone to the gatekeeper's lodge to visit his cousin, and there had been no sign of Victoria's brothers either. But they would have plenty of time to visit in the coming days. It was much more important to get the house livable and get everyone settled in.

Out on the lawn, on a quilt spread out in the sunshine, Hannah Barentine sat sewing and humming quietly to herself. All four of the children were lying on the quilt fast asleep. Beside them Minerva Wilcott, Victoria's cousin, was curled up as unselfconsciously as the children, her little pink mouth slightly open as she slept.

Next to Shiloh, Cheney was in another deck chaise reading *Bleak House,* her favorite Dickens novel. Between their chairs, calm for once, Sean and Shannon lazed—not sleeping, just lolling about.

Suddenly Shiloh made a noise as if he were straining to breathe, jerked upright, and his eyes darted around, though Cheney could tell he wasn't really seeing anything.

"Did you fall in the river?" he blurted out.

Cheney would have found it amusing except for the fact that Shiloh never talked in his sleep, never awakened in confusion, and in particular never seemed to be caught so off-guard and alarmed. "No, darling, no," she said quietly. "You fell in the pool."

His head swiveled toward her, and though his gaze was intense, she still sensed that he wasn't truly looking at her.

"Did someone die?" he demanded.

"What? No—no, Shiloh. What's the matter?" She reached out and took his hand, which was knotted into a tight fist.

He flinched a little and then blinked. His face relaxed somewhat, but when he spoke, he sounded tense. "I had a bad dream. It was dark and cold; freezing damp cold . . . someone was dead." He frowned.

Cheney came to kneel by his chair, noting that her parents and Hannah had heard the alarm in Shiloh's voice and were watching with concern. "It's all right," she called out calmly. "Just a bad dream." Her parents still looked grave—they had known Shiloh long enough to know he wasn't the kind of man to let a nightmare affect him so strongly— but they turned politely away and went back to reading their newspapers. Hannah started humming again, and one small part of Cheney's mind registered that she was humming "Shall We Gather at the River," one of Cheney's favorite hymns.

"Shiloh, you just had a dream, and I'm not surprised it seemed so real. You fell into the pool, remember? I'm sure it was cold and dark, and your denims are still sopping wet. I'll bet you're getting chilled. That's probably why you're dreaming about being cold." She took both of his hands in hers and noticed that his fingers were warm. He didn't seem chilled at all.

He stared at her upturned face and then said automatically, "Yeah, that must be it." His gaze bored into hers, as if he were asking her a question.

Cheney felt confused for a moment, reacting to some sort of communicated distress from Shiloh, but then with relief she said, "And of course, Mr. Bettencourt almost fell off the roof. He could have died."

Still Shiloh gazed at her quizzically and started to say something. But just then Jauncy and Sketes came out of the kitchen, talking a mile a minute rather loudly, and walked toward them. Cheney, who was not given to affectionate displays in public, rose quickly and settled back into her chaise longue. Shiloh, his face now with its customary expression of secret laughter and heavy-lidded good nature, turned to watch them come across the courtyard. They were an odd twosome, to be sure: Jauncy, the small, dapper, precise British gentleman's gentleman, and Sketes, the rotund, red-cheeked, voluble Mrs. Santa Claus, as Cheney had once unforgettably dubbed her. Both Shiloh and Cheney watched them with amusement and clear affection.

But they were not in such good humor. "Mr. Shiloh! Mr. Shiloh!" Sketes started saying from twenty feet away.

"Yeah, Sketes, what's the problem?"

They huffed nearer, and Jauncy took his turn: "It is intolerable, I tell you, Mr. Irons-Winslow! It cannot be borne. No, it really cannot!"

"Can't be born?" he said blankly.

Cheney said under her breath, "Can't *bear* it."

"Oh."

When they reached his chair, they both started talking at once.

Shiloh raised his hand. "One at a time please. Ladies first. What's up, Sketes?"

"Mr. Shiloh," she said, gasping a little, "I have only just discovered that there is not a stick of firewood on the place! I used what I had in the kitchen to do tea, and what have I only just discovered?"

"That there's no more firewood?" Shiloh offered.

"Not a stick on the place!" she cried. "And what's more, how am I supposed to arrange for everyone's baths? With no Christian plumbing? I have one teakettle. One!" She held up one ruler-straight forefinger to illustrate. "One teakettle. To heat up baths for four ladies, two gentlemen, four children, seven servants, and two dogs?"

Shiloh jerked up straight. His change of fortune from penniless orphan wanderer to married man of substance with family had not changed him much; but one thing he did insist on now was a daily hot bath. "One teakettle!" he fumed. "That's it! Mrs. Buchanan's gotta tell me what kinda people *lived* in this crazy house!"

"Dirty people, I'll wager," Sketes said triumphantly.

"Okay, everyone, don't panic," Shiloh said, swinging his legs over to rise and then staring down at his stocking feet. "PJ, go get my boots. I gotta do something, and I can't do it barefooted."

Calmly Cheney asked, "Sketes, there are no waterpots in the servants' workroom?"

"No, ma'am. Not a pot for water, for washing, nor for cooking, except in the kitchen. And they're a mean and meager collection, I'll tell you."

"I have worse news than that," Jauncy said dramatically as he pulled the paper out of Shiloh's boots and handed it to Sketes, who automatically began to fold it neatly, and then bent over to help Shiloh get his boots on, making a face. Helping Shiloh put his boots on was Jauncy's least favorite duty. He always almost got pushed over.

"Can't be worse than not having hot baths," Shiloh grumbled. He pushed, and of course Jauncy almost got pushed right over. "Sorry," Shiloh said, though he didn't sound it.

"I'm sure," Jauncy muttered under his breath. "And . . . sir . . . ugh . . . Mr. Lott's trick knee—oof—tells him that . . . there'll be rain tonight." He straightened with relief, the boots now on.

Shiloh stood up and stamped, as men and horses do to seat their shoes. "Lott's trick knee is ruling my life these days, it seems."

"No, dear, that would be me. Remember?" Cheney said sweetly.

"Huh? Oh yeah, I remember you. My wife, right? Okay, PJ, so Lott's trick knee is warning of rain. And that means . . . ?"

"Cold rain. Falling damps. Chills," he said darkly. "And no fires." With heavy meaning, his eyes slid toward Irene Duvall. She and Richard were sipping tea, pretending not to listen, but they couldn't help but hear, of course. Richard had put his newspaper up in front of his face, but Cheney knew her father and could see the slight shaking and knew he was laughing.

"Aw, man . . . Okay, go tell some tomfools who want to go skylarking that they can shoot down the chimneys," Shiloh said.

"Shiloh!" Cheney said with alarm.

"If they'll rig manropes, like anybody but big Frog dummies would know, and then they'll be all right." Then, in a quieter voice, he said, "Cheney, we've got to have fires. It's warm here during the day when the sun's shining, but it's still February. That means the nights will be chilly, and when it rains, it will be damp and cold."

With a glance at her mother, who was still coolly ignoring them but who Cheney was certain understood everything that was going on, Cheney nodded. "I don't suppose we could get a chimney sweep out here to clean them all today, could we?" There were four chimneys, aside from the detached kitchen chimney, which was the only one that wasn't completely blocked up with what looked like centuries of soot.

"Don't think so, Doc," he said. "Don't worry, I think even that crew learned something from Bettencourt hanging out like the wash blowin' in the breeze." He turned back to Jauncy and Sketes. "Just make sure that they block the fireplace in the rooms before they give it both barrels! If they blacken up another room like Bettencourt did the parlor, I think poor Mallow and Fiona might have apoplexies."

The blood-curdling scream that had come after Auguste Bettencourt shot down the chimney was from Mallow O'Shaughnessy, Irene's servant. She had just finished cleaning every single piece of furniture in the parlor, she had polished the floor, and she had rehung the draperies after taking them down and brushing them—strictly following Jauncy's orders—when an enormous cloud of soot had exploded out of the fireplace and covered every single inch of the room—and Mallow herself—with finely powdered oily black soot. She had screamed. Upstairs in what was to be Cheney and Shiloh's bedroom, Fiona had just finished cleaning it when the fireplace had spewed soot all over her and the room too. While Mallow was a fiery Irish girl, Fiona was a shy, quiet one, so she didn't scream. She just cried, the tears making clean little furrows down her blackened face.

"Okay," Shiloh went on, "I'm going to get us some firewood if I have to go chop down all the cute little lime trees and burn 'em. But first I'm going to go talk to those Espy people again."

"Oh, Shiloh, leave them alone. They obviously don't want to have anything to do with us," Cheney said uneasily.

"I don't care. It's not like I'm gonna ask 'em to lift a finger," he retorted, rising and stretching. "I'm just going to see if they can tell me where I might get some firewood. It'll be easier than just heading out with my ax. Sean! Shannon! C'mon, get off your duffs. If I gotta go to work, so do you." He went off whistling "When Johnny Comes Marching Home," the tune that the watch Cheney had given him so long ago played. He still loved that watch, and he still loved that song. The dogs, their long ears flapping every which way, frolicked and ran and generally acted like silly puppies, which they still were despite the fact that they weighed forty pounds.

Shiloh noted as he neared the servants' cottages that they looked meaner and more squalid in the bright sunshine than they had the night before. With a start he realized that Jauncy, Sketes, Fiona, Mallow, and the Barentines were probably going to be staying in these cottages; and guiltily he thought, *Well, it didn't take me very long to turn into a spoiled, thoughtless robber baron, did it? All of the servants have been working like pure fools on the Big House, seeing to everything that we need . . . and there's no telling what kinda sad shape their cottages are in!*

It was with a dark forbidding expression that Shiloh banged on the Espys' door, and though he had no intention of intimidating them—after all, his ill humor was with himself, not with them—it did make Jerome Espy's sad hound-dog features pale with dread when he opened the door and saw Shiloh's face. When Shiloh saw his expression, it startled him, and deliberately he said very kindly, "Mr. Espy, I'm sorry to bother you again, but I did need to ask you a couple of questions, if you've got the time."

Suspiciously Espy muttered, "Flo, she sees to the Big House, mostly. I see to the gardens and stables and groves and such." His grim expression lightened the tiniest bit as he watched Sean and Shannon nose around behind Shiloh. As if they sensed his attention, they both looked up at him alertly, their gazes clearly assessing whether he was a threat. Sean's and then Shannon's long whipcord tails started to wag in their friendliest figure-eight pattern that moved their entire backsides. Shiloh turned around and saw, with some surprise, their obvious friendliness to this prickly man. The dogs weren't very good guard dogs—they were too gentle for that—but neither did they so openly show friendliness to strangers.

"They like you," Shiloh said quietly. "You have dogs, Mr. Espy?"

"No," he said with clear wistfulness. "Mr. Grider, he didn't take to dogs."

"That's too bad. Dogs can be just like friends and family."

"Guess so," Espy said, watching the dogs with clear regret. Slowly he lowered his hand, palm up. Shiloh stepped aside to let the dogs come sniff him. Cautiously Sean lumbered up, checked the man's outstretched hand, and then stuck his big round head under it to be scratched. Shannon came up, and the two puppies then pushed each other aside to get the attention. With a shock Shiloh saw a shy smile slowly come over the man's cadaverous face.

Instinctively Shiloh stood very still so as not to distract or startle the dogs and let Mr. Espy pet them as long as he wanted. With a certainty that came often to Shiloh, he suddenly knew: *He's lonely, and he's sorrowful. Whatever has happened to these poor people? Why are they suffering so?*

Espy finally looked up, and it was as if he had somehow grown younger in these few unguarded minutes playing with Sean and Shannon. Quietly he said, "They do ease the suffering."

"What?" Shiloh said, startled at the echo of his thoughts. But Jerome Espy merely looked at him with eyes that were again shuttered and secretive, so Shiloh cleared his throat and said, "I was just wondering, Mr. Espy, if you could tell me where I might buy some firewood. Today, hopefully."

Espy's dead gaze went past Shiloh to the Big House. There were two sailors on the roof, and several more down on the ground yelling up at them good-naturedly. Every window was opened, and through them one could see either a servant or a sailor working. Sketes was back on the kitchen path emptying out a pail of water.

"Mister, how many servants you got?" Espy asked in wonder.

"No—they aren't all servants," Shiloh said hastily. "I have—I own a ship, and this is some—most—of the crew. They pitched in to do spring cleaning for us. Extra cleaning that I'm sure you and Mrs. Espy couldn't possibly do."

"You're right about that," he grumbled. "But you're makin' them sailors do housework? For nothin'?"

Shiloh reflected that Jerome Espy must make a poor wage indeed. Now that he saw him in harsh unforgiving sunlight, Shiloh could tell that every scrap of clothing he had on—his breeches, his vest, his shirt, his threadbare sack coat—was as thin as paper from many washings, and everything had at least one darn. Finally Shiloh said, "No, Mr. Espy, I believe in paying people a good wage, whether they're servants or sailors. If you don't mind me asking, are you and Mrs. Espy available to help us out? The sailors will have to return to the ship this evening, for they'll be sailing out for the Caribbean tomorrow. And we do have our own servants, but it is a big house and we could use your help. I'm sure Mr. Grider is paying you in his absence, but—"

Bitterly Espy burst out, "Him! Payin' us one pennyworth more than he hasta! Not likely! Lemme tell you something, Mr. Iron or whatever your name is, Flo heard them sailors talkin' of you payin' them a *whole dollar* for the day and givin' 'em beef and bacon besides! Is that the truth?"

Taken aback, Shiloh stammered, "Well, yes, Mr. Espy—"

Now with righteous indignation the man stepped closer to Shiloh and said, "Did you know that old devil only paid us *eighteen cents* a day? And we been working for him for *eleven year*! Eleven whole year that miserable old—" His muddy eyes blazed, but then the fire died out. His thin shoulders sagged, and he stepped back, mumbling mournfully again, "But we got a roof over our head, and . . . other things too, I guess. . . ."

Shiloh sensed that the deep grief almost overcame the man again. Finally he said evenly, "As I was saying, Mr. Espy, we could certainly use your help, and Mrs. Espy's, too. If you could see your way to working for us while we're here, I could offer you a dollar a day plus some stores."

His head snapped up. "A dollar a day? Each, or for both of us?"

"Each."

The man's Adam's apple throbbed painfully. "You . . . you mean it, mister?"

"Yes, I try always to mean what I say, Mr. Espy."

"We'd be . . . we'd—me and Flo—would be more'n happy to do whatever you need us to, sir," he said humbly. "I could . . . I could fetch firewood right now if you'd care to pay fifteen cent for a rick and let me take the wagon up to the Nielsens'."

"Is it good wood?"

"Seasoned hardwood, sir," he answered, now with a semblance of eagerness.

"Sounds good," Shiloh said with clear relief. "So those stores I was talking about, suppose you go ahead and buy a cord and take a rick or so out of it for the servants' quarters. I hear on good authority there's going to be rain tonight. You need help hitching up?"

"Sir? No, sir, I gen'ally do it my own self," he said, seeming amazed that a person of Shiloh's exalted position would even think of offering help.

Shiloh nodded briskly. "Get to it, then, Mr. Espy. And if Mrs. Espy's feeling at all able, I know our cook Sketes could use some help in the kitchen." He turned and happily called the dogs.

But Mr. Espy caught up with him and plucked at his sleeve. "But Mr. . . . er . . . Iron—it's almost five o'clock. I'd imagine . . . I . . . don't suppose . . . me and Flo would be makin' a dollar today, would we? At this late hour?"

Shiloh grinned. "Are you a God-fearing man, Mr. Espy?"

"Huh?" His face shut down again with the old bitterness. "No, I ain't," he said firmly.

"Too bad. I wanted you to read a story," Shiloh said airily. "If you've got a Bible around someplace, you might want to take a look at the book of Matthew, chapter twenty. Story about some people working in a vineyard. That'll answer your question."

He turned and went off whistling "When Johnny Comes Marching Home."

Espy stared after him and then muttered darkly to himself, "Maybe Flo's got one layin' about somewheres. . . . Ain't he an odd bird, though?" He turned and went back into the cottage, his step lighter than it had been in months, maybe years. He called into their darkened bedroom, "Hey, Flo? Wanta earn a dollar?"

"What you talking about, Jerome? Who ever could earn a whole dollar, 'cept that crazy bunch of sailormen up at the Big House! Don't that just make my head pound, thinking about—"

"Flo," he said softly, coming in to lay his gnarled hands on his wife's bowed shoulders, "Mr. Iron-what's-his-name offered us both a dollar a day. Cash money. To help out all them other servants! Not to be the only two poor hands on the place, mind you, but to work with—I b'lieve I counted seven of 'em!"

She looked up at him, her lined face suddenly with a trace of hope. "You—you don't mean it, Jerome!"

"I do," he said. "I'm off to the Nielsens' right now to buy firewood. And he said he'd give us a good bundle! *Give* it to us!"

Tears came to her already reddened eyes. "And me? He said I could work and earn a dollar a day too?"

"He did, Flo. He said ..." He hesitated and sucked his teeth thoughtfully. "Flo, you got that old Bible of your daddy's around here somewhere?"

"Bible? What you want that for? Like it's gonna do us a bit of good!"

"I got a question Mr. Whatsit said I could find in the Bible."

"He did, did he? And you think the Good Lord's gonna give us anything—answers or anything else—after what we done? After what *I* done?"

"Flo, Flo, don't get to cryin' again," Jerome said softly. "This is something good that's come to us. Now where's that Bible got to? Maybe it's time, Flo. Time for us to be getting it out and reading it again, like we used to."

Flo wiped her eyes with the corner of her apron and then stood up. "I hid it," she said with arid humor, "from myself, I guess, up in the closet. And you tell me, Jerome, if you get any answer from it. I won't believe it till I see it." She left the bedroom, and he could hear her splashing water in the kitchen, washing her tear-streaked face.

Jerome reached up into the top shelf of the closet and pulled out a huge family Bible bound in black leather. It was old, so it showed use, but he and Flo hadn't read it for many years. Her father had been a devout Christian, and he had entered all the births and deaths and marriages in it. And he had read it until the time came to give it to his daughter when she married.

Jerome sat down and thumbed slowly through it, savoring the feel of the thick parchment pages and the aged dry smell of them. He found Matthew twenty and read slowly, his lips moving.

After he finished he looked up and muttered, "All right, then, Lord. I'll say a thanks for this, but then we'll see ... we'll see."

CHAPTER FIVE

Jezebel

"I CAN HARDLY BELIEVE that this is the same fountain and pool," Irene marveled. "It's really lovely."

"Now it is," Shiloh agreed. "But yesterday when I fell in I coulda sworn I saw a couple of mud cats down there."

Irene laughed, but Richard Duvall looked puzzled. "What are mud cats?"

"Poor old Billy Yank," Irene teased. "He's never known the exquisite pleasure of fried catfish."

"That's a cryin' shame," Shiloh said.

The three were taking a leisurely walk in the formal gardens that were laid out in the front of Sangria House. Apparently none of the owners had ever found it necessary to have a carriage drive up to the front door, so the entire front grounds of the house—which stretched about a quarter of a mile down to the south groves—were landscaped in formal gardens. Now, after the winter and presumably under Louis Grider's indifferent care, all of the flower beds looked straggly and half dead. The front of the house was a sad sight, indeed, compared to the east courtyard and the lush green lawn. Shiloh had found out that the lawn had been cared for by Jerome Espy, since that part of the grounds fronted right onto his cottage.

But yesterday Calvin Lott and a crew of determined sailors had drained the fountain pool and scrubbed the pool, sides, and fountain with borax until it gleamed with the tawny beige color of the coquina stone instead of the moldy moss green that it had been. They also improvised a pump to siphon the natural spring that fed the fountain, so the water flowed vigorously again, a cheery four-foot-high spray that splashed prettily onto the wide bowl and then cascaded down into the pool.

That alone improved Sangria House somewhat. With the silent fountain, the still, sullen pool, and the forlorn gardens, the view of the house from the front had seemed like a relic of the Old World, dead and forgotten, inhabited only by sad gray ghosts.

Shiloh surreptitiously studied Richard and Irene as the trio made their slow promenade around the fountain admiring it. Richard looked much better; his face didn't seem so lined with exhaustion and, Shiloh suspected, pain. Richard never complained, but Shiloh, Cheney, and Dev could all see the strain on his face and in his posture when the arthritis in his hip flared up. Aside from heavy dependence on a cane and the more pronounced limp, his face, which was usually marked with sun creases and laugh lines, seemed sallow and strained. Today, Shiloh noted with satisfaction, he had good color, his gray eyes were brighter, and his limp was much less pronounced.

He studied his mother-in-law. She still was very pale and obviously weak, for she leaned heavily on Shiloh's arm, even though they had been walking for only a few minutes, and that very slowly. But still, she did appear to have more energy than she had had in months. The bouts with influenza and the dismal New York winter had sapped her strength considerably. The measure of just how concerned they had been about Irene Duvall, Shiloh reflected, was that both Cheney and Dev Buchanan—two doctors who barely took time off to eat and sleep—had agreed to take extended holidays in Florida this spring. Neither of them, nor Shiloh, of course, had said such to Irene or Richard, but they and Victoria had discussed Irene's grave weakness and inability to recover strength and vitality. Richard, too, had been more affected by the severe winter than ever before.

Shiloh roused himself to listen as Irene turned to him. "That poor Mr. Bettencourt's fall was very nearly a tragedy, wasn't it? If it hadn't been for you, Shiloh, he might have been injured terribly, or even killed."

"Aw, Bettencourt's so full of himself he prob'ly woulda bounced," Shiloh drawled.

"What I still can't understand is how you jumped up to the second story of the house," Richard said. "Dev and I tried and tried to recall exactly what you did, but neither of us could."

"To tell the truth, I don't remember how I did it either." The three stopped and looked up at the second story porch with the low wrought-iron railing. Bemused, Shiloh murmured, "I probably couldn't do it again for love or money."

"I'll bet you could if you had to. Just as you did yesterday," Richard said firmly.

"Maybe." Shiloh shrugged as they resumed their walk. "Funny what you can do when there's nothing left for it but just to put your head down and get it done. That's one thing I admire about the doc. No matter what it is, big or small, when she gets her head set on it, she just gets it done."

In her sweet voice Irene said, "She gets that from her father. They are both very determined, hardworking people."

"Luckily, she got her looks from you," Richard sighed.

"Lucky for me," Shiloh said gallantly, sketching a bow to his mother-in-law.

Irene smiled and nodded an elegant acknowledgment to him, but then she said, "Richard and I think that Cheney is lucky too, Shiloh. No, not lucky—blessed. We're very proud of you."

"Thank you, ma'am," Shiloh said quietly. "You can't know how much that means to me."

They walked around the fountain twice more, but then Shiloh noticed that Irene was slowing down and Richard was leaning more heavily on his cane. "Why don't we go inside and get something cool to drink?" he suggested. "It's actually hot out here, thank the Lord. I like snow but not ten feet of it for five months."

They started back around the house. "That's hardly an exaggeration. I think this was the worst winter I've ever seen in New York," Richard grumbled.

Irene sighed. "I thought that perhaps it's just that we're getting old, Richard. But now that we're down south again, it's made me remember that sometimes the winters up north are very cruel and the entire world isn't covered with ice and snow for months. At any rate, I certainly feel much better. I even feel better this afternoon than I did this morning. Now I wish I had gone with Cheney and Victoria and Minerva to visit the dear Rainsfords."

"Oh, you know them?" Shiloh asked with surprise. "I didn't realize. I just kinda assumed that Mrs. Buchanan was introducing Cheney to them."

"No, the Rainsfords are from New York," Richard explained. "Sam Rainsford is the fourth-generation banker of New York City Bank and Trust. Well, I guess you could say now that his sons are the fifth-generation bankers. Anyway, Samuel Rainsford helped me out when I started Duvall's Tools and Implements way back in 1832. They still have most of our banking business. The Steens, of course, have connections to every banker on the

East Coast, which is why Victoria is acquainted with them."

"Ahh," Shiloh said, "*those* Rainsfords. I've seen City Bank and Trust, St. Augustine, in town. Is that one of the Rainsford banks?"

"Sure is. Samuel and Ivy moved down here some time ago. When was it, Irene?"

"Eighteen-fifty," Irene said promptly. "I remember because they came to our ten-year anniversary party. Don't you recall? And Sam was so ill; his respiratory distresses had gotten so bad that he could barely breathe. Our anniversary is April eleventh, and it seems that Samuel and Ivy moved not long after that."

"You're right," Richard said thoughtfully. "It was thought he had consumption, but that proved to be an incorrect diagnosis, thankfully. He is asthmatic and is prone to having catarrh go down into pneumonia, but he says the sea air does him good."

Shiloh gave Richard a quick assessing glance, but he and Irene went on blithely reminiscing about their old friends. It had given Shiloh a start to hear him talking about consumption, because that was what Cheney and Dev had feared was wrong with Irene. But evidently Richard and Irene were blissfully unaware of this. Shiloh was glad; they had taken a good deal of trouble not to show their grave concern over Irene, and now it seemed that their worries might have been misplaced. It would have done neither Irene nor Richard any good to have known it. *Guess that's a good example of withholding a preliminary diagnosis for the sake of the patient and his family,* Shiloh reflected from his new vantage point of physician-in-training. *Makes sense, but how do you know when to tell them and when not to tell them? I'll have to ask the doc. . . .*

". . . to seeing your cousin Bain Winslow, and of course Beckett and Carsten, tomorrow night for dinner," Irene was saying to Shiloh. "I just hope that Sketes doesn't have too many inconveniences. I know the arrangements have been difficult for the servants."

"So do y'all know Mr. Grider?" Shiloh asked curiously.

"No, he's an old family friend of the Steens," Richard answered. "He's originally from Boston and was a business connection of Henry's. Irene and I haven't met him or his family."

"Family?" Shiloh repeated with surprise. "I didn't know he had a family. I never asked Mrs. Buchanan about him. I was just kinda picturing him like . . . like Ebenezer Scrooge," he said with sudden Dickensian inspiration.

"Oh, I don't think so," Irene said thoughtfully. "I have the impression that he's about Richard's age, though I think his wife is much younger. She is his second wife, you see. I don't know the particulars about his first wife, but I understand that he was a widower. He has no children, but he has three sisters who are also in his household."

They went back into the house by the rear servants' entrance, of course, since the monolithic front door was still locked. Shiloh hung behind, closely watching Richard make his way up the narrow steps that had no handrail. Again he growled inwardly at them not being able to use the front door. *It's just dumb,* he thought. *Such a stupid inconvenience, and what's the idea anyway? All of us are trooping all over his house. It's not like we're gonna steal stuff if we come in the front door, but we sure won't as long as we're dragging in and out of the back door!*

As soon as they got inside they heard the dogs.

"Now what's all that commotion?" Shiloh grumbled. "Excuse me, Miss Irene, I'll just slip on by you and go see about them."

The dogs weren't barking—Irish wolfhounds didn't bark much, as a rule—but he could hear them "talking," as he called it. They made melodious little whines, on a definite scale, from low in their throat to high pleas. It did sound just like the rise and fall of human voices except without words. But now they were, like unruly children, talking too loudly in the quiet house, and Shiloh could hear them scratching.

He went through the dining room and down the hallway. Sure enough, there they were at the cellar door talking and pleading and jumping up to drag their paws down the door in long beseeching let-me-in scratches. Fiona was struggling to pull them away, whispering darkly, "You're going to wake the children, and then what will happen to you? I'll tell you what will happen to you! Mr. Jauncy will lock you up in the workroom again, and won't you just be sad silly little babies then!"

They didn't look like babies, these big lanky dogs with enormous heads and paws and lolling tongues. Every time poor Fiona got one of them pulled away, the other wormed around her legs and jumped up to scratch the door and whine again.

"What's all this?" Shiloh said sternly as he came up the hall.

Immediately Sean and Shannon stopped wiggling and hung their heads with abject shame. But one of Sean's ears got stuck up on top of his head, and Shannon had her pink bows on her ears, so it was very difficult for Shiloh to keep his stern tone. "You—" he began, but it came out as a snicker, and both dogs' heads snapped up alertly. Their liquid black eyes brightened, and Sean promptly jumped up on the door and started talking again. Shannon, ludicrously, bent her front half down, keeping her back end up in the air, flattened her head on the floor, and stuck her long nose in the crack and started sniffing loudly. Then she jumped up and looked up at Shiloh with the wolfhound's perpetual grin, as if to say, "Did you see? Aren't we clever?"

He couldn't help it; his face cracked in a grin.

"Mr. Shiloh!" Fiona said. "You'll only encourage them!"

"I know, I know. Okay, kids, enough showing out. What are you carrying on about anyway?" He reached for them, intending to grab their collars and take them outside for a walk to calm them down. But then Shiloh, Fiona, and both dogs froze as if they were suddenly paralyzed.

Behind the cellar door they heard *meow . . . meow . . . meow . . .*

"That's a cat!" Shiloh exclaimed. "No wonder they were—Aw, man! How are we gonna get that cat outta there?"

"I-I don't know, Mr. Shiloh," Fiona said helplessly.

Irene and Richard came down the hall. Sean and Shannon bounded to meet them; they especially loved Richard because he sneaked them tidbits from the table when he thought Irene and Cheney weren't watching. Richard bent to pet them and looked at Shiloh questioningly.

"Shiloh," Irene asked, "what's wrong?"

"There's a cat in the cellar."

"A cat—oh dear," she said sympathetically.

As if the cat heard her, they heard a faint mournful *meooooow . . .*

"Oh dear," Irene said again, this time with distress.

Shiloh looked at the oak door and then at the ornate iron faceplate of the lock and the large keyhole. He bent down and ran his fingers over the faceplate.

Richard came to stand beside him and peruse the lock mechanism too. "The Spanish were very skilled and precise ironsmiths," he said thoughtfully. "You see that the lock is not fastened to the door with nails or brads? My guess is that a carpenter carefully cut a hole in the door exactly sized to the interior locking mechanism, and the faceplates have small spikes on the back side surrounding a precise cutout of the keyhole. That way the lock could be installed with one side of the faceplate attached and the other faceplate hammered in to fit. Over the years the wood would naturally swell to greatly tighten the fit."

Shiloh sighed. "You're saying that there's no way to take the faceplate off."

"Probably not," Richard answered.

"All right. What about cutting the bolts?"

Richard shrugged. "Probably could, but I would hesitate to do that, Shiloh. It is, after all, not our property. It would be a shame to ruin this lock. Every one in the house is a work of art, you might say."

"I know," Shiloh said with ill humor. "Okay, that just leaves one option. The cat must die."

Fiona's face drained of all color, and she gasped. Even Irene looked startled for a moment. Then Irene said soothingly, "He's just teasing you, Fiona. Now why don't you go see if you can find Mr. or Mrs. Espy? Because, of course, we're going to have to find a locksmith to open the door."

"Yes, ma'am," Fiona said and, with one last frightened fawn's look at Shiloh, fled down the hall.

Sean and Shannon wagged so hard that they started figure eights. Then they started scratching at the door and talking earnestly again, staring up first at Shiloh and then at Richard. "They can almost talk," Shiloh sighed.

"Very nearly," Richard agreed. "Don't you just hate it when the dogs are smarter than you? But what I don't understand is why they didn't take on like this all night."

"By the time Cheney and I took them upstairs it was late, and all of us—even Sean and Shannon—were exhausted," Shiloh said. "But I think that the cat may not have come up here by the door until today. I know I didn't hear a cat in the house last night, and I think I would have if it had been crying to get out. I just wonder how long the poor thing's been down there. Do you know when Mr. Grider and his family left?"

"No. I don't recall Victoria saying, do you, Irene?" Richard answered.

"No, dear," she said. "I think that you gentlemen can handle this crisis by yourselves, so I believe I'll retire for a little rest before dinner. No, no, dear, Mallow will help me, and I can manage the stairs perfectly well. Shiloh, for shame, you must stop teasing that child Fiona. You'll scare her to death." She went around the landing, and they heard her soft tread on the stairs.

"She's better," Richard said happily. "I'm glad we came. So glad."

Meow, said the cat.

Fiona came back with both Mr. and Mrs. Espy in tow. Shiloh spoke gently, for he did know that he—like all men except for Richard Duvall and, oddly enough, Bain Winslow's servant, Sweet—intimidated the shy Fiona. "Why don't you go on back upstairs and finish getting ready for the ladies' return? They'll probably be back soon, and they'll want to rest before dinner." Gratefully Fiona did a small curtsy and disappeared.

Shiloh turned to the Espys, who were watching him and Richard warily. "There's a cat stuck in the cellar," he said bluntly.

Jerome and Flo Espy stared at him.

"We have to get it out."

Both of the Espys dropped their gazes to stare at the floor.

Shiloh and Richard exchanged half-irritated, half-humorous looks. "You try," Shiloh said.

Jerome Espy's head snapped up. "We ain't half-wits. That there must be Jezebel. Stuck in the cellar."

Shiloh nodded patiently. "Jezebel. Mr. Grider's cat, I guess?"

He shrugged. "Good ratter."

Shiloh waited for a little more information, but it appeared that none was forthcoming. He sighed. "We can't leave the cat in the cellar. We have to get her out. The only way I can think of to do that is to get a locksmith out here to open the door."

Jerome Espy frowned darkly and looked down at his wife, who pursed her lips and shook her head. "Old Bebley's the only locksmith in town, and he wouldn't come out here to let a starvin' child outta the cellar, much less a cat. Mr. Grider accused him of making keys to come out here and rob him . . . or something like that. Anyways, Old Bebley said he wouldn't ever set foot on the place."

"Then we must find another locksmith besides Old Bebley," Shiloh said as reasonably as he could. "What's the next nearest town that would have a locksmith?"

Again the Espys exchanged dark portentous glances, and Mrs. Espy pursed her mouth again, but they said nothing.

After what seemed like a long time, Richard said, "Is it Jacksonville? Um . . . Tallahassee? St. Petersburg, maybe?"

"Back side of nowhere?" Shiloh rasped. "Look, Mr. Espy, I don't understand what the big problem is here. Just say the name of the nearest town. Please."

Jerome Espy pulled his gaunt shoulders up straight. "Now look here, Mr. Irons-Winslow, just because you're payin' us don't mean you can disrespect us. Me and Flo are trying to think of what to do, you see, and there's no call for you to go on like we're some kinda pure fools."

One good quality about Shiloh was that he could see when he was wrong, and he could apologize handsomely and sincerely. He stuck his hand out and said, "Sir, you're right. Ma'am, please pardon me for speaking to you so disrespectfully. You've been nothing but a lady, and I am so very sorry for forgetting that. Mr. Espy, please accept my sincerest apologies for being rude to you and your wife."

Jerome Espy couldn't have looked more dumbfounded than if someone had hit him over the head with a flatiron. He stared blankly down at Shiloh's hand, and then his own gnarled fist slowly clasped it. Shiloh shook it firmly, and then he turned to make a small bow to Mrs. Espy, who suddenly looked very pleased and even blushed a little.

Richard Duvall smiled to himself and thought, *Old as I am, my son-in-law just taught me a lesson: Nothing disarms even an implacable enemy faster than honesty and humility.*

A moment later another thought occurred to him. *Now why do I think that the Espys are enemies?*

But with the next sentence Richard's odd impression was confirmed. Jerome Espy's face hardened again, and he said curtly, "There's a bunch of Spaniards settled just over the river, and there's a young locksmith by the name of Benito Muñoz that could likely help you."

Then, before Shiloh had time to say a word, Jerome Espy took his wife's arm and turned her smartly around, and the couple went down the hall and disappeared.

Shiloh looked blankly at Richard. "Guess I'm going over the river in search of Benito Muñoz."

"Are you?" Richard replied. "Which river?"

"Dunno."

"Which settlement?"

"Dunno."

"Then I'm not going with you," Richard joked. "It sounds like you'll be gone for a long time."

Shiloh sighed. "Guess I'll have to chase the Espys down again and ask them to be a little more specific."

Sean and Shannon, who had continued to scratch and whine at the cellar door, both whipped around at the same time and ran down the hallway, their nails clicking on the wooden floor. Shiloh and Richard heard the back door open and a high-pitched giggle.

"Sounds like the ladies are home," Shiloh said. "Maybe Mrs. Buchanan knows a little more about this settlement."

Cheney, Victoria, and Minerva, all wearing visiting dresses, came down the hallway, followed by the dogs. Cheney had explained to Shiloh that morning that visiting dresses were at basically the same level of formality as walking dresses, only the wearer was making calls rather than going on a promenade. Shiloh, puzzled, had asked, "S'pose you take a promenade to a friend's house and then call on her? Whaddya call the outfit then?"

"Afternoon dresses, of course," she had promptly answered. "Because one would not take a promenade in the morning or evening, and one makes morning calls in the afternoon."

"But—aw, forget it," Shiloh had grumbled. "You look beautiful in whatever you call what you're wearin'."

He was right, because Cheney did look lovely in what was called Havana brown poplin, a creamy dark shade with a hint of an olive tint. The rich brown highlighted the delicate coral blush of her cheeks and made her green eyes brilliant. The dress was trimmed with myrtle green bows, a wide velvet sash with a long fringe, and Vandyke ruching around the hem. One of Cheney's signature accessories was the shoes she often bought to match the trimmings of an outfit. For this visiting dress she had bought heeled lace-up boots of soft suede leather dyed the exact shade of myrtle green to match the trim of the dress.

Victoria and Minerva looked lovely too. Victoria's dress was made of a brand-new fabric just introduced in January called satin jean, a finely twilled cotton with a satiny gloss. Her dress was white with a crisp navy blue stripe, trimmed with thick faille navy blue bows. The overskirt, which was caught up on the sides in gathers, was hemmed with a fringe of sterling silver ornaments. Minerva glowed in a frosty pale violet.

"Hello, Father, Husband," Cheney said gaily. "What are you two doing skulking around here in the dark hallway?"

"There's a cat in the cellar," Shiloh answered. "Sean and Shannon found it. Her."

"A cat?" Minerva repeated in amazement. "However did a cat get in the cellar?"

He shrugged. "I guess she lives here. Her name is Jezebel."

"Oh dear," Victoria said, "and we have no key."

"Exactly," Shiloh agreed. "Mr. and Mrs. Espy said there's a locksmith nearby who might be able to come in a hurry. But they didn't tell me where the settlement is. I was wondering, Mrs. Buchanan, if you would know of a Spanish settlement 'just over the river,' as Mr. Espy said."

"I do," Victoria answered, removing her gloves. "I researched everything about Sangria House and Plantation as well as the surrounding area before I decided to lease it. The name of the settlement is Comales, and it is just across the San Sebastian River. There's a ford due west of here where the river is only eleven feet across and shallow, and the Spanish tenant farmers who work the groves live in a small village just on the other side."

Shiloh nodded. "Okay. Would you ladies be needing the carriage again today?"

"No, we've made the only call we're going to make today," Cheney answered. "But why don't you send Andrew in the cart to fetch the locksmith, Shiloh? You and I can walk the dogs while we wait."

"Sounds good to me."

When Andrew returned with Benito Muñoz, Cheney and Shiloh were supposedly playing fetch the stick with Sean and Shannon. The game had somehow deteriorated, however, into a mad sort of game that was something like tag and something like hide and seek, albeit with a stick. It involved a lot of running and laughing on the humans' part, and a lot of running and panting on the dogs' part. Everyone did seem to enjoy the game.

Andrew pulled the cart all the way up the drive to halt beside the kitchen. A small huddle was on the seat beside him. Cheney and Shiloh, exchanging quizzical looks, went up to the cart.

"Mr. Muñoz?" Shiloh said. "Thank you for coming. We're in something of a mess here, and we surely need your services."

Mr. Muñoz was a small, compact man with glossy dark hair and poor but clean clothes. He wore the shoes woven of rope that so many of the Spanish wore, called *alpargata,* and clutched a small leather case in his lap. He didn't look up or move when Shiloh spoke to him.

Shiloh asked Andrew, "He does speak English, doesn't he?"

Barentine answered in his deliberate way, "Yes, sir. Mr. Muñoz, this is Mr. and Mrs. Irons-Winslow that I was telling you about. Now why don't you let Mrs. Irons-Winslow there take you into the Big House so you can see about that cellar door."

"*Sí, Señor* Barentine," the man whispered without raising his gaze from his tightly clutched hands.

Cheney stepped up as he was climbing down from the cart. "*Buenos días, Señor Muñoz. Muchas gracias por venir a ayudarnos.*" He followed her inside, never raising his head.

"What's with him?" Shiloh asked Andrew as he dismounted and came to pet Joey, the sturdy little work pony that pulled the farm cart.

"I don't know, sir," Andrew said. "He wouldn't even talk to me at first, pretended like he didn't speak English. Then his wife came out, and she was calling to him in English, and he got all upset, sir. He yelled at her to get back inside, and she did an about-face and scurried back into their little shanty. Then he dropped his head and hasn't looked up since. He didn't want to come at all, Mr. Irons-Winslow."

"Then how did you get him here?" Shiloh asked curiously.

"I had to pay him five dollars in advance," Andrew answered in a subdued tone, as if he were ashamed. "He climbed in then, but he's never looked up or said a word the whole time."

"You did well, Andrew," Shiloh said reassuringly. "You had five dollars on you?"

He looked up with a shy grin. "Mrs. Buchanan makes all her coachmen and footmen carry a fiver all the time. She's always said it's for emergencies, and I never quite knew what she meant by that. But I figured today was one of those emergencies."

"You're right about that," Shiloh agreed. "If we can't get that door open, I figure the ladies are going to have us choppin' it down. Tie Joey off there, Andrew, and come inside. I'll have to go up to our room to get some money. I sure wouldn't want you to be without Mrs. Buchanan's emergency pocket money."

They went inside and saw Cheney holding the dogs while Benito Muñoz was on his knees at the cellar door working on the lock. Andrew started to grab the dogs to help Cheney as Shiloh slipped by the small group in the hallway to get to the staircase. But just as they neared, Muñoz suddenly hopped up and pushed on the door. It swung open fast and soundlessly, and a black blur flew out, yowling fit to wake the dead. The poor startled locksmith flattened himself against the wall of the passage, his eyes huge, the whites gleaming in the shadowy hallway.

Sean and Shannon, panting and grinning, pulled away from Cheney and disappeared into the open door leading to the cellar. They heard loud trampling of eight huge paws, and then some odd thumps and a small yelp.

"I'll get a lantern," Shiloh said hurriedly. "Doc, do not try to go down these steps until I get back with some light. Andrew, try to find that cat if you can. I don't want her to turn up under Miss Irene's bed or in the well or something. Mr. Muñoz, thanks, and do get the front door now, please." He brushed past the little cowering man to go to the servants' workroom, where he knew lanterns and matches were stored.

Cheney stood at the top of the stairwell calling down, "Sean, Shannon, we're coming, babies. Don't move . . . don't fall down the stairs . . . we're coming . . ." Sean and Shannon were very good at going upstairs, but somehow going downstairs always puzzled them. They would get their front two paws on a step and their back two paws on a step, but then they could hardly figure out how to move one paw so as to get down another step. It was funny to watch when they were at home—Cheney and Shiloh had often stopped at the foot of the stairs in the town house to see them fidget, trying first one front paw, then a back paw, but then thinking better of it, start all over again with the front, and so on. But now, with the dogs just falling into a black hole, Cheney was frightened they might be seriously injured. Both of them were whining now, but Cheney couldn't tell if they were on the stairs, or near her, or if they were down in the cellar. Their high insistent whines echoed eerily.

Shiloh came hurrying back with a lantern, and together he and Cheney went down the stairs, Cheney holding tightly to his arm.

As soon as they got past the top landing, they felt moist chilly air on their skin, giving Cheney goose bumps. Her voice sounded shaky and uncertain as she half whispered, "How big is this cellar anyway? I can't see a thing beyond the light."

"Don't look right at the light, Doc, it'll blind you," Shiloh said, as nonchalant and confident as he always was, which reassured Cheney. "Yeah, there they are, right over there, I can see . . . something . . ."

They reached the bottom of the stairs, and because Cheney was indeed blinded—all she could see were big yellow spots everywhere she looked—Shiloh led her a couple of steps over a cold brick floor to where Sean and Shannon nosed around and around in frantic little circles, whining in the talking way that they had.

"What is that?" Cheney asked. She could now see the dogs, and she could see that there was an odd lump on the floor around which they were circling and nosing. "A pile of rugs or something?"

Shiloh knelt, holding the lantern over the lump. He looked up, and now Cheney could focus on his face. It was grave.

"Not rugs, Doc. It's a man. A very dead man."

PART II

A TIME TO WEEP,
AND A TIME TO LAUGH

Ecclesiastes 3:4

CHAPTER SIX

Dead at the Scene

"SO," CHENEY SAID DRYLY, "I confirm your diagnosis, Shiloh. It's a man, and he is dead." Kneeling by the corpse, she touched his hand; it felt more like hardened wax than human skin. It was cold.

"Yeah. Do you think it's old Grider?" Shiloh asked uncertainly. He lowered the lantern so they could see the body more clearly.

He was lying facedown and was rather crumpled up, so it was difficult to tell the size of the man's frame. His breeches were plain brown wool. He was wearing a cotton shirt with a vest, and a woolen shawl was tied around his neck. His shoes were leather half boots. He was also wearing a woolen nightcap. He looked small and shabby. They could see almost nothing of his face; it wasn't turned to the side enough to see a profile. In fact, he was almost entirely facedown. One leg was slightly bent at the knee, while the other was straight. His left arm was down by his side, his right arm up over his head.

"I don't know," Cheney finally answered after staring at the body for a while. "He doesn't look at all as Victoria described him to me. She said he was a tall, stern, commanding man, with a shock of thick, shiny white hair. Mr. Louis Grider is, as a matter of fact, a year younger than my father."

"Then this can't be him," Shiloh said, setting the lantern down on the floor and rising. "Maybe it's just a vagrant who saw the empty house and came in to get some clothes. And food," he added, remembering the evidence of the meal in the dining room when they had come in on Monday night.

Sean and Shannon were curiously subdued. As soon as Cheney and

Shiloh knelt by the body, the two dogs had moved back toward the staircase to lie down side by side in sphinx poses, with their paws extended in front of them, their heads lifted alertly. Now, as Shiloh stood up, they came to him and did their usual greeting: Sean butted Shiloh's knees with his head, and Shannon leaned against his legs as if she were fighting a strong wind. "Silly old dogs," Shiloh said affectionately, leaning down to scratch their ears. "You weren't fussing about that cat after all, were you? You were worried about Mr. Corpse, here. But—wait a minute, Doc. This has got to be Grider."

"It does? Why?"

"Because he must have the keys."

Shiloh waited for this simple observation to sink in. Even in the dim lamplight he could see understanding come over Cheney's face. "Of course; he's in a locked room that can only be locked with the keys. Unless . . . unless he was murdered and the murderer locked him in with the keys."

Cheney and Shiloh stared at each other. "Well, if he's got the keys, then it's pretty sure to be Grider," Shiloh finally said pragmatically. "You want me to search him?"

"No, I'm not afraid to do it," she said. "It's just that I hate to disturb the body. Normally the coroner wants to see the body exactly as it is found in order to help him determine the manner of death."

"Yeah, right," Shiloh agreed. "Okay, then. What do you want me to do?"

"Mm . . . just wait for a minute and let me think. . . . I would rather like to find out if it's Mr. Grider . . . and I would like to know how long—I mean, if he's been dead—"

"I know, Doc," Shiloh said, kneeling down again. "I know you're not spooked—you never get spooked—but I figure you'd like to estimate the time of death so you can tell the other ladies that he wasn't down here alive and suffering while we were up there on our merry holiday."

"Something like that, only I figure the only one who might have the vapors over a corpse in the cellar would be Jauncy. And about me getting spooked? You remember me, the little heap of jelly down in the cellar of the hospital, thinking that the moon ghost of Abigail van Dam was tormenting me?"

"Yeah, but you really did have somebody haunting you," Shiloh said darkly. "Just because Pettijohn wasn't dead doesn't mean he wasn't scaring you, and one day he's gonna have to pay for that. Anyway, Doc, are you spooked? Over this, I mean?"

"No, of course not," Cheney scoffed. "I suppose what I'm saying is that I'm going to break the law here, and I would like to have your help, since you know so much more about it than I do."

"Huh? Me? Knowing about estimating time of death?"

"No. Breaking the law. Now let me see . . ." She felt the man's hand that was down by his side. "Nothing in his left hand."

Shiloh felt the man's right hand and then put the lantern up close to it. "He's got something, Doc, but he's got that famous death grip. Lemme see—yep, it's a big round key ring. The keys are under his wrist."

"Don't move his hand or fingers," Cheney cautioned. "If you break the rigor, it will look suspicious. So, I suppose this is Louis Grider."

They both stared down at the crumpled figure for a few moments. Finally Shiloh sighed deeply. "I've seen a lot of dead men in my life. Some I called friends; some I called enemies; some I didn't know at all. I've never gotten over how small and pitiful and defenseless men look when their soul has departed."

"True," Cheney agreed. "But as a doctor, you'll start looking for other things, Shiloh. It's from the dead that we learn most about how to heal the living."

He nodded. "So can you tell anything about his time of death, Doc?"

She frowned. "He's still in full *rigor mortis*. . . ." She leaned close over him and sniffed. "There's a very faint odor of putrefaction." Sitting back on her heels, she made a wry face at Shiloh. "It's no use since he's in full rigor and in this position. To do a good postmortem examination I'd have to move him so much it would be obvious we had tampered with the body. I guess I'd better leave it for the coroner. Perhaps he will allow me to assist," she said eagerly. "I have had so much experience with autopsies at the hospital in the last months."

Shiloh rose. "Yeah, Doc, maybe he will. Betcha he's never seen a fine lady who loves cold, putrid, moldy corpses so much."

"Shiloh! He's not moldy!"

"Might be. It's so dark down here he could be covered with mush-rooms and we wouldn't know it," he rasped. "I guess I'll send Andrew into town to fetch the coroner."

"Mm . . . Shiloh, these are such unusual circumstances that I think it would be better if a 'gentleman of substance' explained the situation to the authorities."

"Yeah? You mean you want me to go wake your father up from his nap?" Shiloh quipped.

"No, I mean you should go, Mr. Iron Head."

"Okay," he said reluctantly. "But just remember that Florida's still under congressional reconstruction, so I might hafta talk to the provost marshal. I didn't do so good with them in Charleston."

"No, you and General Forrest almost got us all arrested, including Rissy," Cheney said. "Try to behave yourself this time, please. I don't want to have to come get you out of jail."

Cheney rose and followed him to the staircase. He stood back courteously to let her go in front of him. "You coming with me, Doc? You've got more substance than I've got."

"You'd better not be talking about my figure," she said caustically over her shoulder.

"Huh? No! No, 'course not! I was talking about, you know, what you said about being a gentleman of substance!"

"Well, I think I am more substantial since Sketes has been our cook. Anyway, I'm just coming up to get some more lanterns or candles. I'm not going to stay down there in the dark with that corpse, moldy or not."

They went to the servants' workroom, and Shiloh started to go out the back door. Then he said, "You know what? We forgot all about the poor little locksmith. Wonder if he's still around."

"You know, Shiloh, his hands were actually shaking as he worked on the cellar door lock," Cheney said. "I tried to put him at his ease, but I got the distinct impression that he was just about scared to death."

"Wonder why? Maybe he'd had a run-in with Grider too. Sounds like that old man was a terror to everybody. Excuse me for a minute, Doc." He left and crossed the dining room toward the hall.

Cheney found a cupboard with several lanterns, all full of oil, and some matches. Gathering three of them up, she met Shiloh in the hallway as she went back to the cellar door.

"The front door's unlocked, all right," he said. "It's standing wide open, and no sign of Mr. Muñoz either."

"You mean he didn't stay to collect his pay?"

"No. Andrew had to pay him in advance to even get him to come. Say, Doc, when he opened this door, did he use a lock pick?"

She looked puzzled. "I don't know what that is."

"Burglar's tools, Doc. To pick locks with when you don't have the key and you want to break in," he explained, speaking very slowly.

"Oh. No. He used skeleton keys. Why?"

"Hmm. Never mind. It's probably not important. You want me to help you with that stuff?"

"No. Please just go on, Shiloh, so you'll be back soon. I'm going to go down there and stay with Mr. Grider. Now that we know he's here, I feel someone should sit with him."

He traced her face gently with one finger. "You're an honorable Christian lady, and I thank the Lord every day that you're my wife. I'll be back as soon as I can." He went back down the passage. Sean followed him, while Shannon stayed with Cheney. This was what the dogs generally did without being told.

Cheney went back down the stairs, slowly and deliberately, since she was holding the lanterns and couldn't hold on to the banister. The lit lantern they had left in the cellar cast a weak sickly glow over the body; very little else could be seen in the deep shadows beyond the lamplight.

"It is like a dungeon down here, isn't it, Shannon?" Cheney murmured. Kneeling again by the body, she lit the three lanterns and then placed two at his head and one at his feet. She took the other one so she could explore, making a slow circumference of the cavernous room.

The first thing she noticed was that there were no windows, not even the high small rectangular windows that many cellars had. She was in the room on the west side and finally made out two sinks, two large tubs, and several wash pots piled on a work counter. *The laundry, and here, of course, are the cauldrons to heat water for bathing. What's this? Oh, it's the outside door. I noticed this door when we were surveying the grounds yesterday. Locked, and as solid as the other doors. Probably the original doors, and the house is . . . what? Over a hundred years old, Victoria said.*

Her eyes were growing fairly accustomed to the dim light, so she went into the next room, a room like a butler's pantry, with floor-to-ceiling cupboards and a waist-high worktable. There was not a single thing in the cupboards or on the table. "That Mr. Grider must have been a terrible miser," she told Shannon, who followed her every step. "Or maybe it was Mrs. Grider. I wonder . . . I suppose the ladies went on to England and are still waiting for Mr. Grider or believe he's on the way. It's sad to think of them waiting for him. . . ."

In the other front half of the cellar was a large storage room, and it, too, was bare.

On the east end of the cellar were the wine racks. There were three long ones along the east side, and in the center rear of the room, two more. They were six feet high and about eighteen feet long. There were hundreds of bottles of wine here, she estimated. "Funny," she mused. "He didn't sell the wine. Maybe he was trying to find a buyer for the entire stock." Cheney gazed thoughtfully down at Shannon, who wagged her tail and grinned. Cheney reflected that the dogs had not seemed to be very agitated, considering it had been a corpse down in the cellar instead of just a simple house cat. But Shannon, and sometimes Sean, had stayed with her down in the cellar of the hospital, which was the laboratory and the hospital morgue. Doubtless the dogs were accustomed to the smell of death. Curiously, Cheney lifted her head and sniffed. To her the cellar smelled dank—the smell of old dampness on stone floors and walls— and the air was cold, clammy, and carried the odor of mildew on the odd wisps of drafts in the room. She couldn't detect any smell of death. She knew, however, that dogs had a more keen sense of smell than did humans, and they could probably smell the dead man long before any human ever would.

Cheney went back to stand at the bottom of the staircase and con- sider Mr. Louis Grider's body. At first—not having a sense of the size of the room—she had just assumed that the man had fallen down the stairs, sustained some fatal injury to a critical organ, and died, perhaps from massive internal hemorrhage.

But now Cheney was not so sure.

Slowly she backed up until her heels were against the bottom step. She set down the lantern, crossed her arms, and studied the distance, the position of the body, and the orientation of the limbs. "Something's not right, Shannon," she murmured softly.

Cheney didn't think that Mr. Grider had fallen down the stairs. She started to make some measurements, draw the body in relation to the stairs, and note the exact position of the limbs, but then she realized that the coroner would do that. It was his job, not hers.

Now she wasn't sure when the man might have died. It was so cold, freezing cold, and damp. . . .

Cheney started so violently that Shannon jumped. *That was what Shiloh had said when he had that nightmare—or daymare, I guess you'd say.* She recalled the conversation:

He'd said, *"Did you fall in the river?"*

"No, darling, no. You fell in the pool."

"Did someone die?

"What? No, Shiloh. What's the matter?"

"I had a bad dream. It was dark and cold; freezing damp cold . . . someone was dead."

"It's just a coincidence," she said loudly. The cellar did not have an actual echo, of course, but like many solid silent stone places, it seemed that whispers, just beyond the edge of human hearing, sounded after one spoke recklessly.

Mentally shaking herself, Cheney went back to the problem at hand. *So when did he die? I could at least narrow it down some . . . if I was very careful and didn't disturb him too much.*

Briskly now, without worrying any more about it, Cheney went to work.

She ran upstairs, but very quietly, for everyone else was still resting, taking an afternoon *siesta,* as she was sure many men and women had done in this house for the last hundred or so years. All of the bedroom doors were closed, and she heard no sound. Her medical bag was in her closet. Snatching it up, she almost flew downstairs. She felt slightly guilty because she didn't want anyone to know what she was doing; at the same time she told herself—and the Lord—that she wouldn't lie about it. If the coroner asked her if she had moved the body, she would tell him the truth. Feeling slightly better, she adjusted the lanterns until they gave her the best light.

First she took note of the *livor mortis,* the irregular reddish discoloration of dependent parts of the body due to the blood settling after the heart stops pumping. It was difficult to check, considering that the body was still in full rigor mortis, but she could see the splotchy markings on the underside of the lower arms—she pushed his sleeves up as far as she could without moving the arms—and his face. It was turned very slightly onto the right side, and though she couldn't lift his head, she could see a thin stripe of livor along his cheek and the corner of his mouth.

Next she took the temperature of the body to gauge the degree of *algor mortis,* or the cooling of the body. It normally took approximately forty hours for the body to cool to the environmental temperature. She had no idea what the temperature of the room was, but that could be determined at any time. She jotted down the body temperature of fifty-three degrees, and the time and date—Wednesday, February 27, 3:30 P.M.—in a small notebook she kept in her medical bag.

Next she tried as best she could to see if the rigor mortis was beginning to pass. The stiffening generally began from four to ten hours after death and passed off in three to four days. It began in the muscles around the head and neck, with jaws and eyelids stiffening first; and as it began to pass off, the jaws and eyelids usually were the first to loosen. Very carefully Cheney felt along the man's jawline and then lightly touched his left eyelid. Both were still rigid.

As Cheney was bending over Grider's head, she brushed against the nightcap and dislodged it. Quickly she began to replace it as she had found it, but then she noticed something odd about Grider's hair.

Big tufts of hair were missing. He had odd bald spots all over his head. In fact, even as Cheney moved the nightcap, she could see a large hank of hair inside the nightcap that had evidently come off of his scalp while he was wearing the cap. Then, with some distaste, Cheney saw that the man's head was positively black; he must, indeed, have been filthy, she thought at first. But when she held the lantern close with one hand and gently swiped a clean piece of gauze across his scalp, she saw with amazement that it was not dirt; the skin of the man's scalp actually appeared to be turning black.

His hair was certainly not the silvery white sheen that Victoria had said was one of Louis Grider's most striking features. Slowly Cheney pulled the hank of hair out of the nightcap and held the lantern as near to it as she dared. The hair didn't look right; it was an odd piebald color. It was no use. Cheney couldn't see well enough by the lantern light, so quickly she folded up the hair sample inside a gauze square and put it into her medical bag.

Again she put the nightcap back onto the man's head, gently trying to place it back exactly as she had found it. But once again she was distracted—this time by Grider's eyebrows. She could see his left eyebrow only; and as she pulled the lantern as close as she dared without singeing the man's face, she could see that his eyebrow was extremely odd. *It's just a little tuft of hair . . . it looks as if he might have shaved the inner part and the outer part and just left the middle, but no one would do that. Why would they?*

She was sitting there, staring blankly off into space, wondering why a person might shave only the inner third and the outer third of their eyebrows when Shannon leapt up, went to the foot of the stairs, and started barking.

Cheney jumped up in alarm. She knew that Shannon would not actually attack anyone, but this insistent curt barking meant that someone was coming down the stairs that she didn't like. Cheney heard a man's voice she didn't recognize, a deep raspy voice, and then Shiloh called out, "Doc! Get Shannon, wouldja? The coroner's here and he's gotta come downstairs."

"Of course," she called, frantically replacing Grider's nightcap, then jumping up to grab Shannon's collar and pull her into the empty storage room and close the door securely. "Be quiet, Shannon. You're making a scene," she said severely. Shannon barked twice more and then whined a little. Cheney heard slight sounds behind the door and saw Shannon's black nose shoved underneath the door as far as it would wedge. "Now you be quiet and be good, or I'll leave you down here until we go home," Cheney muttered. Going to the foot of the stairs, she called up, "It's all right now. She's locked up."

She heard an unsteady tread on the stairs and turned for one last guilty glance at Grider. She saw her medical bag right by the body. It was lying open, the gauze pad with the hair in it and her thermometer in the case sticking up. She hurried to grab the bag and shoved it into the bottom shelf of the wine rack right behind Grider's head. Then she whirled around, desperately trying to regain her composure, and saw the coroner, with Shiloh behind him grinning knowingly at her. She assumed an innocent expression.

"Mr. MacDonald, I have the honor of introducing my wife, Dr. Cheney Irons-Winslow. Cheney, may I present to you Mr. Bruce MacDonald, the coroner for St. Johns County."

The first thing Cheney noticed was that the man reeked of liquor. The sour smell hung like a foul cloud around him, and when he spoke, the stench was much worse. He was rumpled. His breeches were unironed, and his sack coat hung messily, one pocket evidently loaded (with a full flask, Cheney thought) and the other empty, which made his coat lopsided. He was fairly tall, about five feet ten inches, wiry and bowlegged. He wore a bowler hat pushed far back on his head, and a few wisps of reddish hair showed thinly around it. He had a bad complexion and bad teeth. His shoulders were bowed, but Cheney didn't know if that was the lethargy of drunkenness or if he was just slightly stooped. She cast a cool sidelong glance at Shiloh, and he grimaced. The meaning was clear: *chronic alcoholic and drunk right now.*

"How d'ye do, eh? Whatsis, little lady? Got a dead body here. You can run along. No need for any little girls having the vapors while I'm seeing about it," he said blearily. "So this is Grider, eh?" He went to stand by the body and stared down at it.

As Cheney watched him, she noticed that he was unsteady on his feet, weaving and bobbing slightly, as very drunk people will do.

"I am a physician, sir," Cheney said evenly. "As a matter of fact, I have had extensive experience in postmortem examinations, and I would like to offer my services to aid you in any way that I can—with examination of the body for the purpose of determining the time and manner of death—"

He turned and glared at her over his shoulder. "Help? A female would-be doctor wants to *help* me? I've been elected coroner of St. Johns County for three years now, missy, and I've yet to need help from any female! Now get along wi' ye—"

Shiloh stepped up and loomed over him, seeming like a gargantuan threatening shadow in the uncertain light of the lanterns. "Mr. MacDonald, you are being rude to a lady. Apologize. Now."

His head wobbling, Mr. MacDonald squinted up at Shiloh's face, his own ravaged features distorted with ill temper. Reflexively he backed up a step, then muttered ungraciously, "Thank ye for your offer, Miz . . . Miz—"

"Doctor," Shiloh pronounced carefully, stepping close to loom over him again. "Doctor Irons-Winslow."

"Dr. IronWinthro," MacDonald pronounced as clearly as he could, considering that he was slurring his words. "But I'll take care of this. S'my job. Beg pardon, ma'am."

He turned back to the body, staring owlishly down. "He's dead, all right. Dead he is. You hear that, Dr. IronWinthro, ma'am? The coroner pronounces him dead at the scene."

"We know he's dead," Shiloh tried to say as politely as he could. "Aren't you going to examine him? Investigate for manner of death?"

"The last time I looked," MacDonald groused as he turned and began to make his unsteady way back to the stairs, "I was the coroner of St. Johns County, Mr. IronWinthro, and not you nor yer wife. The-coroner-pronounces-him-dead-at-the-scene. Thassall you need to know. Thassall you need to hear."

He stepped on the bottom stair, missed it, and stumbled. Shiloh quickly moved to give him a steadying hand, but MacDonald shoved him away, cursing.

"Get your hands off me, you hooligan, or I'll have the provos on ye," he growled, brushing off his sleeve as if Shiloh had soiled it.

Shiloh raised his hands and backed off, rolling his eyes at Cheney.

"No need to call me out, Winthro," he went on grumbling as he made his reeling way up the stairs. "This is Louis Grider for sure and certain, and that fool of a dog ye've got could probably tell that he's dead. And I need a female physician from Noo York, of all the accursed places, to tell me that?"

Shiloh, after glancing at Cheney's *Ask him again!* expression, said, "But, Mr. MacDonald, what have you determined was the manner of his death? And, uh, the time of death?"

MacDonald didn't even turn around. "Report tomorrow. Ain't no need to get in any hurry. Ol' Grider's dead, and he's gonna stay that way."

"Yeah, that was my expert medical opinion too," Shiloh called sarcastically after him.

He and Cheney looked blankly at each other.

Finally Cheney said, "Well, I do assume that someone is coming to get him? Or is that just entirely too much trouble for the coroner of St. Johns County?"

"Well, there was a cart behind us, driven by two men who were in the tavern with Mr. MacDonald," Shiloh answered. "No tellin' how much his drinkin' cronies are getting paid to be ambulance attendants. Yeah. That bunch couldn't *find* an ambulance if they were sittin' in it with a map."

Cheney went back to Grider's body and knelt. "Shiloh—" she began, but then they heard loud uncouth voices, laughing and cursing, at the top of the stairs, and heavy treads as the men started down the stairs.

Shiloh knelt by her and asked in a low voice, "What, Doc? If you want me to, I'll tell 'em they can just wait until you get through here."

She hesitated, staring down at the man's crumpled body. Finally she stood and murmured, "I guess not. It's really not my place. Maybe he wants to do a thorough examination at the morgue. You certainly can't see anything down here, and it's freezing. But do go ahead and get the keys, Shiloh. If Coroner MacDonald wants to charge us with tampering with a body, then so be it. We need those keys."

Shiloh stepped over the body, bent down and loosed the man's four fingers to release the key ring, and then, with a mischievous wink at

Cheney, tossed them into her medical bag, which, Cheney had thought, was invisible in the deep shadows of the bottom shelf of the wine rack. "They won't get lost there, and we'll for sure remember where they are, huh?"

As the two men clumped into the cellar, Cheney muttered, "Thanks so much for your help, Winthro."

"Welcome."

CHAPTER SEVEN

Far Above Rubies

"THIS ROOM SURE LOOKS different from the first time I saw it," Shiloh commented as Sketes began to serve the first course of baked oysters Parmesan. It came straight from the chafing dish, so the fragrant cheese still bubbled.

"I should hope so," Minerva Wilcott said with a theatrical shudder.

"Why is that, Shiloh?" Carsten Beckett asked, his blue eyes wide and innocent. "Did it have the stench of death in it?"

"Carsten, we have said that we will not speak of anything like that at dinner," Victoria said sternly to her youngest brother. Carsten Steen was twenty-one years old, but he looked and behaved more like a teenager. He was much like his father, with a chunky build, thick strawblond hair, mischievous blue eyes, and a wide mouth that seemed continually split into a cheerful grin. It was difficult to believe he was attending New York University, studying banking and finance; he seemed more like the rowdy schoolboy who was always dipping little girls' pigtails into inkwells. Certainly his studies hadn't matured him too much, as he had decided to take an entire semester off so that he and his brother could learn blue-water yacht sailing.

"Vic, I can't believe you're putting on that prim act," Carsten declared. "When Dev talks about things like adipoids and goblins, you never say a word."

"That's because it pertains to his profession," Victoria retorted.

"Goblins?" Richard Duvall repeated to himself with bewilderment.

Cheney leaned across the table to whisper, "I presume he meant *globulins,* Father."

"So now I'm supposed to know what we're talking about?"

"No, Father, now we're *not* supposed to talk about it."

Richard sighed deeply. "I don't know what we're talking about anyway. I never know."

Minerva, seated between the two Steen brothers, was saying to Carsten on her right, "Besides, he said it *looked* different, Carsten, not that it *smelled* different."

On her left was Beckett Steen, who was such a male version of his older sister, Victoria, that it was uncanny. He had thick silver-blond hair, heavy-lidded clear blue eyes, and a fine complexion. Of the four Steen children, Beckett and Victoria were the only two who had inherited Josefina Wilcott Steen's languid grace and innate elegance. "And, Vic, how can you expect us not to talk about it?" Beckett asked lazily. "Finding a corpse in the cellar is so exciting."

"Certainly it is," Victoria agreed. "I for one want to hear all the gossip about it from Cheney and Shiloh; but I do *not* want to hear disgusting details about Mr. Grider's . . . condition," she finished delicately.

Shiloh, at the head of the table, said lightly, "Mustn't offend the ladies, Beckett. All I meant to say was that tonight this room looks warm and welcoming."

Sangria House was over one hundred years old, and in the dining room it showed in the original walnut paneling, dark and gleaming, the exposed blackened beams, and the immense fireplace, where an enormous fire now softened the severe room.

At some point the dining room had been updated, for a pair of French doors faced out onto the back lawn. On this night a dazzling lightning display could be seen through them, and thunder continuously grumbled, but it seemed far away and unconnected to the candlelit room and the splendidly dressed diners. Occasionally raindrops would hiss and sizzle in the fire as they fell down the long, long—and now cleared—chimney.

The dining table was old too and was an unusual piece. Made of the Spanish favorite, walnut, it was so massive it ran almost the entire length of the room. Nevertheless, it was not ornate, as eighteenth-century Spanish furnishings generally were. It was of a surprisingly simple design, with eight legs, squared and heavy, with wrought-iron stretchers running between them across the width of the table instead of the length. The table seated eighteen. The chairs were in the Elizabethan style, with solid backs carved in ornate relief, columnar turned legs, and solid stretchers.

The massive chairs were so heavy it was difficult for a woman to move them. They were obviously handmade in the days when a servant stood behind every diner's chair. All eighteen of them had been lined up against the wall by the sailors after they had cleaned the room, and Sketes had had a time of it dragging nine of them into place for this evening's dinner.

Shiloh sat at the head of the table, with Victoria on his right and his cousin Bain beside her, and then Irene and Richard seated together. On his left sat Carsten, Minerva, Beckett, and Cheney. Cheney, Victoria, and Minerva had agreed to take turns managing and hosting dinners, and tonight was Cheney's turn. As her mother so often did, Cheney had seated the diners at one end, instead of stranding people down the seemingly endless expanse of the table.

"I'm sure this room must have been exceedingly *un*welcoming last Monday night," Bain said in his cultured British accent. "With the storm, and the house being locked up. I suppose we would have done something if we had known you were coming in that night, wouldn't we, Beckett?"

"I don't know what we would have done," Beckett answered with his characteristic languor. "I'm not much for washing up after dinner or airing rooms or tidying up after other people."

"You're not much for tidying up after yourself either," Minerva teased, with the liberty allowed first cousins.

"Oh, as if you are," Carsten scoffed. "You've probably never washed up a single dish in your life."

"And you have?" she asked tartly. She waited a moment while Carsten seemed to be trying to recall if he had ever done such a thing as washing a dish. Then, nodding with satisfaction, she turned back to Bain, who was directly across from her. "But what I don't understand, Mr. Winslow, is why you didn't know that *Locke's Day Dream* was coming in. Carsten told me that the four of you came in on the fifteenth, which was ten days before we got here. Didn't Mr. Grider tell you when we were scheduled to arrive?"

Very carefully Bain answered, "I was not acquainted with Louis Grider, Miss Wilcott."

Shiloh gave him a searching glance. Bain met it squarely with a perfectly expressionless face. Minerva, however, was unaware of the undercurrents between Shiloh and his cousin, and she went on innocently, "You weren't? Beckett and Carsten didn't introduce you? Why not?"

"Minerva, you are interrogating a dinner guest," Victoria said. Turning to Beckett, she asked, "So what did Mr. Grider tell you, Beckett? When you made the arrangements for the gatekeepers' lodges?"

Beckett shrugged slightly. "All he said was that the lodges were unoccupied, so we could lease them anytime we wanted to, on a per diem basis. He said the daily charge would stop whenever your lease started, Victoria, since your lease included the two lodges."

"So when did you arrive?" Victoria persisted.

Airily Beckett said, "This visit? On the fifteenth. That was a Friday, so I paid the rent on the lodges for a week in advance, and then I paid again last Friday."

"So you saw Mr. Grider last Friday?" Cheney asked. "How did he look?"

Beckett answered lazily, "He looked ill. He was stooped and seemed weak. But I knew he was going to England for health reasons, so I didn't think it too odd. He certainly didn't appear as if he might just keel over dead at any minute."

"What about his hair?" Cheney asked insistently. "How did his hair look?"

"His hair? I can't—oh yes, now I remember. He was wearing a nightcap and a shawl, and I recall thinking that he did dress like an invalid," Beckett said. "So I'm sorry, ma'am, I never saw his hair."

"What about his eyebrows?" Cheney demanded. "What did his eyebrows look like?"

Beckett looked puzzled. "His eyebrows? I can't say that I noticed them one way or the other. It's not the sort of thing that men generally take much notice of, Dr. Irons-Winslow, though if I had known that you needed the information, I certainly should have paid more attention," he finished gallantly.

But it was wasted on Cheney, as her green eyes drilled into him. "What about his behavior, Beckett? Was he of sound mind, in your opinion?"

"Cheney, now you sound as if you're interrogating a hostile witness," Irene said gently. "I know that this is hard for you to realize, but most people do not take particular note of a person's eyebrows or meticulously analyze their state of mind."

"Oh, sorry, Beckett," Cheney said. "I'm just curious, considering he was down in the cellar dead, you see."

"Of course, ma'am. My sister has told me that you are prodigiously curious about all things medical, and though I am a poor observer, I will try to answer. Last Friday Mr. Grider appeared to me to be very alert, and he certainly was lucid enough to discuss the rent on the cottages and the money I owed. But he never said anything about when you all might arrive."

"It's very odd," Victoria said. "In his last letter he confirmed he had received my notice that we should be arriving on either the twenty-fifth or the twenty-sixth, and he said that he and his family would be leaving on the twenty-fourth, which was last Sunday. And you're sure, Beckett, that he said nothing of all this last Friday?"

"I'm sure, Vic," he answered with some exasperation. "And the old— I mean, Mr. Grider—took my money for another full week's rent on the lodges too. Guess I'll never get it back now."

"Did you have the agreement in writing?" Victoria asked.

"No, you know I didn't, and don't lecture me for the ten thousandth time about getting everything in writing," Beckett grumbled. "Not everyone is a stickler for that sort of thing. There is such a thing as a gentlemen's agreement."

"Ah yes, the famous gentlemen's agreement," Victoria said solemnly. "It works wonderfully—until the gentlemen disagree, and then they wish they had gotten a written contract, as their sisters had so wisely told them ten thousand times."

"Okay, I get it, Vic," Beckett mumbled.

Victoria turned to Bain and said, "Speaking of these lodges, Mr. Winslow, I hope that the gatekeeper's lodge is not too rustic for you. Mr. Grider assured me that both the north and south lodges were fully furnished and would be thoroughly cleaned and aired. With what we know now, I'm afraid that the state of the cottage may have been quite different."

"It is delightful, Mrs. Buchanan," Bain answered. "I have no complaints at all."

"No wonder," Carsten muttered under his breath, his head bowed over his soup.

"Quiet, Carsten," Beckett intoned in a deep whisper, leaning behind Minerva.

"It doesn't do any good to whisper," Minerva complained. "You're sitting right by me, Beckett. I can hear you."

"Perhaps I was whispering so that others at the table would not hear," Beckett said frostily. "But now we don't have to concern ourselves about that, do we?"

"Aw, I was only talking about old Sweet anyway," Carsten said. "All I meant was that Winslow has a servant at the lodge, and we don't. You didn't ask us if we were satisfied with the south lodge, Victoria."

"No, I did not," Victoria said sweetly. "What about you, Mrs. Duvall? Are you comfortable?"

"I am more than comfortable," Irene answered. "The climate is wonderful; it's difficult to believe that it's the middle of such a terrible winter in the north. I like this place. In fact, I like this house," she added with a twinkle in her eyes, "even if it did have a corpse in the wine cellar."

"One must overlook these minor inconveniences," Beckett said with a sly sidelong glance at his sister, who refused to take the bait and merely gave him a brilliant smile.

"Even my mother is curious about it, aren't you?" Cheney said affectionately. "You brought it up so skillfully and with such delicacy."

"Thank you, dear. And yes, I am wondering about Mr. Grider," Irene admitted. "It seems so extraordinary that his family should go ahead without him and he doesn't tell the servants when we are coming—or even that we *are* coming—and so no preparations are made."

Florence Espy, standing by the sideboard, her burning dark eyes darting from speaker to speaker, shifted restlessly as Irene spoke. As she was taking hostess duty tonight, Cheney was watching Sketes and Mrs. Espy closely as they served. Cheney saw the woman flinch a little, and with horror she thought that Mrs. Espy might actually burst out into one of her odd temper tantrums. But Cheney was underestimating Molly Sketes, who stepped smartly up to the woman and whispered furiously in her ear. Her face reddening, Florence Espy's unhappily down-turned mouth tightened, but she said nothing. Cheney nodded at Sketes—a signal to collect the dishes from the first course and to serve the second—and Sketes once again whispered quickly to Mrs. Espy. With the unobtrusiveness of a long-time servant, Mrs. Espy began to collect the ramekins that had held the oyster dish while Sketes came behind to offer the second course, black bean soup with Boston brown bread. Cheney surreptitiously glanced around the table to see if anyone else had noticed the small drama. It appeared that no one had except her mother, and Irene almost, but not quite, winked at Cheney.

With an air of angelic innocence, Carsten said to Irene, "But, ma'am,

Mr. Grider's family didn't go to England with him. Or . . . er . . . without him. Or—anyway, his three sisters, and his wife, are lodged at Mrs. Fatio's boardinghouse."

Victoria looked surprised. "They are? And you have made their acquaintance?" She turned to Beckett, the older—and somewhat more responsible—brother.

"We are acquainted with Mrs. Grider, aren't we, Bain?" Beckett brightened. "And we've been introduced to the sisters."

"I'm certain that in his last letter to me, Mr. Grider said that his wife was accompanying him," Victoria said thoughtfully.

"Well, she didn't," Carsten said.

"Of course she didn't, you ninny, because he's dead and she's not," Minerva said with a superior air.

"Min, nobody thought she would accompany him when he died," Carsten taunted her. "What was she supposed to do? Throw herself on his funeral pyre or something? Anyway, we saw her at Mrs. Fatio's today. Mrs. Fatio has a courtyard where they serve sangria every afternoon instead of tea."

Victoria's normally languorous gaze grew sharp. "What? Mrs. Grider was having sangria in the courtyard with you two the day after her husband is found dead?"

"Well, yeah," Carsten answered uneasily. "Winslow was there too. Weren't you, Bain?"

"I was," Bain answered carelessly. "We were just offering her our condolences. She is greatly saddened and distressed by her husband's death."

"Uh-huh," Shiloh said to Bain, narrowing his eyes suspiciously. "My guess is that Mrs. Grider is much younger than her husband. Much, much younger."

"I wouldn't know," Bain said, again speaking in the painstakingly cautious tone he had used before when he spoke about Mrs. Grider. "I was not acquainted with Mr. Grider."

Hastily Cheney put in, "Well, I certainly am surprised to hear that his . . . er . . . family is here. You knew Mr. Grider, Victoria; do you know his sisters?"

"No, I don't," she answered. "I only met Mr. Grider once. He had come to town to attend to some business affairs, and as it was on a Saturday, he called on Father at home. Mother and I were receiving too, so Father introduced us. But that was many years ago, when his first wife was still living. I never met her or Mr. Grider's sisters. But now that I know they are all here, I must call on them to offer our sympathy."

"We did that, Vic," Carsten said with surprising meekness. "Honestly. We called on the sisters and Mrs. Grider and offered the family's condolences and assured Mrs. Grider that we would notify Father. And we did. We telegraphed him this afternoon."

"Very good," Victoria said with approval. "Did you ask him if he would like one of us to attend the coroner's inquest, to represent the family?"

"Fortunately, that ordeal won't be necessary, Mrs. Buchanan," Bain said. "There won't be a coroner's inquest, because his verdict was death by misadventure."

"What?" Cheney said, astounded. "Death by misadventure?"

"Yeah, and how do you know all about it, Bain?" Shiloh demanded.

"Mrs. Grider told us," Bain answered. "The coroner told her that Mr. Grider had fallen down the stairs and broken his neck. And this afternoon, when we made our condolence call, she told us."

Cheney's and Shiloh's eyes met, and she shook her head almost imperceptibly. Shiloh looked rebellious for a moment—it was inevitable that he and Bain would be at odds, considering their past—but for once, Cheney was the moderating influence over Shiloh. He half smiled at her, and she could see him relax. Politely she asked, "And so, Mr. Winslow, did Mrs. Grider tell you when the funeral is to be?"

Bain answered with mock gravity, "As a matter of fact, she did, Mrs. Winslow. It's to be tomorrow at three o'clock."

"But I still don't understand," Minerva said plaintively. "Beckett, you met Mr. Grider—before he died, I mean—"

"Yes, luckily it was before he died, Min," Beckett answered solemnly.

"So what was he like?" Minerva persisted.

"Well, he was alive at the time," Beckett said lazily.

"Oh, Beckett, you're as bad as Carsten!" she snapped.

"What'd I do?" Carsten asked, bewildered.

"Nothing, this particular time. But you will, of course, because you always do," Minerva answered smartly.

"I don't!" he argued.

"Of course you do," Minerva retorted.

"But—"

Ignoring them, Victoria said, "Cheney, did you, by any chance, have an idea of when Mr. Grider died? Because I hate to think of him down there, dead, while we . . ." Her voice trailed off.

Cheney's mind was racing, so she didn't notice Victoria's discomfort. "I did just take a look at him, you know. Naturally I was very curious, so I sort of did a cursory examination—just to know about the time of death," she added quickly. "I believe he died either very late Sunday night or in the early hours of Monday morning." Then she became very thoughtful and stared down at her bread plate. She had cut one piece of bread into triangles and was absently arranging them into different geometric designs with her fork.

Victoria said with relief, "So he did pass away before we arrived. That's good to hear."

Abruptly Cheney asked, "Shiloh, you did say that someone had left the remains of a meal, here in the dining room?"

"Yeah, and an empty wine bottle. Say, Doc, that must have been why he went down to the cellar, to get another—"

But Cheney, obviously not listening, interrupted him to turn to Sketes and demand, "Did you clean it up, Sketes?"

Sketes's eyes grew round with surprise that Cheney had spoken directly to her, and she made an awkward little curtsy and mumbled, "Yes, ma'am."

"Did you keep any of it?" Cheney demanded.

"What?" Sketes asked, aghast. "Keep it? After it was all a-moldy and after that devil rat had been snacking of it? No, sir, Dr. Cheney, I did not!"

"Good gracious, Cheney, what a thing to ask," Victoria protested.

"Hmm? Oh. Oh yes, sorry," she said absently. She was watching Bain Winslow because he was watching her. His eyes were hooded as his gaze had fallen on her, and his tawny eyes glittered. But then, so quickly that she thought she might have imagined it, his face relaxed into the familiar lines of cool composure.

"I knew it. I knew there was a rat," Minerva wailed. "I heard Mr. Lott telling one of the other sailors about it! Oh, Mr. Irons-Winslow, please tell me that you killed the rat! Please don't tell me that the rat was down there with Mr. Grider, because if the rat got hungry . . . and . . . and—"

"Uh—the rat's dead," Shiloh stammered.

"But *where* did he die?" Minerva demanded.

"She—Jezebel—killed the rat, Miss Wilcott," Shiloh said as reassuringly as he could.

"That's right. We found him. We found the rat, and we found the cat," Cheney muttered to herself. "The cat had killed the rat, and the cat is fine."

"Cheney, darling, I don't know what you're talking about, and I am fairly certain that I don't want to know," Irene said as pleasantly as she could.

"Oh, sorry," Cheney said. "I was just thinking out loud."

"Don't, dear," Irene said.

"No, I won't," Cheney promised.

"But, Cheney," Victoria said, frowning, "you sounded shocked at the coroner's verdict. You don't think that Mr. Grider died of a broken neck?"

Cheney was still moodily staring at her plate, playing with her bread. Everyone else had finished eating the second course too. Irene sighed, caught Sketes's eye, and signaled her to pick up the second course and serve the third course—tomato and hickory nut salad on shredded lettuce with mayonnaise dressing. Irene noticed that Sketes was paying close attention to the diners and trying to catch Cheney's eye, but Mrs. Espy seemed to be listening to the conversation with dreadful fascination, her eyes wide and stark, her lips pressed together so tightly that it seemed they might bleed.

Finally Cheney answered, "No . . . no, I don't."

There was a shocked hush at the table; the only sound was Sketes picking up the soup dishes. Cheney looked up, and everyone was staring at her. The only person who didn't look stunned was Shiloh, and he was studying her thoughtfully. When he spoke, he addressed her as intently as if they were alone. "Doc, I didn't think his neck was broken either. But do you think it's possible that it was fractured but it wasn't displaced? And that the coroner found it when he did the autopsy?"

They stared at each other while the other diners politely went on eating, though they were listening attentively. Finally Cheney murmured, "I suppose it's possible. But do you think that's the truth, Shiloh?"

He frowned. "I dunno, Doc." After a few moments he addressed the entire table in his old easy manner. "We didn't think his neck was broken. Of course me and the doc checked him over, you know, just to make sure he wasn't just knocked out or something. We didn't know who he was, remember, so we didn't have any idea how long he might have been there. For all we knew, he was some thief who might have broken in to steal the sangria and had sampled a little too much of his ill-gotten gain."

"So there wasn't any blood or twisted racked limbs or horrid green stuff?" Carsten said with relish, eyeing Minerva slyly.

"Carsten, that is quite enough," Victoria said with exasperation. "I declare, Dart and Alex have better deportment than you, and they are only two years old."

"But, Vic, we do want to know what Dr. Irons-Winslow thinks about Mr. Grider's death," Beckett said.

"That is fine, but she doesn't have to tell all about blood or twisted racked limbs or *anything* that is green," Victoria said firmly. Turning to Cheney, she asked, "So, Cheney, how do you think Mr. Grider died?"

Shiloh noticed that Bain stopped eating and was watching Cheney avidly.

"I don't know, really," Cheney answered. "I wish I did know more."

"Victoria, you did say that Mr. Grider was traveling to England to try to find some treatment for his health?" Richard asked thoughtfully.

"Yes, sir. In his letter he related that he had engaged a specialist in Bath, a Sir Wallace Maggard, who is purportedly a world-renowned hydropathist," Victoria told him.

"What's a hydropathist?" Minerva asked Cheney.

"A person who has an empirical system for treating diseases with water," Cheney answered.

"So does that tell you anything about the nature of his complaint?" Minerva asked.

"Not a thing. These hydropathists claim to be able to treat anything from cancerous tumors to catarrh with water."

"So no one knows what the diagnosis of Mr. Grider's illness was, exactly?" Richard said.

Victoria murmured, "I can't recall that he mentioned any diagnosis in his letters. I wonder if he used a local physician."

Her eyes went to Florence Espy, who was again following the conversation with unwavering attention. Victoria would never breach the rule of etiquette that disallowed direct conversation with the servants during a meal, a rather absurd principle dictating that some superior supernatural force blessed the gentry's entertainment, and therefore the servants need not be spoken to. Of course conversation did always take place between the hostess and the servants, albeit mostly by sign language, as if that were not much more primitive than spoken words. Still, the hostess and the diners were supposed to pretend that the servants weren't there, and so, according to tradition, Victoria merely looked in Florence Espy's general direction and raised her eyebrows, and Mrs. Espy answered by a small shake of her head.

"I suppose we'll have to ask his family about his ailment," Victoria said. "Likely he wouldn't trust a local physician."

By now Irene and Victoria could clearly see that Cheney was so lost in thought that she had completely forgotten her duties as hostess, and Shiloh was looking at Irene with mute appeal, for he was still somewhat inexperienced in guiding a table. Irene made a very elusive signal to Victoria—a mere twitch of an eyebrow—and Victoria responded with a slow blink. Shiloh marveled.

Victoria went on smoothly, "I believe that we've exhausted the subject of Mr. Grider's health and death. Let's talk of something more interesting—such as jewels, perhaps. A subject dear to my heart. Cheney, I believe that is the most stunning ruby I have ever seen. You wear it so seldom, it's a treat to see it tonight."

Cheney roused from her brown study and looked down at her left hand. She was wearing her wedding ring, a 5.26 carat ruby. Cheney didn't wear it very often; she wore no jewelry at all when she was working, and unless she was having a lazy stay-at-home day, she always wore gloves, as ladies must. The rectangular stone had a complex step cut, and it simply would not fit underneath gloves. On this night she and Shiloh had decreed that they were having an informal dinner—only five courses. The ladies had all worn semiformal dinner dresses, but the long over-the-elbow gloves had not been required.

Now Cheney looked up and smiled brilliantly. "This stone is so important that it has a name. It is called 'Saopha of Mong Kut.'"

"How utterly romantic," Minerva sighed. "A ruby with a name!"

"Even I don't have a ruby with a name," Victoria said enviously.

Carsten grumbled, "You girls are silly. Don't you even want to know what the name means? It might mean 'dirt of the streets' or 'eye of the buzzard' or something."

"Actually, it means 'Prince of the Winding Valley' in Burmese," Bain said. "The words themselves are Shan, which is an ethnic group in Burma, and they used to be the royal tribe. So I would assume that the stone is ancient, from the time of the Shan kings." He eyed Shiloh knowingly. "Well done, Locke. It is indeed a prince of a gem. Did you go on the Oriental run and buy it?" The Winslows' ships in the Pacific made runs from Hawaii to the Far East and back to San Francisco.

"No, actually your father—my uncle Logan—did me the great service of finding that stone for me," Shiloh answered. "I had asked him to find something unique, and something very precious, for Cheney's wedding ring. And so he did."

Cheney moved her hand back and forth as the diners watched, mesmerized. The great stone glinted darkly in the candlelight, the deep-stepped facets glimmering. "It is amazing," she said softly. "Even in this dim light, it still is a true crimson. It's as if it has a light of its own."

"Actually that's not far wrong, Mrs. Winslow," Bain said. "Burmese rubies of the first quality—which that stone obviously is, I can see it even from here—are prized for their fluorescence, which is a term for how highly they glow in strong light. Burmese rubies often fluoresce so strongly that in daylight they do seem to actually glow."

"Cheney's does," Victoria said with satisfaction. "I see you know something of the properties of gemstones, Mr. Winslow."

"I do," Bain answered. "My family—that is, Winslow Brothers Shipping—has had some jewel trade from the Orient from time to time in a small way."

"It is your family," Shiloh murmured quietly, then, in a normal tone, went on, "Uncle Logan assured me that the stone was genuine, and I took him at his word. I wouldn't know a real ruby from a goose egg."

Bain smiled at him with what seemed to be true affection. "You would probably never get close to a real ruby, Locke. The jewelry trade in the Far East is cutthroat, and I mean that literally. And not just from Malay pirates. The traders lie and cheat, and the beggars standing around when you patronize a jeweler follow you when you leave, hoping to steal whatever you have bought, and besides that, the Burmese king would probably kill anyone who was caught selling—and buying—one of these rubies."

"What!" Cheney and Shiloh said in unison. "You mean this ruby is from illegal trade?" Shiloh asked.

"The Burmese kings, since about 1600, have taken as their personal property all rubies above a certain size," Bain answered. "King Mindon Min, who has reigned since 1853, is no different. Although the East India Company has paid him silver for the rights to purchase gems at Mogok, he still has guards who oversee every stone that comes out of the mines. And besides, if I'm not mistaken, that stone truly is very old, and therefore must have been part of the royal treasury at some time." He shrugged. "It probably has been stolen at some time or maybe several times. Most Burmese rubies are. It is said that you can buy more Burmese rubies in Siam than you can in Burma."

Shiloh grinned. "Actually, Uncle Logan did tell me that he bought this stone from a jewel merchant he had known for many years—in Bangkok."

"Where's Bangkok?" Minerva asked breathlessly.

"Siam," Bain answered.

"Ohh," Minerva said. "But however would you know, anyway, if you were getting a real ruby? Much less one with a name and a pedigree?"

Bain answered, "Miss Wilcott, if Mrs. Winslow will indulge us, some bright day, in the sunlight, I will show you the things about her beautiful ring that are a witness to its quality and therefore add credence to its name."

Minerva Wilcott might have been a little scatterbrained, but she had some experience with men such as Bain Winslow, though perhaps not men quite as smooth and elegant as he. Still, she answered cautiously, "Yes, I'm certain we would all like to know exactly how such things are determined about gemstones, Mr. Winslow."

Instead of being put off, Bain looked amused. "It is an interesting subject, Miss Wilcott, and as Mrs. Buchanan said, one that happens to be of some interest to me too. Did you know, Mrs. Buchanan, that it has been determined that a spectroscope may be used to examine gems? In contrast to simple visual examination, this is a foolproof way to determine if the gem is real and also to identify the true color of the gem."

"I have heard of this, Mr. Winslow," Victoria said, "and in fact I have seen a demonstration. An acquaintance of ours—Jeremy Blue—is attending the Columbia School of Mines and is getting his degree in geology. His class has been learning the science of spectroscopy, and I was asked to lend them some of the family gemstones for a demonstration. I was quite interested in it, and I am convinced that it is the tool of the future for the jewel trade. At any rate, Mr. Winslow, Cheney doesn't have to worry about a scientific examination of her ruby. Aside from the clear fluorescence, it is also a deep rich crimson. It is transparent and flawless."

"Is it?" Bain said, his left eyebrow winging up, as the Winslow men's tended to do. He stared at Shiloh and said in a low voice, "Then, if it is the true pigeon's blood ruby, Locke, it must be very dear indeed."

His meaning was clear: it must be very expensive indeed. Of course no gentleman or lady ever talked about the cost of anything; it was considered crude and ill-mannered.

Shiloh grinned. "Very dear, maybe. But not as dear as my wife: 'Who can find a virtuous woman? for her price is far above rubies.'"

Bain, for once, looked disconcerted. Hastily Shiloh added, "It's in the Bible, Bain. Proverbs."

"Ah," he said, recovering his elegant manner. "I don't know the verse, or indeed anything about the Bible; but I believe you, Locke." He nodded to Cheney, who smiled at him. "Far above rubies," he repeated in a low murmur. "That is very dear indeed."

"Poetry," Cheney said with a hint of embarrassment. "Proverbs is a very poetic book. It also has quite a lot of sound medical advice, such as 'A merry heart doeth good like a medicine.'"

"And beauty tips too," Minerva declared, "because it also says that a merry heart maketh a cheerful countenance. That would make you prettier, wouldn't it?"

"Yes, and that is one reason why you are so pretty, Minerva," Victoria said affectionately.

Suddenly Cheney frowned, and her green eyes narrowed as if she were studying something extremely important, though she was staring into space. "Countenance . . . his face . . ." she muttered. Abruptly she turned to the servants and said, "Mrs. Espy? By any chance did Mr. Grider have lice?"

CHAPTER EIGHT

Ashes to Ashes; Dust to Dust

"WHAT A DREARY FRIDAY," Irene murmured as she stared out the window of the carriage. "Perhaps by this afternoon it will clear." Louis Arthur Grider's funeral was scheduled for three o'clock that afternoon, the first of March. It was now nine o'clock in the morning, and it was misting, the soft, sad rain that was nothing like raindrops falling; it was simply a dampness in the air. The sky was a nothingness gray, and the light was tired. The only color outside was the deep green of the fertile river valley, which looked much more like the Deep South than the seaside. Old huge live oaks with their long trailing beards of Spanish moss stood still and silent, the shadows under them deep and secretive. Richard and Irene were going into the city on King Street, the old road that ran west from St. Augustine all the way out to the St. Johns River and the river and railroad junction of Tocoi. The smell of damp rich dirt and wet green grass filled the small carriage.

"You look pale, Irene," Richard said with concern. "Are you sure you feel up to doing this?"

"It's not a question of whether I feel like it, Richard. You know that we must do this." They were going to pay a condolence call on Louis Grider's widow and his three sisters. That morning everyone had decided that because of the awkward situation—the party living in the bereaved family's home—representatives of the families should attend the funeral, and they should invite everyone to Sangria House after the services for tea and a light repast. But when Cheney saw the raw damp day, her mother's pale face, and her father's more noticeable limp, she had insisted that they shouldn't go out to stand in the mist and get soaked and chilled at the graveside service. Irene had consented to stay at Sangria House and prepare for the funeral attendees, but she had decided that she and Richard must call on Mrs. Grider and the sisters to introduce themselves and then to invite them to Sangria House after the service.

"At such a difficult time, I'm sure they feel awkward and uncomfortable. Richard and I must call on them first so they won't be surrounded by people they haven't even met," Irene had said firmly. "We'll be fine, Cheney."

Louisa Fatio's boarding hotel was on Aviles Street, in the old part of the city. A Spanish merchant named Andres Ximenez had built the two-story coquina house in 1798 and had operated a public hall on the ground floor while living above it with his family. In the 1820s the house had been converted to a boarding hotel and had been operated by a series of gentlewomen. Louisa Maria Fatio bought it in 1855 and opened the dining room to the public. It was considered to have the best food in St. Augustine. Though not a luxurious place, it was comfortable and enjoyed a genteel reputation.

Mrs. Fatio had generously allowed the widow and three sisters to receive condolence callers in her private sitting room. A shy Spanish maid with lovely dark eyes took Richard's cards and went upstairs, then returned and escorted them to the sitting room, a modestly furnished room with sheer curtains on the windows, though no light shone in on this listless day. A small fire in the fireplace brightened and warmed the room. Four women silently occupied two of the four wing chairs and a horsehair sofa that were all adorned with handmade doilies.

The youngest of the four rose and came to Irene's side as they entered. "I am Aimee Grider," she said simply. "Thank you so much for coming, Mrs. Duvall, Colonel Duvall."

She was an attractive woman in her midtwenties. Tiny and small-boned, she had a delicately etched face, finely modeled, with a Renaissance madonna-like quiet beauty. Her hair was a deep chestnut color. She had dark winged eyebrows on a wide forehead, a thin patrician nose, and a wide mouth. Her eyes were dark, with thick luxuriant lashes.

She lowered her eyes in what might have been a modest expression, but instead she seemed closed-in, secretive. Her voice was soft and pleasing, with a deep velvet tone that was unusual in a woman.

Irene reached out and took one of Mrs. Grider's hands and held it. "My husband and I wish to express our deepest sympathy and offer our sincerest condolences for your loss, Mrs. Grider."

"I am grateful. May I introduce you to my sisters-in-law?" Taking Irene's arm, she turned to the three women and performed the time-honored ritual of social introduction.

Letitia Ann Grider Raymond was the eldest sister, in her early fifties. Tall and thin, with a proud bearing, she may have been the female version of Louis Arthur Grider, as Victoria had described him to Irene, with angular features, thick silver hair, a cold elegance. Her eyes, a sharp blue, were not red-rimmed; in fact, Irene thought she detected a certain animosity in her acknowledgment of the introduction.

The middle sister, Muriel Grider, was of medium height; her etched features resembled her elder sister's somewhat, but they were softened, less imperious. She had hazel eyes and thick dark hair streaked with telltale strands of bright silver. Her demeanor was not as proud as Letitia's, but she did seem aloof.

The youngest sister was a complete surprise to Irene; only later did she learn that Phillipa Mae Grider and Muriel Grider were half sisters to Louis and Letitia. They had the same father but different mothers. Phillipa was almost voluptuous compared to her sisters. She was in her early thirties, the same height as Muriel, with ample curves and a small waist. Her eyes were dark, and she had been weeping, Irene saw. She had dark hair and the prominent jawbone and sharp cheekbones of the Griders, but her mouth was more generous and her features were softer, more feminine. She had none of the proud carriage and cold reserve of her sisters. In fact, Irene noticed that the youngest sister's eyes seemed continuously filled with tears, her face lined with deep sorrow.

The introductions done, the expressions of sympathy given and accepted, Mrs. Grider urged them to sit down, so Irene and Richard took two of the wing chairs.

"Of course we understand that you must have many things to attend to today," Irene said, "so we won't intrude upon you for very long."

Richard said, "Although we have only just met, I would like to offer my services if there is anything I can do for your family."

The young widow looked up at him through her thick lashes. "How very kind of you, Colonel Duvall. But the arrangements are all made, and there is nothing else to do now."

"You will let me know if I can offer you any assistance," he said.

"Of course," the widow said softly.

Mrs. Raymond, the eldest sister, spoke. "I hope you are finding Sangria House to your liking?" It was said with an intonation of clear bitterness.

Irene thought that the comment was in poor taste and addressed to the wrong people. As it was, she and Richard were guests of Victoria Buchanan, and if Mrs. Raymond had objections to the lease, she should address them to Victoria.

But Richard Duvall, of course, would never take note of a lady's ill manner, particularly under such circumstances, so he merely said, "It is a fine house, Mrs. Raymond, and the grounds and the groves are beautiful."

Quickly Irene moved on to the second purpose of their visit. "It occurred to us that you may not be in a position to offer any hospitality at this time, Mrs. Grider, so Mrs. Buchanan and I and the other ladies in our party would like for everyone who attends the services to come back to Sangria House for tea and a light repast. I have not been well, and my daughter, who is a physician, has advised me that I should stay indoors, so Richard and I plan to stay at Sangria House and prepare for the funeral party. The young people in our group are planning to attend the graveside services, so our family will be represented by our daughter and our son-in-law and Mrs. Buchanan, who is our daughter-in-law. It would honor us if you would all accept our hospitality as a gesture of our sympathy and consent to come."

"How very thoughtful of you both," Mrs. Grider said graciously. "I will come."

Letitia Raymond actually looked rebellious for a moment, and Irene thought she might respond rudely, but Muriel shot her a warning glance, and Mrs. Raymond's severe features settled into her customary coldness.

Phillipa wiped her eyes and said in a thick voice, "You are so kind. My sisters and I appreciate your solicitations ever so much. Of course we will come to dear Sangria House, for a memorial to our brother."

Irene saw a flicker of something—anger? bitterness? disgust?—in Letitia Raymond's eyes, but the woman quickly dropped her gaze, as did her sister Muriel. Neither of them said another word.

After a few more polite exchanges with Aimee Grider, Irene and Richard took their leave. When they were back in the carriage and clattering down King Street, Irene finally said, "Well, that certainly was nothing like what I expected."

Richard frowned. "What do you mean? What did you expect?"

"I expected to see a grieving widow and family. That is generally what one expects to see when a family is bereaved."

"Hmm. They weren't very sad, come to think of it, were they? Except maybe the youngest sister—what was her name?"

"Phillipa. And I'm not certain about the depth of her grief either," Irene observed coolly. "But at least she did display some semblance of sorrow."

"Irene, you believe that even though they may not actually be sorry that he's dead, they should put on a show of grieving?" Richard asked hesitantly. "Don't you think that's deceitful?"

"It is a polite deceit and not a transgression, Richard. It's like all of those things we said—offering our sincerest condolences, our deepest sympathy, offering to help in any way. It's not exactly true, is it? We didn't know him, and we don't know them, and therefore we don't actually feel deeply about Louis Grider's death. But civilized people behave in a decent manner. And I believe that people who have lost a member of their family, no matter how they truly feel, should behave decently, and yes, that means displaying a sensibility of their loss. Particularly to strangers who are only trying to be kind and who are not close confidants."

"You're right," he said. "You're always right, Irene."

She turned to face him and took his hand. "Am I? Well, then, I'll tell you one thing more, sir. That young widow wasn't only showing a lack of grief. She was flirting with you, Richard."

He was so dumbfounded that his jaw actually went slack and his mouth dropped open. "What! No, no, Irene, that can't be right!"

Her green eyes sparkled, and she squeezed his hand playfully. "You just finished saying that I'm always right."

"But ... but ... that can't be right! I'm old enough to be her father!"

"Louis Grider was only one year younger than you are."

"Who?" Richard mumbled absently. He was trying to recall the conversation with the widow and the sisters. Like many men, he had barely noticed anything at all, because he was mostly struggling to recall the women's names and listening to his wife for cues as to when he should speak and when they were taking their leave.

Irene giggled, a silvery light laugh that sounded as if it came from a much younger woman. "Lou-is-Ar-thur-Gri-der," she pronounced very slowly. "You remember? The Body in the Basement? The Corpse in the Cranny?"

He grinned. "Oh yeah. The Stiff in the Cellar."

"We're awful, simply awful," Irene said with an attempt at sobering up. "We shouldn't be joking. It is serious."

"You mean grave?"

"Stop it, Richard! We've been around our son-in-law too much, I think. We sound just like him."

"Sure, blame it on the men. What about your daughter? Out of nowhere she demands to know if Louis Grider had lice! During dinner! What was that all about?" he grumbled.

"I don't know. I thought she said something about his eyebrows, but I could be mistaken. I was just trying to make her be quiet at the time," Irene said with exasperation. "Very well, I agree that Cheney—*our* daughter—can be just as improper as Shiloh. In fact, women can certainly be just as ill-mannered as men. Such as Mrs. Grider. She was flirting with you, Richard. And you're telling me that you didn't even notice?"

He lifted her hand to his lips. "Irene, I'm telling you that I barely even saw Mrs. Grider, because I just don't want to see any other woman but you. I never have, ever since the first time I saw you. So yes, I'm telling you that I didn't notice her attempts at flirtation, and even if I had, I probably would have laughed out loud."

Irene smiled, pleased with him. "No, Richard, you're not that old."

"Not because I'm too old for her," he said gravely, "but because next to you, she just fades away. Every woman does. That, I can assure you, my dear, I have noticed."

San Sebastian Cemetery was on a small bluff overlooking the San Sebastian River. The small private cemetery was on land that belonged to Sangria Plantation, and the Spanish family that had built Sangria House, the Becerra family, was buried there, as were other Spanish families. Cheney noticed headstones with family names such as Oliveros and Muñoz, the name of the locksmith who had opened the doors to Sangria House and then disappeared as if the entire thing were a magic trick.

Beckett Steen and, surprisingly, Bain Winslow seemed to have helped the widow and family with the arrangements. Beckett, Carsten, and Bain had stopped by just after luncheon to tell them the time of the graveside service and how to get to the cemetery.

"Why don't you just come with us?" Victoria had asked.

LYNN MORRIS & GILBERT MORRIS

"We're escorting the family," Beckett had answered. "Also, the minister performing the service is at Mrs. Fatio's, so we've made arrangements for him to ride out with us."

Cheney had thought it was a little sad that the minister performing the ceremony had never actually met Louis Grider. Reverend Osborn was an Episcopalian minister who had come to St. Augustine for his health and had been staying at Fatio House for several months. He was a young man with kind eyes, thick glasses, and a frail appearance.

And so they now stood on a lonely hillside in the mist, witnesses to the timeless ceremony of committing a body back to the earth. "'In the midst of life we are in death: of whom may we seek for succour, but of thee, O Lord . . .'" Reverend Osborn read the poignant burial rite from the Book of Common Prayer.

Cheney and Shiloh held hands; not because they were grieved, for their participation in the memorial was, as Irene had said that morning, a simple gesture of civilized mankind. But the solemnity of the words, the listless light of the day, and the silent solitude of the little hillside graveyard were sobering. Cheney reflected that it was very sad, for most of the witnesses at the last memorial of this man were strangers who, by simple coincidence, were connected to him by a business relationship: she and Shiloh, Victoria, Minerva, Beckett, Carsten, and Bain. There was, of course, his immediate family—Mrs. Grider, Letitia Raymond, Muriel Grider, and Phillipa Grider. But the only friends of Louis Grider's who cared to attend were Samuel and Ivy Rainsford. Samuel Rainsford, at seventy years old, still had an elfish look, with his round face, small nose and mouth, and still-bright blue eyes; but on this sad day in the soft mist, he was pale, his eyes dulled, and he leaned heavily on the arm of a gentleman whom Cheney didn't know. He was a tall, thin, earnest-looking man with a thick shock of unruly brown hair and a scholarly air.

Samuel Rainsford and his wife Ivy still held hands. She was a lovely much younger woman, small and delicate, with still-creamy skin, a halo of silvery gold hair, a graceful and elegant carriage. They stood huddled close to the sisters. Cheney made a mental note to speak to them after the service and discourage them from coming to Sangria House afterward. She would explain to Mrs. Grider and the sisters that she had advised them to go home for Mr. Rainsford's health.

Cheney had been closely watching the widow and three sisters, for naturally she was extremely curious. But all four of the women wore heavy veils, and because the light was so dim, no impression at all of the faces underneath the black organza veils could be discerned. Her mother had given her a description of the women, so she could fairly well tell them apart, in spite of their anonymous clothing.

One of the black-clad veiled figures, Cheney knew, must be Mrs. Grider. Her outline was youthful, with that indefinable voluptuousness of a young woman. And Bain and Beckett stood very close on either side of her; Carsten lagged behind, looking ill-humored and awkward. Behind and to the widow's left the three sisters were lined up *like blackbirds on a clothesline,* Cheney couldn't help but think. The two taller, thinner ones stood stiff and defiant, their shoulders thrown back. The younger sister, Phillipa, stood with her head bowed. Sometimes a soft sob escaped, and often she reached under her veil with a handkerchief to wipe her eyes. But the widow and the other two sisters never showed any sign of weeping.

But Cheney could hear weeping. It was far off, a mere whisper, as if a sorrowful ghost were passing by, its soft cry floating in the air. It was oddly quiet on the little hill; no birds, no sound of wind; even the river below made no glad rushing sounds. The grim day was as still as if nothing lived or breathed there. But Cheney was sure she could hear a woman softly crying. Her eyes met Shiloh's, and she knew he was thinking, *I hear it too.*

His gaze went over her shoulder, grew intent, and then he made a very slight nod and turned back around. After a moment Cheney, as unobtrusively as she could, turned to look behind. A small woodland separated the graveyard from the groves, a narrow strip of hardwoods, mostly live oaks and elms. Underneath one of the oaks, leaning against its enormous mossy trunk, was a young woman. She wore black, had dark hair, and was almost invisible in the deep shadows of the mighty tree; but her face, when she lifted her head, shone pale in the gloom. She was weeping.

Cheney turned back around.

Reverend Osborn stepped forward, cast a handful of earth on the coffin, and recited from memory in a slow, quiet voice:

"In sure and certain hope of the resurrection to eternal life
through our Lord Jesus Christ,
We commend to Almighty God our brother
Louis Arthur Grider;
And we commit his body to the ground;
Earth to earth, ashes to ashes, dust to dust.

The Lord bless him and keep him,
The Lord make his face to shine upon him
and be gracious unto him,
The Lord lift up his countenance upon him and give him peace.
Amen."

"The Lord be with you," Reverend Osborn said to the people.
"And with thy spirit," the small group responded.
"Let us pray," the reverend said and recited the Lord's Prayer.
Cheney quickly turned around. But the weeping woman was gone.

It was awkward, but somehow Irene and Richard managed to get everyone introduced to everyone, and they all went to the dining room. Cheney made a mental note to herself. *My mother is a very wise woman. This situation is so awkward it would be laughable if it wasn't tragic, but she figured out how to fulfill our social obligations and make it as smooth and comfortable as possible for everyone.*

It would have been impossible to have a sit-down dinner for the funeral attendees because the rules of a dinner party dictated that one must be animated and engage your dinner partners at all times. No one in mourning could—or should—be subjected to that sort of social obligation so quickly. So Irene had asked Sketes to prepare a buffet of bread and butter, cold meats and cheeses, two beefsteak pies, orange-cranberry muffins, and a sponge cake. All of the food was on the sideboard that stood in one corner of the dining room. Jauncy and Sketes had moved a small dining table from the servants' workroom into the dining room, covered it with a white cloth, and put both the tea service and the coffee service on it, along with cups and saucers. In this informal atmosphere, everyone was free to eat or drink as they wished and to seat themselves wherever they wished. Sketes and Fiona served the food at the sideboard, and Jauncy prepared the coffee and tea.

Cheney got herself a cup of tea and then hung back, waiting until the Griders settled themselves. Cheney stood in front of the French doors, which were centered on the long north wall of the large dining room. The sideboard and tea table were in the corner on her left.

She was very curious about the women. Ever since she and Shiloh had found Louis Grider's body, she had had an uneasy feeling about his death. The extremely quick—and, Cheney stubbornly thought, incorrect—coroner's verdict and now the apparent absence of grief in the dead man's family all increased Cheney's disquiet. Observing the women didn't do much to ease her mind. Letitia Raymond and Muriel Grider got tea, moved to the dining table, and sat down, casting ill-favored looks about the room.

The tall man, whom Richard Duvall had identified as Mortimer Pendergast, Esquire, Louis Grider's attorney, went to sit with the two sisters and was obviously expressing his condolences. But the little group appeared exceedingly awkward. Letitia Raymond paid scant attention to the man, barely glancing at him when he joined them. Muriel Grider immediately dropped her gaze and remained silent, her hands fidgeting in her lap. Oddly, Pendergast never looked at Muriel; instead he kept his gaze fixed on Letitia, even though she wasn't looking at him. The oddity was such that, rather than the two—Muriel Grider and Mortimer Pendergast—giving the impression of indifference, their very pointed refusal to look at each other only highlighted the tangible tension between them.

When Mr. Pendergast finished his soliloquy, Muriel Grider didn't look up; Letitia Raymond didn't look around. He sipped from his cup of coffee, rose and bowed awkwardly, and went to the buffet.

Victoria stopped to speak to the two sisters, but Cheney could tell even from across the room that her reception was frigid. Victoria made a couple of remarks, smiled, and then went to sit with Phillipa Grider at the other end of the table. The younger sister had loaded up a plate and was sitting alone, staring disconsolately at the food. Her face still bore the signs of weeping. She roused when Victoria joined her and even became animated as, it appeared, she fawned upon Victoria. Mortimer Pendergast tentatively sidled up to them, and Victoria made a gracious motion for him to join them. Cheney, with a start, thought that Phillipa Grider's expression as she looked up at the lawyer became waspish, even hateful. But then she saw Cheney watching and nodded, her expression now full of woe. Cheney automatically smiled back at her.

Mrs. Grider, her eyes downcast in evident modesty, stood at the fireplace just to Cheney's left with Bain and Beckett and Carsten dancing attendance on her. Carsten had fetched her tea while Aimee Grider talked to the other two men. She was not laughing, or giggling, or coquettish in any way, but neither were her downcast eyes or slow, graceful gestures indicative of a woman in mourning. With a start Cheney realized that the woman, though she was not exactly pretty and certainly not beautiful, nevertheless had a sensuality about her that greatly appealed to men. Normally Cheney was not so analytical of other people, either men or women. Her mind, whenever she paid attention to the complex relationships of human beings, was generally more taken up with their physical health rather than their emotions or passions. In seeing Aimee Grider's sybaritic effect on men, she was fairly certain this was the first time she had ever taken such particular note of another woman.

With this sharp new vision she studied Shiloh's cousin Bain Winslow and intuitively knew that he recognized Aimee Grider's siren attraction and, with some amusement, indulged himself in it. On the other hand Cheney could now clearly see that Beckett and Carsten Steen had no notion that the young widow was practicing her wiles on them, probably for her own amusement. Cheney saw Beckett leave the group and hurry to the sideboard to get a slice of sponge cake. Cheney watched Aimee Grider and Bain exchange coolly amused glances, and Cheney then knew, with an unpleasant shock, that Mrs. Grider and Bain were both playing a cruel game of watching the Steen brothers' infatuation with the widow and were laughing at them. And instantly Cheney thought, *They're lovers! It's in their looks, their expressions, the way she gazes up at him through her lashes, the way he stands so close to her and she allows it . . . and they're laughing at poor Beckett and Carsten, eager little lapdogs that they are.*

Shiloh came up to Cheney on her left side then with the lawyer. "Mr. Pendergast," Shiloh said, "I have the honor of making known to you my wife, Dr. Cheney Irons-Winslow. Cheney, may I introduce Mortimer Pendergast, Esquire. He is the Grider family attorney."

"How do you do, Mr. Pendergast," Cheney said politely, giving him the correct nod required for ladies to acknowledge the introduction of a gentleman with a very tentative connection.

"I am well, ma'am, and I am honored to make your acquaintance," he said, sort of bending from the waist and bobbing his head. He had none of the masculine grace to make his bowing smooth; he was angular and jerky in his movements. With his long legs, sharp eyes, and rather spiky hair, Cheney was irresistibly reminded of the blue herons that stalked the lowland salt marshes.

"Excuse me, Mr. Irons-Winslow," he went on in a deprecating manner, "but to be perfectly accurate, I was Mr. Louis Grider's attorney. I have never had any dealings at all with his widow or sisters."

"I see," Shiloh said. "Pardon me."

"Certainly."

An uncomfortable silence fell on the three. Shiloh, Cheney noticed, seemed to be distracted; he wasn't looking at either the lawyer or her. He kept looking around behind his back. It was very unlike Shiloh. One of his virtues was to give his undivided attention to whomever he was with, making them feel important and interesting. Cheney couldn't help but strain to look around behind him, trying to figure out what was distracting him. All she could see was the sideboard, with Sketes and Fiona serving. Then she did note that Fiona's color was high, her dark eyes wide and stark, and she was watching the group of men surrounding Aimee Grider. In particular, Cheney now saw, her gaze was fixed on Bain Winslow. But then, conscious that she and Shiloh both were being extremely rude to Mr. Pendergast, with an effort she turned her attention back to him.

Though her mind was buzzing with about a hundred questions, she could not think of anything to ask the lawyer about Mr. Grider that couldn't be construed as gossip, or at the least as impertinent curiosity. She was noting with some surprise that the man was much younger than she had first thought. Observing him from a distance, his stooped shoulders and fussy mannerisms gave the impression of his being an older man. Now she saw that he was probably in his midthirties.

Mortimer Pendergast, Esquire, aside from his gauche appearance and manner, had very little social grace, it seemed, and stood awkwardly staring from Shiloh to Cheney and back again. He was obviously taken aback because of Shiloh's sudden inattention and also her own mumpish silence. Finally she smiled as brilliantly as she could manage and asked, "Mr. Pendergast, are you from St. Augustine?"

"Yes, ma'am," he answered with desperate gratitude. "The Pendergasts are an old family; we came here from England during the British occupation of 1763 to 1783. My great-great-grandfather, Henry Mortimer *Horatio* Pendergast, came from Liverpool, where he was a solicitor. He married a St. Augustine woman, my great-great-grandmother, Alberta Lindley Finch, of the St. Augustine Finches. . . ."

With this, Cheney had a fleeting vision in her head of a flock of little birds all named Mortimer, for it seemed that all of Mr. Pendergast's patriarchs were named Henry Mortimer, with only one middle name differing from their fathers'. His own was Henry Mortimer *Albert* Pendergast, named after his native St. Augustine great-great-grandmother Finch's father.

Shiloh continued to fidget, turning to look at the sideboard, at

Fiona—Cheney now suspected that Shiloh was worried about her—and then back to the other side of the room, where Bain and Aimee Grider carried on their little games for anyone who was observant enough to see.

With supreme effort Cheney turned her attention back to Mr. Pendergast's solemn drone. "Is that so, Mr. Pendergast? How interesting. And so what was your great-grandfather's patronymic?" she asked, all the while turning slightly so she could see Fiona.

Mr. Pendergast said with pompous surprise, "Patronymic, yes, that is correct, Mrs. Irons-Winslow. I beg your pardon. I don't believe I've ever met a woman—that is, a lady—who knew the correct terminology for the convention—"

Shiloh interrupted him and said curtly, "Please excuse me, Mr. Pendergast, Doc," and took off to the sideboard.

Cheney watched him in amazement. He went straight to Fiona, standing directly in front of her with his back to everyone else.

Mr. Pendergast faltered, then said, "Well! He's certainly in a hurry, isn't he? If you'll pardon me, Dr. Irons-Winslow, I believe that's the trouble with young people these days. They are in entirely too much of a hurry and are much too demanding. They must have everything, and they must have it right now. It's our permissive society, I tell you. In my father's day, as he tells me very often, things were vastly different. Now, as I was saying, the patronymic convention of families is extremely interesting, as in my own with the slight variation of the *third* given name differing from the father so that we do away with the tiresome enumerating of male descendants but still incorporate family names. . . ."

Cheney tried again to pay attention, but suddenly she noticed that Letitia Raymond had risen, gone to the door into the library, which was on the far side of the room, looked around furtively, and then quickly glided to the hallway and disappeared in the shadows of the dark passage.

Perhaps she just wants to go into the parlor or the morning room and be alone for a few moments, Cheney thought.

But the way the woman had looked as she slipped out of the room— she definitely looked shifty, as if she didn't want anyone to notice her leave-taking—made Cheney very suspicious. Abruptly she said, "Would you please excuse me, Mr. Pendergast?" Shoving her teacup and saucer into his hands, she followed Letitia Raymond.

As she swept around the long dining table she heard Mr. Pendergast say faintly behind her, "Well! Young people these days . . ."

Cheney went into the hallway. Ahead of her in the vestibule, candles were burning; and behind her, in the dining room, several candelabra were on the table, the sideboard, and the mantel, giving some light at either end of the passage. But the day was so dim and gray that the passage was nearly dark. Still, she could see the faint outline of the cellar door. It was open. She heard the unmistakable sound of heels on the steps and the creak of the wooden stairs.

For a moment she debated whether to say anything to the woman—after all, Cheney supposed, it was her house—but then, with sudden alarm, she went to the open door and called down, "Mrs. Raymond? Mrs. Raymond, please don't go down there without a light!" Cheney couldn't see a single thing on the other side of the cellar door; it was simply black.

But she heard what sounded like an embarrassed intake of breath, and Mrs. Raymond appeared on the top landing, her face frozen in a bitter expression. "There are lamps down there, Mrs. Irons-Winslow, in the cupboard behind the wine racks. Surely you know that. Surely you have gone over every inch of the house."

Cheney stood aside to let the woman back into the passage. As politely as she could, she replied, "Actually, Mrs. Raymond, no, I did not know about a cupboard. I haven't searched the cellar, or the rest of the house, for that matter. My only concern is that you shouldn't be going down the stairs without a lamp."

Mrs. Raymond drew up stiffly, her shoulders thrown back and her chin lifted. "I simply wanted to go down to the storage room. I believe some of our property is stored there, and I would like to get a few things. This is my house—mine and my sisters', I mean. After the reading of the will tomorrow, you and everyone else will know it, and no one will have any right to stop me from going anywhere in my own house."

Evenly Cheney said, "Ma'am, I certainly wouldn't try to stop you from going downstairs. The only thing I am trying to stop you from doing is *falling* down the stairs. So please, help yourself to one of the lamps or candles up here."

Cheney turned and went back down the hallway into the dining room. She went to her mother, who was sitting with Phillipa Grider and Victoria. But she noticed that Letitia Raymond, still with the stubborn defiant look on her face, returned to the dining room right behind her.

She didn't go down there, Cheney mused. *I wonder what that was all about. Because I do know that the storage room is completely empty. Maybe she doesn't. Maybe she actually doesn't know where their personal possessions are . . .*

if maybe Mr. Grider disposed of them or stored them or packed them up or something . . .

In that case, why was she sneaking? *Why not just ask one of us? Maybe, maybe she's embarrassed. Yes, that must be it. Maybe Mr. Grider made a big scene and kicked them out, and she's embarrassed to ask perfect strangers if they know where her things are. I certainly would be very ashamed in that case.*

But Cheney knew that Letitia Raymond was not embarrassed or ashamed. She was angry, bitterly angry.

And Cheney couldn't help but wonder why.

CHAPTER NINE

Realties, Residuals, and Ruses

"AT LAST SHE SAYS she feels hungry," Cheney said wearily as she, Sketes, and Mallow came down the stairs from her mother's room. "Sketes, please make her bran tea first and serve it to her, and Mallow, you must make sure she drinks all of it. Sketes, then try some gruel and add a tablespoon of sherry. And would you bake a custard? No nutmeg, please, just a bland custard."

"Of course, Dr. Cheney, I'll fix Miss Irene anything you can think of."

"And how are you doing with the eighteenth-century brick oven in the kitchen?" Cheney asked, half curiously, half teasing.

"I'll tell you something, Dr. Cheney, that there would not be any baked food coming out of that kitchen if it weren't for Flo Espy," Sketes answered. "If she weren't here to tell me the hots and warms and quicks and slows of that there brick monster, all of us might be eating cake batter and burnt roasts and unleavened bread."

"I doubt that very seriously, Sketes, but I am glad Mrs. Espy is here to teach you. I'm sure it must be very difficult to ... um ... learn the ... different oven ... things," Cheney said lamely, as she barely knew the difference between a brick oven and an iron cookstove. She had never cooked on either one, or on anything else, for that matter. The closest she had ever come to cooking was when she and Shiloh toasted Sketes's crumpets over a fire.

Tentatively she went on, "Mallow, I know you are not a cook, but it would help my mother if you would learn to fix some simple dishes for invalids, such as Sketes will be preparing."

"Oh yes, ma'am, Dr. Cheney. I want to learn to take good care of Miss Irene. She's like a mother—" Mallow stopped and quickly looked away from Cheney. They had reached the first floor and were going down the dark passage, so Cheney couldn't see her face at all, but she could hear the sudden anxiety in her voice.

"Like a mother to you?" Cheney finished gently. "I'm glad, Mallow, and I'm not surprised. My mother is a very loving and giving Christian lady. And now I know that you will take very good care of her."

Mallow O'Shaughnessy had been an orphan; her mother had died at her birth, and her father had died when she was six years old. He had a cancerous tumor in his stomach, and he had taken Mallow to Behring Orphanage as soon as he got too ill to take care of her. She had stayed until she was sixteen, and then Irene Duvall had hired her as a downstairs maid. But she had been such a good companion and, lately, nurse to Irene that she was quickly evolving into a lady's maid-companion.

As they came into the dining room, Sketes and Mallow made a quick bobbing curtsy to Cheney and went out the door into the servants' work-room, as there was a covered walkway from there out to the kitchen. The day was dark and chilly, and it rained steadily. On the dining table and the sideboard, even though it was ten o'clock in the morning, several oil lamps were lit, their globes cheery yellow balls in the dim, stern room. Shiloh, Victoria, and Minerva were seated at one end of the dining table, sipping coffee and reading newspapers in the lamplight. It was so dim in the room that one could barely see the unlit far end of the table.

When Cheney came near, Shiloh jumped up and held out the chair on his right, as he was seated at the head of the table and Victoria and Minerva were seated together on his left. Fiona and Jauncy stood at the sideboard, which held several covered dishes, along with platters of cold meats, buttered bread, cheeses, one huge platter of artistically arranged red and green apples and green grapes, and the coffee service.

"Here, Doc," Shiloh said, "we waited for you. I'll get your breakfast. Want coffee?"

"Please," Cheney said, sinking into the chair. "Good morning, Victoria, Minerva. It was so nice of you to wait breakfast for me."

Victoria was rising, waving Fiona away. "No, no, Fiona, just get Cheney's coffee. Min and I can help ourselves. How is Miss Irene, Cheney?"

"She's better. She's actually hungry. I sent Sketes and Mallow to cook some dishes for her that I know she likes. Father's sitting with her right now, reading the paper to her. Thank you, Fiona." Cheney sipped the steaming coffee gratefully.

Everyone fixed their plates, Shiloh said a short blessing, and immediately Victoria pressed Cheney. "Do you think it's another relapse?"

Cheney answered, "No. She had a low-grade fever late last night and just a touch of congestion last night and this morning. No coughing, no inflammation of the throat. I think that she is simply in a weakened condition from the nearly continuous bouts of influenza that she had in January and February. Yesterday, as you know, she went into town, got damp and chilled, and then came back here and made all the arrangements for the funeral party and generally exerted herself too much, and so she has a minor catarrh. Very minor. In fact, she's already better than she was last evening."

After the funeral attendees had left Sangria House at about six o'clock the previous evening, Irene had immediately retired, and Cheney had seen that she was ill and had taken over her care. Bain, Carsten, and Beckett all returned to town with Aimee Grider and the sisters, and they didn't come back to Sangria House. Victoria and Minerva spent the evening with the children and had a tray with them before bedtime. Richard and Shiloh ate the dinner that Mrs. Espy had cooked and then walked the dogs and played chess until late. So none of them had had a chance to talk since their "party" yesterday with those who had attended Louis Grider's funeral.

Cheney hungrily ate bread and butter, apple slices, and grapes. The fresh fruit was good, brought in from the West Indies by ships almost every day. St. Augustine and Jacksonville were getting to be busy ports. Just this year, many visitors from the North had fled the icy blast of winter and had come to Florida. Many of them, like Victoria, were beginning to consider having winter homes in the agreeable subtropical climate.

"How are the children?" Cheney asked rather worriedly. "Are they well? No runny noses? No coughs?" Though she didn't think that her mother had relapsed with influenza, she wanted to be sure that none of the household was showing any symptoms.

"They're fine, Cheney," Victoria reassured her. "Minerva and I watched them like mother hawks last evening, and then we went to the nursery to have breakfast with them this morning. Not a single cough, sneeze, nor runny nose did we see."

"Good," Cheney said with relief. "It sounds as if the children's state of mind is as strong as the Griders'. At least that of the widow and Mrs. Raymond and Miss Muriel Grider. Not a tear or runny nose did I see from them."

"They weren't exactly prostrate with grief, were they?" Minerva commented. "I noticed that myself. I thought it very curious that they weren't sad that Mr. Grider had died. But Miss Phillipa Grider surely did weep. I saw her applying her hankie up under her veil often during the service, and then her eyes were so swollen and reddened when she was here. And I noticed she had so much food on her plate that I couldn't understand how one could weep and eat at the same time, particularly in such quantities. The food, I mean, not the weeping. Anyway, it didn't matter at all. She didn't eat anything anyway. She just pushed things around on her plate and looked very unhappy. Do you think that ladies cannot eat while they are unhappy, Dr. Cheney?"

Her mouth twitching, Cheney replied, "That's a very good question, Miss Wilcott, and one for which I have no answer. What do you think, soon-to-be-Dr. Irons-Winslow?"

Shiloh answered, "It's been my experience that women—ladies, I mean—when they're upset, can pick at their food till it returns to the dust from which it came, while men can eat everything else while they're waitin' on the ladies to finish." To underscore his words, he took a great juicy, crunchy bite of apple.

"That's not a very scientific observation," Cheney said, "but in this case I don't think you can apply the wasting-away rule to grieving women. I noticed that Aimee Grider didn't eat one thing except a bite of sponge cake, and she certainly showed no signs of grieving."

"No, she didn't at all," Minerva declared. "And, Mr. Irons-Winslow, she shows such a marked regard for your cousin, Mr. Bain Winslow. I personally thought it might have been . . . um . . . *un peu vulgaire, c'est ça?*"

Quickly—Cheney fleetingly thought that it was much too quickly for her easygoing, drawling husband—Shiloh said, "Really? I didn't notice that, Miss Wilcott. Here, may I get you more coffee? No, no, I'll get it. I'm going to fix myself a fresh cup anyway."

He grabbed Minerva's cup and his own and went to the sideboard. Cheney noticed that he said something in a low voice to Fiona, whose cheeks were burning. Fiona, her eyes downcast, nodded slightly. Though Shiloh had said nothing to Cheney about Fiona—Shiloh would never discuss a lady's private distress—Cheney had finally caught on to the fact that Fiona had a crush on Bain Winslow, and his presence, particularly his warm attentions to Aimee Grider, upset her.

Cheney realized that her husband didn't want their conversation to be overheard, so she said rather loudly, "Well, I'll tell you this, Victoria. Letitia Grider Raymond may want us out of *her* house, but I certainly hope you have a lease airtight enough that we can stay, for a few days anyway. My mother needs some rest, and I sincerely hope that by tomorrow she will also have some sun and maybe some sea air."

Victoria looked surprised. "Her house? She said that to you?"

"Why, yes. It was the oddest thing," Cheney said thoughtfully, "and I still have no idea what she was doing." She told them about Letitia Raymond heading down the cellar stairs in the dark. "And so she said that, after the reading of the will today, everyone would know it was her house. Hers and her sisters', I think she did say."

"Interesting," Victoria said, speculating. "Aimee Grider told me yesterday that after the reading of the will today, everyone would know that the house was *hers,* and she had absolutely no desire to return to it, and so she hoped that I would purchase Sangria when the lease has expired. I do have a purchase option, for Mr. Grider evidently didn't intend to return here."

Shiloh, returning to the table with two cups of coffee, stopped midstride, his face comically surprised. His eyebrows arched high and his blue eyes rounded. Then, recovering himself, he set Minerva's coffee down and threw himself into his chair again. "You think that's interesting," he drawled, "wait'll you hear what Mr. Mortimer Pendergast, Esquire, told Colonel Duvall."

"All about his great-great-grandfather Henry Mortimer *Horatio* Pendergast, I'll bet," Cheney grumbled.

"Yeah, but besides that, Doc. He told Colonel Duvall that no one—not even he—knows what Mr. Grider's will says. He said he's the executor, but he has no idea what's in the will. He said he's supposed to notify interested parties to be present at the reading of the will, but he didn't even know who the interested parties were." Shiloh was obviously relishing the surprise. "Hey, for all he knows, Mr. Grider may have left Sangria House and Plantation to Jezebel the cat."

"Good heavens!" Victoria exclaimed. "That man left his affairs in the biggest coil I've ever heard of! It's scandalous!"

Minerva said uncertainly, "But . . . then . . . how is it that both Mrs. Grider and Mrs. Raymond each believe that he left the house to them?

They must have at least talked of the will with Mr. Grider."

"Maybe they talked of wills before; and maybe Mr. Grider first left it to one and then changed his will to leave it to the other; or maybe he just misled them," Shiloh said dramatically. "But none of that matters anyway, because he made a new will. On Saturday, the twenty-third of February."

Cheney's cup rattled against the saucer. "What? That was . . . last Saturday? And Mr. Grider died on Sunday?"

"Sure enough, Doc. You said."

"But tell us about the will and Mr. Pendergast," Cheney insisted. "Because, you know, Shiloh, if Mr. Pendergast saw Mr. Grider that Saturday, he may have been the last person to see him alive."

She turned to Victoria and Minerva, who looked puzzled. "Shiloh talked to the Espys, and they told him that the sisters moved to Mrs. Fatio's boardinghouse that Saturday morning. And the last they had heard, Mrs. Grider was staying with Mr. Grider and then they were sailing to England on Monday. But then later that morning they heard Mr. and Mrs. Grider shouting at each other. Mrs. Grider called Mrs. Espy into her bedroom, where she was throwing things into her trunk. She told Mrs. Espy that she was going to Mrs. Fatio's boardinghouse, and Mrs. Espy was to have Mr. Espy saddle her horse and send her things to Mrs. Fatio's in the cart. And then she left, and Mr. Espy took her trunks to the boardinghouse.

"When he got back, Mr. Grider called the Espys in, gave them the money he owed them, and dismissed them. He said that he wouldn't be needing them anymore. They said they never saw him again."

"On that Saturday morning," Minerva said, frowning.

"Yes. Now, Shiloh, this is the same Saturday that Mr. Pendergast was out here making a new will, right?" Cheney asked. Her eyes were sharp, her gaze intense.

Shiloh answered carefully, "Yes, last Saturday. The twenty-third. Mr. Pendergast had gotten a letter, sent by post messenger on Friday, requesting that he come out to Sangria House at three o'clock Saturday afternoon."

"Ohh, he came out here?" Cheney repeated. "It is getting more and more interesting."

"Uh-huh. So he does. And he said there was not a soul in the house except for Mr. Grider and a Spanish priest, Father Manuel Escalante. And Mr. Pendergast said that Mr. Grider didn't waste any time. He took them into the library and told them to witness his signature. He had a signature page, and he signed his name. Then Mr. Pendergast signed it as a witness, and then Father Escalante signed it. Mr. Grider told Mr. Pendergast that it was his new will, and that he was sealing it, and he didn't want anyone to open it until after his death and funeral. He gave Mr. Pendergast a copy and Father Escalante the other copy and sent them on their way."

"But—is that sort of will legal?" Minerva asked doubtfully. "I mean, I thought you had to have a lawyer make it out, with all the realties and residuals and ruses and things . . ."

"Ruses?" Cheney repeated under her breath, but Minerva was breathlessly going on.

". . . and don't you have to sign it in blood or something?"

"Minerva, dear, you've seen *Faust* entirely too many times," Victoria said, her eyes alight. "It's called a holographic will, which simply means it is handwritten by the testator. It's perfectly legal, as long as it is correctly witnessed. And it sounds as if this will was correctly witnessed. Two disinterested witnesses, both—or at least one, a priest—of unimpeachable character, and a testator of sound mind."

"When he reads that will, it's going to be quite a shock to someone, or maybe all of the someones," Cheney speculated.

"If he reads it," Victoria murmured, looking down into her coffee cup as if she were trying to read tea leaves. "Even I don't know if that would be illegal or not."

"What, what? Tell, tell," Minerva pleaded.

Victoria looked up and focused again. "Mr. Pendergast didn't have much to say to me; somehow I escaped Great-great-grandfather Pendergast. After our introduction he had the impertinence to ask me if I had paid Mr. Grider in cash for the amount of the lease. I've thought about it since then and wondered if perhaps Mr. Grider hasn't paid his attorney and if Mr. Pendergast was wondering if there were funds available to collect his fees."

"That old shyster!" Shiloh blustered. "'Woe unto you, lawyers! for ye have taken away the key of knowledge . . .' and I forgot the rest, but it was really bad, I remember."

"We've been studying Luke. Can you tell?" Cheney said, rolling her eyes. "You don't think that Mr. Pendergast might refuse to read the will, do you? Can he do that?"

"I don't think so," Victoria answered thoughtfully. "I believe that once someone dies, the estate must be settled. If the executor refused to perform his duties, I'm sure a probate judge would simply appoint someone else. Anyway, it wouldn't make any sense for Mr. Pendergast to refuse to reveal the terms of the will. He will be able to submit a claim against the estate for his fees, if any are outstanding, and therefore he will, of course, be the first creditor to be paid."

"But . . . but Victoria, however did you answer him? How very rude of him to ask you such a thing," Minerva declared.

"I answered, 'Mr. Pendergast, as you are Mr. Grider's attorney, I believe you should ask him about his commercial transactions.' And he said, 'But he's dead.' And I said, 'Exactly.' That abruptly ended the conversation."

"But, Victoria, what did you do then?" Minerva asked impatiently.

"Oh, then I excused myself and left him. That's when he stalked over to Shiloh and cornered him. He's so funny looking, with his long long legs and that high-stepping gait of his, and doesn't his hair stick up all straight? I thought he looks just like those grumpy blue herons you see around here all the time."

"Oh! I thought that too, Vic! I did!" Minerva cried.

"So did I!" Cheney declared.

"Oh, brother," Shiloh muttered, rising yet again to get some more grapes from the sideboard. Jauncy was standing there with a foolish grin on his face. "D'you hear 'em talking about that poor man, PJ? 'His long long legs,'" Shiloh mocked Victoria in a low whisper, "and 'his hair sticking up all straight.' No telling what they say about us behind our backs, huh?"

Jauncy, silly grin intact, murmured, "I think they are perfectly delightful young persons, sir. And I am certain that you would not be at all upset to hear what they say about you, Mr. Irons-Winslow."

"Huh! Fat chance," Shiloh grunted. His plate heaped high with apple slices and grapes, he had just turned to say something to Fiona, whose cheeks were still red, when they heard the back door open and noisy laughter echo in the quiet house.

Victoria said darkly, "My brothers, laughing like hyenas as usual. Shiloh, would you go tell them to tone it down to a low roar before they disturb Miss Irene?"

But Carsten and Beckett, and Bain along with them, were already coming into the dining room. Now that Cheney knew about Fiona's attachment to Bain, she too felt protective of her, so she watched her carefully as Bain came in. He winked at Fiona; she blushed and dropped her head, but not quickly enough to hide a delighted smile.

Beckett called out, "Oh, good, I'm starved, Vic. Sketes said she thought there was enough fruit and bread and cheese for us till she gets some eggs and biscuits made." Beckett and Carsten immediately made for the sideboard, while Bain came to the table and made gallant greetings and bows to the ladies.

"Please join us, Mr. Winslow," Victoria said, extending her hand prettily for him to bow over. "My brothers are like rude schoolboys, and I am gratified to see they have not corrupted you. As you can see, we are having a very informal late breakfast because Miss Irene is not well and is resting. Beckett and Carsten, if you disturb her, I'm going to make you go away, and I'll tell Father to withhold your allowances for a decade or two."

All three men—even Bain, who rarely showed any sincere emotion—immediately turned concerned faces to Cheney. "Miss Irene's not well?" Beckett said in a much quieter voice. "Is she very ill again, Mrs. Winslow?"

"No, I think she just exerted herself too much yesterday, and she does have a bit of catarrh," Cheney answered. "She just needs some rest."

"Oh, sorry we were so loud," Carsten said guiltily. "We'll be quieter. It's just all the excitement over old Grider's will, you see. The whole town's buzzing. And poor Mrs. Grider, she's upset. Very upset." He popped a grape into his mouth and turned back to piling his plate high with fruit and bread and cheese.

Beckett, who was also helping himself generously, said in sepulchral tones, "And from what I gather, Vic, we're going to be served some sort of probate court order concerning the property and contents of the house."

"I expected that," Victoria said. "I've already wired Father to advise me about legal representation concerning the lease and our situation regarding Sangria House. I imagine one of the attorneys will be down to attend to it."

"Victoria, it would seem that this is turning into a quagmire for you," Cheney said. "Are you sure you don't want to just pack everyone up and—I don't know, we might find a hotel, or—"

"No, Cheney," Victoria said firmly. "I don't want Miss Irene to be upset, and I believe that she likes it here. I like it here. And besides, this is the first time I've ever been able to persuade Dev to take an extended holiday, and he is going to take it here, with all of us, including your parents. Don't worry, Cheney. The lease is airtight, regardless of the circumstances of the Grider family. The attorneys saw to that before I ever became a party to it. And now one of our lawyers will, I'm sure, be glad to come down and take care of all of the legalities for us."

Shiloh turned to Bain. "So what about the will, Bain? What is it that has everyone in town talking about and Mrs. Grider so upset?"

Bain, who had helped himself to a few grapes and an apple, settled down by Cheney. "We don't really know the particulars," he answered. "We were in town, down at the docks, seeing to a couple of things with the boats. We heard that somehow the will was not really favorable to Mrs. Grider or to the sisters."

"There was talk of a sizable bequest to one Dolores Espy," Carsten said dramatically.

"Dolores Espy?" Victoria repeated quizzically. "What connection is she to Mr. and Mrs. Espy?"

"Don't know," Carsten answered, rather shortly and thickly because his mouth was full. "But I expect Aimee's going to need some consolation. We're going to Fatio's this afternoon to call on her and commiserate. Maybe we'll get the story then."

"Oh yes. I'm sure Aimee can hardly wait to confide in you," Minerva said, rolling her eyes.

"She does," Carsten insisted. "I can be trusted with a lady's confidence."

Shiloh was watching his cousin during this exchange. Bain was eating languidly with a particularly innocent expression. As the animated conversation continued, Bain watched everyone with sharp, watchful eyes, though his expression remained bland. Cheney, Shiloh noticed, didn't say another word. She sipped coffee and stared into space.

After everyone had finished eating and Beckett, Carsten, and Bain were taking their leave, Shiloh walked them out. They left by the servants' entrance, as it was so much more convenient than the lofty front door. When they came into the workroom, Shiloh said quietly, "A word, Bain."

He looked rebellious for a moment, but then shrugged and told Beckett and Carsten, "Go ahead, gents. I'll be along in a moment." They left.

Shiloh frowned and said in a low voice, "It was Mrs. Grider, wasn't it."

"What do you mean?" Bain asked.

"You know what I mean. The night we arrived. It was her, wasn't it, at the cottage with you."

Bain stepped closer to Shiloh and said tightly, "I never tell tales about ladies, Locke. Somehow I think you understand that."

Shiloh relented, just a bit. "Yeah, I guess I do. But, listen, Bain. Mrs. Grider's husband died in, shall we say, *mysterious* circumstances. And you had *better not know anything about that.*"

Bain bristled. "I told you, I never even met the man."

"Yeah. And I noticed that even that night, when he was dead in the cellar, you were partying with the merry widow, and you were speaking of him in the past tense. I remember all too well. You said, 'I was not acquainted with Mr. Louis Grider,' and 'I have no idea what his plans were.'"

Bain's tawny eyes narrowed as he stared up at Shiloh. "Locke, you are assigning entirely too much importance to some careless things I said, just as sometimes ladies tend to give entirely too much weight to things that are said. Do you understand me? I had nothing to do with Louis Grider at all . . . and I have, shall we say, a very tenuous connection to Mrs. Grider. It is such a tenuous connection that I have no reason at all to wish Mr. Grider dead."

Shiloh stared down at him, their locked gazes practically sizzling in the air. Then, after long moments, Shiloh relaxed. "I believe you."

"Thanks ever so much," Bain said sarcastically.

"But c'mon, Bain, she is married," Shiloh said.

"Not now," Bain answered smartly. "And just for your information, I'm finding that to be an awkward situation for me. Oh no, Locke, don't give me that holier-than-thou look. Don't tell me you've never been *friends* with a married lady before."

"I have not," Shiloh declared indignantly, but then he continued hesitantly, "well, except for that one lady in New Orleans, but I didn't know she was—aw, forget it! Anyway, Cousin, I think you'd better step lightly. My wife has some hard questions about Mr. Grider's death, and if I were you, I'd keep that in mind."

Now Bain did look thoughtful. "I will, Locke. Believe me, I will."

Chapter Ten

Dark, Dank, Damp, and Drear

BY THE TIME SHILOH FINISHED speaking to Bain and returned to the dining room, the ladies were finished with breakfast. Victoria, Cheney, and Minerva all agreed that they must go change clothes, for they were all wearing morning robes.

"I don't get it," Shiloh said as he and Cheney climbed the stairs to their bedroom. "It looks like a nice dress to me. And we're not going anywhere, are we? So why do you have to change again?"

"Mm? Oh. Um—it's just the rule."

"Oh yeah. One of the ladies' dresses rules. The ones that were practically handed down on stone tablets to Moses, along with the Ten Commandments."

"It does seem like that sometimes . . . especially when you have to change six times a day," Cheney said vaguely, then grew silent again.

Shiloh watched Cheney as she stepped very slowly, her eyes narrowed with concentration, staring at a point always at least six feet beyond. Automatically she went into their bedroom, a nice roomy one with a generous closet. All of the bedrooms had massive four-posters with mosquito netting, rush mats on the floors instead of rugs, and generous chests and armoires for storage. The walls in all of the bedrooms were of the same coquina stone that formed the outside walls; in the bedrooms the stucco was painted pleasing warm colors—pale yellow, peach, a rich buff. But on this rainy morning the room was so dim that everything appeared different shades of gray. Shiloh lit a lamp.

Still in a brown study, Cheney walked to the window and stared out at the steady rain. Shiloh came to stand behind her and put his hands on her shoulders. She reached up and took one of his hands, and they stood there for a while, just watching the raindrops on the old thick windows trickling down as if they were melting.

"What are you going to do this morning?" Cheney asked.

"I dunno," he drawled. "I hate it when I can't go out and play. I thought I'd go bother Andrew and Mr. Espy while they're doing their chores, and see the dogs. But I'd have to swim to the stables, looks like."

"Mm," Cheney said absently. "I wonder . . . I wonder what the will said."

"I expect we'll find out. One thing we do know: he left something to the Espys. That's kinda strange, considering they didn't even go to his funeral. Or the reading of the will."

"Obviously they didn't know," Cheney said thoughtfully. "They would be some of those 'interested persons' that Mr. Pendergast was worried about."

"This whole thing has been really a 'moil and coil,' as Sketes says."

"Yes, it has. Shiloh?"

"Mm-hmm?"

"I'd like to check the cellar again. Just . . . look around."

"You mean check the scene again, huh, Doc," he murmured.

Cheney stiffened slightly. "I didn't say the crime scene."

"Neither did I. But we're both thinking it now, aren't we?"

She turned and put her arms around his neck, and he rested his hands on her waist. She made a face at him. "I hate it when you do that."

"No you don't. You love it. And so do I." He kissed her, and then she pulled away from him.

"I'm going to hurry and change clothes," she said. "This morning robe certainly isn't suitable for bumping around in the cellar."

"Doc, don't tell me that ladies have an investigating-a-murder-scene toilette," Shiloh rasped.

She giggled. "No, it's not quite that bad. But I do have to change into an at-home afternoon dress. Would you go find Fiona and ask her to come?"

"Sure. Then I'll gather up all the lanterns I can find and get 'em oiled up and lit. Meet you in the cellar, Doc." He went out the door, blithely whistling "Shall We Gather at the River."

About half an hour later Cheney came down to the cellar with her medical bag and notebook. Shiloh had lit four lanterns and placed them on top of the wine rack that fronted onto the stairs. Hands on hips, he was gazing around the dark cavern, frowning. "This is one dismal dungeon. Dark, dank, damp, and drear."

"You're right about that, Winthro," Cheney said, amused. She stopped at the bottom of the stair, holding her medical bag with both hands in front of her, simply staring around the room. "Yes, this looks about right. The lighting, I mean. In my mind I've been picturing the room with more light, as if I saw more details, but now I realize that I only saw those details when I took the lantern and held it close up to something. Like the entrance to the laundry room," she said, pointing over to her left. "I thought I could see it, but I can't."

Shiloh nodded. "Okay, so what you're trying to do is re-create the scene."

"Yes. And that way I hope to recall everything about the body in true detail and not invent anything that I thought I saw. Now, I had put the lanterns . . . one at his feet, two at his head, and I was holding one. Let's try that." She set her medical bag down on the bottom step and then came forward to help Shiloh place the lanterns. "Here—yes, that one at his head must have been about here—or—I don't know. Just set it down here. The other one was down at his feet."

"Doc, that can't be right. He woulda been ten feet tall," Shiloh said as she placed a lantern at the absent corpse's feet. "Here, I think it was about here."

"No, no, Shiloh, you're thinking about his short leg, the one that was flexed," Cheney argued. "Victoria said he was about six feet tall, so let's just measure six feet—no, that won't work. He was all crumpled up." Owlishly they both stared down at the floor. The stone paving was icy cold and damp. "It's no use. I need a corpse," Cheney complained.

"I don't have an extra one lying around," Shiloh said, "but I'll volunteer, if you want."

"No, you're too big, and besides, I need you to help me remember. I think if we can re-create the scene, we'll be able to recall exactly how he was placed. And I would only rely on the memory if we both recall it the same way," Cheney said urgently. "You know, Shiloh, I'm beginning to think that this is extremely important."

He nodded. "I think so too, Doc. All right. Gimme a minute." He took off, bounding up the stairs.

It startled Cheney, and she thought, *Hope he's not going to go kill someone for me.* Retrieving her medical bag, she took out her notebook and reviewed the scanty notes she had made when she had done her quick examination of the body while Shiloh had gone to get the coroner. *"Internal temperature, 53 degrees . . ."* *I'll have to ask Shiloh if we can get an atmosphere thermometer and see what the temperature of this room is.* *"Full rigor mortis, no sign of passing, eyelids and jaws still in full rigor. Livor mortis well advanced."*

Cheney looked up and stared into the space above her head. She was standing, facing the first wine rack directly in front of the stairs, about ten feet away from the bottom step. The racks were so tall that she couldn't see the top of them. With idle curiosity she pulled out a bottle and was surprised to see that it had no label. She tried another, and another, all from the row that was about waist high. None of the three had a label. Then she tried one from the row above it, and it did have a label. With some difficulty, lifting the lantern high, she read: "'Sangria de Becerra 1869.'" She started to check more of the bottles, but then she heard her husband's firm tread on the stairs, and Phinehas Beddoes Jauncy's cultured British tones drifted down. ". . . likes angora, not alpaca, begging your pardon, sir," he was saying frostily.

Shiloh bounded down the stairs, followed by a mournful-looking Jauncy. "Hey, Doc, PJ volunteered to be the body."

"Let us say I was pressed into service, Dr. Irons-Winslow," Jauncy muttered. "And Mr. Irons-Winslow did assure me that there was absolutely no blood involved. Either in the death itself or in the re-creation. Correct?"

"No blood at all, Mr. Jauncy," Cheney said as solemnly as a person could who was struggling mightily to hold back a fit of the giggles.

"None on the floor where the remains came to rest?" he asked cautiously.

"None," she assured him. "The remains had no blood at all. On the exterior, I mean. None had come out, I suppose you'd say."

Jauncy winced then squared his shoulders and looked up at her again. "If you're certain none had . . . er . . . escaped the . . . er . . . his person."

"Not a drop."

He nodded and looked down. He was holding a plaid flannel blanket folded over his arm. "Mr. Irons-Winslow said I might lie down on one of your robes, ma'am, but I adamantly refused to wallow around on this cold, filthy floor on one of your fine new cashmere lap robes that Mrs. Buchanan bought for you."

"He made me go get a horse blanket," Shiloh said. "Figured it was the least I could do."

"The very least," Jauncy agreed. "Very well, shall we proceed? Over there?" He pointed to the floor in front of the first wine rack, where Cheney was standing.

"Yeah, that's it, PJ. Right in front of where the doc's standing."

He sighed. "Am I to be tied up and gagged this time?"

"Huh? No, no, PJ, that was only 'cause you scared my horse half to death with your umbrella," Shiloh said, in reference to how he and Jauncy had met. Jauncy had tried to mug Shiloh down at the Hudson River docks one cold night, and his only weapon was his fine silk umbrella with the eagle's-head handle. Balaam, Shiloh's horse, had shied when Jauncy had brandished the umbrella, and it had accidentally popped open. Balaam had knocked Jauncy out when he reared, so Shiloh had thrown the little man over his saddle and hurried him home. But then, when he got home, he discovered that Jauncy had lice, which may have been the actual cause of Shiloh deciding to tie him up and gag him and throw him on the floor of the parlor. Of course, Shiloh had built an enormous fire in the parlor before leaving Jauncy to take an almost-boiling bath and wash his hair four times with various antivermin preparations.

"You had to tie him up and gag him because Balaam was frightened?" Cheney teased. She was still amused at the different reasons Shiloh had given at various times for tying up and gagging the small innocuous Jauncy.

"But he had—aw, forget it," Shiloh rasped. "PJ, you're just postponing the inevitable, my friend. It's time to die."

"Oh, very well," he grumbled. Fussily he laid the blanket down on the floor. Cheney knelt to help him straighten it, as he insisted that every single crease be smoothed down.

"Now, how is this?" she asked.

"Just fine for a horse," Jauncy mumbled under his breath.

"But not for a hearse?" Shiloh punned, grinning.

"Yes, yes, American humor," Jauncy said. "On my back or facedown, Dr. Irons-Winslow?"

"Facedown, please."

"How did I know you were going to say that?" he asked the air above him. As it was obviously a rhetorical question, neither Cheney nor Shiloh answered.

He lay down, and Cheney and Shiloh began positioning him, much as they had done the lanterns earlier.

"Here, Doc, this hand was down, remember? And this hand was up, yeah, straight up. The elbow wasn't bent. But—wait, something's not right."

"It's the angle, Shiloh. Somehow the plane of his body was different. Perhaps if we moved the head around a little more this way?"

"Pardon me," Jauncy said, his words sort of mushy as he was obediently lying with his nose down on the floor. "But I am not actually dead, ma'am. I can hear you, and I'm sure I can move my head as you wish without anyone yanking on it."

"Sorry," she said. "Then could you sort of scoot—or—"

"No, Doc, his head's right," Shiloh asserted, ignoring Jauncy's protestations. "It's his feet that are pointing wrong. We need to—"

"Please, allow me," Jauncy said desperately.

"Wait a minute, Shiloh. We forgot. I had hidden my medical—I mean, I had put my medical bag in the wine rack, down on the bottom shelf. And it was only about six inches from the top of his head. . . . Put it there, in that one empty cubbyhole. That's it! His head was right there, and his face, though it was all smushed down on the floor, was angled this way so that I could see the livor mortis along the nose and cheek. This way—"

"I cad do it byself, ba'ab," Jauncy said as Cheney positioned his face.

"Of course. Sorry," Cheney said again.

"Right. Now, PJ, put your left hand down by your side, palm up. Right hand up over your head . . . Hey, yeah, Doc, see, his fingers were almost touching the wine rack. I remember now, when I grabbed the keys. So then . . ."

They both stood and, like some carelessly cruel harpies, studied the body on the floor, lit by the lurid lanterns. As one, they took one step back, then another.

"Over by—" Cheney began.

"—the steps," Shiloh finished.

They walked to the bottom step, turned, and again studied their manufactured corpse.

"That's it," Cheney said softly. "That was exactly what I saw."

"Me too," Shiloh agreed.

They were quiet for a few moments. The only sound they could hear was Jauncy's breathing. It had a little whistle in it, probably because his nose was smashed against the floor.

"Do you think he could have fallen down the stairs?" Cheney mused, "and landed there? In that position?"

"I . . . dunno, Doc," Shiloh said hesitantly. "It doesn't look right. The body just doesn't look that . . . that disturbed. If you get me."

"I get you," Cheney said. "What you mean is, the position of the body in relation to the stairs, and the state of the body itself, do not suggest that he suffered a violent mortal trauma."

"I meant that? Guess I'm a lot smarter than I knew."

Jauncy sneezed. "Bless you," Cheney said absently.

"Thag you."

"But you know, Doc, it's not impossible either. I mean, we can't prove that he didn't fall down the stairs, can we?"

"Not exactly . . . I can't think of a way to disprove it, or rather, any kind of *in situ* experiment to prove or disprove it."

Jauncy lifted his head. "I am not tumbling down the stairs for you to see if I live or not, or how I might land. Ma'am. Sir."

"Aw, c'mon, PJ, get in the spirit of the thing," Shiloh cajoled him.

"Yes, so very amusing," Jauncy said, smushing his face back down on the blanket.

"Guess we could toss a dog down the stairs," Shiloh suggested. "They bounce pretty good."

"Yes, I'm sure you would toss Sean or Shannon down the stairs," Cheney scoffed. "Remember? Sean already tumbled down here, a few steps anyway. At least, it sounded like it. We couldn't see our hands in front of our faces—oh, my goodness!"

"What, Doc?"

She turned to him. "Shiloh, with all the trouble we've had with lighting down here, it just struck me—Mr. Grider—"

"—had no lantern, and don't I just feel like a pure fool for not thinking of that," Shiloh finished in a disgusted voice.

Ignoring him, Cheney went on, "Now, Mrs. Raymond was sneaking. The reason she didn't use a lamp is because she didn't want anyone to catch her coming down here, and I still haven't figured that out. Anyway, she left the door at the top of the stairs open, so that may have given her enough background light to get down the stairs.

"But when we found Mr. Grider, the door was closed and locked, and only Mr. Grider had the keys, so he must have done it. Why would he have closed and locked the door, because then he would have been in absolute darkness?"

"The answer is he wouldn't have," Shiloh answered softly. "No one would have." He took the lantern, held it up high, and walked to his right, following the wall around to the corner of the first wine rack. "Of course," he said, shaking his head. "Here, Doc." Cheney came to stand beside him, and there, mounted on the wine rack about seven feet up, was a small flat shelf. On the shelf was a sturdy lantern. Shiloh opened the glass door, lifted the wick holder out, and stuck his finger down in the well. "Dry as dust," he said. "I'll betcha anything that they keep this lantern up at the top of the stairs. When they come down, they light it and put it up on this shelf. When it wasn't up there, Mrs. Raymond probably figured it would be here. Anyway, that's what Mr. Grider did. He lit it at the top of the stairs, locked the door behind him, and carried it down here, and died. So it burned until the oil was gone."

"Of course," Cheney said quietly. "And of course, that means that Louis Grider did not fall down the stairs."

Faintly Jauncy said, "For which I am exceedingly grateful. So, Dr. Irons-Winslow, may I stop being dead?"

"You may, Mr. Jauncy. Thank you for your service. You are an excellent corpse. If I ever need one again, I shall call upon you first."

He stood, groaning a bit, and then gave her an elegant, courtly bow. "Dead man at your service, ma'am. Anytime."

He folded up his horse-corpse blanket, and went—in an unseemly hurry, Shiloh thought—back up the stairs.

Cheney sat on the second step and looked around the room. It was indeed a depressing place. It smelled of mold and mildew. The shadows, in the flickering uncertain flames of the lanterns, seemed alive and threatening. The air was chilly, with occasional odd icy drafts that made the skin crawl. As Shiloh sat beside her, she took his hand, which was warm and rough and very comforting, and whispered, "This is a terrible place to die, all alone and in the dark."

"Sure is," he said in a low tone matching her own. "It's really bothering you, isn't it? Grider's death and the coroner's verdict."

"Yes. It's bothering you too, isn't it? You know that it's wrong, all wrong."

"Maybe," Shiloh said cautiously. "But why don't you tell me anyway? Just say what bothers you, Doc. Let's talk about it."

Cheney took a deep breath. "All right. With any death, Shiloh, three things need to be determined: the cause of death, the mechanism of death, and the manner of death. The *cause of death* refers to such things as a gunshot wound, or heart attack, or drowning, or a terminal disease. The cause of death is the specific incident that effected the death.

"The *mechanism of death* is the particular bodily dysfunction that actually causes somatic death. For instance, if the cause of death was a gunshot wound to the heart, then the mechanism of death would be a massive rupture wound to the heart, causing internal bleeding and asphyxia.

"Finally, there are four *manners of death:* homicide, suicide, accident, and natural. So if you think about it, you can understand that a coroner who has no medical training or experience will be able to pronounce the manner of death in many cases without a physical examination. But in many cases, the cause of death and the mechanism of death must be determined first by a medical professional before the manner of death can be decided. And I believe that Louis Grider's death is one of those that does require a competent medical practitioner to do an autopsy to determine cause of death. As we've said, Shiloh, he might have fallen down the stairs and broken his neck. But that needs to be determined by a pathological examination, not by peering down at the body and taking a wild guess. The coroner didn't do the most elemental, simple things to assess the manner of death. I don't even think he looked at the body."

"I'm not too sure he could see the body," Shiloh rasped. "Or maybe he was seeing two or three and just picked the middle one. Anyway, Doc, if I've understood what you've said, Coroner MacDonald ruled that the manner of death was an accident, the cause of death was a fall, and the mechanism of death was a broken neck. That it?"

"That's it exactly, Winthro."

"And so it was wrong and wrong and wrong. Right?"

"Right. And besides that, let's not forget that just now we also ruled out the *object* that the coroner ruled was the causation of the misadventure. In other words, the *crowner* mistook the *deodand*."

"Doc, I'm not up on my Latin yet," Shiloh grumbled. "Speak English."

"Sorry, but it is English," she said in a lighter tone. "Medieval English, to be precise. Originally the official who investigated deaths was called the crowner. And the deodand was the item or event that initiated the death. In other words, if a man fell off a ladder and died from a head injury, the ladder was the deodand. Which, by the way, reverted to the Crown."

"You mean the rich king would get the only ladder the poor widow and children had left?" Shiloh said. "They never change, do they? The rich. Just like old Ahaz and Naboth's vineyard. You just know a king of England really needed some poor serf's ladder."

"Exactly. Anyway, the crowner had deemed that the deodand in this case was the stairs. And we have proved with very little doubt that he was wrong."

"Yeah, we have. So if not the stairs, what was the deodand?"

She turned and looked up at him, her face full of doubt. "I don't know. But I do know that an autopsy would have determined that. And that also bothers me, Shiloh. I'm not sure what the law is here, but in New York, a medical examination must be done in all cases of deaths that are ruled accidental. Even if Mr. Grider obviously had a broken neck, I would think that at least an examination of the spinal cord would have been done."

"Yes, Doc, you would do that, at the very least, because you are very thorough and thoughtful in your work," Shiloh said gravely. "But if it's not the law in Florida, then I get the impression that Crowner MacDonald isn't going to go to any trouble makin' extra work for himself."

"Probably true," Cheney murmured, "but that brings me to my last objection to this whole mortal coil. There were some oddities about Mr. Grider. I showed you his hair, Shiloh. Not only the gross loss of hair but the odd coloration. And his eyebrows. Those are two very important observations I made in just a few moments, in the half dark, in a very cursory examination. Who knows what else could have been learned with a thorough autopsy."

"True," he agreed. "But, Doc, what about the hair and eyebrows? Do you know what caused that?"

"I have my suspicions about the hair, but I've never seen anything like his eyebrows. And now all I have is speculation—idle, useless speculation," Cheney said darkly.

"Okay, I understand what you're *not* saying," Shiloh said. "The word that begins with *p* and ends with *oison* and a nasty death. But, Doc, the man had been sick for some time, hadn't he? Maybe he had something weird you've never heard of. A hair- and eyebrow-killing disease."

"Maybe," Cheney said, "but I don't think so. And even so, Shiloh, his death is still suspicious. You know that when people have a terminal illness or condition—I'm not talking about the virulent plagues, like cholera and typhus—they don't just get up one day, get dressed, go down to the cellar, and fall down and die. They deteriorate over a period of time until they enter the terminus, and then they are generally so ill they can't get out of bed or perhaps even move."

"You're right, Doc. You're exactly right. But what about a sudden heart attack? Or a massive apoplexy?"

"Possible, but I would say not too probable here, again from the particular attitude of the body, but regardless, an autopsy would show that. An autopsy should have been done on that man, Shiloh. It's not right that he was just packed up and stuck in a box and buried without any regard for his passing," she finished passionately.

He studied her and then asked quietly, "So what do you want to do about it, Doc?"

"I—don't know. Yes I do. Let's pray, Shiloh. Let's pray that God will give us wisdom," she said, taking his hand in both of hers again.

"Good idea," he agreed and immediately bowed his head. "Dear Lord, my beloved wife and I want to ask you to help us with this problem. We didn't know this man, Lord, but we believe that a wrong has been committed here, and we want to know how to right that wrong. We don't want to be proud or pushy, Lord, because we know that you are always gentle, and you've taught us not to take authority to ourselves that doesn't belong to us and not to take up burdens that we're not meant to bear. So please let us know what to do, we humbly ask in your name. Amen."

Cheney prayed, "Thank you, Lord, for leading us always. Thank you for my family and friends and especially for my husband. Teach us your ways, Lord Jesus. Guide our footsteps only on the paths of righteousness. In Jesus' blessed name we pray. Amen."

They opened their eyes and looked at each other. Shiloh said, "You know, the other day we read, 'I am the way, the truth, and the life.' Jesus is the Truth, Cheney, so we've always got to seek and honor the truth."

She nodded and smiled up at him. "I believe God has spoken to us, Shiloh. I know we have to try to find out the truth about this man's death. But I still am not sure where to start."

"I am," he said. "With the wisest man I know. Let's go talk to your father, Doc." He rose and offered his hand to help her up. "One thing about your father," he asserted, "is that, for a Billy Yank, he's got pretty good sense. And some good connections. If Mr. Crowner MacDonald only knew that one day the president of the United States might hear from his friend Colonel Richard Duvall that the crowner had messed up the deodand, he mighta changed his tune!"

PART III

A TIME TO KEEP SILENCE, AND A TIME TO SPEAK

Ecclesiastes 3:7

CHAPTER ELEVEN

Cause, Manner, and Mechanism

COLONEL RICHARD DUVALL sat down on a wrought-iron bench in the shady courtyard of Government House and looked around the quiet square. The seat of government of St. Augustine was in the oldest part of the city, and Government House perfectly portrayed its Spanish origins. The two-story building was made of coquina stone and had weathered to a pleasing faint pink. The window frames and shutters were all painted black, and the upper story windows had the uniquely Spanish black wrought-iron windowsill balustrades.

With idle pleasure Richard studied the tiny courtyard. A great native live oak lent a gracious shade alongside tall royal palm trees waving gently in the morning breeze. Underneath these giants grew blue iris, which had been brought by Spaniards who loved the glowing blue flowers above all, and which had become sacred to the native Timucuan Indians, who had used the roots for medicine. On the afternoon breeze Richard caught the spicy-fresh scent of rosemary and saw the plain little plant, which looked much like a weed, growing underneath the bench. It had been transported here by the English in their occupation of 1763–1783. Pink azaleas bloomed profusely, a gift from the Far East and also transported here by Englishmen from the East India Company. A huge white orchid, an escapee from the southern swamps, climbed the mossy trunk of the live oak.

Irene likes it here, Colonel Duvall reflected. *It is a gracious old town. We're both getting older, and there's no doubt the New York winters are getting harder to bear. Maybe we should consider a winter home down here. I'll talk to*

Irene about it tonight. After spending the day on the beach, she might have a better idea if she'd like to winter here.

The previous day, Sunday, had again been chilly and dreary and rainy, but Irene had insisted that she had recovered from her weakness and fatigue on Saturday, since she rested quietly the entire day and had a good night's sleep. So everyone attended the church that Samuel and Ivy Rainsford attended, a plain, homey little Methodist church on the banks of the San Sebastian River. Ivy had invited everyone to come to their beach house the next day if the weather was good. This Monday morning had dawned bright and clear and warm, so Cheney, Victoria, Minerva, and Irene had all decided to take Ivy up on her offer.

The town of St. Augustine had been built on the mainland, but because of the barrier islands, its shoreline fronted inlets instead of the ocean. Samuel and Ivy Rainsford had purchased a fine old Spanish *hacienda* just a mile from Sangria House, but they had also purchased a stretch of shoreline on Anastasia Island and had built a small *cabana* for lazy days on their private beach. Both Ivy and Samuel Rainsford loved the seaside; they spent many days napping and reading on their chaises underneath sturdy canvas umbrellas. Richard Duvall thought wistfully that he wished he were with Irene and the other ladies, reading the fine leather-bound edition of Homer's *Odyssey* he had found in the library of Sangria House or playing with his grandson—for so he considered Dart—and his two adopted granddaughters, and snacking from the great basket Sketes had packed for them.

I can join them when I finish here, Richard thought sturdily. *Duty calls and must be answered first.* He rose with some difficulty—his joints were still sore, as the rheumatism always seemed to flare up when it rained—and went into the cool shady offices of Government House. He passed by the door with the engraved nameplate: *PROVOST MARSHAL GEN. GEORGE MEADE,* for he knew that General Meade was not in St. Augustine at the moment. He went farther down a dim hallway to the black door bearing the more humble sign: *Deputy Provost Marshal Major Micah Valentine.* After knocking he heard a rather harassed voice bid him to come in.

Richard opened the door, stepped in, stuck his hand out, and began, "Good day, Major Valentine, I am—"

But he was, it seemed, curiously swarmed by a large, eager young man. "Yes, yes, I know. You're Colonel Richard Duvall. I have been trying to figure out how to wrangle an introduction ever since I saw you at church yesterday—I know you won't remember me—sorry, sir, please, please sit down—is this all right?—I'll just clear away—"

"It's quite all right, Major Valentine, I'll just sit in this chair," Richard said, hiding his amusement. "It would probably be better if you sat there." Major Valentine was frantically clearing away the detritus that always collects on the desk of a very busy man, for he was trying to get Richard to sit in his chair, which was of fine padded leather. The two seats in front of the desk were simple wooden ladder-back chairs, but Richard managed to disentangle himself and sit down on one.

"Of course, sorry, sir, it's just that I—it's just such an honor to meet you, sir," Major Valentine said, rushing back around the desk to sweep some papers and journals out of the way. Then, rather abruptly, he sat down and leaned over the desk, clasping his hands. "I know you won't remember, sir, but we have actually met before."

Richard Duvall searched his face. He had an honest round face, thick curly brown hair, sincere brown eyes. He was tall and barrel chested, and the hands clasped so earnestly on the desk were like hams. He was, Richard judged, probably in his early thirties, though his boyish looks and eager ways made him seem younger.

The light dawned on Richard's face. "I do remember you, Major Valentine. Fort Donelson, correct? You were General McClernand's courier. I apologize, for I had forgotten your name, but now I do recall seeing you there, and at Shiloh too, if I'm not mistaken."

"No, no, there's no need for apologies, sir. I was only one adjutant among many in those days," he said quickly. "I'm just surprised—and flattered, sir—that you remember me at all."

"I think that we'll remember that time, and those men, all our lives," Richard said quietly. "At least I know I will. And now, since I have a rather unpleasant request to make, I'm happy to see a familiar face."

Major Valentine looked surprised. "Unpleasant request? Sir, I can't imagine what you need, but I assure you, I'll be happy to do anything you ask if it's in my power to grant it."

Richard nodded. "Thank you, Major. This is a difficult problem, but I'm confident that we can find a solution. Are you aware that I and my family have leased Sangria House for the remainder of the winter?"

"No, I wasn't aware—oh. Mr. Grider's death. What an unfortunate welcome."

"It was unfortunate, of course, but since we weren't acquainted with the gentleman it hasn't affected us so deeply that we can't enjoy our holiday. But we have encountered—a difficulty, you might say."

"Concerning Mr. Grider?"

"Concerning his death. To be precise, the cause of his death."

"Oh," Major Valentine said uncertainly. "I thought that the coroner ruled his death resulted from a fall down a flight of stairs. You have a difficulty concerning that?"

"I do," Richard answered. "You see, Major Valentine, my daughter is a physician. As it happens, she and her husband found the body in the cellar—it was my son-in-law who came to fetch Mr. MacDonald. At any rate, my daughter has had some experience in postmortem examination, and she came to me yesterday to tell me that she has grave doubts concerning the coroner's ruling of cause of death."

"She does? Are you saying that she—and you, sir—believe that Mr. Grider was murdered?"

"I have no opinion at all, because I have no experience in such things. I didn't even see the body," Richard cautiously replied. "However, my daughter did stress to me that she isn't questioning the coroner's ruling of accidental death. That, she says, is actually termed 'manner of death' and is more a matter for a legal investigator to determine than a physician. She insisted that her doubts have nothing to do with the alleged fall down the stairs; if I understood her correctly, it is actually what she calls the 'mechanism of death'—the physiological process that caused death—that she questions. She doesn't believe Mr. Grider's neck was broken. But she doesn't know what he died from, because only an autopsy could determine that. And Mr. MacDonald performed no autopsy; in fact, my daughter said that he did no examination at all of the body at the scene, which, I understand, is the correct procedure in any case."

"I see." Major Valentine frowned; it sat heavily on his cheerful face. "So, sir, the unpleasant request you must make is that Louis Grider's body be exhumed and an autopsy be performed?"

"It is," Richard answered simply.

"Have you, by any chance, spoken to the widow or the family about this?"

"No, I haven't. We are barely acquainted with them—we only met them the day before the funeral—but even if they were friends, under these special circumstances we believe that appealing to the authorities first is the proper thing to do," Richard said. "Neither I nor my daughter is aware of the laws of the state of Florida, nor do we know if any laws were actually broken by the coroner. But legality is not the sole consideration here. Cheney, my daughter, believes that it is only just that Mr. Grider should be properly examined, the cause and mechanism of his death determined, and the manner of his death investigated, if necessary. And I agree with her."

"I agree with you both." Major Valentine paused and stared into space. "But this is truly going to cause some fireworks. Or more fireworks, I should say." He focused back on Richard. "You've heard, I presume, about the will."

"Actually, we had heard some rumors that it was . . . unconventional," Richard said cautiously. "And evidently the ladies of the family were in high dudgeon after the reading."

"Yes, that makes—Sir, what is 'high dudgeon'?" Major Valentine asked abruptly. "I have always wondered."

Richard looked comically surprised. "I haven't the faintest idea. We'll have to ask my wife, or my daughter. They always know things like that. They speak French, you know."

"They do? Then they would surely know," Major Valentine said with endearing ingenuousness. "Anyway, Colonel Duvall, our provost judge is Colonel Lawrence Allard. Have you met him?"

"Why, yes. He was one of General Meade's most trusted staff advisors all through the war. Certainly I remember him."

"Yes, he's a good man. Anyway, he is our provost judge, and he has advised me that to probate Louis Grider's will may be a long process. He said there were some singular clauses in it that were going to require investigation. And he said that there are already claims against the estate, including one from Mr. Grider's personal attorney, who is also the executor—"

"Ah, Mr. Pendergast," Richard said solemnly. "I have met him. And you say he has filed a claim against the estate?"

"Yes, but his is not particularly controversial. It's merely for his last meeting with Mr. Grider, which had taken place shortly before his death, and so Mr. Pendergast had not had the opportunity to present him with a bill," Major Valentine explained. "But other claims have been filed too, which must be investigated: several by his tenant farmers; by four of the tradesmen in St. Augustine, and by—coincidentally, it would seem—the coroner, Bruce MacDonald, and his brother, Robert MacDonald."

"Is that so," Richard murmured, his gray eyes narrowing. "That is interesting. Is it a large claim, may I ask?"

"Not really, but before I go on, sir, I would like to assure you that I am breaking no confidences nor violating any laws here," Major Valentine said. "All of this will be in today's newspaper. Probate court is not confidential. The public has a right to attend, and I'm sure you know that the settlement of an estate is published exactly so that any and all claimants may have an opportunity to file. At any rate, Bruce and Robert MacDonald claim that Louis Arthur Grider overcharged them three hundred dollars of interest on a loan. It is a minor sum, but from what I understand, there was some sort of ongoing feud, a bitter one, with the coroner and his brother and Mr. Grider, so it may not have been simple carelessness on the coroner's part to hurry and get Grider buried and gone."

Richard nodded, his face grave. "Then I am sure that my daughter is right. A postmortem examination should be done by a party who can remain objective."

"I agree, Colonel Duvall. And about the Espys, sir. They are still living on the estate, correct?"

"Yes, and they both continued to work for us on Saturday and yesterday, and we didn't like to question them concerning Mr. Grider's will," Richard replied. "They didn't mention it and neither did we. My wife and I thought that perhaps it might be a long interval before the estate is settled, and probably the Espys couldn't afford to stop working until they could realize their inheritance."

"A reasonable assumption," Major Valentine said dryly, "except that Jerome and Florence Espy's inheritance is not, at this time, exactly clear. In fact, the only perfectly clear bequest in the will is to their daughter, Dolores Espy. She inherited Sangria House and Plantation. And her son, who is named Timothy Espy, inherited the sum of twenty thousand dollars, which has been placed in a trust for him in a bank in Boston. The trust's administrator is Dolores Espy."

"Good heavens," Richard exclaimed. "We didn't even know the Espys had a daughter. But what about the man's wife? And three sisters? They weren't mentioned in the will?"

"Oh yes. Judge Allard said there were provisions for them in the will, but there were problems with all of the other bequests besides the ones for Dolores and Timothy Espy. And unfortunately for Miss Espy and her son, the will cannot be probated in part; it must be done in total or else the entire document will be declared invalid and the disposition of the estate done by the court. But Judge Allard said he believes the will is valid and executable, only it is a complex document and rather obscure.

He wouldn't try to quote it to me; he is having it copied and asked me to study it and offer him my advice concerning an investigation into some clauses of the bequests. In fact, he thought it might be necessary to issue court orders concerning the property, both for the house and some of the contents. I just didn't realize that you and your family, sir, were the tenants at Sangria House."

Major Valentine settled back in his chair, which creaked comfortably and the leather rustled. After a thoughtful few moments he went on somberly, "And now, sir, after the information that your daughter has so thoughtfully brought to my attention, I must say I do have many questions. I'm not exactly sure of the laws concerning the coroner's investigation in Florida either, but perhaps having martial law in this case is not such a bad thing. I would like to speak with your daughter so that I may document a physician's expert opinion, and then I shall order the exhumation."

Richard said wryly, "My daughter will be very surprised that anyone besides her family considers her opinion to be an expert one. As you might imagine, her reception as a lady doctor is not usually so warm."

"Sir, if your daughter has any part of your courage and sense of honor, I know that her opinion will be all the testimony I need to order an exhumation," Major Valentine replied. "And if I may be so bold, after seeing the beautiful lady at your side in church and the other young lady who so closely resembled her, I must confess that just to meet them would be a pure pleasure."

"I appreciate that, Major Valentine," Richard said. "But still, you may want to keep my son-in-law in mind when you express those sentiments to my daughter."

"Ah yes. The blond giant?"

"Yes."

"I am persuaded, sir, to be the soul of discretion. In fact, may I request that *you* express my admiration to your daughter? When the blond giant is not present, of course."

"In this case, I believe that the saying 'Discretion is the better part of valor' may apply, Major Valentine. As it happens, I am instructed by the ladies to ask if you will join us for dinner tonight, at which you may meet my daughter and the rest of our party. And the invitation includes your wife, of course."

"I'm not married, Colonel Duvall," the young man said, "and it would be my great honor to attend dinner tonight."

The two men rose, and Richard offered his hand. Major Valentine shook it hard enough to jar Richard's teeth, but he managed to say, "We'll see you tonight then, at nine o'clock. And, Major Valentine, it will be our pleasure."

CHAPTER TWELVE

Black Cards

"EN GARDE, MONSIEUR!" Cheney warned, and then began her ferocious attack.

Shiloh parried her initial line of attack with a rather clumsy *parry of quarte,* and then he stepped back as she lunged. The needle-thin foil cut the air one inch away from his vest. His own foil shot forward as he attempted a parry called *envelopment,* which was meant to sweep Cheney's blade in a full circle by a circular motion engaging the upper third of her blade. Instead, he engaged the strongest part of her blade, the *forte,* down near the hilt, and the button at the tip of his foil locked hers. Before he realized what was happening, he had whipped her foil out of her hand, and it went dancing above their heads. Shiloh had to push Cheney out of the way so he could catch it before it hit her head.

Unfortunately, she sat down hard in the sand. "Black card!" she cried, the name of the gravest offenses in the sport of fencing. "No pushing!"

"Sorry, Doc, but I was just—" He was holding both of the foils in his left hand now and was puzzled as to how to tuck them under his arm so that he might help Cheney up. It was a tricky thing, considering that his right arm was tied behind his back.

Cheney glowered at him, then hopped up as nimbly as a child. It helped that she was wearing the fencing costume Fiona and the sailors of *Locke's Day Dream* had made for her. The daring split skirt, made of fine stout linen, allowed her more freedom of movement than most women ever dreamed of. In the front and back was sewn a flap, attached at the waist and gathered to give the appearance of a full skirt. Because she was so proud of the sailors and Fiona, she also wore her fencer's vest with

LDD embroidered in gold and navy blue thread instead of the traditional small red heart. They had also made her a perfectly fitted glove. Shiloh had bought her mask. Now she pulled it off, breathing hard from exertion. Her cheeks glowed, her green eyes were brilliant.

Stalking toward him, she held out her hand. Mischievously he tossed her foil up in the air, allowing his own foil to hang on his thumb, caught Cheney's by the blade just close to the hilt, then held it out, hilt first, and bowed.

"Showboat," she muttered. "I could have caught it."

"With your head," he teased.

"Perhaps instead of tying one hand behind your back, I should gag you," she said, tossing her head. "It may not handicap your fencing, but it would give me some semblance of peace of mind."

"But then how could I tell you how beautiful you look with the sea breeze teasing your hair that's on fire, the murderous look in your green eyes, and your silver rapier glittering dangerously in the sun?" he asked.

Whipping her foil in a figure eight, listening to the dangerous hum with satisfaction, Cheney answered, "At least you're paying attention. Sometimes it seems that you can parry without even looking up. It's just not fair, Shiloh. Your reach is too long, not to mention your legs."

"I could get on my knees," he suggested. "I could be the Iron Stump."

"Funny," she said sourly. "How about if I tie both of your hands behind your back, blindfold you, and tie your feet together? I might be able to beat you that way. Oh, forget fencing. It's no fun if you have to handicap your opponent. Especially if he keeps beating you anyway. Let's go down there and shoot that big log that washed up."

She untied his hand, and with relief Shiloh reached up and pulled off the wire mesh mask. It was hot. "Yeah, I feel like shootin' something myself," Shiloh agreed. "That log does look like it needs killin'."

They ran to the canvas pavilion set up on the beach. Ivy Rainsford and Irene Duvall sat in chaises underneath it. Baby Lisette was asleep in a wicker basket conveniently placed by Irene's chair. Out on the beach, Dart and Alex built sand forts and made explosion sounds from artillery pieces made out of shells. Sean and Shannon ran up and down like the foolish puppies they were, their long tongues lolling, their enormous ears flopping. Occasionally they ran into the surf and tried to bite the incoming splashing waves.

Hannah Barentine was looking like a pretty farm maiden in a blue dress with a crisp white apron and wide-brimmed straw hat. She was writing simple words in the sand for fun little English lessons for Solange, who had spoken only French when the Buchanans had adopted her just two months previously. The girl was learning English vocabulary, grammar, and spelling at a much more advanced rate than other children at seven years old. She was a rather plain little thing, with wispy blond hair and sad brown eyes. But she was not nearly so thin and bedraggled as she had been when Shiloh and Dev had found her. In the bright sunlight, laughing as she and Hannah wrote in the warm sand with a stick, she was almost pretty, Cheney thought, as she and Shiloh came into the cool shade of the pavilion.

Locke's Day Dream had supplied the pavilion and the chaises, and Shiloh, shunning the servants, had insisted that he could handle all the baggage and setting up the canvas canopy himself. Nearby Victoria and Minerva had set up easels and were painting seascapes. Quietly, so as not to awaken the baby, Cheney and Shiloh put their foils into the velvet-lined cases and got their guns—matching Colt .44 revolvers—and ammunition out of one of the storage lockers they had brought. "We're going down the beach, Mother," Cheney said quietly. "Are you all right? Need anything?"

"No, darling, you run along and shoot your guns," Irene said. "We shall all feel much safer when you've killed the log."

Cheney giggled, then she and Shiloh, holding hands, ran off down the beach. Sean and Shannon bounded after them, looking like small galloping ponies.

Ivy Rainsford's gaze followed them. "Cheney has become a perfectly beautiful woman, Irene. And your son-in-law—what an intriguing man! Not to mention handsome. In your letters you told me that he was, but he's quite different in person—so vibrant and energetic. They seem to be very happy."

Irene regarded her friend with affection. Ivy Gainsborough Rainsford, at fifty-six years old, was nine years older than Irene. When she had been a young much-sought-after socialite in New York, she had been an acknowledged beauty, and the beauty, now mellowed and made softer with age, was still there. She had still-lovely creamy skin, a halo of silvery-gold hair, long elegant fingers, a graceful carriage. Many men had been disappointed when she had consented to marry Samuel Rainsford, a balding, short, rotund, rather elfish man fourteen years her elder. That had been forty years ago. Irene thought that Ivy, too, still seemed happy in her marriage.

"I believe they are," Irene answered rather wistfully. "As I've told you, Cheney has never been in the habit of confiding in me. She keeps very much to herself. But yes, they do seem to be happy together." She turned back to her friend. "What about you, Ivy? Are you still happy living here?"

"Oh yes. Sometimes I miss living close to the children," she answered, then, with a sly sidelong glance at Irene, added, "but we now have eighteen grandchildren and three great-grandchildren. I don't miss having them around all of the time."

"Oh no? I can't imagine why not," Irene said with an innocent air. She glanced at the children playing on the beach and then reached down and smoothed Lisette's black springing curls. "For my part, I'm very happy to have Dart, and now Solange and Lisette, living nearby. But perhaps I wouldn't be so happy if this blessing was multiplied by seven."

Ivy giggled, a very youthful sound. "Perhaps not."

It was odd that the two had become such fast friends almost as soon as they had met. When one knew the mother and daughter, it was easy to see that Cheney Duvall's reserve was not so unusual, because she had inherited it from her mother. Irene normally did not form such close relationships easily, but she and Ivy Rainsford had had such a warm rapport on short acquaintance that Irene had simply accepted, and been grateful for, the friendship. It had also been strange that the companionship had endured so many years when it was conducted mostly through letters. But Irene still felt as close as ever to Ivy Rainsford, even though it had been five years since they had seen each other.

"Irene, tell me something," Ivy said, her blue eyes lit with girlish eagerness. "Would you and Richard consider moving here? I know that you like St. Augustine, and it would be a happy dream to have you living nearby."

Irene turned to look down the beach. They could see Cheney and Shiloh, who had taken a few shots at the hapless log but now seemed to be playing a mad game of tag through the surf, with the dogs first running from them and then running after them. The sound of Cheney's laughter and Shiloh's deep baritone sounded faintly over the rhythmic rush of the waves and the soft whisper of the sea breeze. She looked over at Victoria, her lovely, gracious daughter-in-law, as she serenely painted. Then she shook her head. "Richard and I couldn't possibly leave New

York. Both Cheney and Dev have decided to make their lives there."

"But?" Ivy said slyly.

"But," Irene said with a smile, "we are here. Cheney and Dev have managed to find a way to take some time off. And Richard and I are very, very glad to be out of icy, snowy, frozen New York."

"It is lovely here, isn't it."

"It is."

"So wonderfully warm."

"Yes."

"The sun, and the sea . . ."

"Yes."

"And so you'll move here?" Ivy said quickly.

Irene smiled. "I understand that a lot of families from the North are vacationing here during the winter. Perhaps it would be nice to—"

"Have a winter home here," Ivy finished for her. "That's how Samuel and I started, you know. He, too, started to find the winters unbearable when he got older. We spent five—or was it six?—winters here before Samuel retired. And when he did, we couldn't move here fast enough. I've never regretted it, even though sometimes the summers are very hot and our social life has been, shall we say, very slow."

"Really?" Irene said with surprise. Ivy Rainsford had always been a very sociable creature. Even though the Rainsfords lived in New York, they had had friends in Boston, Philadelphia, Detroit, and of course Washington. The newspapers used to document their attendance at many social functions, and before they had begun wintering in St. Augustine, they'd had a summer residence on fashionable Cape May, New Jersey.

Irene continued, "But why, Ivy? I know this is actually a rather small village, but haven't you made friends here?"

"Yes, we have," she answered. "But life is slower here, less frenetic. The social rounds are much less demanding; generally, the most activity on my social calendar is a dinner party on Friday and a church picnic on Sunday. And now you know, dearest Irene, why I so badly want you to move here," she added slyly.

Irene smiled. "To add to your social calendar? I doubt that very seriously, Ivy. Anyway, as delightful as this day is—and with your charming company, of course—the prospect of vacationing here is beginning to look more attractive all the time. But you must tell me, Ivy, for I admit I'm shamefully curious. What about the Griders? After all, they are your nearest neighbors. Are you and Samuel close friends with them?"

Ivy turned back to stare out at the endless ocean. "Close friends? I think so, yes. At least Samuel and I still consider them close friends. But Louis had . . . distanced himself, I suppose you might say, in the last few years, from almost all of his friends, not just from Samuel. When Louis's first wife, Penelope, was alive, we were all—including Letitia and Muriel and Phillipa—much closer. After Penelope died and Louis married Aimee, we did not see nearly as much of them. Even my friendship with his sisters has waned in the last years. Aimee and the sisters and I still call on each other once a month or so, but it's more of a social convention than anything else."

"I understand," Irene said quietly. "Richard and I have known couples like that too. Sometimes it just happens that people drift apart."

"Perhaps," Ivy said uncertainly. "But it wasn't so much drifting apart as it was that over time, they all seemed to change. All of them, even Aimee. Of course she was barely eighteen when Louis married her back in 1864, so it is not too surprising that a young woman would change and mature as she came into her twenties."

"I never met Mr. Grider, but didn't Victoria tell me that he was the eldest of the siblings?"

"Yes, that's right. He was fifty when he married Aimee."

"I see. Was it the usual *mariage de convenance*—poor family, distinguished lineage, ample marriage settlement?"

"Not exactly. That would seem to be more her mother's story than Aimee's. Her father is Martin Dalrymple—you know of the Boston Dalrymples? Founding Fathers, Boston Tea Party, and so on. And her mother is Belinda Adler—"

"Of the Boston Adlers, the fabulously wealthy Boston Adlers," Irene finished for her.

"Yes. Anyway, the Dalrymple family's fortunes were increased mightily when Belinda married Martin; but I must say that there is one twist on the old story, and that is that Martin Dalrymple may be many things, but he is no wastrel. He is a shrewd investor and capitalist, and so Aimee does not come from a background of genteel poverty. But even if she had, I never got the impression that Aimee was forced into a marriage against her will. Though she was so much younger than Louis, she seemed happy enough."

"Did she?" Irene asked. "The difference in their ages is unusually wide. It would be strange for a girl that young to be truly happy with a man of fifty."

Ivy frowned slightly. "I suppose so. But when they first got married, I believed that Aimee was much like I was, you see. Even though the difference in our ages is not nearly so much—I was seventeen when I married Samuel and he was thirty—everyone thought that it was a marriage of convenience. But they were wrong. I was never the kind of woman who longed for danger and high passions and melodrama and swooning," she said with delicate distaste. "I had so much respect and esteem for Samuel, and when he asked me to marry him, I felt honored. He has always made me feel secure and cherished. Over time my respect for him has grown into a deep and abiding love. And I believed that Aimee's temperament was much like my own when I was young—calm and contented with a faithful, mature husband."

"Calm she is," Irene said evenly, "but contented she is not."

Ivy turned to Irene, her gentle blue eyes wide with surprise. "How did you know? How could you know?"

"It was easy. When we made a condolence call on the grieving young widow, she flirted with my husband. Oh, she is very subtle, very skillful, but in my opinion women like her are never quite subtle enough. It's all too easy to recognize them for what they are."

Ivy stared at Irene for a few moments longer and then broke into genuinely delighted laughter. "Oh, dear, I cannot imagine how Richard reacted! Was he perfectly horrified?"

"No, he was perfectly blind, deaf, and dumb," Irene answered dryly. "I don't think he would have realized what she was doing if she had thrown herself at his feet and sworn her undying love."

"No, of course Richard would have been utterly dumbfounded. He is that sort of man. He never sees any woman but you, and never has, I imagine."

"I am blessed," Irene said, "that he is so blissfully ignorant of women's wiles. Anyway, Ivy dear, I suppose it didn't take you long to see what kind of woman Aimee Grider truly is?"

"Long enough," Ivy answered. "There were a few times when I thought Aimee was treating even Samuel with a little too much familiarity, but he was all of sixty-four years old when she arrived here, so I told myself that I was just a foolish old woman, imagining things. After all, what could she possibly hope to gain from flirting with Samuel? Her own husband was only fifty then and much more vigorous and commanding. And Louis was fully as wealthy as we are, so I knew that Aimee couldn't have been angling for Samuel's money."

With surprise Irene asked, "The Griders are that well off? Good heavens, Ivy, Sangria House is certainly not spartan, but neither is it the kind of house that I would expect an extremely wealthy family to have."

"Well . . . I did say that *Louis* was wealthy," Ivy said carefully. "And Sangria House is much like Rainsford House, isn't it? We have a large house with nice furnishings, but somehow as you get older the kind of lavish stuffy opulence you see in the best homes in Boston and New York seems rather tiresome."

"Ah, so Louis Grider was a miserable miser."

"Irene! I said no such thing!"

"No, you would never say anything unkind," Irene said with affection. "But I know you, Ivy, and besides, I sort of gathered that Mr. Grider was a penny pincher from being at Sangria House. Little things, such as the cheap candles and much-mended mosquito nets. Thin threadbare rugs in the servants' quarters. The lack of care of the grounds. And, of course, Shiloh told me and Richard that Mr. Grider was paying the Espys only eighteen cents a day. No wonder they are so thin. They were probably starving."

"It is true, he seemed to get more and more . . . thrifty as the years went by," Ivy said. "But Aimee always seemed to have the newest, most fashionable clothes and hats and gloves and shoes, and she often bought jewelry and such things as expensive stationery and bed linens and even expensive imported foods and wines. Perhaps Letitia and Muriel and Phillipa didn't have such a generous allowance, but it is understandable that a man would be more generous with his wife than with his sisters."

"Is it?" Irene said thoughtfully. "I was under the impression that when people grew miserly, they were generally miserly to everyone, from tradesmen to their own family."

"Perhaps, but Aimee made certain that Louis didn't try to . . ." Ivy's sweet voice trailed off. Her cheeks colored a delicate rose, and she dropped her eyes.

Quietly Irene said, "You know, Ivy, Cheney believes that there are some crucial unanswered questions concerning Mr. Grider's death. As a matter of fact, Richard has gone into town to see the deputy provost marshal and make some inquiries, and I believe the authorities will take his concerns seriously."

Ivy looked up then. "Are you telling me that there is likely to be an investigation?"

"Yes. And I am also fairly certain that Mr. Grider's body will be exhumed and a proper autopsy done—I hope by Cheney. Under the circumstances I don't regard information about the Griders as malicious slander, Ivy. You know me, and I know you, and we are not cruel backbiting gossips. Something odd happened in that house; I'm sure of it, and personally I hope that Richard and Cheney and Shiloh will find the truth as quickly as possible. Anything you can tell me that would help would be, in my opinion, an assistance to them."

Ivy nodded and again stared out at the sea. "You know, Irene, I can't say I'm shocked. As you say, something odd happened in that house . . . but it wasn't just when Louis died. As I said before, the Griders have changed. They've all changed, in the last—I suppose most noticeably in the last year.

"But first you must realize how Aimee used to be and why I did think she was a serene and contented girl. It's because she really did seem to be when Louis first married her. Don't misunderstand me. She was never shy. She was always very sure of herself. For instance, it seems that the true love of her life is horses. She's an excellent equestrienne, and she even works in the stables, tends to her mares when they're foaling, attends to her own tack—you know, you've known true horse people before. That's what Aimee is, and Louis has always—apparently happily—financed her dealings. Over the years she's bought and sold and bred horses and kept a fairly substantial stable, and Louis always seemed rather proud of it."

"Yes, there are four horses and one pony in the stables now," Irene said. "Our three young gentlemen guests leased them from Mrs. Grider, and they assured us that all of the horses are of high quality."

"Yes, that is truly Aimee's passion," Ivy sighed. "Until—but I get ahead of myself. Anyway, for about five years the Griders seemed to be doing fairly well. Letitia and Muriel had some, shall we say, stiffness in their attitude toward Aimee, but that is only to be expected. They probably felt very insecure when Louis brought home such a young wife, and Aimee is not the type of person to go out of her way to ingratiate herself to anyone, particularly her much older sisters-in-law."

"What about Phillipa, the youngest sister?" Irene asked curiously.

"She and Aimee have always seemed to get along well. I could never detect any restraint between them at all. And Louis, well, he was always a severe, rather cold man, so there was no outward warmth in his behavior toward his sisters. But he did provide for them, and he has done so ever since their father died in 1855, and that alone is an admirable thing,

I think. Anyway, Louis did thaw out with Aimee. He did seem to be deeply in love with her, and his conduct toward her was always . . ."

"Besotted?" Irene supplied. "Older men with very young wives usually do appear to be."

"I suppose so," Ivy agreed. "It was unusual for Louis to be quite so . . . indulgent. And Aimee always did treat him with extravagant affection. It was very odd."

"What do you mean, odd?"

"It was so out of character for both of them," Ivy finally answered. "Louis didn't seem to be the type of man who would be, as you say, besotted. And Aimee has never seemed to be the type of woman who would gush. But there you have it. That is precisely how they treated each other, even though they were nothing like that when they weren't together. It was so jarring that even Samuel noticed it—you know how men are so unobservant, Irene—and Samuel is one of the least perceptive men that has ever stumbled around on this earth."

She and Irene shared small knowing laughter. "Yes, he is perhaps one of the few men who can compete with Richard in that area," Irene said. "But both of them are sharp-eyed enough in other ways. Go on."

"Well, as I said, I called on Sangria House and they called on me, and we had dinner together every two weeks or so, and often we and two other couples—the Ketchums and the Ewings—had dinner parties, sometimes picnics here at the beach. This went on until—let's see, it must have been around the first of last year. Yes, as a matter of fact, I recall now that it was a New Year's dinner at Sangria House last year, 1869, about the second or third of January, I think. Louis had aged some that year because he had had a protracted illness in November. I never quite understood what his particular ailment was, but once Letitia told me that their mother had died because she was of a very frail constitution, and when she caught smallpox, she went downhill quickly and died. Apparently Louis had convinced himself that he had the same frailties and was very vulnerable to any ailment, so he often took to his bed with even the slightest catarrh or influenza."

"Oh, really," Irene said speculatively. "That is very interesting. I want you to tell Cheney later all you know about Mr. Grider's illness, because the information he gave Victoria when she leased the house was very sketchy. Naturally we didn't want to question his sisters or his widow too closely."

"Of course, though I don't know much more about the particulars,"

Ivy said. "I did notice, though, when he was ill, for he generally disappeared from our society for a month or more.

"Anyway, we were at Sangria House for a New Year's celebration, and the Ketchums and Ewings were there too. Aimee was burbling along—yes, this is the same Aimee. I'm telling you that her and Louis's behavior when they were together was almost giddy. All of a sudden the room grew unnaturally silent. I was seated at the other end of that enormous slab of a table, and in this sudden quietness I heard Aimee saying, 'My poor Louie has been so very ill that he's left quite weak and spent. He was unable to even go into town and attend to the banking. Isn't that right, Mr. Rainsford? His afflictions are so many and heavy that he hasn't even been able to attend to the plantation. Letitia has been taking care of all of the Sangria business. I never see enough of my poor Louie when he's ill; and I know it's so difficult for him too. Isn't it, darling? You never neglect me unless you are very, very ill.'"

"Aimee Grider said all that drivel?" Irene said. "The same Aimee Grider who was as modest and downcast as a nun during the funeral?"

"The same," Ivy said positively. "And Louis just sat there and stared down at his plate and never said a word. Of course it was the most shameful performance I've ever witnessed. But as I said, Aimee is subtle, and there was no word or phrase that one could actually object to. But it was the flamboyant manner in which it was said that made it so reprehensible. Of course it must have mortified Louis, but he never said anything except to mumble, 'I am much better now.' It was pitiful stuff, especially considering that Louis had always been a proud, even arrogant, but commanding man. Aimee had reduced him to a pitiful little weakling with that one speech. And that was the beginning."

"I see. So the miserliness, the protracted ailments, the meaningless penny pinching started then?"

"Yes," Ivy said very quietly. "And that was the month when Aimee began to have an affair. His name was Captain Scott Feldhaus, and he was a dashing, careless, reckless sort of man. Oh yes, he's from Boston, and we know him and his family well. But take my word for it, Irene, he didn't seduce Aimee Grider. I saw her that month, before she began the affair and afterward. That dinner party was before she began it, and later I realized that she had finally grown weary of her husband, and this was the most effective means she had of making him smaller, not only in her eyes, but in everyone's. In some way she was justifying herself. I saw her after she began the affair with Captain Feldhaus, and she was defiant. She made up her mind what she wanted, and then she went and got it."

"But, Ivy, what about poor Mr. Grider? Surely he found out?"

Ivy looked troubled. "I have wondered about that time and time again. I could never detect the slightest change in Louis's behavior toward Aimee. During her affair, she still cooed and simpered to Louis, and he still seemed just as helplessly besotted as he had ever been. To this day, I believe that either he did not see or he simply refused to see."

"As that so-wise man Matthew Henry said, 'None so blind as those that will not see,'" Irene said. "What about Mrs. Raymond? And the other sisters? Surely they knew. Wouldn't they have told their brother of his wife's infidelity?"

"I don't think they would," Ivy answered slowly. "I don't think they would have dared. As you said, Irene, there are those who just refuse to see. Telling them what is in front of their eyes doesn't mean they will see it, and usually, when people are in a willful self-deceit, they don't appreciate anyone disturbing their delusion. As another very wise man said about Israel, 'Prophesy not unto us right things, speak unto us smooth things.'" Ivy's serene features wrinkled for a moment, and she murmured, "Now who said that? Where is that in the Bible? Isn't it frustrating when you can remember the verse but not where it is?"

"We'll ask Richard when he gets here. He'll certainly know. He knows so much of the Bible," Irene said, her gaze going hopefully behind them toward the path down to the beach from the cabana. "I hope he's not long. He so wanted to come with us, but he would do the dutiful thing first, of course. Anyway, Ivy, go on about the sisters."

Obediently Ivy continued, "Letitia is a woman much like Louis; she is somewhat calculating and cold, and if I'm sharp enough to know that Louis would hear nothing against his wife, then certainly she is. Muriel is not as shrewd as Letitia, but the same would be true of her. Phillipa is not like the others; she is vulnerable and insecure, and it would never occur to her to cause any trouble with Aimee. At any rate, the affair was somewhat short-lived, and I thought afterward that perhaps it was simply a wild fling of Aimee's, just something she did to see if she could."

"I suppose, when Captain Feldhaus left, she showed no signs of regret? No loss?"

"No. None. As a matter of fact, I think she was relieved." Ivy turned to face Irene, her blue eyes clear and uncharacteristically hard. "You understand, Aimee would never confide in me nor anyone else. I never spoke of this to anyone, and no one ever had the audacity to bring up the story to me. But Samuel and I often invite the soldiers that we know here to the beach and to the house for parties and dancing. I saw Aimee and Scott together, and though neither of them showed the least sign of their secret, I knew, and that was when I truly understood what kind of woman Aimee is. No, she didn't care when Scott's term of enlistment was up and he went back to Boston to marry a sweet girl that he'd been betrothed to for years. Aimee didn't mind because she had gotten him and then had tired of him. But what I didn't understand then was that she was evidently ready for a new conquest."

"So she was," Irene said slowly. "And I can even tell you who the new man is."

"You don't have to. It's your son-in-law's cousin, Mr. Bain Winslow. Isn't it?"

Irene looked surprised. "Why, yes, I believe so. But how did you know?"

Ivy's mouth grew into a tight line. "Because they met at my house. Beckett and Carsten called on us as soon as they arrived in St. Augustine, back in January, the first time they sailed in. And when they did, Aimee happened to be calling on me, and I saw her look as soon as she had been introduced to Mr. Winslow. And he saw it too, of course. He would recognize a woman like Aimee instantly."

"Yes, he would," Irene sighed. "He surely would. As most men do. That's what women like Mrs. Grider never understand; men see them for what they truly are, not for what they think they are. They think they are mysterious, seductive, intriguing *femmes fatales*. But men—and generally women—know that they are nothing so exotic. They are, to put it bluntly, simply easy. Even the ones who do not seem to be vulnerable to falling in love, as it appears Mrs. Grider is not."

"Well, she wasn't in love with Scott Feldhaus," Ivy said tightly. "He just seemed to be an acquisition she strove for—not to be crude—but much as she works hard at finding and acquiring good horseflesh. But Mr. Bain Winslow—I've seen them together a lot in the last two months, Irene. And this time I'm not so sure that Aimee's in control of that little *mésalliance* as she was with Scott, and even her husband."

Startled, Irene asked, "You mean you think that Mrs. Grider is in love with Bain?"

"I do."

"But, Ivy, do you think—is it possible she could have wanted to get her husband out of the way if she has fallen in love with Bain?"

Ivy shrugged, but it was a curiously affirming gesture, instead of an expression of ignorance.

Both of the women turned their faces toward the restless sea. Though the sky was a peaceful blue, the Atlantic, as always, was a cold gray. The wind had a chill in it; the sun was bright and warm, but just at the edge of their perception they knew that with just the right draft, they would grow cold.

Irene pulled her shawl tighter around her shoulders. "You know, dear Ivy, I hope that Mrs. Grider didn't kill her husband because she thought she and Bain would live happily ever after. That would be an extremely cruel irony."

The women turned to watch Shiloh and Cheney, who were now skipping in zigzag patterns, trying to dash away from the lapping tide. The dogs didn't quite understand the game, but they did understand running in a silly way, and so they joined in. Irene couldn't help but smile.

"Mr. Bain Winslow is not like your son-in-law, is he?" Ivy said. "He doesn't strike me as the faithful, loving husband type."

"No, he's not; but then again, neither was Shiloh until he was saved and started walking with the Lord. No, that's not quite true. Shiloh has loved Cheney for a long time, and I believe that in his heart he has been true to her ever since they met. But anyway, it's my impression that his cousin Bain is quite a rake, and he would regard Aimee Grider as fair game."

Ivy sighed. "That would be because Aimee has made herself fair game. Foolish, foolish girl."

"I just hope," Irene said in a low voice, "that soon we don't find out she's much worse than that."

CHAPTER THIRTEEN

Pro Hac Vice, or *For This Occasion*

"OOH, HE'S LOVELY," Minerva said as she peeked out the window. "I've always thought men looked so splendid in full dress uniform. And isn't he perfectly huge—oh, dear!" As if she had been shot, she jerked back from the window and ran to her chair, her satin dress rustling busily. "He saw me! He looked up to the window and grinned, and then made this odious little salute. The impudence! Perfectly scandalous!"

Victoria smoothed her skirt and said serenely, "Oh, certainly, Min, he's the one who's scandalous, to acknowledge seeing you ogling him from behind the curtains."

"I was not ogling him," Minerva retorted indignantly. "I was merely observing him."

Victoria, her blue eyes twinkling, mimicked, "'Ooh, he's lovely.'"

Minerva tilted her chin and looked down her nose at Victoria. "As I said, I was merely observing that he was lovely."

The assembled company heard the front door open and the murmur of voices, Jauncy's low respectful murmur, and Major Micah Valentine's muted bass. They grew silent and looked expectantly toward the door of the parlor.

This room—the parlor or drawing room—was the most formal in Sangria House. The draperies covering the two windows that looked out on the front gardens were of heavy red velvet, from floor to ceiling, with tiebacks of gold rope with large tassels. All of the furniture was ornate, hand-carved walnut, heavily ornamented. The upholstery of the settee, wing chairs, and side chairs was of the same crimson velvet as the draperies. This was also the only room in the house that had a woolen rug, a

159

fine Alcazar carpet that must have been over two hundred years old, for it was faded, but it was still thick and plush.

One rather unusual feature of the room was a round ball-and-claw-footed oak table centered in front of the fireplace and covered with an upholstered tablecloth with long heavy gold fringe. Four armless side chairs were drawn up to it. Irene had speculated that it was a sort of worktable, where ladies could sit and sew or trim hats and drink tea. Along one wall were an upright piano and four side chairs. In one corner by the fireplace was the settee, facing two wing chairs and two ornate armchairs. Irene had ordered the grouping arranged so that it could seat the six of them and their guest. She sat by the table in a side chair; Shiloh and Cheney were on the settee; Richard sat by the fireplace in one of the comfortable wing chairs; Minerva and Victoria sat in the plush armchairs, which left the wing chair across from Richard for Major Valentine.

The door opened and Jauncy stepped in, bowed elegantly, and said in stentorian tones, "Major Micah Valentine." The major came in, and Richard hurried to meet him and shake his hand.

"Major Valentine, prompt to the minute, as every good soldier must be," he said. "Allow me to introduce you . . ." Richard proceeded with him around the little group, performing the intricacies of formal introduction.

Major Valentine did look very imposing, if not exactly lovely, in his full dress uniform of a major in the United States Army. His frock coat of dark blue was so precisely tailored that it had no crease or untoward wrinkle, while the seam of his light blue trousers was as sharp as a knife. With his gold epaulettes, the rank insignia of embroidered oak leaves, the double row of gold buttons, the gold sash with the fine fringe, and the cavalry sabre, he cut an extremely imposing figure. When Richard introduced him to Minerva, her cheeks colored, but Major Valentine never made the least sign of acknowledging her window peeping. He only bowed deeply and murmured, "At your service, ma'am."

"Please join us, Major Valentine," Irene said, elegantly motioning to the empty wing chair. "We are having tea, which is, I know, an unusual custom to indulge in before dinner, but one which we have come to enjoy." She nodded a signal to Jauncy.

"Delighted, ma'am," Major Valentine said, settling into the armchair. For the next few moments the company evaluated their guest as he was memorizing them, an inevitable ritual of humans when meeting a stranger, although in refined company such as this it was very discreet and practically instantaneous.

Richard and Shiloh were wearing black dress suits, frock coats with stiff white shirts and smart bow ties. The ladies all wore satin, with the graceful low necklines and long trains of evening wear. Victoria wore an icy blue satin, Irene wore a light pearl gray satin, Minerva wore a bright glossy peach, and Cheney positively glowed in jade green, one of her best colors, which made her skin look like alabaster and her hair like muted fire.

These initial appraisals only took a few seconds; then, as the host, Richard said, "We've only been here a few days, Major Valentine, but we do like St. Augustine. How long have you been stationed here?"

"A little over a year, sir," he answered. "I like it here too—the warm climate, the beaches. And the townspeople are, I find, quite hospitable in spite of the fact that they are under martial law. It has been such a pleasant experience that I have written to my parents and asked them to consider purchasing a winter home here. We live in Chicago, and the winters can be brutal."

"Indeed they can," Irene agreed. "This winter, in particular, has seemed harsher than we can remember, but then again Richard and I have wondered if it is not simply that we are getting older instead of the winters getting worse. Either way, we have surely enjoyed the mild weather down here. Are your parents at all interested in moving to St. Augustine?"

He grinned, and it was particularly engaging coming from such a great bear of a man. "They weren't at first, but I am what you might call stubborn, and I believe I'm either persuading them or just wearing them down so much that they will eventually give in."

"You are from Chicago, sir?" Minerva asked. "Then you must be acquainted with our Uncle Porter Wilcott."

His brown eyes alight as he turned to Minerva, he answered, "Why, yes, my family is acquainted with the Porter Wilcotts. You say Mr. Wilcott is your uncle, Miss Wilcott?"

"Yes, he's my father's brother, and Mrs. Buchanan is my cousin, and her mother is Mr. Porter Wilcott's sister," Minerva answered all in one breath. "So we are practically related, are we not?"

"We—you mean, you and Mrs. Buchanan are practically related?" Major Valentine murmured, his wide brow wrinkling. "But—you said you are cousins, didn't you? I mean, aren't you?"

"Exactly," Minerva asserted. "And so we are practically related."

Victoria looked amused. "Don't worry, Major Valentine, our family connections often confuse my little cousin. May I ask your parents' name? I am acquainted with most of our Chicago Wilcotts' friends."

This comfortable conversation ultimately revealed that Victoria and Micah Valentine had actually once met at the funeral of an elderly Wilcott gentleman who had died in 1845.

"I can barely recall Cousin Tyron Wilcott. I was just a child," Victoria said quickly, for she had been very vague about her age for years now. She was actually thirty-two years old, which would have made her seven years old at the funeral, but Victoria generally gave the impression of being not quite thirty, and so at times like this she usually skipped over exact details.

Major Valentine's brown eyes twinkled; he might look like a great gentle bear, but he was by no means as slow as one. "And no wonder, Mrs. Buchanan. As I recall, you were a very small girl, with big blue eyes and a halo of silver-blond curls, hiding behind your nanny," he said gallantly.

"And now I remember a great tall boy with brown curls who kept teasing the girl standing in front of him at the graveside," Victoria said. "Could that have been you, Major Valentine? Pulling on that poor girl's hair, and once, didn't you yank on one end of the bow in her hair so that it came untied and fell out?"

"Guilty, I'm afraid. That was Miss Mary Louise Leighton, and she still hates me," he answered.

"I doubt that very, very much," Minerva said. "She would be foolish to carry a grudge for so long. I remember Cousin Tyron Wilcott's funeral too, and I would not have been at all angry if you had pulled on the bow in my hair."

"Minerva, dear," Victoria interjected, "Cousin Tyron Wilcott's funeral was over twenty years ago, so you could not have possibly been there, much less remembered it."

"Perhaps I'm thinking of some other Cousin Tyron Wilcott," Minerva said carelessly. "But still I wouldn't have been angry at Major Valentine."

"You are very kind, Miss Wilcott," Major Valentine said.

Jauncy came in then with the tea service and set it on the round table. Irene poured, and Jauncy served. Shiloh went to stoke the small fire; night was coming, and the room was growing chilly. He stood and took his cup of tea. "Thanks, PJ," he said, setting the cup on the fireplace mantel and leaning against the ornately decorated lintel. "I see that you're cavalry, Major Valentine. What's your outfit?"

"Fourth Illinois Cavalry," he answered with pride. "Then, when the war was over, we were integrated into the Fourteenth. And you, sir?"

Shiloh answered quietly, "Sergeant, Army of Tennessee, Confederate States of America."

"My son-in-law was one of Forrest's boys," Richard said with evident pride. "One of his bodyguards, as a matter of fact."

Major Valentine looked up at Shiloh, his eyes wide, his expression unfathomable. For a moment Cheney was afraid the major may say something derogatory; the old enmities were far from healed, even though the War Between the States had ended almost five years ago.

Suddenly Major Valentine bounded up, his hand outstretched. "Sir, let me shake your hand. We chased you all over creation, and it's a pleasure to finally meet one of Forrest's best. At last I know that you were not a company of ghosts, as it did seem many times."

"No, it's my pleasure, Major," Shiloh said, eyes glinting. "We were not ghosts, sir, just fast and hard riding."

"And hard fighting too," Major Valentine said ruefully. "Were you at Shiloh, sir? I actually saw General Forrest as he retreated in the Fallen Timbers, when he pulled that poor dead Billy up on his saddle and used him for a shield. . . ."

Richard Duvall, who was at the Battle of Shiloh as an aide to General U. S. Grant, stood up and joined the animated conversation as Shiloh and Major Valentine began to break up the fireplace matches into small sticks to use to illustrate the arrangement of the forces. Little bits of bark from the logs stacked by the side of the fireplace represented the rise and fall of the ground, and teaspoons suggested the boundaries of the terrain at this epic battle in a little-known bit of woods that surrounded tiny Shiloh Church, Tennessee. The three men went on talking and pushing their little pieces of battle remembrance around on the mantel until Jauncy announced dinner.

Richard and Irene, according to age-old tradition, led the procession into the dining room, while Major Valentine happily escorted both Victoria and Minerva. Shiloh and Cheney brought up the rear. Richard assumed the head of the table, with Victoria, Shiloh, and Cheney on his right and Minerva, Major Valentine, and Irene on his left. The long table had been covered with three snowy-white polished linen cloths and set with an old set of Meissen china that had been stored in the workroom. A silver chest had been unearthed in the cellar, and Jauncy had polished for two solid days. Now the heavy, intricately designed silver glinted in the muted light of two dozen candles in two silver candelabra set on the table, surrounded by glossy magnolia leaves and pink azalea blooms.

Richard said a blessing, and the diners prepared to eat.

Irene and Cheney, across from each other, exchanged meaningful glances. Near the head of the table, on the opposite side from Irene, Victoria could see Irene but not Cheney, but she watched Irene's face intently. As was the etiquette at formal dinners, the ladies unbuttoned the first three or four buttons on their long over-the-elbow gloves and then pulled the fingers and thumb out so that the hand part of the glove might be pulled all the way off and tucked into the glove on top of the hand at the wrist. Cheney had never had a pair of gloves that fit over her wedding ring, the great 5.26 carat ruby, but Victoria had designed a glove with a small pleat just at the bottom end of the third finger, left hand, with a tiny button at the side of the finger. She had ordered this special pair of gloves from her glover in Paris and had meant to give them to Cheney for her birthday in April; but when Victoria received them just before they sailed, in January, she decided to give them to Cheney on the occasion of their first formal dinner at Sangria House. Victoria was a generous friend and rather childlike in her pleasure at giving gifts. Now Irene watched Cheney carefully, while Victoria watched Irene, as all three ladies arranged their gloves. Cheney unobtrusively unbuttoned the finger button on the side of her third finger and then unbuttoned the first four buttons at her wrist. Smoothly the fingers came out of the glove, and she pulled the glove over the large ring without a hitch. Irene smiled very slightly and nodded at Victoria.

Shiloh, who was privy to all of this difficulty over Cheney's ring, watched and marveled at the ladies. Such sophisticated nonverbal communication was far, far beyond the reach of mere mortal men.

Jauncy served the first course, a delicious fried cake of shallots and crabmeat, flavored with pepper, butter, and Parmesan cheese. Sketes called it Crab Lorenzo, though she had never specified who Lorenzo might be. The small cakes were fried in the chafing dish, put on buttered toast, and served hot. Sketes quickly fried up the cakes, and Jauncy served.

"I believe this is the best crab dish I have ever tasted," Major Valentine said to the air above him, as was correct, since he could not address Sketes directly.

Irene said, "Thank you, Major," but Sketes was the one who looked vastly pleased.

Major Valentine continued, addressing Cheney across the table. "Your father told me, Dr. Irons-Winslow, that you speak French, Spanish, Latin, and Greek. That is an impressive list of languages, so we are certain you would know exactly what 'high dudgeon' is."

Cheney laughed, a sweet, light sound that Shiloh loved. "With such a recommendation, I am ashamed to say that I must disappoint you. I have no idea of the origin of the term, sir, but I do know the mental picture it conjures. I hope my father was not saying that he had observed me *personally* in such a state?"

Major Valentine smiled at her, and Shiloh became very alert. He could see that Major Valentine admired all of the beautiful women at the table, but he imagined he saw a special regard in the major's warm brown eyes. His steely blue gaze caught the major's, and Valentine seemed quickly to cool off. *Maybe we're not such slouches at nonverbal communications as I thought,* Shiloh reflected with satisfaction.

With perhaps more formality than before, Major Valentine answered, "No, as a matter of fact, your father just observed that the Grider sisters had appeared to be in such a state the day that the will was read. But perhaps this is not fit conversation . . . ?"

Minerva said with a small pout, "I don't know why we shouldn't talk about the will and even the death of Mr. Grider, including all the disgusting details. Dr. Irons-Winslow, Mr. *soon-to-be* Dr. Irons-Winslow, Dr. Buchanan, and their partner, Dr. Cleve Batson, all talk about the most gory things at dinner. Indeed, sometimes I think they save up the most gruesome things particularly *for* dinner. I shouldn't think talk about a dungeon could compare with eyeball jelly and liver juice."

Major Valentine agreed. "No, ma'am, a dungeon could not in any way compare with those."

Cheney, hiding a smile, said, "I am sorry, Minerva, but now that you're practically one of the family you will have to get accustomed to discussions about such things as . . . um . . . liver juice. At any rate, I believe Major Valentine was actually asking about the phrase 'high dudgeon.' Not a dungeon. And now that you've brought it up, Major Valentine, I am vastly curious about the phrase. Does anyone know where it comes from?"

"I read the word in Shakespeare," Irene said. "If I'm not mistaken, it was in *Macbeth,* so I looked the word up in the *Oxford Dictionary.* The word *dudgeon* is actually a type of wood used especially for dagger hilts. The origin of the phrase 'high dudgeon' to indicate a state of extreme indignation is unknown."

"Well, I should certainly be in high dudgeon if I were stabbed with a dagger," Minerva said. "And didn't I tell you, Major Valentine, that we would soon be talking of something about dead people's bodies or how they get dead? Did I not warn you?" She turned an appealing gaze up to him.

With some trace of the indulgent affection that everyone seemed to evince toward Minerva after they had known her for even a short time, he answered, "Indeed you did, Miss Walcott. And if the conversation distresses you, I'm certain we can all agree to wait until after dinner to continue."

Cheney did not look at all agreeable, but Minerva looked vastly pleased. "Oh no, sir, you are very gallant, but I want to know about poor Mr. Grider too. Are you going to dig him up and let Dr. Duvall—her friends and family still call her Dr. Duvall instead of Dr. Irons-Winslow, for her husband is studying to be a doctor too, so we wouldn't want to confuse the two. . . ." She appeared to get lost, as it were, in her parentheticals, and so she regrouped and finished, "—and let Dr. Duvall cut him up?"

Major Valentine looked so comically surprised that everyone else smiled. He recovered quickly and said, "As a matter of fact, I have done more than that. Judge Allard ordered an exhumation tomorrow." He spoke to everyone, but his gaze rested on Cheney with a rather assessing expression. "Dr. Irons-Winslow, if it is agreeable to you, I do have a warrant from the provost judge, on both my recommendation and your father's, naming you Provost Medical Examiner *pro hac vice,* and ordering you to perform a medical examination of Louis Arthur Grider. Would you accept this warrant?"

Surprised and pleased, Cheney said, "I would be honored, sir." She turned to Richard. "Thank you, Father. I can't tell you how much this means to me."

Minerva rolled her eyes. "See, Major Valentine? She and Dr. Buchanan love to cut up dead people and then tell us all about it at dinner!"

"It is curious, Cheney," Richard said, "that you are so excited about doing an autopsy. But anyway, you are certainly welcome."

Shiloh frowned. "I'm nowhere near up on my Latin, Major Valentine. What's the deal again, with the warrant?"

"Pro hac vice," Major Valentine repeated proudly, carefully enunciating properly: *proh-hock-veechay*. "And now you know all of the Latin that I know. It means 'for this occasion.' Dr. Irons-Winslow is warranted a provost medical examiner title for one autopsy, on Louis Arthur Grider."

Shiloh turned to grin down at Cheney. "So now you're a provost marshal. Do I hafta salute you, Marshal?"

"No, Winthro," Cheney replied smartly. "Just falling to your knees when I enter the room will suffice. So, Major Valentine, do you have the facilities to do the autopsy at the Castillo?"

He frowned. "I-I'm not sure, Dr. Irons-Winslow. I suppose none of us thought about it. Our regimental surgeon has a small office, with the regular supplies and medications, I suppose. Would that do?"

"Oh no. I need a laboratory, with a good microscope and a good Bunsen burner," Cheney said, growing excited. "And, of course, an examination table, one that is tilted slightly so that the fluids . . . um—"

"There, I knew we would get around to the blood and jelly and juice," Minerva said triumphantly.

"Sorry," Cheney said and then continued, "I do have my scalpels and saws, Major Valentine, but I will certainly need these facilities and some supplies. Let's see, nitric acid, carbolic acid, and . . . what is it?—some mineral . . . zinc, I believe, isn't it, Shiloh?"

"I dunno," Shiloh said. "Nobody knows what you're talking about, Doc."

"Oh," Cheney said, looking rather guiltily around the table. "I suppose I could wait to give you my list of requirements, Major Valentine."

"That might be best, ma'am," he said. "You'll have to write it all down anyway."

"Speaking of that," Richard said, "did you, by any chance, Major Valentine, bring us a copy of Mr. Grider's will? I don't suppose we actually have a legal right to it, but it seems that we all got involved in the thick of it."

"As I told you, Colonel Duvall, the will is a matter of public record now, and as tenants of the house, you have become deeply involved—whether you meant to or not," Major Valentine answered. "Of course this house is included in the will, so I'm afraid I also have some judicial orders concerning some parts of the house and some of the contents. I thought after dinner we might discuss all of that, and since it so closely concerns all of you, Judge Allard and I agreed that you should have a copy of the will available to you and your attorneys, if you wish. I did understand, didn't I, Mrs. Buchanan, that you have a documented lease for Sangria House and Plantation, along with a purchase option?"

"I do," Victoria answered. "My attorney assured me that the document is perfectly correct and legally binding, both upon me and the lessor."

Major Valentine nodded. "Of course. So under these circumstances, you are in fact an interested party of the will, bound to the inheritor of the estate just as you were to Mr. Louis Grider when he was alive."

"Correct," Victoria said. "Naturally I have consulted with my attorney, and he sent a letter special delivery to assure me that I have legal standing to bind the inheritor to the lease, and to the purchase option, if I wish."

"That, too, is my understanding," Major Valentine said. "But I must admit that my understanding stops there. And when you have had an opportunity to read the will"—here he addressed the entire table—"I hope that you will understand more than the rest of us have. Judge Allard is mystified, the inheritors are mystified, and even Mr. Grider's own attorney has no idea of the meaning of some parts of the will. Mr. Grider himself composed this will, you know; his attorney didn't draw it up."

"But, is it just nonsensical?" Victoria asked curiously.

"Not at all," the major answered. "He was evidently in his right mind, and the bequests themselves are perfectly clear and legal, as far as Judge Allard can see. But the document is, well, shall we say, it is cryptic. I must confess that I hoped, since, after all, you are such an educated, learned company"—he smiled down at Minerva—"that you all may be able to decipher the mystery."

Dinner continued in this pleasant manner, and when the last cloth had been drawn and the only course left was coffee and nuts and cheese, Irene suggested, "Perhaps we may have our coffee in the drawing room? If the gentlemen would care to join us, I know that we ladies would appreciate the company."

Richard, Major Valentine, and Shiloh all rose to pull back the ladies' chairs. "I for one have never cared for the custom of the ladies leaving us men on our own," Major Valentine said.

"Neither have I," Shiloh agreed as Cheney took his arm. He and Major Valentine, in the course of dinner, had come to an unspoken understanding: Shiloh understood that Major Valentine admired Cheney very much, and Major Valentine understood that Shiloh would kill him if he showed that admiration too ardently. It was the simple sort of agreement that men of honor could come to over dinner.

They retired to the parlor, with Richard and Irene leading. As they entered Irene turned to speak to the rest of them. "Although we're all behaving in a very civilized manner, I'm sure we're all indecently eager to hear Mr. Grider's will. Why don't we sit at the table and have Jauncy serve the coffee there, and perhaps Richard could read aloud the famous—or infamous—last will and testament?"

"No one here could be indecent, ever, Mrs. Duvall," Major Valentine said in a quiet baritone. "It is time for that poor gentleman's dying testament to be known and understood by honorable and caring people. Whatever he was in life, he deserves that the truth be known about his death and his dying wishes. And I think that he would appreciate consideration from Christian people such as you."

Chapter Fourteen

Last Testament

IN THE DRAWING ROOM Shiloh built up the dying fire as Major Valentine pulled the side chairs up to the table. Richard fetched one of the large candelabra from the dining room and set in new candles. Jauncy, meanwhile, set the coffee service on the table, along with a large platter of assorted nuts, cheeses, crackers, and grapes artistically arranged on it. Finally everyone settled down, snacking and enjoying the strong Moorer's Jamaican Coffee, a product imported by Winslow Brothers Shipping that the Duvalls and the Irons-Winslows favored.

Major Valentine pulled the sheets of fine parchment out of his tunic. "This is a fair copy by one of Judge Allard's clerks," he said quietly. "Colonel Duvall, would you please read it to us?"

Richard began to read, and after reading only the first three lines, he was interrupted by exclamations and questions demanding what it meant.

"'Fair is foul, and foul is fair,'" Richard repeated thoughtfully. "It's a quote from something—it's enclosed in quotations—but I'm not quite sure what it means, to tell the truth. Let me . . . one moment, please . . ." He read to himself, flipping the page and skimming through. Then he looked up at Major Valentine quizzically.

The major shrugged. "We don't know what it all means, sir." Then addressing the others, he said, "Aside from some oddities, such as that quote, there are other strange phrases in the will, and there are also some numerical sequences that, so far, no one has been able to decipher at all. If Colonel Duvall could simply read through the will as it is, including the numerical notations, maybe something will occur to one of you here. Who knows?"

"This makes sense," Irene agreed. "Read it through, Richard."

"Very well, here goes:

"LAST WILL AND TESTAMENT
OF LOUIS ARTHUR GRIDER

"'Fair is foul, and foul is fair.'"

"I, Louis Arthur Grider, being of sound and disposing mind and memory, not being actuated by any duress, menace, fraud, mistake, or undue influence, do make, publish, and declare this to be my Last Will and Testament. I.7.8–12

"I appoint Henry Mortimer Albert Pendergast, Esquire, as Executor of this my Last Will and Testament. My Executor shall be authorized to carry out all provisions of this Will and pay my just debts, obligations, and funeral expenses.

"*Miss Dolores Martha Espy* I.4.5–11

"I will, give, bequeath, and devise all real property designated as Sangria House and Plantation, including but not limited to the house, outbuildings, winery, land, groves, and fruits, to Miss Dolores Martha Espy and her heirs and assigns forever.

"All of my books, maps, newspapers, and articles, along with the personal journals, correspondence, and sundry other items which I have placed in the lockbox in the safe in my study, I will, give, bequeath, and devise to Miss Dolores Martha Espy, in the hope that she will always continue her search for knowledge.

"*Timothy Mordred Espy* IV.2.27

"I will, give, bequeath, and devise the sum of monies at present on account in New York City Bank and Trust, the principal of ten thousand dollars and including all profits accruing to the sum from investment of said monies by City Bank, to Timothy Mordred Espy, a minor child, to be held in trust until he reaches the age of twenty-one years. I hereby appoint Miss Dolores Martha Espy, the minor child's mother, as administrator of the trust, in the knowledge that she will continue to be mindful of his needs and requirements. II.3.97

"*Jerome Espy* IV.3.209–210
"*Florence Espy* V.1.46–49

"To my servants Jerome and Florence Espy I will, give, bequeath, and devise the contents of the lockbox I have placed in the safe in my study, on the condition that they are found to be not guilty of any crime after my death. If one of them shall be found to be guilty of a crime after my death, this bequest shall be directed to the other; if both of them shall be found to be guilty of a crime after my death, this bequest shall be considered null and void and the said lockbox shall be included in the residuary clause of this Last Will and Testament.

"I will, give, bequeath, and devise all of the rest, residue, and remainder of my estate, of whatever kind and character, and wherever located, as follows:

"One-half to my wife, *Aimee Belinda Dalrymple Grider,* I.5.62–65, and the other one-half to my sisters, I.3.32–37, as follows:

"One-third to my sister *Letitia Ann Grider Raymond;*

"One-third to my sister *Muriel Darlene Grider;*

"One-third to my sister *Phillipa Mae Grider;*

"on the condition that they are found to be not guilty of any crime after my death. If one of them shall be found guilty of a crime after my death, then the bequest to them shall be considered null and void and such bequest shall be apportioned equally among the innocent parties of the residuary clause.

"If all parties to the residuary clause are found guilty of a crime after my death, the bequests to them shall be considered null and void, and the residue of my estate shall be added to the bequest to Miss Dolores Martha Espy.

"Any and all debts of my estate shall first be paid from my residuary estate.

"I desire to be buried in the San Sebastian Cemetery, with as little expense or ceremony as may be.

II.3.90–94

"I revoke all former wills by me made, declaring this only to be my last. In witness whereof, I, Louis Arthur Grider, have hereunto set my hand and seal, this twenty-third day of February, in the year of our Lord one thousand eight hundred and seventy.

"Louis Arthur Grider
"'In the great hand of God I stand . . .'

"Signed, sealed, published, and declared this twenty-third day of February, in the year of our Lord one thousand eight hundred and seventy, by the above named Louis Arthur Grider, for and as his Last Will and Testament,
"In the presence of us.

"Henry Mortimer Albert Pendergast, Esquire
"Father Manuel Escalante"

"What an extraordinary document," Victoria said. "Is it, in Judge Allard's opinion, a legal and binding will?"

"He believes so," Major Valentine answered. "Of course, any will may be contested by any of the beneficiaries if they can establish a sound judicial question. In this case, it would seem, they may question Mr. Grider's state of mind."

Quietly Minerva said, "Then I think they would be making a mistake. It seems to me that Mr. Grider went to very great pains to create this document in exactly the way he did. It obviously took a clear, calculating mind to reason out the terms; and though some of it seems very obscure, I'm sure that the quotes and numerical quotations are actually some references that are very very clever. As he says in the beginning, 'Fair is foul and foul is fair.'"

With a hint of surprise that then turned to admiration, Major Valentine regarded Minerva and said, "Very astute, Miss Wilcott. What seems foolish may in fact be clever."

She batted her eyelashes up at him with exaggerated coyness.

"You know, that does make sense, I think," Richard said. "Consider this: Grider suspected that someone was trying to kill him—someone close to him. But ranting and raving about it might seem as if he was going lunatic. And he didn't want to disinherit anyone who was innocent. So he constructed the will in this way, hoping that the authorities would catch on and be alerted, and in the investigation of the meaning of the will, they would figure out that they needed to investigate his death."

"Which is exactly what's happening," Major Valentine said with wonder. "With the help of the illustrious learned company here, of course, in particular Dr. Cheney Irons-Winslow." He made a small bow in her direction. "But Judge Allard did say that the instructions regarding the possible criminality of the beneficiaries were going to cause some problems. I mean, if one wanted to be scrupulously literal, one could wait for the rest of the beneficiaries' lives to see if they committed a crime or not, so the will would never be probated. But now we know that he was probably talking about whoever was trying to kill him. In that case, to obey the spirit of the testament, we have to wait to find out who killed him—if someone did—before the beneficiaries can collect their inheritance."

"Except for Miss Dolores Espy and her son, Timothy," Minerva said. "Mr. Grider apparently had no qualms about them."

"Very true, Miss Wilcott," Major Valentine said, "but a will cannot be probated in part; it must be executed as an entire document."

"But what about them? Who are they?" Minerva asked, her wide brow furrowed slightly. "She's a 'miss,' so she is not married, but she has this son, whose last name is . . . ohhh," she finished, blushing a little. "Oh yes, of course. Miss Espy, with a son named Espy . . . the main beneficiaries of Mr. Grider's will. I understand. But . . . But—oh, dear, what a . . . what a—"

"Mortal coil," Irene said with peculiar emphasis. "Mortal coil, from *Hamlet*. Would you all excuse me for a moment, please?" She jumped up, and Shiloh, Richard, and Major Valentine almost fell over trying to get out of their chairs as she hurried out of the room.

The three men looked at each other with surprise and puzzlement and then took their seats.

"That was a lot more like something the doc would do than Miss Irene," Shiloh said.

"Very true. I don't know that I've ever seen Irene just jump up and dash out of a room," Richard said, mystified.

Cheney sighed. "As usual, she was much more graceful than I am when I jump up and dash somewhere. It was more like she rose and glided away."

"Is glided truly the past tense of glide?" Minerva wondered.

"What do you think it is, dearest? Glid?" Victoria said.

"No, of course not," Minerva scoffed. "Glade, maybe?"

At this point, perhaps fortunately for Minerva, Irene came back into the room carrying an open book, frowning down at it. The men hopped up again, and with an impatient movement she signaled them to sit down and she regained her chair. "'Fair is foul, and foul is fair,'" she quoted triumphantly. "Act 1, *Macbeth*."

"It sure is," Shiloh agreed. "Now I remember. I've read it three or four times since the doc got me addicted to Shakespeare on one memorable sea voyage."

"Ugh," Cheney groaned. "Don't remind me. I've never been so seasick before, and may I never be again. Shiloh read *Hamlet* to me—what was it? Three times? Four times?"

"At least. But it turned out all right—for me anyway—because it took me that long to get the hang of Middle English. Helped later, too, when I smarted up and started reading the Bible."

"King James was a big fan of William Shakespeare," Richard said. "Shakespeare's acting company was designated the King's Men soon after King James succeeded Queen Elizabeth to the throne. Oh yes, King James was quite a loyal fan and patron. If I'm not mistaken, Macbeth was an actual person, and Banquo was one of King James's ancestors."

"That's very true, which made the way Shakespeare portrayed the politics in *Macbeth* rather . . . skewed, shall we say," Irene commented.

Minerva looked mystified. "I read *Macbeth* once, but I don't remember anything except that Lady Macbeth said a word that I was taught ladies did not say, something about a spot on her hand. What was the story about again? Besides the spot?"

"It's a tragedy, a fairly gruesome tale," Victoria said gravely. "Three witches prophesy to Macbeth, who was a great lord, that he would be king of Scotland; they also prophesy that his friend Banquo would not be king, but his sons would be. This prophecy so corrupts Macbeth that he and his wife murder the king of Scotland and then murder Banquo and try to murder his son, and they also murder another kinsman's family, including his young son. Macbeth does become king, but it is a costly victory for him. His wife dies, probably by her own hand from guilt, and Macbeth's crimes are found out, and he is murdered by one of his own subjects. After his death Banquo's son becomes king. All of the witches' prophecies come true, but only through evil means, when evil triumphs."

"Gracious, no wonder I can't recall the story," Minerva said with a little shiver. "I probably forgot on purpose so that it wouldn't give me nightmares."

"'Macbeth does murder sleep,'" Irene murmured. "Act 2, scene 2." She was thumbing through the book, a handsome edition of 1860, printed on thick parchment and bound in a rich oxblood Moroccan leather. "Oh yes, here's our old friend the dudgeon. Act 2, scene 1: 'I see

175

thee still, and on thy blade and dudgeon gouts of blood . . .' It is a bloody tale, a dark tale, but I still believe Shakespeare was possibly the greatest poet in the world. Mr. Grider was obviously a Shakespeare fan too. This book is well read. Several passages are underlined."

"And what was that last quotation, on the signature page?" Cheney said, taking the copy of the will from Richard. "Yes—'In the great hand of God I stand. . . . ' Isn't that in *Macbeth* too, Mother?"

"It is, isn't it? Let me see, yes, Banquo, act 2, scene 3."

"That's it, that must be it. Could the numerical notations indicate lines from *Macbeth?*" Cheney asked, her eyes bright. "Here, let's look. The first one is by Dolores Espy's name: I.4.5–11. Read act 1, scene 4, lines 5 through 11, Mother."

Irene turned the pages of the book, and her eyes softened. "He's got it underlined in red ink.

". . . very frankly he confessed his treasons,
Implored your highness' pardon, and set forth
A deep repentance. Nothing in his life
Became him like the leaving it. He died
As one that had been studied in his death
To throw away the dearest thing he owed
As 'twere a careless trifle."

"He repented of his wrongs to her," Minerva said softly. "It would not have been seemly to do it personally, for he was still married. What a noble and honorable way to say he was wrong and how sorry he was."

"It also seems he repented of the way he had been living," Irene said. "By all accounts he was a grasping and greedy sort of man, with no interest at all in living a godly life. But perhaps the reason—or one of the reasons—that he used this quote, and the one about being in God's hand, is because he repented and asked the Lord to save him before he died."

"That's a very good possibility," Major Valentine said. "I know Father Escalante, and he is a humble, dedicated Christian. Even though Mr. Grider wasn't Catholic, I have always thought that one reason he asked Father Escalante to witness his will was so that he might ask him to pray with him. I had intended to ask Father Escalante about it when we called him to witness the will, but we were all so dumbfounded by it that he got away before I could speak to him."

"Oh, I hope Mr. Grider was saved and knew the Lord Jesus," Cheney said fervently. "It . . . it was a lonely death. How I hope he knew the Lord's comfort and peace."

"I believe he did," Irene said firmly. "Any man who ended his last will and testament with what sounds like a sigh of relief that he's in God's hands has to know the Lord Jesus. Now, what about the next notation? Was it by the boy's name?"

"Yes, there are two: the first one is act 4, scene 2, line 27," Cheney said.

"'Father'd he is, and yet he's fatherless,'" Irene read.

Major Valentine shook his head in a gesture of admiration. "Do you know what Judge Allard thought? Of course we're assuming that Timothy Espy is Louis Grider's son, but in the will Mr. Grider never came right out and owned up to the boy. Judge Allard said that if Louis Grider had maintained that Timothy Espy was his son in the will, the wife and sisters could contest the will and try to make Miss Espy prove that the boy was Grider's son, which is just about impossible. Besides, someone like Miss Espy might never have the grit to stand up to the Griders in court. But since Mr. Grider never clearly said that Timothy was his son and simply made Miss Espy and the boy beneficiaries with no qualification, there is no ground to contest it—except if Mr. Grider was not in his right mind. And I think with what we're finding out here, no one can say that he wasn't coherent and, incidentally, also very intelligent."

Cheney pointed to the next notation by Timothy Espy's name. Irene looked it up and with a grave expression read, "'Your royal father's murder'd.'"

A long heavy silence ensued. At length Minerva sighed and said softly, "Did you notice the little boy's name? His middle name, I mean. It's Mordred. That was the name of King Arthur's illegitimate son. Louis Grider's middle name is Arthur. Miss Espy may have been only a servant, but evidently she is well read. Didn't the will say something about that?"

"Yes. He left all his books and articles to her, hoping she would continue her search for knowledge," Major Valentine said. "I've read that will so many times, trying to puzzle it out, that I've practically got it memorized. Now I'm very curious about all these quotes from *Macbeth*. Aside from the connections to the will, it's just really fascinating. What's the next one?"

"The beneficence to Mr. and Mrs. Espy," Cheney said. "Here, by Mr. Espy's name: act 4, scene 3, lines 209 through 210."

Irene turned pages and then read:

"Give sorrow words. The grief that does not speak
Whispers the o'er-fraught heart and bids it break."

"That man is a man of few words, and he does sorrow so," Shiloh said, his gaze distant, his voice soft. He was recalling the odd moments of instinctive knowledge when Jerome Espy had been playing with the dogs and had echoed Shiloh's thoughts. "What about Mrs. Espy?"

The thick fine pages rustled, and Irene said in a quiet voice, "The doctor who attends Lady Macbeth says to her:

"Go to, go to! You have known what you should not."

"The gentlewoman who attends Lady Macbeth says:

"She has spoke what she should not,
I am sure of that. Heaven knows what she has known."

"There is something about the Espys, some history with Mr. Grider, and I don't think it's only about Miss Espy and the boy," Shiloh said, narrowing his eyes and staring into an unknown distance. "Something else, something that deeply affected all of them."

"Perhaps now they may be able to confess their sins, as Mr. Grider did," Minerva said. "This is all so very sad."

"I'll bet the next quote may not exactly be sad," Cheney said dryly. "It's by Mrs. Grider's name. See, Mother, here."

Irene and Cheney were sitting by each other, so Cheney pointed out the notation, and Irene found the passage. "Oh, dear," Irene said with genteel distress. "This is—well, I'll just read:

"To beguile the time,
Look like the time; bear welcome in your eye,
Your hand, your tongue; look like th' innocent flower,
But be the serpent under't."

"Who said that?" Minerva asked. "That's not at all nice."

"No, it's not, Min," Victoria said, hiding a smile. "Lady Macbeth said it, and she wasn't a very nice person."

"She was certainly not a lady that we would receive," Minerva said delicately, "would we, Victoria?"

"Well, that is rather difficult, you see, dearest. What Mr. Grider was implying is that Mrs. Grider might be like Lady Macbeth—who was a murderess—and we have received Mrs. Grider, you know."

"Ohh," Minerva said, her blue eyes huge and round. "That is difficult. I shall just have to leave that up to you and Mrs. Duvall. You would
never, never do anything wrong, I'm sure."

"At least not Mrs. Duvall," Victoria said slyly.

"Foolish girls," Irene said. "Let's go on. What's the next one,
Cheney?"

"One before the clause concerning the sisters. Here, Mother, I.3.32–
37."

"Yes, I was afraid of that," Irene said with no small irony.

"The weïrd sisters, hand in hand,
Posters of the sea and land,
Thus do go about, about,
Thrice to thine, and thrice to mine
And thrice again, to make up nine.
Peace, the charm's wound up."

"The three witches, huh," Shiloh muttered. "That's pretty harsh."

"I guess he thought they were trying to murder him," Richard said
in a rough voice. "And he may have been right, for all we know. It would
be hard for a man to suspect such treachery from his own family. And,
whatever kind of man he was, he did give his sisters a home and sup-
ported them."

"Perhaps he was mistaken," Minerva said with distress. "Not that he
was a lunatic, but perhaps he was just really very sick and having illu-
sions."

"Delusions," Cheney gently corrected her. "And if that's true, there's
a very good chance that a postmortem examination will prove it, Min."

"Isn't there another notation?" Major Valentine asked.

"Yes, one more, at the end of the testament," Irene answered with a
glance at the paper Cheney still held and turned to it in the book.

". . . for from this instant
There's nothing serious in mortality:
All is but toys. Renown and grace is dead,
The wine of life is drawn, and the mere lees
Is left this vault to brag of."

Major Valentine said heavily, "Sounds like Louis Grider was a mel-
ancholy man. Well, speaking of vaults, sort of, Judge Allard has ordered
that I inventory and seal some of the items that pertain to the will until

the probate is finished. Judge Allard strictly instructed me to tell you, Colonel Duvall, that he intends absolutely no disrespect to you and your family. These precautions are being taken so that there will be no misunderstandings among the inheritors of the estate."

Richard grinned, a boyish expression that lit up his handsome but somewhat severe features. "Judge Allard doesn't think we're going to drink up all the sangria, eat all the oranges, beat the servants, and steal all of the gold Grider hid under his mattress?"

Major Valentine answered gravely, "I'm sure Judge Allard wants to make sure that the three sisters get to do all of that."

Minerva giggled. "Can't you just see Mrs. Raymond drinking all the sangria?"

Everyone chuckled.

"Come to think of it," Cheney said, "she was trying to sneak down into the wine cellar when everyone was here after the funeral."

Suddenly Major Valentine was very intent. "She did? Did she tell you what she wanted?"

Surprised at his gravity, Cheney replied, "Why, no—no, she didn't. I didn't question her, of course. I just stopped her because she was going down the stairs without a lantern, and I was afraid she would fall. But she seemed embarrassed that I had seen her, so she turned around and went back into the dining room."

"She said nothing at all?" he asked.

"Well, she said that there were lanterns downstairs, and that I knew that, and I was just trying to stop her from . . . from whatever she was going to do," Cheney replied.

"Told you. They think we're going to steal the silver and horses," Richard insisted.

"Actually, sir, you may not be too far wrong," Major Valentine said. "You see, Mr. Grider's money has sort of . . . disappeared."

Everyone stared at him blankly.

Finally he continued, "Judge Allard wanted to have a complete list of all of Mr. Grider's assets, you see, because the residual clause of the will means that everything besides the specific bequests will need to be inventoried and valuated so that they can be equally distributed among Mrs. Grider and the sisters. So Judge Allard ordered Mr. Grider's bank— City Bank and Trust of St. Augustine—to submit to the court a statement of Mr. Grider's accounts. And the balance currently is about nine dollars and some change. Samuel Rainsford told Judge Allard that Mr.

Grider had been withdrawing large amounts in cash, beginning in the last week of January, and continuing all through February. You know, of course, because you are friends with the Rainsfords, that Mr. Rainsford is retired from active participation in the bank, even though he owns it. It's just that Mr. Ewing, the bank president, thought it so odd that he alerted Mr. Rainsford. To withdraw high sums in cash requires some notice to the bank, because often they don't keep reserves enough to cover their own requirements if withdrawals are extremely large. It was odd, because normally a person with such a large balance will simply ask for bank drafts to take to his new bank when he moves. But Mr. Grider just walked out of the bank with greenbacks."

"I have to ask," Victoria said dramatically. "How much?"

"About a quarter of a million dollars," Major Valentine said.

The only sound was a low whistle from Shiloh. Then he asked, "And you mean no one knows where he stashed it?"

"We don't know where it is," Major Valentine answered carefully. "We're not sure whether the ladies do or not. But Judge Allard is going to be interested to hear that Mrs. Raymond was going down to the cellar for some reason . . . and that was before the will was read too. You see, she took care of the Sangria Plantation business when Mr. Grider was ill. Evidently he wasn't in the habit of letting his sisters or his wife know much at all about his business, but sometimes he had to let Mrs. Raymond know some things. At any rate, now you can see why Judge Allard is a little anxious that Mr. Grider's assets don't get misplaced. Any more than they are already."

"Do you want to search the house?" Richard asked.

"Not really. Not now. But I am curious," he said, turning to Shiloh. "In the cellar, did you notice anything odd? Was there any evidence that Mr. Grider had been digging up the floor or perhaps chiseling into the walls? Anything like that?"

Shiloh shook his head. "The floor is flagstone, and from what I've seen, they're all original, which means they're old. I think we would have noticed if any of them looked new." He looked at Cheney for confirmation, and she nodded. He went on, "The walls are coquina, and I didn't notice any place that looked disturbed or different. Of course, the light's not good down there, and I wasn't particularly looking."

Major Valentine looked thoughtful. "Have any of you seen anything in the house that might indicate a hiding place? Floorboards pulled up? A locked cupboard with no key? Anything like that?"

They looked at one another. "There was a locked trunk in the master bedroom," Richard said. "After we knew that Mr. Grider was dead, we thought that it must have been packed for his trip, but of course he never left. When Shiloh got the keys, he opened it up to confirm it. It's still there. We didn't go through the entire trunk, but it did look as if it was just his clothing. Other than that, I don't suppose we have noticed any likely hiding place at all."

"Well, we're not going to try to search for the money right now," Major Valentine said. "We're hoping that someone, somewhere, will have an idea about it; otherwise, we're looking at an almost impossible task. I mean, it could be anywhere within a fifty-mile radius of the bank. Anyway, Judge Allard wants to first find out exactly how Mr. Grider died. No one's going to get a single copper until we know that. But if you should happen to find a great big pile of money, we'd appreciate it if you'd let us know."

"Yeah . . . yeah, I guess we'd do that," Shiloh drawled. "Prob'ly."

"Figured," Major Valentine said with a smile. "Now, Colonel Duvall, would you please witness the inventory and seals I'm obliged to do?"

"Of course," Richard said.

Mischievously Victoria said, "You see, Major Valentine, I'm of a more mercenary mind than everyone else here, so I happen to know what you mean. You're going to go through Mr. Grider's desk, open his safe and those boxes, go through them, and list the contents. Now, you don't think that the ladies here are going to let you men rummage through those things without our help, do you?"

"She means that we all really want to know what's in those boxes for the Espys and Miss Espy, and in the safe, and if there's any money in there, and how much it is," Minerva said in one breath. "Oooh, maybe he put his quarter of a million dollars in the safe!"

"That would make too much sense," Victoria murmured. "With that poor man's tortured mind, his money might be buried ten feet deep in an unmarked hole or stashed in a hollow log. Or it may be the wallpaper in the dining room—who knows?"

"But the wallpaper in the dining room doesn't look like money," Minerva explained to Victoria.

"It was just a whimsical example, dear Min," Victoria said, her eyes alight. "Like you."

"Oh, I see," Minerva said with satisfaction. "And so, Major Valentine, shall we retire to the library to do the seals and things?"

"I would be honored if you would allow me, Miss Wilcott," Major Valentine said, rising to help Minerva with her chair and offering her his arm. Her blue eyes brilliant and her cheeks flushed with pleasure, she took his arm, and they led the way down the hall to Louis Grider's library.

It was a stern, thoroughly businesslike room. The desk was a dark mahogany banker's desk with brass fittings. On the desk were a clean blotter and a marble inkstand with two pens and a cut crystal inkwell. The walls were lined with bookcases, and they were filled with books, all of them finely bound in leather, some with gold or silver lettering. It appeared that Mr. Grider was not a collector of books; he was an avid reader. The books were not first editions or collector's items or antique editions; they were books meant for reading and had been read. Richard had already spent hours poring over the collection and had seen with interest, considering that Louis Grider's personality seemed to have been severe and unimaginative, that he had evidently had a richly literate mind. The books ranged from Plato's *Dialogues* to Mark Twain's *Life on the Mississippi* to an imposing twenty-book collection on insects by various famous and learned entomologists.

There was one small storage closet in the back of the room, and the freestanding safe was in it.

"The combination was in the copy of the will that Mr. Grider gave to Father Escalante," Major Valentine said with a trace of amusement. "It wasn't in the copy that he gave the lawyer. So, Colonel Duvall, I'm going to open the safe, and I'm going to write down what I find, and I'm also going to say it as I list it. I'll require you to listen to my verbal affirmation, watch me take the inventory and list it, and then witness as I put the various items under court seal."

"I understand," Richard said. He stood at the door of the tiny room; Major Valentine could barely squeeze into it and squat down to the safe. He opened it on first try, but as they suspected, the only things in it were two small tin boxes, labeled in Grider's compact neat handwriting—one labeled "Dolores Espy" and one labeled "Jerome and Florence Espy." They weren't locked. In the one for Dolores Espy was a stack of one hundred dollar bills and several envelopes tied together with a black ribbon.

"Five thousand dollars in cash," Major Valentine said carefully, "and envelopes. Looks like personal correspondence in Mr. Grider's handwriting, so I'm not going to read them. In the box labeled 'Jerome and

Florence Espy'—" he hesitated as he counted the stack of bills—"there's five thousand dollars in cash and one envelope containing what looks like a letter from Mr. Grider, so I won't read it."

He and Richard finished the formalities, the listing, and the sealing, and then came back out into the room.

Shiloh said, "I've kept the keys, but we haven't used them. The front door has an inside bolt, so we lock that at night. We don't bother to lock the back door because the servants usually come in before any of us are up. The dogs would alert us if anyone tried to come in during the night." He held the keys up and jingled them, a heavy iron ring with at least twenty keys. "Guess the keys to the desk are on here."

After several tries they found the key that unlocked the desk drawers. Generally, in desks with locking mechanisms, the center desk drawer, when unlocked, releases two rods that extend to either side and down the back of the side drawers. But in Grider's desk they were not at all surprised to find that each drawer had a different lock on the front of the drawer, each requiring a different key. They found the plantation papers, journals, and ledgers, the bank records—but with no convenient notes about where Grider had put the cash he had withdrawn—and a small metal box in the bottom left-hand drawer that contained about fifty dollars in silver and small bills. "Just petty cash for the household needs," Major Valentine said as he noted it.

When they finished the inventory and seals, Major Valentine took his leave, as it was getting very late. "I'll come pick you up in the morning, Dr. Irons-Winslow, Shiloh, and take you to Duff's Apothecary, where we have arranged for you to do the autopsy. It was a lovely evening, in spite of the rather grim tasks we were obliged to do."

Minerva, her eyes like stars, said, "Good night, Major Valentine. Perhaps I may see you tomorrow when you come to pick up Dr. Cheney and Shiloh?"

"It would be my fondest hope, Miss Wilcott," Major Valentine said, and then, rather boldly, bent and brushed his lips against her gloved hand.

"Lovely," Minerva sighed. "Perfectly lovely."

CHAPTER FIFTEEN

Grief and Grievances

"MISS IRENE . . ."

Irene heard the faint cry and looked up from her book. "Oh dear, Mallow, is that you?" she said, rising from the easy chair by the window and hurrying to the door of the bedroom. The lower half of a body was evident, with two small, plump freckled hands clutching a veritable tower of folded linens. No puckish Irish maid could be seen. Irene took a stack from the top of the tower, and at least she could then see Mallow's glowing red hair. "Don't move. I'll come back and get more," Irene instructed. "How ever did you get up the stairs?"

"I didn't, really," Mallow answered, her voice slightly muffled, as the linens were still stacked high enough to cover her face. "At least, not like this. I made three trips to the top and stacked them . . . but I thought I could at least make it to the bedroom with all of them."

Between them they managed to get all of the linens onto the bed. There were two dozen sheets and two dozen pillowcases of a thick and very smooth material, all of them plain white. Now that she could see and move and breathe, Mallow fingered the fine fabric with pleasure. "These feel ever so lovely," she sighed. "And even if they almost smothered me, at least they do smell heavenly."

Irene picked up a folded sheet and smoothed her hand over it, savoring the softness of the fine fabric. "It's a rather new material called 'satin duchesse.' Victoria swears it makes the best bed linens she has ever known. My daughter-in-law insists that only white linens should be used, that the dyes are unhealthy to breathe in. I must say that I'm coming to believe she is right; these just smell clean, don't they? Dyes do have a scent, I believe, even after several washings. Anyway, Mallow, surely you didn't take all of the linens that Victoria ordered, did you?"

"No, ma'am, the order came in a cart. I think there were enough linens for the whole county," Mallow said, carefully refolding and stacking the linens in small manageable sets. "Did you know that Mrs. Buchanan had one of their ships—the Steen ships, I mean. I think it was called the *Maid of Aspinwall*—come to St. Augustine specially to bring us bed linens? Did you ever hear of such a thing?"

"I have, yes," Irene answered with a smile, "since I have known Victoria. The Steens sometimes do treat their merchant fleet as their own personal gigs. Gigs, my son-in-law taught me that," Irene added with an endearing girlishness. "That's the name of the captain's little boat that he uses to go back and forth from ship to shore."

"Gig," Mallow repeated meditatively. "Captain's gig. I'll remember. Anyway, Miss Irene, you go ahead and sit back down and read your book. I'm going to change the bed since we have all these fine new linens. But wherever am I to store them?"

Irene settled back in the chair and took a thoughtful sip of the tangy lime-lemonade that Sketes had made fresh that morning from fat, juicy Sangria Plantation fruit. "Mm, you know, Mallow, Richard's closet has a very high shelf that is not tall, but I believe it is deep. We've stored nothing up there because it's too high even for Richard, but I think it would be fine for the bed linens. Why don't you get Shiloh to put them up there for you, dear?"

"No, Miss Irene, Mr. Richard's trunk is in just the right place that I can stand on it," Mallow said, going back and forth to the left-hand closet with the linens. She was stacking them on one side of Richard's great steamer trunk so that she could stand on the other side and hand the linens up onto the high shelf. Richard and Irene were using the master bedchamber, and it had two fairly large closets. Both of them had been empty when they arrived, but each had a single rod for hanging clothes. So Mallow had put Richard's clothing in the left-hand one and Irene's in the other.

Mallow was a feisty, sweet-natured Irish girl, known to be rather talkative. But Irene didn't mind. She found the girl to be refreshingly honest, with a native wit that amused Irene even when she was unwell or felt low, as she sometimes did.

Mallow continued, "And there's not a soul on the place, Miss Irene, anyway. Dr. Cheney and Mr. Shiloh have gone off to do their autopsy, Miss Victoria and Miss Minerva have taken the children on a picnic, and of course you know that Mr. Richard is in town. I don't mind, though. I'm getting this lot stacked as neat and nice as you please. Did Miss Victoria overdo it a little, I'm wondering?"

Irene had gone back to puzzling out an obscure passage in Ezekiel, for the book she was reading was the Bible, but having been married for many years, she had developed the knack of listening with one part of her brain while another part worked on something else. "Yes, it seems that she feels badly, as if she failed in her hostess duties because we could never find any bed linens. I think they're probably stored in the servants' cottage, the one where all of the Grider family's things are, but even if we had them, I think Victoria would have bought all new ones anyway. It seems that Mr. Grider was . . . very thrifty, and so they probably would not have been up to Victoria's standards."

"No, somehow I don't think that Mr. Grider would have splurged on satin duchesse sheets and pillowslips," Mallow said dryly. "Hello, what's this?"

Irene looked up with interest at the change in Mallow's tone. "What is it, Mallow?" She couldn't actually see the girl, as the four-poster bed with the draperies blocked her view of the closets.

"It seems not quite every single thing got stored in the servants' cottage," she answered. "There's a ladies' complexion powder tin shoved way in the back of this shelf."

"Oh? Well, this was Mr. and Mrs. Griders' bedchamber. I suppose Mrs. Grider put it up there and forgot it."

"P'raps," Mallow said slowly. "But, Miss Irene, it's only about half empty. That's kind of odd, isn't it? I mean, if it was full, you'd think that she might have bought this tin before she ran out of the old one and then have put it up here to keep until the old one ran out. But since it's half empty, you'd think it was the one she was using. . . . Did she just sort of lose it?"

"Perhaps she put it up there, somehow it got shoved to the back of the shelf—and she forgot about it?" Irene speculated.

"Maybe . . . but . . . I don't know, Miss Irene. This powder smells funny."

"What?" Irene said sharply. Putting aside her book, she got up and hurried to the closet. "Here, Mallow, give it to me, please." The girl was still standing on Richard's trunk. Obediently she handed the tin down to Irene.

It was unmistakably a commercial preparation. The tin's label read:

"Antoinette's Milk of Roses Facial Powder." There was a picture of a white rose on it. Irene went back to her chair, sat down, and studied the label by the strong afternoon sunlight. It was an old label, smudged on one corner, and another corner was coming up. Slowly and carefully she twisted off the top. The powder was fine; some motes puffed up as she lifted the lid. Cautiously she lifted her nose, closed her eyes, and smelled the air above the tin, being careful not to breathe in any of the powder. It did have an odd chemical smell, very faint. Commercial preparations of ladies' face powder were made of zinc oxide. Generally some sort of perfuming was added to the ground mineral to give it a pleasing scent. Although Irene had always used a private preparation of rice powder and talc that Dally Clarkson made for her, she knew of zinc oxide face powder. This didn't smell like any she had ever seen. She replaced the top and put the tin on the side table by her chair.

Mallow finished putting the sheets up and prepared to strip the bed. Curiously she asked, "Did it smell funny to you, Miss Irene?"

"It did. And in the bright light you can see that the powder has a peculiar gray tint," Irene answered. "Don't touch it again, Mallow. In fact, I think—yes. Mallow, empty a hatbox that will hold this tin, and then go ask Mr. Jauncy to come here, please." Irene took a piece of her notepaper and quickly wrote a note to Cheney.

Mallow took one of Irene's hats out of a round hatbox and then gave it to Irene. Very carefully Irene replaced the top onto the tin and put it and the note into the hatbox. Mallow was just leaving to go get Jauncy when a discreet knock sounded at the bedroom door. It was Jauncy, holding the card salver.

He bowed elegantly, as he always did. "Miss Mallow, Miss Irene has a caller. Is she receiving today?"

"I'm not sure, Mr. Jauncy, but won't you come in? Miss Irene just now asked me to fetch you."

"Of course." He came in and Irene came to him, carrying the hatbox. Bowing, he said quietly, "At your service, madam."

"Yes, thank you. Mallow, take the salver, please. Jauncy, I want you to take this out to Andrew and ask him to take it to Cheney and Shiloh, please. I believe he knows where they are performing the autopsy."

"Yes, madam, at Duff's Apothecary," Jauncy said. "And the caller, madam?"

Irene took the card from the salver Mallow held. It was a frilly silly thing, with a fat Cupid shooting a bow and arrow toward a big blurry bunch of what Irene supposed were pink roses that formed the cutwork border of the card. *Phillipa Mae Grider, Sangria House, St. Augustine, Florida,* it read in spidery flowery script.

She looked up in surprise. "Just Miss Phillipa?"

"Yes, madam," Jauncy answered.

"All right, thank you, Jauncy. Go on down and show Miss Grider into the parlor and beg her indulgence. I'll be with her in a few moments. Then take the box out to Andrew, and also please ask Sketes to make tea."

"Yes, madam," Jauncy said and left.

Irene hurriedly changed from her morning robe into a more suitable receiving dress, a pretty cream-colored percaline frock, sprigged with tiny pink and yellow flowers and trimmed with a fine, intricate creamy lace.

Phillipa Grider was in the parlor, but instead of sitting and serenely waiting for Irene, she was pacing, her head bent, staring down at her hands. She was wearing black silk, of course, since she was in mourning. Her hat was a chip straw, dyed black, with a small brim and a long gray veil. The only thing that relieved the oppressive black was the wrinkled, worn white handkerchief she carried, twisting and worrying it with both hands. Irene was shocked to see that Phillipa wasn't wearing gloves and the hem of her dress was torn in one place so that the tail end of the skirt dragged the floor. Although the three sisters did not dress richly, in the two times Irene had seen them, she had noted that they were meticulous in their dress, their hair was always styled, their accessories correct.

Phillipa, the youngest Grider, was a woman whose prettiness was not attributable to the particular formation of her face, but to the combination of feature and expression. Her eyes were well formed, a warm dark hazel color. Her brow was wide and smooth, her nose and mouth small and delicate. But now, when she stopped pacing and looked up as Irene came into the parlor, Irene thought that Phillipa looked as if she had been weeping for a long time and hadn't slept either. Phillipa was pale, with bruiselike shadows under her eyes. Her thick dark hair, which was usually so attractively arranged, looked wispy and carelessly coiffed. Her smile of greeting was halfhearted. "Good afternoon, Mrs. Duvall. I'm so glad you agreed to see me. I wasn't certain of your at-home days."

"Oh no, Miss Grider, under the circumstances I would be more than happy to receive you, or Mrs. Grider or your sisters, any time," Irene demurred graciously as she went to Phillipa's side and took both of her hands. "Please, sit down. Jauncy will bring tea shortly. I hope you will join me?"

"Yes—yes, of course. Tea sounds wonderful. Is Mr. Jauncy that wonderful English butler? He was serving after the funeral. . . ." She bent her head and began to weep softly.

"Miss Grider, I am so very sorry for your loss," Irene said quietly. "What can I do to help?"

Phillipa pressed her sodden handkerchief to her eyes. "There is nothing, of course. There is nothing anyone can do. Perhaps I shouldn't be making calls yet, but I'm afraid that my sisters and . . . Aimee—I mean Mrs. Grider—are not suitably fulfilling our obligations of gratitude. I simply had to come to thank you for all of your kindness to us."

"I am glad to see you, Miss Grider, but I can assure you that, as far as I and my family are concerned, it's not necessary to strictly observe the formalities just now." All the time Irene's mind was racing, for Phillipa Grider was not observing any formalities, strictly or not. Ladies always sent notes of thanks when they were in mourning; they never made social calls, particularly alone. Irene continued, "We understand that this is a very difficult time for you all. We don't expect anything from you nor Mrs. Grider nor your sisters, except to let us know if we can help you in any way."

"No, no, that's not why I'm here," Phillipa said, too hastily. "I don't want anything. I just wanted to say thank you and . . . and—but, Mrs. Duvall, I just don't understand! I simply must ask you why your daughter insisted that my poor brother's rest be disturbed in this cruel manner. For what possible purpose? Why in the world would Dr. Irons-Winslow do such a thing?"

Although Irene was uneasy with these questions, she gave no sign. "Miss Grider, I am unaware of how you were notified of the exhumation, but I would have thought that it would be carefully explained to you."

"Oh yes, that nice Major Valentine has been very solicitous," she said with a jerky wave of her hand. "He said that it was because of that awful coroner, Bruce MacDonald, being so careless. But why should I and my sisters and Aimee have to suffer because of that? Even if he didn't . . . didn't . . . have an . . . accident, he—what I'm trying to say is, Louis was ill, very ill. I took care of him, you know. I always nursed him when he was ill."

"No, I didn't know that. It is difficult caring for a chronically ill person, even if it is a family member," Irene said.

"Oh, I don't suppose you could say that Louis was *chronically* ill," Phillipa replied fretfully. "But he was ill a lot. He inherited his poor health from his mother. You do know that Muriel and I are half sisters to Louis and

Letitia? We have the same father but different mothers. Louis and Letitia's mother died when they were children. She had a frail constitution, and Louis is the same. I mean, Louis was the same." She teared up again and wiped her eyes but then quickly went on, "I'm the only person that Louis would allow to be near him when he was ill. Aimee would usually move out of their chambers, into the tiny little guest bedroom, when Louis was sick. She is not the sort of person to be a good nurse, you see."

"It does take a special person," Irene agreed gravely. "My daughter and son, for example, are excellent doctors. But they are dismal nurses. On the other hand, my maid Mallow is a very good nurse. She is calm and competent and works quietly and takes care of you without fussing all about. It strikes me that you may be that kind of nurse too, Miss Grider."

"Oh yes, that's exactly the kind of nurse I tried to be," Phillipa said with the only sign of animation Irene had seen in her yet. "Louis could be a difficult patient. He was demanding, but he didn't like fussy, flitting women. Not that Aimee or Letitia or Muriel are fussy or flitting, quite the contrary. Aimee, in particular, is very calm and controlled. Normally, I mean. In the last two months she has been curiously . . . mm, I suppose *busy* may be the word I'm searching for. Not flitting, mind you, but busy."

"Busy," Irene repeated.

"Yes. Busy. Isn't it odd? She seemed to be just going languidly along, much as our lives always were, small and quiet, each day a routine. Aimee has her horses, which she loves, and Louis did indulge her very much in that area and others. Oh yes, he adored her so! He allowed her to buy and sell horses just as she wished, with never a second look at the ups and downs, shall we say, of horse trading." She frowned with distaste. Ladies, of course, were rarely called "horse traders," and when they were it was generally meant as a deadly insult. Phillipa glanced at Irene with eyes still tear-stained but now also watchful.

Irene said nothing and carefully guarded her expression so as not to give away the distaste she felt for the way the conversation was going. She knew that Phillipa had ulterior motives for this visit, and Irene wanted to learn as much as she could from the woman. *It is amazing how much one can learn from simply listening and observing,* she reflected as she gave Phillipa an automatic smile.

"Yes, the horses are all quality animals, my husband and son-in-law tell me," Irene said. "I believe Mr. Bain Winslow told all of us that Mrs. Grider had been kind enough to allow him and Beckett and Carsten Steen the use of the saddle horses while they are here."

"Oh yes, she's been very generous with Mr. Bain Winslow," Phillipa said. Now she had an absentminded air and didn't meet Irene's eyes as she spoke. She motioned with her handkerchief and stared out the front windows.

Irene was still trying to think of something to say that was at the same time innocuous and also leading when Jauncy came in with the tea. By the time this ceremony had been properly observed and Irene and Phillipa were sipping tea, Irene had thought of her response to Phillipa's last rather indecorous comment.

"I have been friends with Ivy Rainsford for many years now. She tells me that your brother was very much in love with Mrs. Grider, and it seemed that she made him very happy," Irene said innocently. "Ivy said that Mr. Grider did indulge Mrs. Grider somewhat, but that is not too uncommon for an older man with a younger wife. And she is much younger than you all, is she not? Perhaps there is such an age difference that Mrs. Grider is simply—misunderstood."

"Misunderstood?" Phillipa practically snorted. It appeared she had recovered admirably from the sorrow that had threatened to overwhelm her only minutes earlier. "Believe me, the only person who ever misunderstood Aimee was my poor brother. Everyone else understands her only too well."

"Really? I'm surprised, Miss Grider. It seems to me that when two people are happily married, they must know and understand each other extremely well. For how else can they sustain a marriage?"

"My brother thought he knew and understood Aimee," Phillipa said shortly. "And she was smart enough to keep him happy in his blindness. Until recently, that is. As I said, last month she seemed to suddenly get very *busy* and was rather neglectful of our brother. And then she decided that she didn't want to go to England with him. That's why he made her leave, you know. Because she had gotten too busy for him, with her new friends and all—you know, the Steen boys and particularly Mr. Winslow. They were—that is, are—the very best of friends, I suppose you might say, although others might say . . ."

This was getting entirely too personal—and malicious—for Irene's sensibilities. Wryly she reflected that she would not make a very good investigator, for she simply couldn't continue the conversation. Although she and Ivy Rainsford had discussed the affair between Aimee Grider and Bain Winslow, it was different. Irene did want to learn all she could from Ivy because she knew that it would help with what everyone now knew was a murder investigation. And Irene knew and trusted Ivy; she was no gossip. But Phillipa Grider's conversation was growing simply sordid.

Firmly she said, "Perhaps you weren't aware that Mr. Bain Winslow is connected to my family? It is by marriage, but still, even though he is distant, my husband and I are coming to regard him as a connection because of the great esteem we hold for our son-in-law, Mr. Irons-Winslow. Shiloh is Mr. Bain Winslow's first cousin. Would you like a slice of orange sponge cake? Our cook, Sketes, makes the most wonderful cakes and pies and sweets. I'm sure you will enjoy it."

"Well, perhaps just one," Phillipa replied. She seemed unabashed at Irene's gentle rebuke. "It does look very good."

Irene served both of them a small ladylike piece of cake, and they spent a few moments talking about the cake, how fluffy it was, how the cooks managed to make cakes rise in the century-old brick oven.

"Mrs. Espy always wanted us to replace that old oven," Phillipa said. "But I must say that it does still bake excellent cakes, does it not? My brother wasn't the sort of man to spend money on things that were not needed or useful. He was an extremely shrewd businessman and managed his affairs with an attention to detail and a carefulness that simply bemused me. I am not inclined to be a good businesswoman, like my half sister, Letitia. She took care of Sangria House and even the plantation and winery when Louis was ill. She is an excellent businesswoman, I suppose. I'm so lamentably ignorant that I wouldn't know how to judge such things, but my brother did. Just as I was the only person he allowed to nurse him, Letitia was the only person he allowed to attend to the family business when he could not."

"Oh, really?" Irene said politely. "That's very interesting."

"Interesting? Perhaps. But for poor Letitia it was quite maddening. Although she could do everything required to run the household and even Sangria Plantation, the minute my brother was able to get out of bed, he would dismiss her as if she were a parlormaid and step right back in without ever giving her one iota of credit or gratitude. Although Letitia—nor I nor my sister Muriel—ever dwelt upon it, of course Letitia had a perfect right to expect that Louis would at least make arrangements for her to take over Sangria Plantation. And now look what he's done! With that insane will, and everything left up in the air, and his own wife and sisters unsure of where they stand!" Her voice had slowly risen to a near hysterical pitch, so with a quick sidelong glance at Irene, Phillipa's brow smoothed, the fire went out of her eyes, and her voice, once again, sounded soft and low. "I suppose you know about the will," she half whispered, as if she were ashamed.

"Yes, since we are tenants of the house and Mrs. Buchanan has a lease with a purchase option, we have become what is termed 'interested persons,'" Irene answered evenly. "As a matter of fact Major Valentine was here just yesterday and brought us a copy of the will. He also had some court orders regarding some of the personal property of the estate."

Phillipa looked down and twisted her tortured handkerchief. "I suppose by that you mean the boxes that are in the safe. Naturally it would greatly add to my sisters' peace of mind were we to know the contents of those boxes."

Irene said nothing; she merely kept her expression pleasant and stayed still while the woman sitting next to her fidgeted.

After a few moments' hesitation, Phillipa went on, "My sister Muriel's fiancé advised her that we should have a legal right to at least peruse the pertinent documents and records that pertain to our case."

"I'm sorry. Who is your sister's fiancé?" Irene asked politely.

Phillipa seemed very surprised. "Why, it's Mr. Mortimer Pendergast. Louis's attorney. I just assumed that you knew, since you and your party are so intimately involved with the case, as you say."

"I believe I said that we are interested persons, a legal term," Irene said, correcting her gently. "Anyway, it is possible that Mr. Mortimer Pendergast is exactly right. I wouldn't know, and I doubt very much that any of us, except perhaps my daughter-in-law Mrs. Buchanan, knows enough of estate law to be able to judge such a thing. But the problem, Miss Grider, is that there is a court seal on the contents of the safe, on the safe itself, and on Mr. Grider's desk. My husband witnessed Major Valentine's inspection of the contents of the safe, the safe itself, and the desk and then was served with the court order. So I'm sure you understand that there's not much I can do to help you. If you—or anyone, for that matter—would like access to the safe, I suppose you would have to obtain an order from the probate judge. Perhaps since Mr. Pendergast is your sister's fiancé, he will be able to help you ladies with the legalities."

Phillipa shook her head. "No. Mr. Pendergast would never do that. He and Muriel don't want anyone to know that they are . . . *involved*. And Mr. Pendergast, of course, theoretically represents my brother, as executor of his will, and so to help us would be a breach of ethics, wouldn't it? Muriel and Mr. Pendergast think it would look suspicious. Certainly they didn't want my brother to know. He would definitely have been suspicious. They don't seem to be very well suited, after all, do they? And they are so very secretive, it does seem odd, since there is nothing that anyone could possibly object to . . . except for my brother, of course. He would naturally have been upset."

"Upset? Why should he have been upset? Miss Muriel is of age, and I assume that Mr. Pendergast is a suitable man, with nothing objectionable in his background. I understood members of his family have been lawyers here in St. Augustine for many years."

"Oh no, my brother would not have found Mr. Pendergast objectionable on personal grounds," Phillipa said, shrugging. "It would have been on business grounds. He looked at everything from the business standpoint. If Muriel had been betrothed to Louis's attorney, naturally Louis would have felt that Mr. Pendergast's loyalties would have been compromised, and he would have forbidden the match. And he likely would have dismissed Mr. Pendergast."

"I see," Irene said. "It seems your brother was something of a hard taskmaster."

"He was. But such things didn't really affect me, you know. As I said, there was no danger that I was going to try to take his business away from him, or betray him, or steal anything from him," Phillipa said, now in a cool and calculating manner. "All I ever wanted to do was take care of him. That was all. I just wanted to stay with him and take care of him."

"Admirable," Irene said in the same sweet tone she always used. "But in that case, Miss Grider, how was it that Mr. Grider decided he didn't want you to accompany him to Europe? Since he was ill, it would seem that he would particularly want you, his trusted nurse, to go with him."

To Irene's dismay, Phillipa burst into tears, jumped up, and began pacing again.

"They . . . they turned him against me!" she cried. "They were all of them so selfish, so greedy of their own wants that they didn't think about mine at all! Aimee, who wanted to stay with her new obsession. Muriel and her bony oily beau, for shame, at her age! And Letitia, who simply couldn't leave Louis alone about Sangria Plantation and how she should have it! Finally Louis just sent us all away!"

Phillipa did seem truly devastated; she stopped pacing, bent her head, and began to sob. Irene rose, put her arms around the woman's shaking shoulders, and said quietly in her ear, "Miss Grider, I am so very sorry for your troubles. Please sit down. I am going to have Jauncy bring a brandy for you. Perhaps it will calm you, and then you may want to stay here for a while and rest."

Irene led Phillipa haltingly back to the sofa as she talked. The woman practically fell onto the sofa and looked back up at Irene with haunted eyes. "I loved my brother, Mrs. Duvall. I . . . I . . . hope you can believe that."

"I can. Please, just stay here and try to calm your mind, Miss Grider. I'll return in only a few moments."

Irene slipped out of the room, closing the door behind her. Before fetching Jauncy, she stared into space for a few moments, thinking hard. *Something has been wrong with this entire conversation. What exactly is it? It's out of sync, discordant, like a pianist out of time or an actor missing his cue. It throws off the timing of all of the actors. . . . Is that what I am? Just an actor in her play?*

Jauncy came out of the dining room then and walked down the hall. He had gone several steps before he saw Irene, and when he did, his pace quickened and he looked concerned. "Miss Irene? Is something wrong?"

"Something definitely is, Mr. Jauncy," she said grimly. "Would you please bring a brandy for Miss Grider? She is feeling unwell."

"Certainly, ma'am," he said, whirling to hurry to the library, where the only liquor in the house was stored. He turned again, however, to ask, "Miss Irene? May I bring you something? You look a little pale yourself, if you don't mind my being so bold."

"No, thank you. I'm fine, Mr. Jauncy. Only vastly puzzled, I suppose, and no spirituous liquor will help that. Just the brandy for Miss Grider, please."

"Yes, madam." Jauncy turned to hurry on into the library.

As Irene returned to the parlor, she thought quickly, *No, it's not acting. She really is distraught. Aside from her sorrow, her state of mind is obvious from her dress and appearance. But what is it about this entire conversation? Something false, something contrived—*

And then the realization jolted Irene. *She has led the entire conversation. She has—intentionally, I believe, in spite of her distress—managed to provide both of her sisters, her sister-in-law, and the attorney with grievances against Louis Grider.*

Grievances . . . which could mean motives . . .

For murder.

PART IV

A TIME TO CAST AWAY
STONES,
AND A TIME TO GATHER
STONES TOGETHER

Ecclesiastes 3:5

CHAPTER SIXTEEN

Where Death Rejoices

"IT IS MY HONOR to make known to you Dr. Cheney Irons-Winslow," Major Valentine said with the gravity proper for such important introductions. "Dr. Irons-Winslow, may I present to you Dr. Clyde Duff, a physician of long standing here in St. Augustine, and his brother, Merle Duff. Mr. Merle Duff is the apothecary who has graciously consented to allow us to use his laboratory for the autopsy."

Cheney acknowledged the introductions as Major Valentine then went on to repeat the ritual with Shiloh. Dr. Duff, the elder brother, was tall and slender, his hair gray, his nose thin and slightly hooked, with a thin mouth and grim eagle eyes. Merle Duff had no resemblance to him at all, as sometimes happens. He was shorter, of medium height and build, with sandy brown hair and bright brown eyes. The main difference between the two, Cheney noted, was that Dr. Duff looked bitter and unhappy, while Merle Duff looked genial and easygoing. Major Valentine had told Cheney and Shiloh as he had escorted them into town that the Duff brothers had been very successful men of some means, although they were not considered wealthy. The Duff family had owned several hundred acres of land on the other side of the San Sebastian River, with one grand plantation home. Merle Duff had built another about a mile away from the old family home.

But both men had joined the Army of the Confederate States of America, and after the war the Reconstruction government had heavily taxed the Duff family holdings, as it had done to almost all men of property in the Confederate States. The Duff brothers could not pay the taxes, and so carpetbaggers had bought the land and the two homes for three hundred and sixteen dollars. Ironically, the carpetbaggers who had bought the Duff properties were Robert MacDonald, a Freedman's Bureau agent in St. Augustine, and his brother, Bruce MacDonald, who was the coroner. It was for the purchase of the Duff family holdings that the MacDonald brothers had become indebted to Louis Grider.

Cheney took an appraising look around. The storefront was typical of small apothecary shops from time immemorial: shelves and cases full of exotic powders and herbs, glass bottles filled with tinctures and solutions of every color, mysterious jars of brown glass with labels carefully handwritten in Latin, and the ever-present tart chemical smell. It was very small, however, with the glass-fronted counter facing the front door and set back only about five feet. Behind this was a curtained entryway that Cheney assumed led into the laboratory where Mr. Duff mixed his remedies and prescriptives. The shop was so small because it was actually half of what his original storefront had been. After they had lost their land and homes, the Duff brothers had divided the two-story building in half; Dr. Duff's office was next door and the two Duff families lived in tiny flats on the second floor.

The introductions completed, Dr. Duff said in a gruff voice, "I would offer my services if you had need of them, Dr. Irons-Winslow, but since you, Mr. Irons-Winslow, are going to assist, I shall take my leave. Good morning." The bell on the door jangled jarringly as he pulled the door shut.

Ruefully Cheney watched him go. She was accustomed to curt dismissals from male physicians. Merle Duff said quietly, "My brother is very busy, you see. We still have quite a lot of patients all over St. Johns County, and many of them can't come into town. He spends most of his days riding around the country."

"Of course," Cheney said, smiling at the jovial younger brother. "And speaking of patients, I'm eager to get started on mine, if you wouldn't mind?"

"You are?" Mr. Duff blurted out. "Of . . . of course, Dr. Irons-Winslow. This way, if you'll permit me." He lifted the counter flap, and Cheney and Shiloh followed him to the back. Shiloh looked back at Major Valentine, who was rather hastily opening the front door.

"Whatsa matter, Major?" Shiloh called. "You aren't gonna come give us a hand?" He and Major Valentine had come to establish a rapport once the major had gotten Shiloh's grim nonverbal warning and had stopped watching Cheney with such open admiration.

"No, sir, I most certainly am not," Major Valentine retorted. "I don't want to see, I don't want to know, I don't want to do anything except deliver the report to Judge Allard. I don't even want to read it."

"Girly muffin," Shiloh said.

"That's right," Major Valentine answered defiantly and left.

The back of the store was dominated by a large cluttered desk and a worktable that had a Bunsen burner installed. A high autopsy stand on rollers was beside the worktable. Bins and carboys and crates full of stock took up much of the floor space. A number of items were set out neatly on the worktable, including a microscope with a heavy-duty oil lantern next to it, a tray of slides, a grocer's scale, an apothecary's balance, a stack of blank writing paper, two neatly folded oilcloth aprons, a mortar and pestle, a selection of both tin and ceramic bowls and basins, and much more.

Eagerly Merle Duff said, "I hope I've gathered everything you might require, Dr. Irons-Winslow. I've never attended an autopsy, and though my brother observed dissections in medical school, he has never performed one, so I wasn't sure what was needed."

Cheney set her medical bag on the worktable, casting a critical eye over the items so neatly arranged there. "Mr. Duff, I can see that you have everything I requested and have also added some items that will surely prove handy."

"I hope that you have the proper surgical instruments, Dr. Irons-Winslow," he added, "for of course I never stock such expensive and seldom-needed items."

"Actually, I did bring everything that I need here to St. Augustine," Cheney answered, pulling a black velvet roll from her bag, while Shiloh put a small square valise on the worktable. "My husband and I have traveled quite a bit, and I have learned from hard experience that it's wise to bring all of my implements." The black velvet roll contained ten scalpels of various sizes, all newly sharpened and glittering dangerously, while the valise contained surgical tools such as saws, catlings, retractors, and large bone knives.

Mr. Duff's eyes widened, for though he had seen scalpels and surgical instruments before, he had never seen such quality workmanship, nor had he seen a lady who seemed so comfortable with the grim tools. Cheney selected a large scalpel and tested it against her thumb. "Wonderful," she breathed. "Shiloh, if you decide not to be a doctor, I believe you could make a fine living going around and sharpening surgical instruments."

"Huh, that's too much hard work," he grumbled. "Especially these fine-tooth saws. To get a really good edge on 'em you have to sharpen every little V separately. Hey, Mr. Duff? There's a couple of things I think we might need if you could rustle 'em up for us."

"My husband has been my assistant for several years," Cheney explained. "He's studying to be a physician, but he's already a very competent surgical assistant."

"I see," Mr. Duff said agreeably. "I'll be glad to 'rustle 'em up,' Mr. Irons-Winslow, whatever they are."

"Do you have Carr's Carbolic Compound? We need at least a gallon, I'd say."

"Why, yes, I do stock Carr's, in quart bottles, and I think I have four." He pulled the canvas curtain aside to go back into the shop.

Cheney was already putting the oilcloth apron on. "I'm so glad Mr. Duff thought of these. I would hate to get anything on my clothes, and I had completely forgotten about a coverall, which I did not bring on holiday anyway."

"Yeah, Doc, it'd be a crying shame for you to get liver juice on your dress, as Miss Minerva says." Shiloh pulled the bibbed apron over his head. "It's a really pretty dress, and you look pretty in it. Like peaches and cream."

"Thank you," Cheney said, pleased. Shiloh always gave her such nice compliments, never automatic, always spontaneous and truthful. It was a quality in Shiloh that Cheney treasured and determined that she would never take for granted.

She did look fresh and pretty. Nothing about her appearance hinted at the somber job she was about to perform. She was wearing a tangerine-colored skirt with four rows of tightly gathered white lace flounces and a white blouse with a ruffled cravat, a cameo brooch, lace-trimmed cuffs, and small delicate shirring. She had already taken off her peach-and-white striped jacket with an open corsage that fit tightly at the waist, along with her gloves and a snappy little hat that was little more than a diadem of white velvet with a drape that came gracefully under her chin. The climate appeared to agree with Cheney too; her auburn hair was glossy, her complexion seemed to glow with health, her green eyes sparkled.

Mr. Duff came back in, four quarts of Carr's Carbolic Compound cradled in his arms. "Yes, I do have four on hand," he said, beaming.

Shiloh took them, uncorked one, poured it into a large basin, and began selecting certain scalpels and knives to throw into the amber-colored liquid. "So, Mr. Duff, have you submitted a bill to the provost marshal for all of your stuff here? It's by their warrant that the doc is ordered to do this autopsy, so they're paying the expenses."

"Oh, that's very good news," he said with obvious relief. "I didn't know, exactly . . . er . . . since I volunteered . . . um—I shall certainly send them an itemized bill."

"Yes, you must do that," Cheney said, glad that Shiloh had thought of this; it was obvious that Mr. Duff could hardly bear the expense of all the supplies by himself. "You must carefully list every little thing we use, Mr. Duff, and I will be glad to sign the statement. I am so happy that you have such a good microscope—it is a Roentger, is it not? You must also include a fee for usage of your instruments."

"Gladly," Mr. Duff said, polishing his fine microscope for at least the hundredth time that morning.

Cheney continued, "In fact, now that I'm thinking of it, I don't quite understand why we are here, doing this autopsy, using your things, Mr. Duff. Isn't there a morgue? And doesn't the coroner's office have a budget for this kind of thing?" Shiloh had poured out another basin full of carbolic acid, and Cheney rolled up her sleeves and started scrubbing her hands and arms. After Shiloh got all the instruments in the basin, he started scrubbing up too. Mr. Duff watched them with interest but roused himself to answer Cheney's question.

"I have no idea what the coroner's office's budget has in it or where the funds for it may be going," he said with some spirit. "But Hagley's Funeral Parlor has the only morgue, you might say, in the sense that they have a room where they clean the bodies and do the embalming. But Mr. Grider made no allowance for his remains, as I understand it, and the widow didn't seem to want to spend an extra dollar for Mr. Hagley's services, so he refused to allow the autopsy to be done at his place. Major Valentine asked my brother and me if we would help out, and Mr. Hagley did allow me to borrow one of their tables. And so here we all are."

"Yes, here we all are," Shiloh repeated, "except for one little detail."

Mr. Duff looked distressed. "Oh dear, have I forgotten something critical?"

"Doubt it," Shiloh answered, drying his hands and looking

quizzically around. "Not forgotten, just displaced, maybe. Where's Mr. Grider?"

"Oh yes, I mean, no, I haven't forgotten him," Mr. Duff said with relief. "It's just that—Dr. Irons-Winslow, I don't mean to imply that you are indelicate, but after all, he has been deceased for eight days now, and this is a small shop, and it is rather warm, and the . . . er . . . *aroma,* shall we say for lack of a better word—"

"'By this time he stinketh: for he hath been dead four days,'" Shiloh quoted. "If it's good enough for Lazarus, it's good enough for me."

"Uh . . . yes, of course," Mr. Duff said uncertainly. He had never met a doctor like Cheney, or a soon-to-be-doctor like Shiloh. He didn't know whether to laugh or be very solemn, but in the next moment he found out, because Cheney threw back her head to look up at Shiloh and teased, "It may be good enough for you, Winthro, but I'll bet you wouldn't want Mr. Grider in your parlor either. Is he outside, Mr. Duff?"

"Yes, in a small yard with a little herb garden that my brother and I keep," he said with some embarrassment. "It is fenced in, Dr. Irons-Winslow, so it affords some privacy. It's not as if I have him out there on display. The gravediggers simply dumped the coffin back there, and I started to . . . take him out and—perhaps—clean him up, but I wasn't certain if that would be proper."

"No, you were right to leave it to me," Cheney said kindly. "As a matter of fact, there is a sort of legal chain of custody that should be preserved here. I'm surprised—well, perhaps I'm not very surprised that the men who exhumed the body didn't observe the legal niceties. They work for the coroner's office, I presume? I thought so. I understand that Mr. MacDonald is exceedingly displeased that Judge Allard ordered an autopsy."

"Well, he'll have to get in line and wait his turn along with everyone else who's exceedingly displeased," Mr. Duff said with a somewhat surprising asperity. "Because there are a lot of people objecting to the autopsy, including Mr. Grider's widow, his sisters, his creditors, even his attorney. Seems like all they care about is his will, not his death. At least that is how they're all acting, is what I've heard."

Cheney was surprised. Mr. Duff did not seem to be the kind of man to indulge in unfounded gossip. "But, Mr. Duff, is everyone spreading this story about all of these people? That they are all acting in a questionable manner that implies some sort of guilt? Because I never implied, never even hinted, that Mr. Grider's death is suspicious. I have simply maintained that his death is unexplained and that a proper autopsy will explain it."

"It's not a story, Dr. Irons-Winslow, it is fact," Mr. Duff asserted, tilting his chin. "All of the persons I mentioned have communicated their displeasure either to me or to my brother, who, himself, had very little charitable feeling toward Mr. Louis Grider. You see, Mr. Grider called him out to Sangria House for a consultation three years ago. My brother told him that he had a common catarrh with a slight fever. Mr. Grider believed that he was seriously ill and my brother was just an ignorant country doctor who was unable to diagnose his particular ailment. There was some bitter wrangling, because Mr. Grider complained to several prominent people in town and did, in fact, attempt to blacken my brother's reputation. Also, he never paid my brother's fee," he added.

"This man seems to have alienated just about everyone he came into contact with, including his own family," Cheney said regretfully.

"It would seem so," Mr. Duff agreed. "At any rate, my brother has very little desire to get caught up in the . . . er . . . fracas over Mr. Grider's death. I know that it was a relief to him that his services were not required. As for the other people, I don't know what's wrong with them," he concluded. "Shame on them, I say. What's wrong with finding out the truth about how Mr. Grider died? Everyone deserves that. No matter how they lived, the truth about their deaths should be noted, their passing marked with clarity and dignity."

"Bravo, Mr. Duff," Cheney said softly. "My beliefs exactly. I hope and pray that soon we'll know the truth, even if it is only noted and honored by us here. Now, would you please help my husband get Mr. Grider?"

"Of course," he said. "I've made this ramp down the back steps so we can roll the table out." Shiloh and Mr. Duff rolled the table outside while Cheney watched. Mr. Duff had already taken the nails out of the top of the coffin, so with a minimum of trouble they loaded the body onto the table and rolled it back into the laboratory.

"Now, with my sincerest gratitude, Mr. Duff, I will release you from this somber task," Cheney said, smiling.

"Why, you're more than welcome, Dr. Irons-Winslow," Mr. Duff said, bowing a little, his honest brown eyes shining.

Shiloh sighed to himself; he could see that yet another man was smitten by his gracious and beautiful wife.

Duff went on a little shyly, "But . . . I was wondering . . . if it would be possible—I know I couldn't actually *help* you, Dr. Irons-Winslow, but perhaps I might just observe? I should really like to."

"You would?" Cheney said with surprise. "Usually medical students are the only people who can honestly say they like dissections."

"Perhaps," the little apothecary said, "but I confess I have a very curious mind. Don't get me wrong—my brother is the doctor in the family, and I like my little shop and my patrons; most of the people who are my customers I have known all my life. It's just that I do study, as much as I can, the *materia medica* and chemistry. That is why I did indulge myself with such a fine microscope. And I am fascinated with anatomical studies. I think that it would help me to see some of these organs and tissues that I'm always reading about."

"In that case, Mr. Duff, you are welcome to observe," Cheney said. "And now, since I and my husband have not come to know you very well yet, but together we are getting ready to perform a task that is, by its very nature, one of delicacy, I would like to make something clear to you, sir.

"We are Christians, Mr. Duff, and we believe that each of us is God's creation, formed and given life by Him. We believe that this body we are about to dissect is no longer inhabited by Louis Arthur Grider, that he has passed on to the place where he will spend eternity, and we hope that is with the Lord Jesus Christ.

"This collection of tissue and skin and bone no longer is Mr. Louis Grider but a vessel that we can respectfully, with the proper sense of gratitude to our God for His guidance, learn from. And though we may seem to be lighthearted at times, we do have a sense of the honor that is bestowed on us who learn of God's creation in this way. *Hic locus est ubi mors gaudet succurrere vitae.*"

"Let me, Doc," Shiloh interrupted quietly. "I've really been working on my Latin. It's: 'This is the place . . . the place where death joys—no, where death rejoices to teach those who live.'"

Merle Duff smiled, and his face was alight. "I'm a Christian too, Dr. Irons-Winslow, and I think that's the perfect way to describe what is, as you said, a delicate task that we're about to perform. For my part, I'm honored to have the opportunity to learn, and now I'm thankful to the Lord that we all see this as a way for Him to teach us of life."

"Good," Cheney said, smiling. "I must warn you, however, that since the opportunity for dissection doesn't come around every day, my husband and I had agreed that I would lecture as I work. I hope you won't be bored."

"Oh no, not at all," he said quickly. "In fact, it seems that that would be the best thing, if you were to at least name what we're looking at."

"That's the truth. That's why I asked her to lecture," Shiloh said. "I've assisted at surgeries before, and I know some stuff, but I've hardly ever known one thing under the skin. The epidermis, I mean."

"Me either," Duff agreed. "I have assisted my brother a few times with simple surgeries. And I was in the war, a surgeon's mate. But that's not the same. War isn't the same."

"Sure isn't," Shiloh grunted. "I was a medical corpsman too." They nodded to each other in perfect understanding.

It never failed to amaze Cheney that men had some sort of mystical mutual comprehension about war, no matter how different the men, no matter if they wore blue or gray.

"Then it seems I will have two expert assistants today," Cheney said brightly. "Are we ready? All right, I will make notes as I work, and later I'll write up the formal report."

"But, Dr. Duvall, perhaps I could do that?" Mr. Duff offered. "I have nice handwriting, if I do say so myself. I intended to take notes, if you allowed me to observe—that's why I included the paper and pens with the supplies. But if you would tell me what to write down, I can keep notes while you work, which will surely save you some time. I've studied *Gray's Anatomy,* so I am familiar with the proper names. And I'm a good speller."

"Yes, that would be wonderful, Mr. Duff," Cheney said. "I admit it is difficult to keep my train of thought for the lecture, perform the tasks, and take notes all at the same time. All right, are we ready? Very well. Mr. Duff, note if you please: Examination takes place Tuesday, March 5, 1870, at Duff's Apothecary in St. Augustine, Florida. Time is 8:40 A.M. Subject is one Louis Arthur Grider, male, date of birth August 8, 1814, date of death believed to be either late Sunday night of February 24 or in the early morning hours of February 25.

"Got that, Mr. Duff? All right, Shiloh, if you'll help me prepare him for autopsy, we'll get down to business. . . ." Working together quickly, with little wasted effort and perfect cohesion, Cheney and Shiloh measured Grider, estimated his weight, and noted the general physical appearance of the body, along with a professional assessment of the state of deterioration.

"Now, Mr. Duff, you must very carefully transcribe the observations I am now going to make," Cheney said firmly. "These exterior physical signs will, I believe, be critical to the determination of the manner, cause, and mechanism of Mr. Grider's death."

"Yes, Dr. Irons-Winslow," he said, pen at the ready, his eyes full of curiosity.

"First the neck, Shiloh," she murmured, and he lifted Grider's head from the table and smoothly rotated it in small circular motions while Cheney slid her fingers underneath the neck. After a moment she nodded to Shiloh, and he laid Mr. Grider's head gently back down. In a lecturing tone she said, "Vertebrae in the neck appear to be intact. Coroner's determination of cause of death as a broken neck is therefore questionable. Thorough dissection of the neck and spine is critical."

Mr. Duff finished writing with a determined scratch and then looked up.

Shiloh sighed; even with his gentleness, a large hank of hair had come off into his hands. Cheney said, "Fold it into a gauze square, Shiloh. At least we won't have to shave his head to get samples." She turned to Mr. Duff and recited, "Subject is observed to have suffered from alopecia, both antemortem and postmortem. The gross loss of hair appears to have been mainly antemortem. Upon visual examination, the hair appears to be colored alternately black and white, giving it a distinctive banded appearance. Microscopic evaluation of hair will be included with dissection and microscopic evaluation of tissue and organ samples."

Mr. Duff said nothing, but his expression as he finished the notes and looked up was grave.

"You have seen this symptomology before, Mr. Duff?" Cheney said quietly.

His smooth boyish brow wrinkled, and he answered haltingly, "No, I have never seen it before, Dr. Irons-Winslow, but I thought—I wonder—"

"Go on, Mr. Duff," Cheney said. "This is how we learn. And I believe that anyone who wishes to learn should be encouraged, always. I can see that you have a theory, and I would like to hear it."

He looked gratified and continued with more confidence, "I have read that chronic arsenic poisoning can be evidenced in the hair, with a microscopic evaluation showing the arsenic salts at measurable increments in the length of the hair, and it can be mathematically related to the time intervals in which the arsenic was ingested."

"Very good," Cheney said.

Shiloh nodded, a sign that he was following.

Slowly Mr. Duff continued, "I also remember reading that arsenic can affect pigmentation of the skin. Is it possible that it could also affect pigmentation of the hair? That it could cause such obvious bands of discoloration?"

"That is my theory," Cheney asserted. "As far as I know, there is no recorded evidence of arsenic having such an effect on the pigment of the hair, but it does follow, doesn't it?"

"Yeah, that follows," Shiloh said quietly, "but, Doc, have you ever seen anything like this poor man's scalp? Could the arsenic have discolored his whole scalp like that?"

"It's not dirt?" Mr. Duff exclaimed, leaning forward. "I thought it was scandalous that Mr. Grider would have been prepared for burial in this careless manner."

"No, it's not dirt," Cheney answered. "Shiloh, hand me that magnifying glass. Thank you. Mr. Duff, would you care to observe?"

Eagerly he leapt up, took the magnifying glass, and perused Grider's scalp carefully along one of the large parts of exposed scalp where the man's hair had come out. "It's actually a discoloration of the skin," he mused. "In fact, Doctor, it appears that the roots of the hair follicles—where the hair used to be, at least—are blackened." He straightened, handed the magnifying glass back to her, and stared down at the dead face. "And his eyebrows. What has happened to them? Are you familiar with these signs or symptoms?"

"Not at all," she answered, bending to study Grider's scalp closely. "Shiloh, the lantern, please? Thank you. No, Mr. Duff, I have never seen, heard, or read of these particular symptoms. But with your help, and with the benefit of my husband's shrewd instincts, I intend to find out as much as I can about these peculiarities. But we must take it one step at a time. Now please note: Scalp appears to be discolored a mottled black upon simple visual examination. With magnification of fifteen times, it is evident that the discoloration involves only the shafts of the hair follicles. Also upon visual with fifteen times magnification, abnormality of the hair of the eyebrows is evident. Inner one-third and outer one-third of both eyebrows are missing. There is no evidence of discoloration of hair shaft, as in the scalp. As with the scalp hair, the hair of the eyebrows appear to be completely missing, not shaved or plucked."

Cheney's eyes narrowed with concentration as she surveyed the rest of the body. She asked Mr. Duff to read back a couple of sentences. She nodded with satisfaction and then dictated: "The only other pertinent external evidence is that of matching abrasions on subject's knees."

She and Shiloh bent over, examining them; Cheney pointed to one or two places, and Shiloh gently felt with his fingertips. "The abrasions are still slightly swollen and reddish from inflammation, obviously ante-mortem." Changing to her normal speaking voice, she told Shiloh and Mr. Duff, "If the abrasions had been postmortem, they would now appear to be slightly yellow and the skin would have a distinctive fibrous coating resembling parchment." Cheney's and Shiloh's eyes met, and she nodded. "He fell to his knees, Shiloh. He was standing, he fell to his knees, and then he fell down. Whatever killed him, it was not tumbling down the stairs and breaking his neck."

Mr. Duff said quietly, "You do think he was poisoned, don't you, Dr. Irons-Winslow?"

Cheney answered in a matter-of-fact tone, "It is my theory that the cause of death was from arsenic poisoning, yes. But it is only my theory, and this examination will either confirm or negate that theory, but that is not the reason for performing this autopsy or any other. Cause of death is only one—"

"I know," Shiloh volunteered, then recited: "Manner of death—there are four: homicide, suicide, accident, and natural. Cause of death: the agent or item that induced death, also called the deodand by us learned types. And finally, the mechanism of death: the pathological changes to the body that resulted in death."

"What's a deodand?" Mr. Duff asked, puzzled.

"I'll explain it to you later," Shiloh said airily. "And all about the crowner, who I woulda liked to have crowned with a crowbar. You too, prob'ly."

"At any rate, Mr. Duff, my husband has given you the last three items that you will transcribe for this report, but not the part about the deodand," Cheney said. "Manner of death, cause of death, mechanism of death. It is the mechanism of death that we will determine first by this postmortem examination." She selected a scalpel and leaned over the body. "Actually, it's probably a good thing that he wasn't embalmed by a professional. Sometimes embalming fluid will mask the signs of disease, toxicity, or pathological changes of the tissues or organs.

"For a thorough and comprehensive postmortem examination," Cheney went on as she made the typical Y incision, "there are eight systems that should be investigated. Number one, the general external examination that we have already done. Two, the central nervous system—the scalp, skull, and brain. Three, the endocrine system—the pituitary, thyroid, and adrenals. Four, the respiratory system; five, the cardiovascular system; six, the gastrointestinal system; seven, the genitourinary system; and finally the musculoskeletal system. But because this is not a typical postmortem examination for teaching purposes, I'm going to do the gastrointestinal system first."

Shiloh nodded as he helped her with the abdominal exposure. "So that stuff you asked for—the nitric acid and the zinc—is for some kind of test for poison?"

"Yes, they are. Mr. Duff, I'm sure you will find this interesting, and I would like you to make very careful, comprehensive notes, particularly during this procedure. We are going to perform what's called the Marsh test, named after an English chemist named James Marsh. In 1836 he published a method for converting arsenic in body tissues and fluids into arsine gas, which, incidentally, had already been discovered by a Swedish chemist named Karl Scheele. But Marsh improved on the test, because he was able to convert arsine—a highly unstable gas—back to metallic arsenic, which was a tangible, visible proof of the presence of arsenic. It's much easier to show metallic arsenic to a court than to perform a test in which a whiff of smoke is produced and then disappears in an instant."

"Very interesting," Duff murmured, scribbling furiously.

"It's a very sensitive test too," Cheney continued, "that will detect a very small amount of arsenic. Carefully note the steps of the procedure, and I will tell you how to word the results."

"Okay, Doc," Shiloh said as he finished cutting the cartilages that opened the chest cavity and removed the breastbone and attached rib cartilages.

"Be very careful with that, Shiloh, because we'll do a comprehensive examination later," Cheney cautioned him. "But I want to go ahead and do the Marsh test first, before we get fatigued. It's kind of tricky, so I want to have a perfectly clear head."

"Good idea. So what do we do the test on?" Shiloh asked.

"The liver."

He sighed. "I knew we were gonna get liver juice on us sooner or later."

"If I go up to my flat and make some coffee, could I persuade you to stop and rest for a little while and share my coffee?" Mr. Duff suggested.

"You are so kind," Cheney said. "I would love a cup of hot coffee."

"Me too," Shiloh said. "If you wouldn't mind, Mr. Duff, we'll clean up a little bit and sit down and reconnoiter."

Mr. Duff went to the door—the steps up to his flat were outside—then stopped and turned around. "You won't do anything else until I get back, will you?"

Cheney smiled. "No, Mr. Duff, we won't."

He turned to leave, then whirled once again. "And—you won't say anything important while I'm gone?"

"Naw, we hardly ever say anything important anyway," Shiloh drawled as he took off his apron and began to wipe it down with carbolic acid.

"Humph, I know that's not true," Mr. Duff muttered and then hurried off.

"I think he just called me a liar," Shiloh said.

"He didn't. He just corrected you," Cheney said. "He's a bright, good-natured gent, isn't he? Not like his brother at all."

"I know, but the brother got the best name. Dr. Duff. Dr. Duff—isn't that a fine sound? Think when I get my M.D. I'm gonna change my name to Duff just so's I'll be called Dr. Duff."

"Why don't you just add it to all the rest of your names?" Cheney asked tartly. "You've got so many nobody will even notice if you tack on one or two more."

"Your names too, m'dear," Shiloh reminded her. "Cheney Duff, Cheney Duff . . . Doc Duff. Oh, that's good!"

"Don't even think about it."

They walked outside to get some fresh air. In the back of the double storefront was a postage-stamp-size yard, with three neat rows of small trimmed green bushes. Cheney walked carefully between the rows and knelt to look at the tiny labels stuck on little wooden stakes. "Let's see what we have here . . . anise . . . comfrey . . . meadowsweet. Oh, look, Shiloh, this is boneset! I've never seen the plant. The Indians used it to treat fevers, catarrh, influenza, even rheumatism. I wonder if the natives here—what was the name of the ancient tribe? The Timucuans, that's it. I wonder if they used it."

"Here comes the gardener. You can ask him," Shiloh said, hurrying to help Mr. Duff carry a large covered tray down the narrow steps.

They went in and got the tray situated on Mr. Duff's desk, and Shiloh pulled up two straight chairs from Mr. Duff's storeroom for himself and Cheney. Cheney poured and served, and they drank the hot, strong coffee gratefully.

"Isn't it amazing how refreshing very hot coffee can be even when it's warm?" Cheney said idly.

"And tea," Shiloh added. "So anyway, Doc, now that Mr. Duff's back we won't be telling secrets behind his back; we'll be telling them in front of his front. So poor old Grider wasn't poisoned, huh?"

"He wasn't poisoned by arsenic, Shiloh," Cheney said carefully. But then she sighed deeply. "I was so sure, especially after Mother found the powder in her—I mean, in Mrs. Grider's bedroom."

"Well, the powder didn't contain arsenic," Mr. Duff said, "but neither is it rice powder." Before they had taken a break for coffee, Andrew Barentine had delivered the tin of complexion powder Mallow and Irene had found that morning, and they had performed the Marsh test on it. It was clearly negative.

Then they had microscopically examined the powder. It clearly was not zinc, nor rice powder, nor talc—for Mr. Duff had samples of these ladies' preparations in his shop for comparison—but was some mineral that none of the three of them had ever seen before. Mr. Duff, who was proving to be a very useful assistant, made careful, expert line drawings of each of the microscopic powders and then had made sealed slides of the samples and labeled them. "For complete thoroughness," he said.

"What do we do now?" Mr. Duff asked. "I mean—what are you going to do now, of course."

Cheney smiled at him, and once again Shiloh saw that the man did everything but swoon. "Now, Mr. Duff, we continue with the complete postmortem examination, which, I want to stress to you, we would do regardless of the results of the Marsh test. All that the negative results of the test mean is that the cause of death was not from arsenic poisoning. We still have to find out what caused Mr. Grider to die."

"Wasn't Mr. Grider ill?" Duff asked. "I mean, I had understood that he had been very ill, bedridden, in fact, for most of the month of November, with some sort of respiratory distress."

"All we really know is that he was going to Bath, in England, for hydropathy treatments," Shiloh said. "That could be for anything from a blister on your foot to cancer of the brain, if you believe the pamphlets."

Mr. Duff sniffed. "It's my personal opinion that Mr. Grider was something of a hypochondriac. As far as I know, he had no physician attending him. After he and my brother had their disagreement, Mr.

Grider started medicating himself. He made very regular purchases of sulfate salts. As I understand it from Miss Phillipa Grider, Mr. Grider reflected upon how sulfates do preserve wine for many years; he then conceived that adding additional sulfates to wine may work as a preservative, if you will, for the human body."

"Yeah? What about that, Doc? Could he maybe have overdosed himself on that?" Shiloh asked with interest.

"I doubt it very seriously," Cheney answered thoughtfully. "Sulfate salts are a derivative of sulfur, Shiloh. I suppose large amounts of sulfur would poison you, but it would be almost impossible to take because of the smell and taste."

"True," Mr. Duff agreed. "And sulfate salts are a very weak ester of sulfur, so it would take enormous amounts, I should think, to poison a person."

"So let's forget arsenic poisoning. Once again, we go back to the basics and do a postmortem examination step by step." Cheney stood and pulled her now-cleaned apron back over her head. "And hope—and pray—that we can find out how this man died."

"I suppose we must be thankful that we know how he died," Cheney said wearily. "But it is so frustrating because I don't know *why* he died."

"I can stitch him back up and clean him up, Doc," Shiloh said. "Why don't you sit down and dictate the rest of the report to Mr. Duff?"

"I believe I will," Cheney agreed. "I must admit I am tired." It was almost seven o'clock. The autopsy had taken almost nine hours; they had taken about an hour for a quick lunch at Janie's Café down the street.

Mr. Duff asked hesitantly, "Dr. Irons-Winslow? Is that what you want to do? Because I could help Mr. Irons-Winslow if you'd rather write the report yourself."

She thought for a moment. "No, Mr. Duff, this is only going to be a preliminary report, a sort of continuation of the autopsy notes. I think I shall come back tomorrow, perhaps do some more microscopic examinations of the tissue samples, and do the formal report. In the meantime, if you wouldn't mind, I will just finish dictating to you."

"Of course," he said, getting fresh paper and taking his seat at his desk, pen poised.

"First, so that you'll be clear, understand that the autopsy report is distilled down to three items, as my husband recited before: cause of death, mechanism of death, and manner of death. Remember, Shiloh recited them before?"

"Yes, I do," Mr. Duff said with satisfaction. "I did not know this, so I wrote it all down for my own notes."

"Good. Now, for your own information, the coroner ruled as follows: Cause of death—a fall downstairs. Mechanism of death—broken neck. Manner of death—accident."

"Yes, and so I will have three headings for your report," Mr. Duff murmured, his pen scratching busily. "I'm ready."

Cheney took a moment to arrange her thoughts, then recited slowly: "Mechanism of death was determined to be fatal termination of respiratory processes effected by cerebellar tonsil herniation through the foramen magnum secondary to central herniation."

". . . secondary . . . to . . . central . . . herniation," Mr. Duff murmured.

"That's a mouthful just to say his brain swelled up so much it pushed down into the hole at the bottom of his skull," Shiloh said as he stitched. "Right, Doc?"

"Right," she agreed.

Shiloh straightened and looked at her with puzzlement. "So, Doc, you think the poor guy just—quit breathing?"

"I do," she answered. "I think the swelling reached a critical point and his brain just stopped working. What I can't imagine is how he kept from becoming completely deranged before this point was reached. But he was certainly lucid enough when he wrote his will. Though it was a little eccentric, it was really extremely clever and required no small degree of analytical skill."

Mr. Duff looked up, his face so avidly curious that Cheney thought he looked like a mischievous little boy. But he said nothing, as he was a well-bred gentleman and was also a discreet man who never discussed his customers' medications or preparations, even though apothecaries weren't held to such strict ethics as physicians were. Cheney smiled to herself. "I'll tell you all about Mr. Grider's will, Mr. Duff, if you will be so kind as to make me some more of your excellent coffee after I finish the dictation."

"Of course, of course," he said eagerly. "I must admit I am extremely curious. But I would never say anything to anyone, not even to my brother."

Cheney shrugged. "I would imagine it's going to be in the newspaper anyway, but I will be glad to tell you, Mr. Duff, what we made of Mr. Grider's last will and testament and get your opinion of our analysis. After all, you are proving to be a very intelligent and able assistant. Now, to continue: Mr. Grider's cause of death was an abscess of the brain effected by an unknown toxic agent, introduced by means unknown."

". . . means unknown," Mr. Duff whispered as he wrote.

"Manner of death," Cheney finished in a hard voice, "unknown."

CHAPTER SEVENTEEN

Miasmas

BY THE TIME MR. DUFF'S buggy reached the little road that served as the entrance to Sangria House, it was almost ten o'clock. Mr. Duff turned smartly into the grounds and pulled up to the kitchen, as close as he could get to the back servants' entrance. "Are you sure you wouldn't like me to pull around front?" he asked doubtfully.

"Oh no, we're used to sneaking into the tradesmen's entrance of the Big House," Shiloh said as he lifted Cheney down. "I got my back-door clothes on anyway. Good night, Mr. Duff, and thank you again."

"We are grateful to you for all of your assistance," Cheney said. "And I'll be back tomorrow, Mr. Duff, if I may inconvenience you one more day."

"There is never any question of any inconvenience, Dr. Irons-Winslow," Mr. Duff declared. "Not at all. It's been my pleasure and honor to work with you, ma'am, and I look forward to your visit tomorrow. And, Mr. Irons-Winslow, I hope to see you soon too. Good night."

As he drove off, Cheney looked back at the kitchen where the windows showed a light. "You know, Shiloh, I've just realized how very hungry I am. That must be Sketes in the kitchen, cleaning up. Do you think we should go beg for a crust of bread?"

"I'm starving too, and if I know Sketes, she'll have more than a crust stashed away for midnight raiders," Shiloh said, taking Cheney's arm as they turned around to go back.

"You have information about midnight raids on the kitchen?" Cheney asked suspiciously. "Are you telling me that you leave our bed,

sneak off in the dead of night, leaving me defenseless, snoring and snort-
ing, and go raid the kitchen?"

"Oh sure, and who's the one I had to come find those water crackers
and ripe olives for night before last?" Shiloh asked. "And besides, you
never snore."

"I don't?"

"No. You giggle."

"I do not!"

"You do too. I always wondered what you were giggling about in
your sleep. You don't know?"

"No, I don't," Cheney answered. "Probably laughing at you."

"Prob'ly," Shiloh grumbled. He pushed open the old heavy door of
the kitchen and waited for Cheney to go through first, but she stopped
so short in the doorway that he practically ran into her.

The faint wavering light that Cheney and Shiloh had seen through
the thick windows was from the fireplace, where there was a cheery fire
built. The night was mild and humid, but such a small fire in the huge
maw of the cooking hearth in no way overheated the room. The kitchen
was warm, though, and smelled of lemon wax and fresh bread.

Like all ancient kitchens, this one had a long solid worktable. Seated
on one side of the table on a high stool was Fiona, and on the other side
was Bain Winslow. As Cheney and Shiloh came in Fiona was smiling at
something Bain had said, shyly lowering her head but gazing at him
through her thick dark lashes. When the door opened, Fiona started and
then jumped up in confusion.

Bain looked over and gave them a lazy smile. "Hello, Dr. Irons-Winslow. Hello, Locke. If you've come for a snack, you might get Fiona to
make you some toasted cheese. She is the empress of toasted cheese. But
you may not have mine; you will be obliged to apply to the empress
yourself."

"Bain, what do you—" Shiloh started blustering, but Cheney quickly
interrupted him, moving to Fiona's side.

"Fiona, toasted cheese sounds wonderful," Cheney said, smiling at
the girl and taking her arm. "Generally I'm hopeless in a kitchen, but I
am determined to learn your secret of toasted cheese. Would you help
me make some? Lots and lots of toasted cheese, please. Shiloh and I have
just discovered that we are practically fainting with hunger."

"Of course, Dr. Cheney," Fiona said. She was wringing her hands and wouldn't look up. "I was just—Mr. Winslow was—I mean, Sketes and I were cleaning—"

"It's all right, Fiona," Cheney said softly but with a warning look at her husband, who was looking stormy. "You've done nothing wrong, and besides, you aren't working for me tonight. You're a grown woman. You may do as you please."

Shiloh still looked cross, but he pulled up a stool and sat down at the head of the table. "That does smell really good," he said, eyeing Bain's plate.

"Forget it, Locke." Bain snatched up the last triangle of soft bread thick with melted Parmesan cheese. "And Miss Keane, if you're going to do more anyway, would you please do me another slice or two?"

"Yes, sir," she said faintly. She was whispering to Cheney as they gathered up a fat half loaf of bread, a bread knife, the crock of shredded cheese, and a clean oak cutting board. After Fiona had made Bain's snack, she had quickly cleaned everything up and put it away. In the corner, the cat Jezebel was lapping up the last of a bowl of cream.

"I'm surprised Sketes allows a cat in her kitchen," Cheney said to Fiona.

Fiona smiled. "Actually she's partial to cats, she told me. They always had cats on the boats—for the rats, you know."

"Yes, the same reason Mr. Grider had Jezebel," Cheney said. "He wouldn't allow rat poison in the house, Mrs. Espy said. But I wonder if he allowed its use in the kitchen and stables."

"No, ma'am," Fiona answered. "Mrs. Espy told us that there's none on the place. Even the servants weren't allowed to use anything like that in their cottages. Mr. Grider was afraid of miasmas."

"Miasmas," Cheney repeated ironically. "I'm not at all surprised. In fact, there may be something to that. Ever since we found his body it seems that my brain has been fogged. Maybe it is miasmas. Anyway, let's take all of this over to the table. I can hardly see a thing in this dark corner. Besides, I have to watch my husband every minute."

"Huh, wish that were true," Shiloh grunted, jumping up to carry the food and supplies to the table. Cheney and Fiona washed their hands in the pail of hot soapy water that was a staple of Molly Sketes's kitchen. Shiloh fetched two more plain earthenware plates from a cupboard and pulled a jar out of another. "Uh-huh, I knew Sketes would have some of these bread-and-butter pickles around here somewhere," he said with satisfaction, setting them on the table.

"Mr. Shiloh," Fiona said, "that covered toasting dish is hung on the top of the rack. Would you please reach it for me?"

"Sure." He handed it to her, and Fiona and Cheney started slicing bread and piling cheese on it to put into the flat tray. It had a long handle and a hinged top so that the bread could be toasted over an open fire without getting a smoky taste.

"Isn't it necessary to measure the amount of cheese one . . . er . . . applies to the bread?" Cheney asked uncertainly.

"Not generally, Dr. Cheney," Fiona answered. "Usually you just put some on there so that it looks right."

"But what do you mean, it looks right?" Cheney insisted. "I don't understand how it can look right before it's toasted. When it's toasted, the amount looks completely different than when it's shredded. And does one press it down, sort of mush it together? Because that, too, would change the amount, wouldn't it?"

"Maybe if you could slice the bread, I'll just do the cheese," Fiona said.

"She makes really good tea," Shiloh told Bain brightly.

"Does she?" Bain said with amusement. "How unusual for an American lady. Perhaps, Dr. Irons-Winslow, you might do us the honor of making tea?"

"But I wanted to learn how to do toasted cheese," Cheney said stubbornly.

"Sounds really complicated," Shiloh said. "And we're hungry, remember? You wanna eat tonight, or what?"

"Oh, very well, but you're not fooling me. You think that I can't learn how to make toasted cheese," Cheney said darkly. "I am an educated, intelligent, capable woman, and I could learn to make toasted cheese."

"Of course you could make toasted cheese, Dr. Cheney. You can do anything you set your mind to. I could do the tea," Fiona said hesitantly.

"No," Bain and Shiloh said in unison, an oddly identical tone and inflection coming from two men who, though related, could not be more different. Guiltily they glanced at each other then began mumbling things like, "No, really, Dr. Irons-Winslow—not necessary for you to stand over a hot fire—forget it Doc—Fiona's the empress of toasted cheese, remember?" and so on.

Cheney glared at them. "I'll do tea."

When everything was ready, Fiona finished making sure everything was on the table and began sidling toward the door. Bain called out, "Miss Keane, surely you aren't leaving us? I hadn't finished telling you all of Sweet's and my housekeeping woes yet."

Shiloh, who normally made Fiona somewhat nervous, went over to her, took her hand, made a mocking bow, and led her back to her stool. "Your Majesty, Empress of the Toasted Cheese, please do not deprive us of your royal presence. Besides, if you leave, the doc will make me clean up."

"Oh, Mr. Shiloh, you go on so," Fiona mumbled. But she did allow Shiloh to lead her to her seat. "You know I would have come back and cleaned up."

"I know," he agreed, sitting by her, "but you've done double duty tonight. My cousin and I will wash up so that you ladies may do your evening *toilette* and 'sleep, perchance to dream.' Or, like the doc, giggle."

"Wash up?" Bain repeated. "Do you mean clean up these dishes and things?"

"Yes, that's what I mean, Cousin. It's really very simple. I'll teach you. It shouldn't take any time at all for you to catch on."

"Couldn't I just go fetch Sweet instead?" Bain said plaintively. "He's good at that kind of thing."

"No, see, that's the point, Bain," Shiloh said very slowly, as if speaking a foreign language to a child. "*We* do it *instead* of the servants. I was speaking to Miss Keane in a sportive and breezy manner, in the vein of her being an empress, and so the frivolity just naturally came to be that the royal ladies will retire and we will do the washing up."

"I don't see the humor," Bain grumbled, "but I'm as big a man as you are, Locke, so if you can clean a kitchen, so can I."

Fiona looked very uncertain at this—Bain's irony was heavy indeed—but Cheney smiled. "It takes a man who has no doubt of his masculinity to clean a kitchen. My husband does it sometimes, and he does it very well. I'm certain, Cousin, that you, too, will prove to be very powerful in the kitchen."

"Humph. What about it, Miss Keane? Do you think I'll be a powerful masculine washer-upper?" Bain teased.

"Oh yes, Mr. Winslow, I think you're very, very powerful and masculine. . . ." Her voice trailed off.

Cheney thought she had seen Fiona blush before, but now her fair cheeks were so red she looked as if she had scarlet fever.

Bain grinned devilishly. "Why, thank you, Miss Keane. I would love to discuss this more with you later—"

"Bain," Shiloh said in a low growl of warning.

"—when my cousin is not here to interrupt us," Bain finished, eyeing Shiloh with icy amusement. Then, obviously to draw attention away from Fiona's embarrassment, Bain asked, "So, Locke, I assume you and your lovely lady-wife have finished the grisly task? How about giving us the first dispatch on Old Grider's condition? Besides the fact that he's dead, I mean. Pardon me, Miss Keane, for the indelicacy."

Fiona, whose head was still bent low over her cup of tea, recovered enough to murmur, "Oh, I've heard much, much worse in Dr. Cheney's house, Mr. Winslow."

"She sure has," Shiloh agreed. "Condition of employment: a strong stomach. Anyway, Bain, I don't think we're supposed to discuss the autopsy with anyone."

Bain said in a mock whisper, "Don't let him fool you, Miss Keane. They would tell you everything, down to the last blood droplet, if I weren't here. I'm a suspect, you see. They think that I did the old man in, to steal all the gold hidden underneath his mattress."

"Oh, surely not," Fiona said with distress. "Mr. Winslow could never do such a thing, Mr. Shiloh!"

"Oh, but he could," Shiloh said dryly. "Couldn't you, Bain?"

"Perhaps, if there were enough gold," Bain replied carelessly. "But in this case that certainly did not apply. There was not enough reward at all, not by a very very long margin."

Fiona may have been a young woman—she was nineteen years old—but she was very innocent, so she didn't catch the double meaning of Bain's words. Cheney did, but when she saw that Fiona was unaware, she decided not to make an issue of it and gave Shiloh a warning glance. "At any rate," she said quickly, "I'm afraid there is not very much to tell. Mr. Louis Grider was in fairly good condition for a man of his age and reported frail constitution."

"He was?" Bain said with honest surprise. "I understood he was a very sick man. I mean, that was the whole point, wasn't it? He was going to England for treatment of some serious condition and didn't intend to return, since we're all here at Sangria House and Old Grider obviously hoped Mrs. Buchanan would purchase the place."

Shiloh looked at him curiously. "You mean you really didn't know if he was so sick he thought he was going to die, or if he just wanted to live in England, or if he thought he was so sick he might never be able to stop the treatments?"

Now Bain was the one who spoke very slowly and clearly. "Locke, I have told you that I was not at all acquainted with the man. Not-at-all. I know next to nothing about him."

"Yeah, I know. You've said it about fifty times," Shiloh retorted. "But I thought you might have some idea, since you and Beckett and Carsten have spent some time with the family." He cast a quick glance at Fiona.

Bain shrugged. "Not really. All I knew was that Grider was going to a hydropathist in Bath. I can't blame the ladies for not wanting to go. Bath is a dead bore, I can tell you. It's full of old people and sick people taking the waters for their ailments. Tiresome."

"We had already heard that Mrs. Grider did not wish to leave St. Augustine," Cheney said, "but you said 'ladies.' You mean the sisters didn't want to go either?"

"I got the impression that Miss Phillipa did, but that neither Mrs. Raymond nor Miss Muriel wanted to go. But I don't know much more than that," Bain answered. "So you're really not going to tell us about the results of the examination, Dr. Irons-Winslow? I must say I'm extremely curious. Aren't you, Miss Keane?"

"I suppose so," Fiona admitted. "It's very hard not to be after finding him in our cellar and all."

Cheney said, "I'm sorry, but I couldn't tell you much even if I wanted to. Cause of death is still inconclusive. That is, I believe I know what caused his death, but I wasn't able to substantiate it. There's something . . . something . . . I know, I did know, I heard . . . but I've forgotten it and I just can't quite . . . grasp the connection. . . ."

She was staring very hard at Bain Winslow as her mind obviously tried to zero in on whatever it was she had forgotten. Though many men might have been uncomfortable under the circumstances, Bain was not the kind of man to be easily intimidated. He took a cautious sip of tea, which was still so hot it sent up a thin wisp of steam. "I didn't murder Old Grider, Dr. Irons-Winslow," he said. "That's not what you have forgotten."

Hastily Cheney said, "No, no, that's not it, I know, Bain. I don't believe you murdered Mr. Grider."

For a brief moment Bain's heavy-lidded languorous expression lightened with pleasure, both at Cheney using his given name and at her belief in his innocence. Then quickly his manner reverted to the old lazy cynicism. "Why, thank you, Cousin. Such a glowing recommendation. I'm positively embarrassed."

Cheney's intense gaze was still fixed on his face, though she obviously wasn't listening to him. "There's something—something you said, or did, that keeps trying to come up to the surface of my mind that has to do with Mr. Grider's death. I just can't put it together . . . no, no, I've lost it."

"Doc, you're tired," Shiloh said. "I know, because I'm tired. It has been one long hard day. Why don't you and Fiona go ahead? I meant it. Bain and I can mop this up."

Cheney nodded. "You're right. Maybe when I've rested, my mind will be clearer."

"Miss Wilcott, Mrs. Buchanan, and Mr. and Mrs. Duvall have agreed to join me and Beckett and Carsten for a picnic lunch down at the river tomorrow," Bain said, rising to hand up Fiona from her stool. He took her elbow to walk her to the door, and she looked so happy it seemed that she might simply take flight. "Would you join us, Cousins? And of course you too, Miss Keane. I thought I might bring Sweet. He would love to see you."

Fiona said nothing. Her gaze rested on Cheney with an expression of longing for a moment, and then she dropped her eyes.

"Sounds like fun," Shiloh said. "How 'bout it, Doc? Then tomorrow afternoon I'll take you into town to Duff's, and we'll finish the report and take it to Major Valentine."

"It does sound like fun," Cheney agreed. "And of course, Fiona, you may go. Thank you, Bain."

"You're welcome. Good night, Your Majesties."

———

Although the young gentlemen—Bain, Beckett, and Carsten—had decided to have a picnic and invite everyone from the Big House, it had been up to a woman, Victoria, to organize and plan the event, and of course it had been servants who did all the work. It took several trips with the cart, saddling horses, hitching up the brougham, and even then, the carriage was so crowded with Victoria, Minerva, Richard, and Irene that Cheney and Shiloh decided to walk with the dogs. It was almost a mile to the picnic spot, but Cheney was something of a tomboy, and she insisted that she would enjoy the exercise.

She was secretly glad to have an excuse to wear old comfortable boots, only one petticoat, and a skirt of walking length, which came only to the ankles. Victoria, Minerva, and Irene wore watering-place frocks. They had no train, the bustles were smaller than usual, and they had short sleeves, so they were less formal than other outfits. But still they were trimmed with flounces, ruffles, laces, embroidery, and other delicacies, and of course all three women correctly had all the accessories— shawls, hats, parasols, gloves, fans, reticules—that encumbered them so much they were virtually helpless.

With delight Cheney walked, sometimes ran, alongside the stuffy closed carriage, with only an old chip straw hat with a small brim, comfortably worn leather riding gauntlets—carrying no small purse, no fan, no parasol. She and Shiloh picked up sticks to throw for the dogs, who always chased them but seldom retrieved and returned them. Sean and Shannon were much given to running around in circles, silly wolfhound grins intact, rather than settling down to the serious business of retrieving sticks.

The picnic spot was a stand of four old gnarled live oaks, growing at four corners that formed such a perfect square it seemed as if they had been planted for the purpose. Underneath them the shade was so deep that no field grass or shrubs grew, only a deep carpet of moss. Here the muddy riverbank was narrow, with oaks and weeping willows growing right up to the soft-flowing water. The sun was brilliant, and in the warm still air hundreds of yellow butterflies floated.

"Oh, this is lovely," Irene exclaimed as Bain, Beckett, and Carsten lined up like courtiers, bowing, to hand the ladies down from the carriage. "A perfect day, a perfect place for a picnic."

Bain, on his best behavior, as people tended to be when they were around Richard and Irene Duvall, offered Irene his arm. "We are so very glad that you are well enough to join us, Mrs. Duvall. You only add to the grace and beauty of this place."

"You're very kind, sir," Irene said with composure and took his arm. Though there were pallets of thick quilts laid out for the younger people, Andrew Barentine had thoughtfully brought two of the chaises for Richard and Irene. The servants—Fiona, Sketes, Andrew and Hannah Barentine, and Bain's servant, Sweet—had set up the cart with all the food and supplies at one end of the grove. Bain had also brought a portable stove from his yacht, a large iron tub on a stand. Sweet had built a fire in it several hours earlier so that there was a very hot bed of coals to heat water for coffee and tea, and to keep Sketes's delicious fresh-made bread warm in a tin bread warmer.

Solange, Dart, and Alex, who, along with Lisette, had come down on an earlier trip with Hannah Barentine and Fiona, ran to meet them.

It was about eleven and already very warm. Dart and Alex ran to Shiloh, and Dart, a very precocious two-year-old, yanked on Shiloh's breeches and cried, "Unca Shiloh, Unca Shiloh, swim, swim, swim!"

Shiloh knelt down and hugged both of the boys; Alex Barentine was a little shy, but Dart swarmed all over him as if he were a tree to climb. "If Missy say? Missy say?" Dart insisted.

Since Dart was actually Devlin Buchanan's half-brother, Devlin and Victoria had decided to teach him to call her "Miss Victoria" and Dev, "Brother Dev." But, as children will, he had dubbed them with his own names. Devlin Buchanan was a reserved and distant man, but he had softened considerably when he and Victoria had adopted his half brother as a small, ill baby and had taken to calling Dart "Brother dear." And as the servants always called Dev "Dr. Buchanan," Dart had gotten mixed up and started calling Dev "Doctor Dear." "Miss Victoria" had proven to be a little too much, so Dart had shortened it to "Missy."

Now Shiloh answered, "If Missy says you can, and Alex, if your mama says you can, then I'll take you both swimming."

It took about half an hour for everyone to get sorted out. Beckett and Carsten decided to swim with Shiloh and the boys. Richard and Irene wandered along the riverbank for a slow, ambling walk. Hannah Barentine was just about to give Lisette a bottle, but Victoria decided she wanted to do it, so Victoria, Minerva, and Cheney settled down on a pallet with the baby and Solange. After talking to Sweet and Fiona for a while, stealing cookies out of a covered basket, which made Sketes slap his wrist and then make vigorous shooing motions, Bain came back and threw himself down on his side on the pallet with the ladies.

Cheney studied him with dry amusement. Two men more different than her husband and his cousin could not be imagined. Shiloh was tall and muscular with a good-natured, slow demeanor and was most at home in his faded denims, plain white shirt, old boots, and wide-brimmed cavalry hat. Bain Winslow was of average height and slim, with an intense catlike stare, but most of the time he affected a heavy-lidded languorous air. He always dressed in the very height of sharp fashion. Today he was wearing soft fitted buckskin breeches with English riding boots, a broadcloth waistcoat with a gold chain, a fine linen shirt with full sleeves, and a chocolate brown tie with a small pearl stickpin. He had relaxed enough to take off his coat, a dark brown suede riding jacket. He had worn a hat when he rode, but he disliked hats extremely—they mussed his perfectly coiffed thick curly brown hair—so he had taken it off and had commanded Fiona to fix his hair. Blushing but also giggling, Fiona had quickly fixed it again. Fiona was an extremely skilled hairdresser, and Bain was not at all embarrassed to have a woman dress it. "Sweet brushes it straight back, vigorously, as if he's cleaning a carpet," he had told her, which was what had made her relax enough to giggle.

Watching Cheney with a knowing air, conscious of her perusal, he announced in his perfect British English, "Sketes assaulted me. I came to beg protection from you ladies."

"We're afraid of her too," Minerva said. "We're not going to be able to help you at all, Mr. Winslow."

"Thou shalt not steal Sketes's cookies," Cheney said sternly.

"I've never known much about the Bible," Bain mused, "but I can't recall that one at all."

Solange was half hidden behind Victoria, but now she leaned up and whispered something to her.

"In English, darling," Victoria said gently. "Of course you may help me with Lisette." Victoria was holding the baby, giving her a bottle. She was a lovely chubby baby with dark, almost black, hair that was already glossy and curly. She had enormous dark blue eyes and an angelic complexion. Her half sister, Solange, however, was rather sallow, with mousy thin blond hair. She did have lovely eyes, however, dark, with dark thick lashes and perfect arched brows. "Come around here. Don't be shy," Victoria went on. "And you may give Lisette her bottle."

With a frightened-fawn glance at Bain, she inched around to sit in front of Victoria so that she could hold the bottle. "*Merci*—I mean, thank you, Missy."

Bain watched the two children with mild curiosity. Beckett and Carsten had told him that their sister had adopted two children, but they hadn't told him the entire story about Dr. Marcus Pettijohn and his wife, Manon Fortier. Now, with an uncharacteristic gentleness, he asked Solange, "*Alors, tu es française, Mademoiselle? Comment t'appelles tu?*"

Solange darted a cautious look up at Victoria, who smiled and said, "This is Mr. Bain Winslow, Solange. He is Mr. Shiloh's cousin. It's quite all right."

"He spoke French to me, Missy," she said in a low tone. "Do I—"

"When an adult asks you a question, you must answer respectfully and call him 'sir,' or if the person is a lady, 'ma'am.' If you are addressed in English, you must answer in English. But if the person speaks to you in French, then of course you may answer in French."

Solange nodded, turned to Bain, and looked up at him shyly. *"Je m'appelle Solange Fortier, Monsieur Winslow. Je suis très heureuse de vous rencontrer."*

"Mais non, c'est à moi, l'honneur, Mademoiselle Solange." A long conversation ensued, in which Solange asserted that she was French, that her sister Lisette was also French, that Missy and Doctor Dear had indeed been kind enough to adopt them, and that she was learning English and did not think that it was as pretty as French but that Missy had promised her a new blue dress with lace flounces if she learned enough English to recite Mr. Wordsworth's poem *She Dwelt Among the Untrodden Ways* at one of Missy's dinner parties.

"Ah, then we must certainly practice your English, Miss Solange," Bain said gravely. "For it is my considered opinion that you will look very pretty in a blue dress with lace flounces."

"I am not pretty like my sister Lisette, Sir Winslow," Solange said, matching Bain's gravity. "Or like my mother is pretty . . ." She frowned and then asked Victoria uncertainly, "That is not correct, is it? She is pretty . . . no, no I mean, she *was* pretty." She straightened her shoulders then turned back to Bain and said in a voice that was entirely too hard for her age, "My mother is dead, Sir Winslow. She *was* pretty."

"I'm very sure she was," Bain said, now uncomfortable. He was fully capable of having idle meaningless conversation with children, but his sincerity didn't extend to anything of substance. In fact, Bain Winslow was pretty much like that with everyone, child or adult.

"That's very good English, Solange," Victoria said. "You are doing so well in your lessons. I'm proud of you. You're very smart, you know. And you are not plain. You just have a different prettiness from your sister. There are many, many lovely women, and all of them have their own kind of beauty."

Solange listened to Victoria, rapt, and then said, "This is true, Missy. You and Miss Minerva are very, very beautiful, but so is Dr. Cheney, and she doesn't look anything like you."

"You see? Just like you and Lisette."

Solange nodded, looking down at her half sister and smoothing back her curls from her forehead. "I used to sing to her when I fed her. Shall I sing, Lisette?" She hummed a little introduction and then sang, *"Ombre légère qui suis mes pas . . ."*

Minerva, sitting by Cheney, leaned over and whispered, "She's been staying with me and Master Albini during my voice lessons. She's quite good."

Staring at Solange, Bain said, half to himself, "Good? The child has perfect pitch. Solange . . . Fortier? Is it possible? Her mother wasn't Manon Fortier, was she? The famous French mezzo-soprano?"

Solange turned abruptly. "Sir Winslow? *Vous avez connu ma mère?"* She still reverted to French when she was in a hurry.

Bain recovered from his surprise and made a bow that was no less courtly because he was lying on his side. "I was not so fortunate, Miss Solange. I was merely one of her many admiring fans, for I saw her in the Toulouse Grand Opera House when she sang Amastre in *Serse.* She had thirteen curtain calls, I believe, on the night I was there."

Solange smiled, and it transformed her solemn thin face with a child's delight. *"Mais oui, monsieur, Maman était la plus belle—"*

"English, please, Solange," Victoria said mildly.

Without losing a beat Solange continued, "—and was the greatest singer in Paris, or in the world, I think."

"Perhaps she was," Bain agreed. "She was surely the best mezzo-soprano I ever heard. Did you ever have the pleasure of seeing her, Mrs. Buchanan?"

"No, I didn't."

"She had the most powerful mezzo-soprano and contralto voice I've ever heard in a woman," Bain said thoughtfully. "And you understand that generally the lower-toned voices have a certain edge or roughness in tone that is difficult for a woman to polish completely? Not Manon. Her voice was like oil, like warm oil. Not sweet and syrupy like a soprano's. It was like deep velvet, with a dreamy quality that came through even in *opéra comique.*"

"She could sing lots of men's tenor parts too," Solange said eagerly, expertly taking the bottle out of Lisette's mouth and taking the corner of a handkerchief tucked into her blanket to clean her mouth and a little trickle of milk on her cheek. The baby blinked sleepily up at her and then grinned toothlessly. Solange went on, "She taught me Handel's *Largo* from *Serse. Ombra mai fù . . ."* she sang.

Bain, with a look of amusement, joined her in a tolerable tenor, while

Minerva sang the low tone up an octave, and Victoria, who was a fine soprano herself, joined too. The opera *Serse*, or Xerxes, opened with King Xerxes singing the slow, low song in praise of the shade of a plane tree. The music had become so famous in the years following the first performance of the opera in 1738 that it had become known simply as Handel's *Largo* and was still a popular drawing-room song that, because of its simplicity and low range, could be performed by even the least accomplished young ladies. Even Cheney, who had no musical talent whatsoever, hummed along. Evidently it was a powerful lullaby, for Lisette's eyelids drooped, drooped, and then closed.

Smiling, Cheney took off her gloves, then went to take Lisette from Victoria's arms and return her to her little cradle that was in the back of the cart so Hannah could watch her. Victoria was rather frail, and she had a hard time getting up when she was holding the baby. When Cheney returned, she sat back down and reached up to take off her hat, for the day was growing warmer, and even the small pool of dappled sunlight that shone down through the oak-leaf roof was very warm.

Victoria chided her, "Cheney, you shouldn't take off your hat. Where is your parasol?"

"I didn't bring one," she answered. "Don't fuss, Victoria. I've been tanned before and my husband didn't leave me. And to scandalize you even further, dear Victoria, I'm not going to put those gloves back on. They're hot."

"I'm not scandalized," Victoria said. "I'm accustomed to your ways, Cheney dear. And even if you do get as brown as a little wrinkled sultana and your hands turn into leather, I'll still be your best friend. I'm sure Shiloh will put up with it too."

"Somehow I doubt that my cousin will ever look like a dried-up old leathery woman—particularly after seeing her mother and how much Cheney takes after her," Bain said gallantly.

"Thank you, kind sir," Cheney said. "But I must admit I've never *ever* seen my mother out without hat, gloves, and parasol."

Bain's eyes dropped to Cheney's hands. In spite of the fact that she was a doctor, which meant that she was a working woman and wasn't as meticulous as most women of her class about wearing gloves and soaking her hands in warm cream for two hours every day, she had lovely white hands, with long slender supple fingers and nails with very white tips and pronounced white half-moon cuticles, a fairly rare trait that women particularly envied.

"I don't think you should worry, Cousin," Bain insisted. "You have lovely hands, and especially when that stunning ring graces them. As I've said, I long to see that jewel close up. Would it be terribly impudent for me to ask if I might look at it more closely?"

"Yes, it would be terribly impudent, but impudence I am accustomed to experiencing from the Winslow men," Cheney said with amusement, reaching to take the ring from her left hand. "But that's never stopped me from—oh!"

Bain jumped. "What happened? Did you hurt yourself, ma'am?" He pronounced it "mum" in the upper-class British manner.

"No, no! You said it, Bain, and now I remember!" Cheney said excitedly. "Where's Shiloh? We have to go to town, right now!" She jumped up, chattering, "Of course, swimming . . . over here, isn't it? We must go now. Excuse me, please, everyone." Whirling, she hurried off in the direction of the swimming hole.

Victoria called after her, "Cheney, where are you going? Back to the apothecary's? I didn't think that it was an emergency for you to finish that report."

"No, no, not the apothecary's, the jeweler's," Cheney called back over her shoulder.

Victoria, Minerva, and Bain all stared blankly at one another.

Finally Bain grinned with devilment and said, "I've often thought my cousin Locke was lucky to have married Dr. Duvall. But I must also admit—he's a courageous man."

CHAPTER EIGHTEEN

Poison Is Cold

"SO LEMME GET THIS STRAIGHT," Shiloh said, frowning heavily. "We had to go back to the Big House, I had to hitch up Caliph with your sidesaddle, you had to change into a riding outfit—faster than I thought any lady could change shoes, much less into a whole other costume—and we have to ride hard into town because there's an emergency. And now you're telling me it's a jewelry emergency? I figured the only lady who ever had to rush to a jeweler's in an emergency might be Victoria Buchanan."

Cheney answered, rather breathlessly partly because she had hurried so and partly because Caliph, a spirited black Arab, was trotting briskly. "It's not a jewelry emergency, silly. It's a . . . a . . . I just have to borrow a spectroscope, and the only person who might have one is that jeweler. You know, the one whose receipts were in Mr. Grider's desk. He was an assayer, a metallurgist, an appraiser, and a jewel merchant."

"So it's a spectroscope emergency?"

"No, it's not an emergency. I just—I mean, I'm just excited that I remembered—Oh, forget it, I'll explain later," Cheney said, spurring her horse to a fine gallop. Shiloh, on the big old saddle horse Tocoi, eventually caught up to her and said, "Okay, Doc, but I think we might hafta get Major Valentine to help us out. I doubt if any jeweler is gonna let you waltz in and take his . . . uh . . . stuff out of his store."

"It's not as if I'm stealing diamonds. I just want to borrow his spectroscope for a little while," Cheney argued.

"Uh-huh."

After a few moments, when the only sound was hooves hammering on the road and grunts of the hard-riding horses, Cheney muttered in irritation, "All right then. To Government House first."

Major Valentine was glad to see them, but his welcome faded into puzzlement when Cheney tried to explain what she wanted. "You're saying, Dr. Irons-Winslow, that you need a jeweler to help you finish the autopsy on Mr. Grider?"

"No, no," she said, making herself slow down and organize her thoughts. "There is a tool, a scientific apparatus called a spectroscope, that might help me determine Mr. Grider's cause of death. You know that I suspect he was poisoned, but I determined that he had no arsenic, no strychnine, no chloral hydrate, and no potassium chloride in his body."

"And so, I understand, you were not able to determine cause of death," Major Valentine said slowly.

"True. But I was able to determine manner of death, and he did have all the signs and symptoms of toxicity, so I still believe that Mr. Grider was poisoned. I have remembered another test, for another substance, that might be used as a poison. This test requires a spectroscope. Mr. Duff doesn't have one, but it is possible that a jeweler might, particularly if he is also a metallurgist."

"Ah, you're talking about Cathcart's," Major Valentine said, now leaning forward eagerly. "The sign says 'Metallurgist, Assayer, Appraiser, Precious Metals and Fine Jewelry.' Oh yes, now I remember some of Mrs. Grider's jewelry receipts from Cathcart's were in Mr. Grider's files."

"Exactly," Cheney said with relief. "Do you know Mr. Cathcart?"

"Not Mr. Cathcart, Mrs. Cathcart," Major Valentine said, standing to put on his hat and gauntlets. "And you're right, Shiloh, she would never let you two just barge in and use her microscopes and stuff."

"Told ya," Shiloh said to Cheney.

Ignoring him, Cheney asked, "So you'll go with us and explain to her, Major Valentine?"

"I will, and if necessary, I'll get a warrant for the . . . the . . ."

"Spectroscope," Cheney supplied.

"Spectroscope," he finished with satisfaction. "The widow Cathcart is a whole lot . . . er . . . stricter than Mr. Cathcart was, so I imagine there's going to be a user's fee somewhere along the line. I'll have to see to that anyway."

"So it's actually Mrs. Cathcart who's the assayer and metallurgist?" Shiloh asked curiously.

"She wasn't when the Cathcarts married about thirty years ago. But Mr. Cathcart used to say that she did everything he did just to show him how much better she could do it. And when you meet her, you'll see what he meant," Major Valentine said ruefully. "She's very crisp and businesslike, you might say. But yes, she is a certified assayer and studied metallurgy at the Atlanta Institute of Metallurgy and Mining. She's from Atlanta."

Cheney looked at her watch. "It's already noon. Will we have time to go to the jeweler's and then back to Mr. Duff's? I have to take the spectroscope to Mr. Duff's to perform the tests."

Major Valentine grinned, which made him look like a big sleepy bear. "Ma'am, this is a very small town. Cathcart Jewelers is just about four blocks from here, and it's only a couple of streets over from Duff's. We've got plenty of time. It's not like the big city, where it takes you all day to get from one place to another."

They went down to Bridge Street, and now that Cheney knew she was going to get her spectroscope, she actually enjoyed the short ride. St. Augustine did have an Old World air, and Cathcart Jewelers fit in very well. It was a small, discreet corner shop on a quiet street with respectable merchants and other offices such as surveyors and lawyers. Cathcart's had no vulgar window displays; their sign was hand painted in gold leaf on the glassed door.

As the three entered, a small silver bell tinkled with quiet music. Their footsteps made no sounds on a thick Persian carpet. On each side of the small rectangular room were long glass cases, with gas lamp fixtures attached to the tops of the cases to light the sparkling jewels displayed with an understated elegance on black velvet. Cheney was, perhaps, not the jewel lover that Victoria was, but she was a woman, and she was irresistibly drawn to the displays. They were different from any jeweler's she had ever seen. Rather than pieces of jewelry displayed in a sort of a catalogued manner—diamonds here, rubies there, sapphires in this row—certain spectacular pieces were placed as a centerpiece, with other smaller items surrounding them. The one that drew her, glittering in the center of the case on her right, was a necklace with intricately carved gold rectangles suspended on a heavy flat gold chain. The necklace had a look of the ancient world. Egyptian, perhaps. It was laid out on a raised circular piece; surrounding it, in a sort of glowing halo, was a perfect circle made of gold nuggets. It was as if a gifted artist, such as a sculptor, had designed the displays rather than a merchant.

A man came around from the back of the other case, rubbing his hands briskly. He was short, chubby, and cheerful looking. At first Cheney thought he was in his forties because he was bald on top; but as he neared she could see that he was much younger, perhaps only in his late twenties. He had apple cheeks and the huge fluffy sideburns made popular by the Union general Ambrose Burnside, though his namesake feature had somehow been turned around backward.

"Good afternoon, madam, gentlemen," he said happily. "Welcome to Cathcart's. I am Dexter Nebbins, at your service. How may I help you today?"

Major Valentine introduced himself and Cheney and Shiloh. "We are investigating the death of Mr. Louis Arthur Grider—"

Mr. Nebbins's cheery round face drained of all color, his pudgy hands stopped their gleeful rubbing, and he backed up a step. His mouth opened, closed, opened; his brown eyes grew round and alarmed. Cheney thought, with some amusement, that she had never seen such a perfect example of a guilty response; even two-year-old Dart Buchanan could better assume a look of innocence when he was in trouble.

"I-I never actually did anything illegal," Mr. Nebbins said in a strangled whisper. Lurching forward, with a haunted glance over his shoulder, he asked, "Is it necessary for Mrs. Cathcart to know? I mean, I . . . I never meant to harm anyone, General."

"Major," Major Valentine corrected him sternly. "Now look here, Mr. Nebbins, if you know something about Mr. Grider's death, you'd better just tell us now, or I'll have to take you to the Castillo for questioning."

The pudgy hands flew up in the air, and Mr. Nebbins bounced backward again with alarm. "His death? Oh, no, no, no, Mr.—General— Major, I wouldn't know anything at all about that! Oh, horrors, no. What I know—all I know—all I ever did was give her blank receipts. That's all. I didn't even cut the price of her purchases. I don't have any sort of authority to do that. My aunt would never allow it. She doesn't allow what she calls heathenish bazaar haggling. No, no. All I ever, ever did was just . . . just . . . omit the . . . uh . . . price of the goods on her copy of the receipt."

"Mrs. Grider's receipts, you mean," Major Valentine said carefully.

"Yes, yes. Mrs. Grider's receipts," Mr. Nebbins said, still whispering and glancing with haunted eyes over his shoulder. "On the shop's receipts I always put the true price, which, of course, Mrs. Grider always remitted. Always remitted promptly. And properly. Oh, no, no, no, I wouldn't do anything illegal."

"Mm-hmm," Major Valentine said sternly, and the little man visibly wilted. "Excuse us a moment, Mr. Nebbins." He drew Cheney and Shiloh aside and said in a low tone, "I must be a better interrogator than I thought. A confession already. What he's confessing to I dunno, but he sure is confessing."

With a stifled giggle Cheney said, "I believe I might help you out with that, Major. I think Mrs. Grider used her powers of persuasion to get Mr. Nebbins to give her blank receipts for the purchases she made. Then she could fill in the amounts—the prices she paid—herself, and I imagine she inflated them in order to give an accounting to her husband. She probably got a sort of allowance and accounted to him for the way she spent it."

"Ah, I see," Major Valentine said. "That way she could keep some extra cash for herself, hmm? But what about Mr. Nebbins here? Could that be construed as any sort of crime?"

"Oh, no, no, no," Shiloh said, his blue eyes gleaming. "Arrest Mr. Nebbins? How could you, General?"

Cheney poked Shiloh's side, and he mumbled, "Ow." Ignoring him, she said, "It doesn't sound as if he actually committed a crime, Major Valentine. He didn't even cheat his employer, as he obviously did charge a fair price to Mrs. Grider. Remember, Victoria did comment when she saw those receipts that it seemed Mrs. Grider had been paying too much for her jewelry."

"Yes, I remember now. All right, then, I suppose we'll leave Mr. Nebbins free to live his dangerous life of crime." He returned to the case, where Mr. Nebbins still cowered behind. "Very well, Mr. Nebbins. I and my colleagues don't see any need to question you at this time. However, you must be available for further questions if Judge Allard sees fit, sir."

"Oh, yes, yes, yes, of course," Mr. Nebbins said with vast relief. "But that's all I know about anything. About the Griders."

The major nodded curtly. "Very well. Now, what we would like to know is if Dr. Irons-Winslow may borrow Mrs. Cathcart's stereoscope—"

"Spectroscope," Cheney whispered loudly.

"Spectroscope, I mean," he corrected himself. "Is Mrs. Cathcart here?"

"She's gone to Atlanta to visit her sister, my mother. You see, Mrs. Cathcart is my aunt, and a wonderful woman she is, if I may say so. She'll be back next Monday," Mr. Nebbins blathered.

"I'm afraid that would be too late for our needs," Major Valentine said. "We need you, Mr. Nebbins, to make the spectroscope available to Dr. Irons-Winslow."

"But I-I couldn't possibly, oh, no, no—"

"Oh, yes, yes," Major Valentine said pleasantly. "Because I'm sure Mrs. Cathcart wouldn't wish to be bothered with all these complications about blank receipts and murder investigations. By the time she returns, the spectroscope will be returned, with a nice remuneration by the court for a usage fee."

"Oh! Oh! You should have said so in the first place," he said with vast relief. "Of course Mrs. Cathcart would be happy to allow Dr. Irons-Winslow to use the spectroscope for a reasonable fee."

A user's fee was agreed upon, Major Valentine wrote out the agreement, Shiloh and Cheney witnessed it, and Mr. Nebbins was happy because he knew his aunt would be happy. They left the shop with the spectroscope.

Shiloh shook his head as they mounted up. "Mrs. Grider sure tied poor ol' Nephew Nebbins up in knots, didn't she? Poor fellow. If there ever was an honest man, he sure is."

"How can you be so sure?" Cheney asked curiously. She envied Shiloh's insights into people, even people he had just met.

"'Cause it never even entered his mind to pocket the user's fee," Shiloh answered. "You could tell when Major Valentine started talking about it that he was only thinking about how his aunt would handle it."

"Right," Major Valentine agreed with satisfaction. "He didn't bite on the kickback. I hope poor old Dexter never meets up with a cardsharp who talks him into a nice friendly game of five card stud. He couldn't bluff a deaf blind man."

St. Augustine might have been an old sleepy village, but the traffic between Sangria Plantation and the town that day was enough to liven it up. First Cheney and Shiloh had left their riverside picnic to hurry off on their spectroscope emergency; then, after they had arrived at Duff's, Cheney sent Shiloh back to Sangria; he fetched Andrew Barentine, still at the picnic, to take him to Sangria Plantation winery to fetch their insect powder. Then Andrew returned to the picnic while Shiloh went back to Duff's. Not long after that, Shiloh and Major Valentine dashed into Sangria House, down to the cellar, laughing like two boys, clambered loudly back up the stairs, and rode off again before Minerva could even get her hair fixed to go intercept Major Valentine to invite him to dinner. So Victoria and Minerva sent Andrew back to Government House with a dinner invitation for Major Valentine, and he then returned. Finally, about seven that evening, Cheney, Shiloh, and Major Valentine once again rode down old King's Road to Sangria House just in time for dinner.

Cheney and Shiloh bathed and dressed while Major Valentine had tea with Richard and Irene in the parlor. Finally all the ladies were ready, and everyone settled down to enjoy the first course, another of Sketes's delicious creations, baked brie with paprika.

Victoria, cool and elegant in an airy mint green chiffon and diamonds, said, "We should begin with polite conversational niceties, but everyone here is so consumed by curiosity that I'm afraid I might have a mutiny on my hands, Major Valentine, if we don't hear Cheney's story immediately."

"Actually, I've only heard the end of the story, but I'd like to hear the middle," Major Valentine said. "But I do claim the story rights to Nephew Nebbins."

"Aw, no, no, no," Shiloh objected, his eyes blazing blue with laughter. "I wanted to tell about Dexter."

"Let Major Valentine tell," Minerva said, looking up at the major from beneath her eyelashes. Victoria, whose turn it was to be the hostess, had obligingly placed the major next to her. That afternoon Minerva had carelessly suggested that they invite Major Valentine for dinner, but when she had seen Victoria's polite but brief note of invitation, she had insisted on adding a rather effusive and flowery note of her own.

"Okay, since he's the guest," Shiloh grudgingly agreed.

His deep voice thick with amusement, Major Valentine told all about Dexter Nebbins and the receipts.

"I told you I thought the prices for her jewelry were too high," Victoria reminded them. "So after you three terrorized poor Mr. Nebbins, I assume he must have let you have the spectroscope."

"Yes, and it is a wonderful instrument—such quality workmanship," Cheney declared. "Although I finished with my testing this afternoon, Mr. Duff and I used it to analyze several more substances he had in stock in the apothecary, just for fun."

"Fun," Minerva repeated with disbelief. "Analyzing smelly old chemicals with a scientific apparatus is fun?"

"Well, it's not as exciting as a really thorough autopsy, of course," Cheney said enthusiastically. "But the science of spectroscopy is fascinating. You see, in the early part of the century, the German scientist Joseph von Fraunhofer observed that the continuous spectrum of light was marred by over seven hundred dark lines, which we now call, naturally, Fraunhofer lines. But it wasn't until just a few years ago that Kirchhoff and Bunsen, of Bunsen burner fame, bless him, invented a device . . ." Her voice trailed off as she noticed the blank gazes of the other diners. "Oh. I guess no one really cares about the history of spectroscopy. I beg your pardon. It's just that Mr. Duff and I did get a little carried away."

"When we left he was setting fire to his apron to see what was in it," Shiloh said conversationally. "So you can see that the doc's really kinda subdued. In comparison."

"The problem, Dr. Cheney," Minerva said kindly, "is that you're so smart no one ever knows what you're talking about. It's not your fault, really, and so we all excuse you when you're going on and on about things that the rest of us have no hint of what you're trying to tell us. Like about that Mr. Kerchief and Burner, none of us would understand anything about them and their apron."

Cheney blinked several times. "Thank you, Minerva . . . I think."

Richard, his brow furrowed, asked, "Pardon me? Shiloh? Did you say that Mr. Duff was setting his apron on fire?"

"I did," Shiloh confirmed, polishing off the last of his brie with satisfaction.

Cheney, after a small shake of her head to clear some of the confusion after Minerva's previous speech, said, "You see, a spectroscope, by vaporizing substances in a Bunsen burner—Oh, forget it. Using the spectroscope I found that Mr. Grider had been poisoned by thallium."

Cheney stopped for dramatic effect, and Victoria, unruffled as always, signaled Sketes for the second course, a creamy cauliflower soup. Then she said, "Regardless of what Minerva says, dearest Cheney, I am extremely curious how this came about with the spectroscope. One moment we're having a nice picnic, the next you're dragging Shiloh to town in search of a spectroscope."

"I know. I still haven't explained even to Shiloh, I've been so busy— All right, I've been so excited about the spectroscope," Cheney admitted. "This is how it happened. If you'll bear with me, it's truly not a long involved explanation.

"Thallium is a metallic element, discovered nine years ago by an

English scientist, Sir William Crookes. Using a spectroscope, he found a new bright green emission line when burning the dust of a sulfuric acid plant, and that's how he discovered this new metallic element, thallium. There was a comprehensive report published the next year about the discovery and possible new uses for this metal.

"But I had forgotten all this, you see. Then Bain—Mr. Winslow, our cousin," she explained to Major Valentine, "was talking about using a spectroscope to look at my ring, because spectroscopy is fast becoming the authoritative method of determining the authenticity of jewels." She held up her hand, moved it back and forth, and the ruby glowed darkly, mysteriously in the soft candlelight. "It kept nagging at me that Bain had said something that I needed to think about, to remember. Then this morning, when we were talking about my ring again, I remembered. So we went and got the spectroscope, and I found thallium in Mr. Grider's remains. It was odd really, because generally poisons concentrate most in the liver, but for some reason thallium showed up in the kidney tissue, and also, of course in the brain tissue samples."

Cheney abruptly cut short her lecture. Although her parents and Victoria and Minerva were staring at her with that particular glazed look they habitually got when Cheney, Dev, and Shiloh launched into medical discussions, Major Valentine's strong, tanned features had turned pale, and he was looking at Cheney as if she were a slimy bug in his soup.

"Oh, I beg your pardon, Major Valentine. I'm so accustomed to discussing medical topics with my family . . . and . . . they don't mind at all, you know," Cheney stammered with embarrassment.

"I do," Minerva said with a compassionate look up at Major Valentine. "I mind. But no one ever pays attention when I try to tell them how disgusting their globules and spleen spots are."

"No, no, Dr. Irons-Winslow, I didn't mind at all, I just . . . it was . . . I thought . . . I bit my tongue!" Major Valentine finished with sudden inspiration.

"Ahh," Cheney said, nodding. "Very painful indeed. And, Major Valentine, I suggest that you, along with Mr. Nebbins, stay away from the poker table. Anyway, to simplify—and edit—as the coroner pro hac vice, I determined that the cause of death was from thallium poisoning."

The table sobered somewhat. Irene said softly, "So it is certain that he was poisoned by thallium? Where would one get this poison?"

"In the study released about a year after Sir William Crookes found the metal, they were experimenting with some applications, and the report mentioned that they had already found that it was an effective insecticide. Then, sometime later—I don't exactly recall where, in what publication—I did read that a British company had begun producing a new insecticide with thallium as the effective ingredient. So I had Shiloh fetch the insecticide they use at the winery, and it is an English brand called Admiral Turner's Vermin Killer. Mr. Duff carries it, and Sangria Plantation buys it to use in the winery because there are so many insects drawn to the fruit syrup they add to the wine to make sangria, and this particular compound has proven to be very effective. And then"—Cheney glanced meaningfully at her mother—"I found that the substance in that tin of complexion powder in the Griders' closet was thallium, the same concentration of the powdered metal contained in the insecticide."

"Oh, dear, I was afraid of that," Irene said. "But how was it given to Mr. Grider, Cheney? Could you tell that?"

"Actually, I can," Cheney answered carefully, now mindful of Major Valentine's sensitivity. "That is part of a coroner's job, to determine the exact cause of death. In cases of poisoning, there is a fatal dosage, which is usually determined as the amount of the substance that will kill a healthy adult male. In cases of single fatal dosages that result in death, it is generally either accidental, as when a person drinks large amounts of raw whiskey, or it is deliberate, when a person commits suicide by taking a fatal dosage of poison.

"But in poisoning cases, there is also what is known as chronic poisoning, resulting in cumulative toxicity through fatal dosage. This, too, can be accidental, as when people are exposed to some toxic substance, such as lead, in contaminated water. But mostly, in cases such as Mr. Grider's, it is murder. The person has been given very small amounts of poison over a period of time, until the poison accumulates in their body to a fatal amount."

"And so you were able to determine that Mr. Grider had been poisoned in this way? Small amounts over a long period of time?" Minerva asked, impressed despite herself.

"Yes, I was," Cheney answered. "Mainly because of some very odd effects the poison had on his hair and eyebrows. His hair, in particular. It enabled me to estimate a timeline. I think that Mr. Grider had been given small doses of thallium, at irregular intervals, for approximately two months."

"And were you able to find out how it was given to him?" Minerva asked.

Cheney smiled at Shiloh. "With my husband's help, we figured it out. The thallium was ingested, so Mr. Grider had to get it through his food, water, drink, or any other substances he ingested, such as medicines. Shiloh pointed out that it would be very difficult to poison Mr. Grider's food, since his family lived with him and they customarily dined together."

"Of course," Victoria said, growing interested, "they eat as we eat; everyone eats the same dish. It would be almost impossible to poison the food without poisoning other members of the household."

"Exactly," Cheney said. "Also the water. Mrs. Espy also told Sketes that the family generally drank fresh fruit juices, as they are so readily available here. Every morning Mrs. Espy would prepare two pitchers of some sort of juice or punch for the family for the day. Poisoning these would inevitably poison someone else besides Mr. Grider."

"They didn't drink the wine?" Minerva asked with surprise. "They didn't drink their own sangria?"

"Nope. Mr. Grider didn't drink wine, at least not for pleasure, so he decided the ladies couldn't have it either," Shiloh said. "That's what Mr. Espy told me when we were talking about the wine cellar. But Mr. Espy said that sometimes, on special occasions, they would have a bottle of wine, like for Christmas and birthdays. But Mr. Grider did drink a small glass of wine every night. His very own concoction: Sangria de Becerra with a very small addition of sulfate salts. That was what Major Valentine and I came to fetch today, from the cellar—one of his bottles of tonic. The doc tested it, and it had a small amount of thallium in it."

"So you found this poison in Mrs. Grider's tin of complexion powder, in his wine . . ." Minerva said, troubled. "I can't believe it. Mrs. Grider? She's . . . she's . . . respectable! She comes from good family, the Dalrymples of Boston!"

Major Valentine finally spoke up. "It does seem very unlikely, ma'am. I suppose anyone could have planted that powder to make Mrs. Grider look suspicious. If you knew Mr. Grider's reputation, there are any number of people who might have liked to see him in the ground."

"Yeah," Shiloh murmured. His icy blue eyes narrowed as he stared into an unknowable space. "But not everyone who happens to dislike a man thinks he's vermin that needs killin'. Poison's cold, you know it? Poison is cold."

"You know what they say," Major Valentine said.

"I do," Victoria answered evenly. "They say that poison is a woman's weapon."

"Oh dear, you all do think it was one of the Grider ladies," Minerva said with real distress. "I just can't believe it. Surely it was someone else. One of these other men—persons—who had a grudge against Mr. Grider."

"Maybe," Shiloh said, "but there are only a few people that fit the M-O-M. Huh? You mean none of you know what the M-O-M is?"

"The mom?" Minerva ventured.

"Well, yeah, but it's also what the Pinkerton detectives call the murder code," Shiloh said, tilting his straight Roman nose up in the air. "You recall, m'dear, when we made the acquaintance of Max Townsend of Pinkerton's when we had that Central American adventure?"

"Oh yes, that adventure," Cheney said glumly. "Hurricanes, explosion, train wreck—"

"Snakes," Shiloh said with a grimace. "I hate snakes. They love me, though. Anyway, Max Townsend was a Pinkerton detective, and one night when we were playing, well, we were discussing the scientific investigation of crimes. And he said that what the Pinkerton men always look for in unsolved murders is M-O-M. Means-Opportunity-Motive."

"Means, opportunity, motive," Major Valentine repeated thoughtfully. "That makes sense. That makes a lot of sense."

"Especially with poisoning," Cheney said, holding a piece of the third course, a juicy roast beef, in midair and staring off into space. "That would narrow down the possible suspects considerably. In Mr. Grider's case, there might be dozens of people with motive, but only a few of them would have the opportunity."

"But anyone could buy Admiral Turner's Vermin Killer, surely," Minerva protested, "if Mr. Duff carries it."

"Yes, but there are only a few people that would have the opportunity to use it," Major Valentine said very gently to her. "To put it into his wine, Miss Wilcott."

"Ohh, dear, the poor Grider ladies again," she sighed.

"Well, I suppose the Espys too," Irene said. "It certainly seemed that they had motive."

"It would seem so," Major Valentine said, troubled. "I'm not looking forward to the interrogations I'm obliged to conduct. The Grider ladies are—well, they're ladies. And I hate to admit it, but I feel some sympathy with the Espys. That story about their daughter and grandson sounds pretty shabby to me." He frowned, and though Major Valentine was often like a big friendly boy, he could be forbidding, with his imposing size and his heavy features darkened fiercely.

"He tried, though," Minerva said in a small voice. "Mr. Grider tried to make it up to her. In his will, remember."

"Maybe," the major growled. "But I don't think you can make up for being dishonorable."

"Perhaps not, Major Valentine," Irene said, "but then I do think your standard is very high. At any rate, Mr. Grider did not deserve to be poisoned, no matter what his faults."

Major Valentine's stormy dark eyes lightened as he regarded Irene. "You're right, ma'am. Tell me, Colonel Duvall, Mrs. Duvall, would you consider going with me to speak with the Grider sisters and Mrs. Grider? I don't feel quite comfortable interrogating ladies of good repute, particularly when I don't strongly suspect them."

"You don't? You think it was the Espys?" Shiloh asked sharply.

Major Valentine frowned. "I just don't know, Shiloh. I hope I'll know more after I talk to the suspects. What about you, Shiloh? Do you think the Espys are innocent?"

Shiloh sighed deeply. "Aw, I dunno either, Major."

"Then what about this: do you think it's likely that if the Grider ladies are guilty, they would have conspired among themselves to poison him? All of them, or any two of them?" Major Valentine asked.

Shiloh thought for several long moments before answering. "No. No, I don't. Like I said, poisoning is a cold, secret way of killing. It doesn't strike me as the kind of weapon a conspiracy would choose. It's more . . . personal."

"That's what I think too," Major Valentine said, frowning. "And that's why I hoped Colonel and Mrs. Duvall would go with me to talk to the ladies. If one of them does happen to be guilty, chances are there are three other innocent ladies of good repute that I will be obliged to ask very personal, and probably very intrusive and rude questions. I think, Colonel Duvall, that you and Miss Irene would help to give the ladies—the innocent ones—a sense of comfort and dignity."

Richard and Irene glanced at each other, and with the easy communication that comes from living together and loving each other for many years, they both nodded assent at once. "We'll be glad to come, Major Valentine, if you think we can be of assistance," Richard said.

"Besides," Irene said with a hint of devilment in her green eyes, "I always wanted to interrogate a murder suspect. Perhaps I shall get her to confess."

Richard sighed deeply. "I could never lie to Irene, that's for sure. Never even tried. I was afraid I'd burst into flames or a great bolt of lightning would hit me."

"I could never lie to her either when I was a child," Cheney mused. "She can just look at you, and you know she knows the truth, so you sort of curl up and whimper."

"Nonsense," Irene scoffed. "You tried. It's just that you were such an abysmal liar when you were small, dear."

"No, it's you, Mother," Cheney said with affection. "You're such a lady that it affects everyone. They can't look you in the eye and say an untruth."

"Then I'd better not take you to Cathcart's, Miss Irene," Major Valentine said, now with a grin. "Because Dexter Nebbins would probably confess to every death that's occurred since the day he was born."

CHAPTER NINETEEN

The Essence of the Thing

"THANK YOU FOR RECEIVING us, ladies," Major Valentine said solemnly. "I know that this is a difficult time for you. First let me express to you all my sincerest sympathy for your loss."

He looked huge and, truth to tell, intimidating in Mrs. Fatio's homey sitting room. The three sisters, Aimee Grider, and Irene sat down while Major Valentine and Richard stood on either side of the mantel. Though it was only ten o'clock in the morning, it was already very warm, so there was no fire, but the grate had been cleaned and oak logs were already laid for the next cool evening. A breeze stirred the delicate lace curtains, wafting the briny scent of the sea into the room.

As before, Aimee Grider took the role of hostess. Seating herself in one of the wing chairs, her back arrow straight, she looked up at Major Valentine. Her demeanor and expression were proper, even prim, but her voice had a raw edge. "Somehow I think this isn't simply a condolence call, Major."

"No, ma'am, it isn't." He had brought a leather satchel and now laid it on the mantel. Taking a piece of paper out of it and unfolding it with a crisp rustle, he looked around at the ladies. "Yesterday Dr. Irons-Winslow completed her postmortem examination and gave me the final report on Mr. Grider's death. I'd like to read the summary to you." Clearing his throat, he read in an expressionless tone. "'Item: Mechanism of death: Fatal termination of respiratory processes effected by cerebellar tonsil herniation through the foramen magnum secondary to central herniation.'" He glanced up. Aimee Grider looked much the same as before—severe and dignified—but Mrs. Raymond, Muriel Grider, and

Phillipa Grider all looked utterly mystified.

Calmly Irene said, "It is rather indelicate, I know, but I'm sure you all wish to know how Mr. Grider died. My daughter explained it to me. This means that Mr. Grider's brain swelled until such damage was done that he simply stopped breathing."

No sound in the room except for a tremulous sigh from Phillipa Grider.

After a few moments Major Valentine went on, "'Item: Cause of death: Chronic thallium poisoning, resulting in cumulative toxicity through fatal dosage. Item: Manner of death: Homicide.'"

Now a sort of low tremor sounded in the room. Mrs. Raymond drew in a sharp rasping breath, Muriel Grider gasped, then murmured, "Oh no," and Phillipa Grider gave a low throaty moan and bowed her head. Aimee Grider stiffened, her lips pressed together in a sharp line and her thin nostrils flared until they were bloodless white. But she made no sound.

Major Valentine refolded the paper and tucked it back into the satchel. Clasping his hands behind his back, he said, "I would like to speak to each of you ladies separately. Mrs. Raymond, Miss Grider, Miss Grider, if you would excuse us, I'll speak with Mrs. Grider first."

Muriel and Phillipa looked confused, but Mrs. Raymond said in a sharp indignant voice, "You want to question us? About Louis's death? That's why you're here?"

Major Valentine met her hostile gaze squarely. "Yes, ma'am."

"But—No, I won't allow it," Mrs. Raymond said, her voice growing shrill. "I won't! It's absurd!"

"Mrs. Raymond, I would like to ask you and the other ladies some questions," Major Valentine said with no trace of emotion. "I would like to do that here, now. But if you refuse to cooperate, I'm afraid I would be obliged to conduct formal interrogations at the Castillo, and I don't think any of you would want to go through that if it's not necessary."

"No, I can't. I can't," Phillipa groaned, her eyes filling with tears.

Ignoring her, Aimee turned to the sofa, where the sisters sat, and bit off the words, "Letitia, you and Muriel take Phillipa down to my room and give her a brandy to calm her. I'll come get you when I'm finished here."

The older sister looked stormy. "But, Aimee, they—" Abruptly she cut off her words at a savage glance from Aimee Grider. Then Letitia shot up off the sofa, jerked around to stare at her sisters, and grated, "Come along. Let's just get this shameful business over with. Phillipa, please, try to collect yourself." Muriel, her dignified features pale and drawn, took Phillipa's arm and the three sisters left the room. Letitia marched out, her heels clattering hard on the wooden floor, her look at Major Valentine venomous. Neither Muriel nor Phillipa looked up at all.

Aimee Grider had not moved. Her hands were folded gracefully in her lap. In her plain black satin dress she looked even more enigmatic, a younger Mona Lisa.

Major Valentine had decided that to be as plain, simple, and straightforward as he could be was the best plan. And Richard and Irene Duvall had agreed, for his honesty was so apparent that an innocent person could feel no fear of him, and a guilty person could hardly hope to face down such rock-solid integrity.

Irene noted that Aimee Grider certainly showed no fear, but then again, Aimee Grider rarely showed any true emotion at all. She looked up at Major Valentine, apparently simply waiting to answer his questions. Irene did note that Aimee had paid no attention whatsoever to Richard. With arid amusement she reflected that Aimee had no use for Richard now; only Major Micah Valentine was important.

"Mrs. Grider, do you have keys to the wine cellar?" he asked pleasantly.

She blinked several times, the only sign of surprise. "No, I don't. As far as I know, there is only one key, and my husband has it. Had it."

Major Valentine nodded. "So when anyone wanted to go down to the cellar, they had to ask your husband to unlock the door? The inside door?"

"I suppose so. I don't really know. I never went down there."

"Never?"

"I went down in the cellar when I first arrived at Sangria House, when Louis and I first married and he was showing me the house," she explained, her tone cool. "That's the only time I've been down there."

"I see. Mrs. Grider, do you know where Mr. Grider put all the cash that he withdrew from the bank?"

"What? No!" It was the first time her voice betrayed any strain; she sounded angry, but it wasn't a heated anger, rather more an intense irritation, as when one is unpleasantly surprised.

"Did you know that he was taking all of his money out of the bank during January and February?"

"No, I did not. My husband rarely discussed his business dealings with me."

"This evidently had nothing to do with his business, ma'am. We believe he did it because he knew someone was poisoning him and he wanted to hide his money, thereby delaying the probation of the will in the hope that his death would be thoroughly investigated." Major Valentine spoke in an even and distant tone, as if he were reading a boring paragraph in a dull book.

Aimee Grider stared up at him, for he still stood by the fireplace. Her dark eyes met his gaze unflinching. There was a long heavy silence. Aimee didn't drop her eyes.

Major Valentine turned and reached back into his satchel. "Is this yours, Mrs. Grider?" He pulled out the tin of complexion powder that Irene and Mallow had found in the top of the closet.

Her eyes narrowed for the merest instant, and then her brow smoothed out. "I don't know. That is the type of powder that I use, but I have no way of knowing if that particular tin belongs to me or not."

"It was found in your house."

"But I have my own cosmetics here, including my tin of powder. I wouldn't have left my powder at home," she argued.

Major Valentine nodded, then carefully set the tin on the mantel. He turned back to her and asked, "Did you poison your husband, Mrs. Grider?"

"I did not." The answer was brusque and quick.

"Do you know who did?"

"No."

"Do you know why anyone would want to kill your husband?"

She opened her mouth, closed it, spent a few seconds in thought, and then said, "I have no idea."

"No?" Major Valentine said, with evident surprise. "Did you know about Dolores and Timothy Espy?"

She looked startled then but recovered in an instant and resumed her former complacent pose. "No, I didn't. But that all happened years ago, long before I met Louis. It certainly would not have given me a reason to kill him."

"But he left Sangria House and Plantation to them," Major Valentine said. "Surely that makes you angry."

"I don't care about Sangria," Aimee shot back. "I don't want that house or the plantation. And even if it did make me angry, Major Valentine, I didn't know about them until after my husband was already dead. I had never heard their names until the reading of the will."

"But you were angry with him for some reason, ma'am," Major Valentine said, now curt. "You left him. You left him on the Saturday before you were scheduled to sail to England with him. But he died the next night."

"I didn't kill him," she said, matching the major's curtness.

"Why did you leave him?" he shot back at her.

"Because I had decided I didn't want to go to England. We argued, and I left."

"Why did you decide not to go to England?"

"I had—" Abruptly she stopped, and her dark eyes cut to Irene Duvall. "So that's why you're here. To offer Christian comfort to the scarlet woman? To pray for the murderess's evil soul?"

"If you would like me to, Mrs. Grider, I would be glad to pray with you," Irene said quietly. "But that's not why I'm here. My husband and I are here because Major Valentine asked us to come, because he knew it would be difficult for you to talk to a stranger."

She laughed, a harsh rasping short noise. "Don't you think you should have told them, Mrs. Duvall, that women would be much less likely to confess anything to another woman?"

"No, I would not tell them that, because I don't think it's true of all women," Irene said. "I think most women would rather talk to another woman."

For the first time Aimee Grider looked honestly surprised. But, as before, she quickly regained her bland expression and said, "Personally, I have always found men to be more amiable companions and confidants. But, as I have nothing to confide, it's beside the point in this situation."

"Mrs. Grider, you haven't answered my question," Major Valentine said sternly. "Why did you decide not to go to England with your husband?"

She looked back at him and narrowed her eyes. Finally, in a low tense murmur, she said, "You, Major Valentine, already know the answer to that question. As do you, Colonel Duvall, and you too, Mrs. Duvall. So I am going to refuse to give you any further information, sir." She rose, and two ragged red patches showed high on her smooth ivory cheeks. "If you have any more questions for me, you are going to have to either arrest me or have Judge Allard issue a subpoena." With that she swept out of the room.

The three looked at each other. Richard, whose hip was starting to bother him, sat down in the chair next to Irene's. Major Valentine started to say something, but then Letitia Raymond came into the room. She was an imperious woman, and she still looked angry. She went to the wing chair all the way across the room, where Aimee had been, and sat down with a jerky, graceless motion. The corners of her mouth were turned down, and her eyes flashed.

"I didn't kill my brother," she said tightly. "Any other questions?"

Major Valentine looked faintly amused. "Yes, ma'am, I'm afraid so.

Where did Mr. Grider hide all of his money?"

The major's abrupt changing of the subject threw Mrs. Raymond more off guard than it had Aimee Grider. "What? Where did he—I don't know! How should I know?"

"Because you know more about his business than anyone else," Major Valentine answered mildly. "You took care of the house and the plantation when he was ill."

"Yes, and I was good at it too."

"So I understand. So you must have known that he was withdrawing large sums of money from the bank in January and February."

She dropped her gaze to her hands. She held a white handkerchief, but she didn't fidget; she merely smoothed it out over her black bombazine skirt. "Yes, I saw him one day. He came in from town and went into the library. I needed to ask him something, so I just went in. He had closed the door but not locked it. He . . . he had a bag, and he was taking money out of it. Bills, stacks of them."

"Did you ask him what he was doing with such large sums of cash?" Major Valentine asked.

She looked up at him with impatience. "Ask him? Ask Louis anything? No one ever questioned Louis, Major Valentine. He just told me to leave him, and so I did. I never mentioned it to him."

Major Valentine picked up the tin and lowered it down so that it was on Letitia's eye level. "Is this yours, ma'am?"

"What? Why, no. That's the powder that Aimee uses. We can't afford it," she said. "Our allowance is nowhere near as generous as Aimee's."

Major Valentine set the tin of powder back on the mantel. "That's not the case now, is it? You will have a generous settlement from your brother's will."

She snorted. "If that ridiculous document can ever be probated and the estate settled."

"Of course. Mrs. Raymond, why did you go down to the cellar of Sangria House on the day of Mr. Grider's funeral?"

Her eyes widened, and quickly she looked away, out the window and then back at him. "I was going to look in the storage cupboard down there and see if Louis had put the money in it."

"If you had found this money, I'm sure you would have told the probate judge so that it would have been included in the assets of the estate."

"Of course," she said, glancing up at a point just beyond Major Valentine's ear.

"You have keys to the cellar, don't you? Why didn't you just check to see if the money was down there while you were still at Sangria House?"

She looked surprised, then confused. "Keys? I don't have keys to the cellar. No one has keys except Louis. I could never get down there before, so when I saw the door was open, I—"

"Just thought you would check," Major Valentine finished for her. "So the estate could be settled quicker."

She frowned and looked down again at the square of white on her skirt. With long strong fingers she smoothed it again, though the fine linen showed no wrinkle. It was a plain square, with no lace border. Letitia Raymond was not a lace handkerchief kind of woman.

"Are you acquainted with Dolores Espy?" Major Valentine asked.

"I was," she answered darkly. "She used to work at Sangria House. Jerome and Florence told us she had gone to Jacksonville to work. I haven't seen her for years."

"And her son? Timothy Espy? Did you know about him?"

"No, and I still don't know anything about him except that my brother must have been insane to leave Sangria House and Plantation to them," she said with clear distaste. "She's a housemaid! She can't possibly hope to be able to manage a house like Sangria, much less a complex business like Sangria Plantation and Winery."

"You should have had them, Mrs. Raymond?" Major Valentine asked.

"Of course I should have them! After all these years and all I've done for that business, it only makes sense that Louis should have left them to me!" she almost shouted.

"But he was trying to sell out," Major Valentine said softly. "He was going to sell Sangria and move to England. Why weren't you going to England with your brother, ma'am?"

"We had planned to," she said, ducking her head and muttering. "But Louis decided that he didn't want us to go, so he sent us here."

"Did you want to go?"

She hesitated a moment, then burst out, "Of course I didn't want to go! I tried to tell him that there was no need to lease Sangria House, that I could manage the house and the plantation very well until he was well enough to return."

"But he did lease Sangria House, and he did decide not to take you with him but to leave you here," Major Valentine said calmly. "And then he died, and the only will you knew about was the former one. In that will he did leave Sangria Plantation to you, Mrs. Raymond."

"I know that, and I still can hardly believe he would ever do something so foolish as to leave it to that girl!" she said, her severe, sculpted cheekbones coloring scarlet.

"No, you didn't know that. Did you poison your brother, Mrs. Raymond? So that you could have Sangria House and Plantation for yourself?"

"No, no! I didn't. I never would have hurt Louis! How can you say such a thing? How can you even think such a thing?" she demanded angrily. "I did not kill my brother!"

"Do you know who did?"

"No! I know nothing about it!"

"Do you know anyone who might have had a reason to kill Mr. Grider?"

"No, of course not!"

"Mrs. Raymond," Major Valentine said, "it appears to me that you had more reason to wish Mr. Grider out of the way than anyone."

She pulled herself upright, her back stiff, her eyes glinting. "I don't care what you think, sir. I did not kill my brother." Her burning gaze went to Irene Duvall, who was watching and listening with quiet sympathy. "I'm surprised at you, Mrs. Duvall, obviously a well-bred lady, condoning this scandalous interrogation of ladies of good reputation and family! Why do you lower yourself to be a part of this?"

"I don't consider it lowering myself at all," Irene answered. "If it had been my brother, I would want any help I could get to find out who poisoned him."

Mrs. Raymond recoiled as if Irene had threatened to strike her. "I . . . I know I seem unfeeling," she said in a raw tone. "My brother and I were not what one would call close. But I am sorry he's dead, and I—It's a shock, you know. To find out he was . . . murdered. Perhaps my reactions are—I'm not quite myself, you see."

"I understand, Mrs. Raymond," Major Valentine said. "I think that will be all for now. If you would ask Miss Muriel to come in, I would appreciate it."

"Yes, yes." She seemed disoriented for a moment, and then she rose and left the room. Her step was not nearly as hard and deliberate as before.

Miss Muriel Grider came to the door and hesitated. She was wearing black too, of course, since the family was in mourning. She looked as if she had been weeping. Her face was softer, less severe than Letitia's, and she had a sort of delicacy of feature that made her look younger and warmer than her older half sister. She did strongly resemble Letitia, however, which proved that they, as Louis, had taken after their father.

"Please come in and sit down, Miss Grider," Major Valentine said pleasantly.

Muriel Grider was nervous. She sat on the very edge of the chair, the same chair in the corner that was set apart from the rest of the room. The women were trying to distance themselves from Major Valentine and the Duvalls as much as possible. But Muriel Grider seemed to find some reassurance that Irene was there; Muriel's eyes often came to rest thoughtfully on her.

Major Valentine began his questions and got basically the same answers he had gotten from Aimee and Letitia: no, Muriel did not have keys; yes, she had known Dolores Espy when she worked at Sangria House but had not seen her since then; no, she knew nothing of Timothy Espy; and yes, this latest will of Louis Grider's had been a shock to her.

"By the way, Miss Grider, is this yours?" he asked innocently, displaying the powder tin.

"That? Why, no. That's not the powder I use. That's the kind Aimee uses—expensive and imported," she said with ill humor. "I can't afford cosmetics of that quality. Whatever are you doing with that?"

"I just had some questions about it, ma'am. Now, I understand that you never wanted to go to England, and finally you just decided that you would not," the major said. "Why was that?"

Muriel bit her lower lip, and her hands twisted nervously in her lap. "I have personal reasons for wanting to remain in St. Augustine," she finally answered.

He nodded. "One of those reasons is your betrothal to Mr. Henry Pendergast?"

Her eyes opened wide with shock. "How did you know about that? He never told you!"

"No, he didn't. But that is why you didn't want to leave St. Augustine, was it not, Miss Grider?"

"I—yes, I suppose." She stopped, swallowed hard, and then answered simply, "Yes. I wanted to stay here because Mr. Pendergast and I have . . . an understanding."

"But this relationship, this understanding, you and Mr. Pendergast kept from your brother, didn't you?" he asked. "It was a secret engagement."

"Ye-es, I suppose so," she hedged.

"You didn't want Mr. Grider to know because you thought he might disapprove?"

"I believed he would, and so did Henry. My brother was very strict about such things," she said in a tense voice.

"Yes, I believe he interfered with one of your previous suitors, didn't he? In fact, didn't your brother forbid you to see this man, and didn't he tell this man never to see you again?"

"Yes, but that was—that was long ago, when I was much younger. The gentleman in question—it turned out my brother was right. He was not suitable," she said, dropping her head and twisting her delicate fingers.

"In fact, he stopped seeing you after your brother threatened to cut you off without a settlement, or an allowance."

Her head snapped up. "Yes, yes! But that was years ago!"

Major Valentine said very softly, "I know, but isn't that the same reason you kept your relationship with Henry Pendergast a secret from your brother? Because you thought he might cut you off again, with nothing?"

"We decided—It was so ... difficult—my brother was so stubborn ..." she stammered. "It's all because of that awful Walter Raymond that Letitia married! He wasted all of Letitia's money, and my brother never forgave her, and he would never let any gentlemen pay their addresses to me or Phillipa after that! It was awful the way he treated us!"

"So did you poison him, Miss Grider?"

"What? No! No, I couldn't. I wouldn't!" She turned her stricken face to Irene Duvall. "Mrs. Duvall, I know we are barely acquainted, but you seem to be a gentle and sympathetic woman; can't you tell him that I couldn't do such a thing?"

"But someone did, Miss Grider," Irene said. "Someone poisoned your brother over a period of two months. It was done, and Major Valentine must find out who did this terrible thing."

"But it wasn't me! I'm innocent!" she said and then bowed her head with despair. She did not cry, but she seemed truly exhausted.

Major Valentine studied her bowed shoulders, her twisted hands. After a few moments he said, "Very well, Miss Grider, that's all for now. Please ask Miss Phillipa to come in."

Without another word or backward look Muriel hurried out of the room.

Again the three glanced at each other, and Irene whispered, "We'll help you note all of this afterward, Major Valentine."

"Thank you, ma'am. It's been more complicated than I—Hello, Miss Phillipa. Please, come in and sit down."

Phillipa came in, stopped in the middle of the room, looked around as if she were lost, then went and sat on the sofa, near Major Valentine. She would have had to crane her neck up to her right to look at him, but she was right across from Richard and Irene, and she looked at them with tear-swollen eyes. Irene noticed that, as on the day she had come to Sangria House, Phillipa was slightly disheveled; the black string tie of her gray blouse was half untied, her hair was wispy, the coiffure coming loose, and the toes of her black shoes were very dusty. Again she tortured a white handkerchief in her hands, twisting it and fidgeting with it until it was just a wrinkled soggy ball.

To their surprise, in contrast to the other ladies who had simply waited for the questioning to begin, Phillipa blurted out, "Major Valentine, how did you say my brother was killed?"

"He was poisoned, ma'am."

"By what? What was it?" she demanded.

"Thallium, ma'am."

"Thallium? What is that?"

"It is an insecticide and vermin killer," he said, watching her closely.

"But—how could—wait. Is it the insecticide that they use at the winery?" she asked suddenly.

"Yes, it is."

"Then—couldn't it have been an accident? Louis did go to the winery occasionally. Couldn't he have just . . . breathed some in? Accidentally?" she asked in a pleading voice.

Major Valentine shook his head. "No, ma'am, that is not how Mr. Grider was poisoned. Now, Miss Grider, could you please tell me if you had keys to the cellar?"

This conversation was very odd because Major Valentine was behind Miss Grider's right shoulder, and though they were having a dialogue, her sorrowful gaze went back and forth to Richard and Irene Duvall, and then she would drop her head and twist her handkerchief. Now she looked up at the wall above Irene's head.

"What? Keys to the cellar? No, no. I've never had keys to the cellar. Only Louis has the keys."

"What about when Mr. Grider was ill?" Major Valentine asked her. "Didn't he give you his keys so that you and your sisters could attend to things when he was bedridden?"

Now she dropped her head, and her voice was muffled. "No, he didn't give his keys to anyone. He was very rarely so ill that he didn't get up in the morning and open the library and unlock the file drawers in his desk. And then he would lock them back up when Letitia had finished for the day."

"I see. What about his tonic, ma'am? His bottles of tonic down in the wine cellar. Didn't you fetch them for him when he was ill?"

"No. He went down to the cellar himself, got his tonic, and then brought it upstairs. He only took a very small glass once a day, at night. He never left the bottle upstairs."

"So Mr. Grider never gave you his keys when he was too ill to attend to these things," Major Valentine asked her again.

"No, never. Louis was extremely organized, and he had his routines. He didn't like to upset his routines."

"It must have been hard for him, then, to have to sell Sangria House and Plantation and move to England."

"Oh, it was! He was so ill, you know, and he needed special care. That's the only reason Louis would ever have turned his life upside down in such a manner," she said passionately.

"But there's one thing I don't understand," Major Valentine said. "You were his nurse for years, and as you said, he obviously needed a lot of special care. Why didn't he want you to go to England with him?"

Phillipa's face crumpled and tears welled up in her eyes. "They-they turned him against me! They lied to Louis about me! I didn't take his money. I would never take his money!"

"Who lied about you, Miss Grider?" Major Valentine asked.

"Letitia, and then Aimee! They—some money disappeared from the household money that Louis kept in his desk. But I didn't take it! It must have been Letitia, or Aimee, or even those Espys, but Letitia said I must have taken it, and Aimee agreed," she said, distraught. "Why not Muriel? Miss Perfect sneaking around with Louis's lawyer? He would have come closer to knowing about the money than I ever would!"

The tears rolled down her face, and she bent her head to wipe her eyes and nose.

"So you didn't take Mr. Grider's money," Major Valentine said. "I believe you, Miss Grider."

Her head shot up, and she craned to look over her shoulder. "You do?"

"I do."

She turned to Irene. "You believe me too, don't you, Mrs. Duvall?"

"As a matter of fact, I do," Irene said thoughtfully.

"Good, good," she mumbled and then twisted awkwardly around to look up at the major again. "Is that Aimee's complexion powder there?

Whyever would you have Aimee's complexion powder?"

"How do you know it's hers?" Major Valentine asked.

"You have some strange woman's complexion powder?" Miss Phillipa asked with what appeared to be true bewilderment.

"It's—Never mind that now, Miss Grider. I need to ask you a few more questions." Major Valentine clasped his hands behind his back and frowned. Then he repeated in an echo of her previous disapproving tone, "'Those Espys.' What about them, Miss Grider? Did you know of Dolores and Timothy Espy?"

"Know of them? I knew Dolores when she was at Sangria House. Is that what you mean?" she asked, looking blankly up at the wall above Irene's head again.

"No. I mean, did you know of her and her son inheriting the estate from your brother?"

"No, of course not. He had always just sort of . . . implied . . . that Aimee and I and my sisters would inherit everything. It was quite a shock."

"You were shocked at your brother's last will and testament?"

"Yes, very."

"What about the money? Do you know where your brother hid all of his money?"

"I? Know about his money? Of course not. If he thought I would steal household money from him, he surely wouldn't let me know anything about his fortune," she said nervously.

"Were you shocked at your brother's death?"

"Why . . . yes, of course. He . . . had health problems, but he had been doing well for a while, so yes, I was shocked at his death."

"Oh? Were you, Miss Grider? Did you poison your brother, Miss Grider?" Major Valentine asked in a hard voice.

"Did I—did I—? No, no!" she said in a strangled voice. Then she pitched forward, buried her face in her skirt, and began to sob.

Major Valentine and the Duvalls came slowly down the stairs to the vestibule of Fatio House. As it was now just after noon, on their left across the passage they could see that the dining room was filling up. Mrs. Fatio had the reputation of serving the best food in St. Augustine in her café. The men were hungry, but ladies such as Irene simply didn't dine in public, so neither Richard nor Major Valentine mentioned it. Richard asked, "Would you like to sit in the courtyard for a while, Irene?

I'm sure Major Valentine could persuade Mrs. Fatio to bring us a pitcher of her famous iced punch."

"That does sound lovely," Irene said, but added, "I wouldn't like to be there, however, if we would intrude further on the Grider ladies."

"It would be awkward if we were sitting there evaluating the results of our interrogations regarding the murder investigation and all of our prime suspects should join us," Major Valentine said ironically. "But I don't think that's going to happen, ma'am. People don't usually visit in Mrs. Fatio's courtyard until late afternoon."

They chose a wrought-iron table, painted white but now comfortably peeling, underneath an enormous live oak tree. Though the temperature had slowly risen through the morning until it was unseasonably warm even for early March in Florida, still the freshening breeze blew, and it was cool in the deep dappled shadows of the old oak. Rosa, one of Mrs. Fatio's pretty maids, brought a pottery pitcher that tinkled dully with ice chunks and three tall glasses. The punch was a deep true red, sweet and refreshing, with orange juice, limeade, and cherry syrup.

Major Valentine took a long appreciative drink, pulled a sheet of paper out of his satchel, found a pencil in his tunic pocket, and licked the tip in a boyish habit that made Irene smile. He wrote the date at the top of the paper, and she noticed that his handwriting was much like the man himself: large, generous, and careful. "You know, I've investigated four murders since I've been here. Three of them were brawls down at the docks; one of them was a Seminole Indian who tried to rob a shipping office and got shot for his trouble. I've never had to deal with anything like this."

"I think you did a very good job, Major Valentine," Richard said steadily. "You were tactful but thorough."

"Thank you, sir. Now, if you wouldn't mind, I'd like to get your over-view of the interviews. Just your first general impressions, Colonel Duvall."

Richard looked a little surprised. "Me, Major Valentine? I'm just here to offer you moral support and, I suppose, the respectability an old graybeard lends."

"Sir, no one would ever think of you as a graybeard," Major Valentine said. "But I do think you have wisdom, and that's why I asked you to help me with these interviews."

"I see," Richard said. "Very well, I'll try." He took a contemplative sip of his fruit punch, his warm gray eyes unfocused on the distance across the courtyard. "The problem I have is contemplating any one of them as being a murderess. It seems so unlikely, but if you accept it, then you must accept it could be any one of them. In that light, they all said things that were doubtful and behaved in ways that might be construed as suspicious."

"So that narrows it down to the four of them," Irene teased.

Richard chuckled good-naturedly. "Glad I could help out."

Irene insisted, "But you do suspect one of them, Richard, I know."

He stared at her. "Yes, I do. But I'm not sure that the reasons for my suspicions are sound, so I'd rather not say right away. I need to think about it."

"One thing is very true about what you said, Colonel Duvall," Major Valentine said. "After talking to them, I can't rule any of them out."

"Did you think you would?" Irene asked curiously.

"Actually, ma'am, I did. These ladies are such unlikely killers that I thought surely the guilty one would just suddenly look . . . look . . ."

"Evil?" Irene asked.

"Yes, ma'am," Major Valentine said with relief. "Evil. I thought I would just be able to see. I mean, how can a person commit such a cold-blooded murder of a close family member and not be different from the rest of us?"

"They are different from the rest of us," Richard said. "But it just may take time before it shows."

"Yes, sir, that is possible," Major Valentine agreed. "Like Lady Macbeth. She was fine at first, but then she slowly went mad and finally died, probably by suicide. Mrs. Duvall, may I ask your overall impressions of the ladies?"

"Mrs. Grider is bitter. Mrs. Raymond is angry. Miss Muriel Grider is defiant, and Miss Phillipa Grider is . . ." Irene paused delicately.

"A mess," Richard muttered.

"I was going to say 'in deep turmoil,'" Irene said, her sea green eyes twinkling. "But 'a mess' is fairly accurate too."

Major Valentine was writing the ladies' names and Irene's one-word description next to them. "You didn't write down what I said," Richard said in an injured tone.

"That all four of them could be guilty?" Irene said. "Major Valentine, you didn't write that down?"

"No, ma'am. But I am writing down that Miss Phillipa is a mess."

"That's better," Richard sniffed.

"It's just that I don't know how to spell turmoil," Major Valentine said, deadpan. Then flipping the paper, he looked at the list of five questions he had asked the ladies. "I did learn some things. All of them agreed about the key to the cellar, that only Mr. Grider had the key, and it's unlikely that he would have let any of them have his keys. None of them knows where the money is, that's for sure. And I think Mrs. Raymond was the only one who knew that Mr. Grider was taking cash out of the bank and hiding it."

"It's interesting that she didn't try to lie about why she was going down to the wine cellar," Richard mused.

"That's because we already knew the truth," Major Valentine said. "Remember, she did lie to your daughter about it. That day."

"So she did. I had forgotten," Richard said. "But there's one thing I did just realize. Mrs. Raymond did lie. Today, I mean."

"She did? What do you mean?" the major asked quickly.

"I don't think she ever saw Grider with a bunch of money. She said that he was in the library, fresh from the bank with a haul, and that he hadn't locked the library door. But I just don't believe that. Think about it; nothing we've heard about Louis Grider suggests that he wouldn't lock the library door if he was doing something with that money. I mean, the man locked the cellar door behind him even though he was completely alone in the house."

"You're exactly right, Richard," Irene said. "He was a man who was rigid, controlling, and as Miss Phillipa said, he liked his routines. So I think . . . I think that Mrs. Raymond probably was snooping in Mr. Grider's papers. I'll bet she looked at his bank journal and saw the large cash withdrawals." They had all seen Grider's meticulous accounting journals, ledgers, files, and receipts for every facet of his business and finances.

"What other details of the interviews did you notice?" Major Valentine asked them. "Anything that particularly struck either of you?"

Richard's brow creased with concentration. "The tin of powder. Mrs. Grider's answer was very calculated. Perhaps she knew that it was the one with poison in it."

"Then if she's that smart, she would never have left it in her closet," Irene said. "That has always seemed odd to me."

"Planted by the real killer?" Major Valentine asked.

"Perhaps," Irene said cautiously. "I suppose if it was Mrs. Grider she wouldn't have wanted to have a tin of Admiral Turner's Insecticide and Vermin Killer handy, so putting it into a tin of face powder was very smart. And that shelf above the closet is very deep. I would say that the chances of us finding it were small. In fact, if Victoria hadn't ordered so very many sets of bed linens—which is an unusual circumstance—then we probably wouldn't have found it."

"But wouldn't it be very difficult to live with the chance that someone would find it?" Major Valentine asked.

Irene made a graceful dismissing notion with one tiny hand. "If I hadn't been there, I imagine Mallow would have simply thrown it out. And I doubt if I would have paid attention to it either except that Cheney is my daughter, and she is the coroner pro hac vice, and I knew the details of Mr. Grider's death—well, you do see that the chances of anyone taking any note of that powder tin were extremely small."

"So no matter whether it was Mrs. Grider or one of the others, it might have been just a convenient way to hide the powder while they were using it to poison Mr. Grider," Major Valentine grumbled. "So far none of my thorough and tactful interrogations has shown us a thing."

"You got all four of them to admit to a motive," Richard said.

"I did?" the major exclaimed.

"Yes, you did. I know when you think about it, you'll see it."

He looked down at his list. "Yes . . . Mrs. Grider and her—" He stopped abruptly and looked up at Irene Duvall. "I know that he is a relative of your son-in-law, ma'am. Shiloh told me that he honestly didn't think that Mr. Winslow had anything to do with Mr. Grider's death, but he said it was fine with him if I interviewed Mr. Winslow."

Irene smiled her sweet smile at him. "It's fine with us too, Major Valentine. Mr. Winslow has a history, and it's perfectly understandable that you might suspect him."

"You sound very careless about it, ma'am, considering he's a connection. Distant, I admit, but he is connected to your family. Is it because you believe he's innocent?"

"Not exactly," she admitted honestly. "It's because I trust my son-in-law's judgment and integrity. If he didn't believe his cousin was innocent, he wouldn't say it. And he's very astute about these things. If Shiloh says Mr. Winslow is innocent, then chances are he is innocent."

Major Valentine nodded and looked down at his list. "So, Mr. Winslow is Mrs. Grider's motive. And Mrs. Raymond—she didn't know about the last-minute will, so she thought she would inherit the house and plantation if Mr. Grider was dead. Miss Muriel—" He stopped and looked up at Richard and Irene with such honest puzzlement that they had a hard time not exchanging smiles. "Is it possible that anyone could commit a murder for love of Henry Mortimer Albert Pendergast, Esquire?"

"I put her at the bottom of the list," Richard admitted.

"Very well, gentlemen, you may dismiss him, but you're looking at the wrong motive," Irene chided them. "It's not just for love. It would be a matter of security, a matter of self-worth, and a matter of living the rest of her life as an old maid, subject to a strict and controlling brother, or of being married, with a house and a life of her own. And, incidentally, a very comfortable life. Remember, they all expected to inherit, and regardless of the way the house and plantation were bestowed, they all knew that Mr. Grider had a fortune in the bank."

"Okay, I can see that," Major Valentine said slowly. "And that just shows you why I asked you to come along, Mrs. Duvall. I'm not at all clever, you know. No, I don't mean I'm stupid or ignorant. But I'm not very clever about people. Especially ladies."

"Major Valentine," Irene said softly, "there are hardly any men who have ever understood women. You see more than most, I think."

"Huh, I'm trying to learn, but they are mysterious creatures," he rasped. "No offense, ma'am."

"None taken, sir. Now, for Miss Phillipa Grider. Her motive?"

"I don't get her," Major Valentine admitted. "She really seemed to be sincerely attached to Mr. Grider. Maybe she's just putting it on, but to me it looks like she's the only one that cared anything about him."

"It seems that way," Irene said softly. "And he sent her away and wouldn't take her to England with him. He even thought she had stolen from him."

"Yeah, that's a pretty serious betrayal, especially for a dependent lady who's getting older and probably isn't going to get married. And she didn't know about the new will either, so she stood to inherit a bundle too. Hey, maybe I'm learning something after all," Major Valentine said with some satisfaction. Then he grew serious again and said, "You know one thing that I noticed? None of them could, or would, say the word *poison*. When I asked them, they all just said things like 'I didn't kill him' or 'I would never do that.' That word . . . *poison*. Seems like even if you didn't know what it was, you'd know it was something bad. It just sounds evil. Sometimes words reflect the . . . the . . ."

"Essence of the thing?" Richard suggested.

"Exactly!" Major Valentine declared. "Like hiss."

"Deeeep," Richard growled deeply.

"Haunting," Irene whispered.

"Gave me chills," Major Valentine said.

"Onomatopoeia," Irene said.

"Ma'am? Is that like a word for goulash? Sounds like it to me," Major Valentine said.

"A disease?" Richard guessed.

Irene laughed, a sweet sound that made both men smile. "No, it happens to be the name of the phenomena that we're talking about. Words that sound like the truth of their essence. Onomatopoeia. Like poison, as my son-in-law so wisely said, it is cold."

Richard Duvall sighed. "Very true. Cold . . . poison. I admit it. To me, the only one of those ladies who seems cold enough is Aimee Grider."

Major Valentine's eyes went to Irene Duvall's face. "Ma'am? Is that what you think?"

Irene dropped her gaze and said softly, "If it is true, may God have mercy on her soul."

PART V

A TIME TO MOURN, AND A TIME TO DANCE

Ecclesiastes 3:4

CHAPTER TWENTY

Confessions

SKETES STOOD AT the old stove in the Sangria House kitchen the next morning. Her chubby cheerful cheeks were scarlet, because it was already very warm at eight o'clock, and also because she had built a hot hot fire in the stove, as it was time to cook the bacon, sausage, and eggs. The heavy twelve-inch cast-iron skillet on one of the open burner holes was full of bacon and sausage, and it sizzled so loudly she couldn't even hear herself humming "My faith looks up to Thee, Thou Lamb of Calvary, Savior divine! Now hear me . . ."

"That sure smells—" The voice sounded just behind and above her left shoulder. Lightly and quickly for such a short round woman, she whirled and struck out again and again with a wide tin spatula.

"Ow, ow! Sketes, it's me!" Shiloh said, retreating with his hands stuck up in the classic defensive position of a person who's being savagely attacked.

"Oh! Mr. Shiloh! You did give me a start!" Sketes retorted. She stuck her fists on her hips, utterly unrepentant. "For such a big man, you don't make any more sound than that sneaking conniving cat, Jezebel!"

"Sorry," he said lamely.

"So you should be, scaring a poor woman half out of wits," she muttered, turning back to her skillet.

"But, Sketes, I've been coming in here every morning about this time," he said, pleading.

"I know that, sir, begging bacon, of which you're not going to get any today anyways. You . . . you . . . just startled me that bad. Begging your pardon, Mr. Shiloh."

"No, no, it's really okay, Sketes. I'm the one who's sorry. Next time I'll stamp and whistle, knock something over," he joked.

"Yes, sir."

Jauncy came in carrying an armload of the eighteen-inch quarter logs they used in the cookstove. When he saw Shiloh, he hurried to the wood-box, dumped the wood, and began rolling down his sleeves. "Good morning, sir. Please, take your seat and I'll fix your toast. Would you like me to peel and slice you an orange?"

"No, I can manage," Shiloh answered and sat down at the high stool already pulled up to the worktable, where a plain place setting of plate, napkin, knife, and fork was placed next to a big ceramic bowl piled with lemons, limes, and oranges. Selecting the fattest glowing orange, Shiloh bowed his head, thought a brief prayer of thanks, and started peeling.

Jauncy had pulled on his coat and waited for Shiloh's prayer to end and then put a glass of milk, cold from the icebox, by his plate. "Your milk, sir," he murmured.

"Thanks, PJ."

Ruefully Shiloh reflected, *Guess I'm just gonna have to face it. Even when I'm wearing my back-door clothes, I'm not the same back-door guy. What was it they called 'em at Cheney's aunts' house in New Orleans? Not high hats . . . Big Bugs, that's it. I've become a Big Bug.*

Shiloh had not realized exactly when he had suddenly become one of Them—the privileged, the ones the servants waited on, instead of the others, the vast majority of people who never had a servant, never would, and wouldn't know what to do with one if they had. *It's true. If someone had told me ten years ago I'd have a valet, I prob'ly would've busted 'im up just to show 'im I was no muffin with soft hands that needed someone to brush me and dust me.*

It was odd how bereft Shiloh felt when he realized this for the first time. He felt a definite sense of loss, but as he thought about it he began to understand that it was part of leaving boyhood, and the lack of responsibility that goes along with it, behind and facing up to his position in the world as a man. Of course, it was his marriage to Cheney Duvall that had elevated his social status, but this was not just a change in associations that had come along with his more expensive white shirts. It was a path, a life path, that Shiloh had never expected to take, and it had changed him in ways that he had not foreseen. It was not a bad thing, he knew; but he did realize that when your life changes drastically— even for the better—you must always forfeit some other good. In this case, he had gained a life with a woman he loved beyond anything he had ever imagined, a family, and prosperity. He had given up the carelessness and ease of a man alone and beholden to no one.

"When I was a child, I spake as a child, I understood as a child, I thought as a child; but when I became a man I put away childish things," he thought with the pang that comes to all boys when they understand that they have become men.

He had eaten half his orange, staring into space with his deep contemplations of life and change and manhood, when Jauncy set his plate in front of him. It had two pieces of thick toast with butter and six pieces of steaming bacon. Glancing up at Sketes in surprise, she winked impudently at him and turned back around to her still-sizzling skillet.

Maybe, he thought with satisfaction, *I'm only half a Bug. No, that's too disgusting even for a would-be doctor. I'm a Medium Bug, that's it.*

Just the fact that Shiloh was even in the kitchen at this time of the morning proved that he wasn't quite a Big Bug yet. Everyone else was still asleep, or at least they hadn't come out of their bedchambers. But Shiloh woke up early, as he had done all his life. And, as he had done all his life, he still worked hard. He wanted to. For only one short period— when he and Cheney had become estranged, before he became a Christian—had he lived the life of a man of leisure, a man-about-town, a Fine and Dandy. He had hated it, and not just because he had felt sordid because of the late nights, the drinking, the women. He had felt fatigued, and achy, and unwell, and sluggish. He liked to work. He liked to work hard and get tired. When he was home in Manhattan, he rode a lot, a long ride early in the morning along the docks, and usually long rides in the still-developing Central Park on the nights when Cheney worked late at the hospital. Many times he would take Sean, and he and Sean would run and play in the park, so Shiloh, and incidentally the dog, would get plenty of exercise.

The routine here was different, of course, because they were on holiday. Every morning Sketes would fix biscuits, corn bread, fresh bread, either chops or bacon or sausage or ham or a combination of them, assorted fruits, and soft-boiled eggs. By nine o'clock the sideboard in the dining room was loaded. People came down whenever they chose and served themselves breakfast. The food stayed in covered warming dishes on the sideboard until just before luncheon at about two o'clock.

But this was just a little too leisurely for Shiloh. Ever since they had first arrived—and he'd had to work like a stevedore to help get the house habitable—he had gotten up early. Sean usually sneaked out with him, while Shannon would open one sleepy eye and then close it again and stay in bed like the other ladies of leisure in the household. He and Sean would go out to the kitchen to snitch some pre-breakfast snack.

Sketes always fussed at him for stealing bacon, for that was his favorite, and she usually slapped his hand away after the first piece; he rarely got a second. When Shiloh had been a child in Behring's orphanage, bacon was a treat that he could remember having only twice, when some kindhearted contributors had donated enough for the entire orphanage. He could never forget how good it had smelled when the Behring sisters were cooking it, and he would never forget how good his two pieces tasted. He remembered fervently hoping, when he grew up, that he might have enough money to eat all of the bacon he wanted. He had enough money now, and he often ate six, eight, ten pieces of bacon. When Sketes would let him have it, that is.

After his pre-breakfast snack he went out to the stables to help Jerome Espy and Andrew Barentine muck out and groom the horses, and exercise them if no one wanted them that day. Florence Espy had disappeared; they hadn't seen her since the day Grider's will had been read, last Saturday. But Mr. Espy had returned to work. Once he had told Shiloh that Flo had "megrims"—vicious headaches—that kept her in bed, sometimes for days, unable to eat or even drink anything or have any light in the bedroom at all. Shiloh had told him that Cheney would be happy to attend her, and Mr. Espy had responded, in a thoroughly disbelieving tone, that he'd ask Flo about it. It had never been mentioned again.

Shiloh had raised Mr. Espy's daily pay to a dollar and a half. He and Cheney sent over baskets of fruit, and Sketes had baked bread and cakes and once an enormous beef roast and a ham that Victoria had bought and ordered to be sent to them. Mr. Espy always thanked Shiloh; once, after receiving the ham and the roast, he had had tears in his eyes. "Mr. Grider never give us nothing, not even at Christmas," he said. "Flo—Flo and me are grateful, real grateful, Mr. Iron."

"Just call me Shiloh," he had said.

Shiloh finished and thanked Sketes and Jauncy, another habit that set him apart from the general unthinking Big Bugs. Sean, who had slunk out with his tail between his legs while Sketes had been beating Shiloh with her spatula and then dressing him down, was waiting for him outside. "Thanks a lot. You're a great watchdog," Shiloh grumbled as they headed for the stables. Sean looked up at him woefully and whined a little in his throat, a little up-and-down sound that Shiloh recognized as an apology.

Jerome Espy was already mucking out, tossing the dirty straw onto the back of the cart and shoveling the manure into big galvanized tubs. Every day the soiled straw and the manure was taken out to one of the farthest fields, where they were mixed together in a composting square. Once the mixture reached a certain depth, it was left to dry in the sun and then was collected and used for fertilizer. Andrew usually took the cart out to the composting field while Espy and Shiloh groomed the horses and fed them, cleaned the tack, and made sure all the fittings, harnesses, and other tack was in good repair.

"Good morning, Mr. Espy," Shiloh said. "Got an extra shovel?"

In his slow deliberate way, Jerome tossed a pitchfork full of straw onto the cart, lowered his pitchfork, and clasped it with both hands. "Good morning, Mr. Shiloh. I was hoping to have a word with you this morning."

"All right, what can I do for you?"

Jerome Espy swallowed, his Adam's apple going up and down in his thin neck. His dark mournful eyes were narrowed to slits against the bright morning sun, and the thin line of his mouth was tense. "Mr. Shiloh, me and . . . and . . . my family would like to talk with you. Would you do me the honor of coming to my home for a bit?"

"Sure, Mr. Espy."

He nodded curtly, then turned and called into the shadowy stable, "Andrew, me and Mr. Shiloh are going to be gone for a bit."

Andrew called out, "All right, Mr. Espy, I've got it in hand."

Espy leaned his pitchfork against the stable wall and headed off toward the servants' cottages.

Shiloh said, "You better stay with Andrew, boy." Obediently Sean trotted into the stables; he and Shannon adored Andrew Barentine.

Shiloh was mystified, but he followed Espy to his shabby cottage. They went into the parlor, a tiny dark room that smelled of tallow candles and linseed oil. On a worn horsehair sofa sat Florence Espy, along with a young woman with a sweet face and a little boy.

Mr. Espy took a deep breath. "Mr. Shiloh, I'd like for you to meet my daughter, Dolores. And this is my grandson, Timothy. This is Mr. Shiloh Irons-Winslow, what I been telling you about."

"Hello, Mrs. Espy," Shiloh said, and she nodded stiffly. He turned to

271

the young lady, who stuck out her hand with a graceful motion. She was small but curvy, with pretty strawberry blond curls, blue eyes, and a milkmaid's complexion. Her looks and carriage were still youthful, but her eyes were shadowed with either weariness or sadness, or both. Shiloh couldn't tell. She had age lines on her forehead and deep creases etched from nose to mouth, too deep and world-weary for her twenty-eight years. Still, Dolores Espy had a youthful freshness of face.

With something of a shock he realized that Dolores Espy must have looked like her mother before the cares of this world had entangled and embittered the older woman.

"It's an honor to meet you, Miss Espy," he said, bowing over her hand in a gallant old-world gesture usually reserved for grand ladies. He saw the surprised appreciation in her eyes when he rose.

He turned to the boy, who hopped up and stuck out his hand. He was six years old, Shiloh remembered from Louis Grider's will. And even though Shiloh had only seen Louis Grider through the ugly mask of death, he could see him in this boy. He had finer features than his mother or grandparents, with a thin high-bridged nose, a wide forehead, sharp high cheekbones, and a strong angular jaw, all blurred a little with a child's softness, but still sure signs of his parentage.

"Hello, sir," Timothy said nervously. "I'm very glad to meet you."

Shiloh automatically went down on one knee to get on eye level with the boy. Shiloh was six-four, and he was conscious that peering up at the heights was intimidating for children. Shaking the boy's hand solidly, he said, "I'm very glad to meet you too, Timothy."

Timothy regained his seat; his feet stuck out just past the end of the sofa cushion, and Shiloh saw that his shoe soles were much mended.

"Won't you take a seat, Mr. Shiloh?" Mr. Espy said, awkwardly gesturing to a brown corduroy armchair that had a shiny seat and arms. A delicate tatted antimacassar lay along the top headrest. Shiloh sat down and looked at the family with what he hoped was polite interest.

"Would you take some coffee, Mr. Shiloh?" Flo Espy asked in a weak voice. She looked unwell; she was pale and her angular face looked so drawn it was as if the skin were stretched too tightly over her cheekbones and chin. Her eyes were sunken and red.

Shiloh always accepted the hospitality of the house; it was a rule that he had found made people feel more comfortable. "Thank you, I would like a cup of coffee, ma'am."

Without another word Flo rose and went down the hall. The cottage was very small, and Shiloh could clearly hear the clank of a tin coffeepot and the dull sound of earthenware coffee mugs.

"Mr. Irons-Winslow, I've heard a lot about you," Dolores Espy said in a pleasant voice. Shiloh noted that her diction was more polished than her parents' and that she had used his correct name.

"Have you, ma'am? I'm sorry I can't say the same about you. My wife and I had hoped we would make your acquaintance. And yours too, Timothy."

"You can call me Timmy, Mr. Irons-Winslow," he said shyly. "No one ever calls me Timothy 'cept my mother when she's mad at me."

Dolores smiled; it made her look younger. "I don't get mad at you, Timmy. I just get impatient sometimes."

"Huh? What about the thing about the peaches?" he reminded her.

"Well, okay, I was mad then," she said, ruffling his thick blond hair. "Why don't you go outside and play for a while?"

He was obviously eager to be dismissed, jumping up and running toward the door in haste. Just before he hit it, Shiloh called after him, "Timmy?"

"Yes, sir?"

"You like dogs?"

"Oh yes, sir!"

"Then go to the stables. There's a man named Mr. Barentine there. Tell him I sent you to play with Sean. Got it?"

"Yes, sir. Thank you, Mr. Irons-Winslow!" The door squeaked open and slammed shut.

Flo came in with a wooden tray and set it on a rather rickety side table by Shiloh's chair. It held an old blue-spattered tin coffeepot, three brown crockery cups—one with a chipped lip—and a plain brown sugar bowl and creamer. She poured out a cupful of the steaming thick dark brew. Shiloh sniffed appreciatively. "I like strong coffee when it's real fresh," he said. "Just black, please, ma'am."

"I-I like it too," Flo said tremulously, "but it seems like it gives me the megrims sometimes, so I don't often drink it." She fixed two more cups, black for Mr. Espy and one with sugar for Dolores.

"Mr. Espy told me you had those headaches. Mrs. Buchanan gets them sometimes too. My wife is her doctor, you know, and she—Dr. Irons-Winslow, my wife—has a tonic and a soothing compress for the eyes that helps some. I know she'd be happy to attend you, Mrs. Espy, if you should come down with one while we're here."

273

Flo Espy served her daughter and husband and then turned back and listened to Shiloh, her arms crossed. The expression on her face was more like the old irritable Flo. "Your wife . . . would attend someone like me."

Shiloh couldn't help but grin. "Most of her patients are someone like you, ma'am. And me. And she even married me."

Flo stared at him with her gimlet gaze for long moments. And then, almost unbelievably, she began to laugh. It was an old creaky rusty laugh, but it was real, and Flo even slapped her knee. Dolores giggled, and Mr. Espy's mortician-like face cracked into a grin.

Flo sat back down and looked at Shiloh as if she were really seeing him for the first time. Perhaps she was. "I disagreed with Jerome about us talkin' to you, Mr. Shiloh. But I'm of the mind that maybe he was right and I was wrong. That don't happen too often, you know."

"Like mostly never," Jerome muttered.

"That'll do, Jerome," Flo said, but her voice was not as petulant as before; she even sounded a slightly teasing note. "Anyways, Mr. Shiloh, I guess we're all here because we have some confessing to do, and I'm the one with the most to confess. I'd like to go right ahead and get it over with." She hesitated to draw a deep breath.

Shiloh said quickly, "You know, you've never offended me or wronged me, ma'am, and so you don't owe me anything."

"But we do, Mr. Shiloh," Jerome Espy said. "We have wronged you and yours, and some others too. We just think that you've shown us Christian love and mercy, so we chose you, and we hope you'll help us with all the atonements we need to make."

"I'll help you any way I can, sir," Shiloh said.

Flo spoke up again, in a tuneless, monotonous, staccato recitation. "I stole all the bed linens out of the big house. On that Monday when I thought Mr. Grider had already left, me and Jerome used the back-door key and went in. I went straight upstairs and stripped the beds and took the extras out of the closets. And we never looked in the dining room. If we had've, we might have known that Mr. Grider was still there, and we might have found him down in the cellar. I'm sorry, sir, and I've washed all the bed linens and aired them and ironed them and folded them up nice to give back to Mrs. Buchanan."

"All right," Shiloh said easily. "I'll be glad to explain to Mrs. Buchanan. I know that she won't be angry, Mrs. Espy; in fact, she will likely tell you to keep the linens."

"I know that," Flo said tightly. "But I have to give them back."

"Yes, I know. Just don't worry about the linens anymore, ma'am. And you know, even if you had seen Mr. Grider's dishes, would you have thought he was still there? Would you have searched the house for him? Would you have gone and gotten a locksmith to let you in the cellar just in case he was there?"

"No," she replied, "but that don't make me feel any better."

"I went with her, helped her, and I've thought long and hard about that man lying down in the cellar while we were there stealing from him." Jerome choked a little. "It was more my wrong than hers, and I'm sorry, real sorry. We're not going to do things like that anymore, in my house. Ever since you told me to read that story in Matthew, Mr. Shiloh—especially since you've showed us the kind of Christian kindness and mercy that's in the Bible—I've been reading it a lot. And Flo has too, when she can bear it. And before we talk about some other real hard things that we've got to talk about, I'd like to ask you to pray for us, and with us."

"I'll be glad to, Mr. Espy. Could I read you something before we pray?" Shiloh picked up the big Bible that was on the lower shelf of the little table by his chair.

"We'd be pleased if you would," Jerome answered.

Shiloh turned to John 5 and began to read. "Jesus said: 'For as the Father raiseth up the dead, and quickeneth them; even so the Son quickeneth whom he will. For the Father judgeth no man, but hath committed all judgment unto the Son: that all men should honour the Son, even as they honour the Father.'" He looked up at Jerome and Flo, who were listening closely. "Do you understand what that means?"

"I think so," Flo said slowly. "It means that Jesus gives us spiritual life, just like God gives us eternal life when we die. And Jesus is the One who judges us, because God gave Him that authority, and that . . . that . . . privilege."

"Exactly," Shiloh said. "And remember what Jesus said to the condemned adulterous woman? He said, 'Neither do I condemn thee; go and sin no more.' He doesn't condemn us. Ever. He forgives us. Always." He read again: "'Verily, verily, I say unto you, He that heareth my word, and believeth on him that sent me, hath everlasting life, and shall not come into condemnation; but is passed from death unto life.'" Once again he looked up at them and noticed out of the corner of his eye that Dolores Espy was crying softly. To Flo and Jerome he said quietly, "You've heard the Word. Do you believe on Him? Will you ask Him to save you and give you everlasting life, the eternal life that begins the moment you invite Him into your heart?"

Flo bent her head and sobbed, a dry painful sound. "I do. I want to be saved," she cried.

"Me and my wife, we want to be saved, Mr. Shiloh," Jerome said clearly. Slowly he rose and went to the sofa and knelt, clasping his wife's hands. Shiloh got up and knelt next to him.

Jerome prayed: "Dear Lord Jesus, me and my wife Flo want to be saved. We've had a passing acquaintance with you in our lives, Lord, but we want more than that. We've sinned. We've done some awful things, Lord, and we need you to forgive us for all of those sins. We ask that you save us, save our lives now, from our sin and the sin in this old evil world, and save our lives in the world to come. Come into our old cold hearts, Lord, and make your home there, we ask in your blessed name. Amen."

Flo prayed, haltingly, to be saved, and then Shiloh prayed for them and for Dolores and Timothy. When they all rose, Dolores was hugging her mother, and they both wept. "I'm so glad, Mum, so glad. Now I know that you'll be all right. You'll be well, and you'll grow strong, and the Lord will surely bless all of us." She looked up at Shiloh. "I was saved right after Timothy was born, thank the Lord. But Mum and my father have had a . . . longer, harder road."

"I've no excuse," Flo said, pulling a handkerchief out of her sleeve and dabbing her eyes with it. "After all you've been through, for me and Jerome to say our lives were too hard to thank the Lord, that's just our old stubborn hard hearts."

"But, Mum, what I've been through is my own fault," Dolores said gently. "And a lot of what you've been through is my fault." She looked up at Shiloh with a small sad smile. "I'm sure you know about me and Mr. Grider, Mr. Irons-Winslow. Everyone connected with the will does, I presume. No, don't worry, it's not really a big secret. Everyone in Comales knows about it—that's where Timmy and I live, in Comales—and a lot of people in St. Augustine know too. If you knew Louis, you could hardly miss the truth when you see Timmy."

Shiloh cocked his head to one side. "You were in love with him," he said with sudden revelation. "We all thought—we just assumed that he had taken advantage of you. You were at his funeral, weeping. It sounded so sad, such a loss . . ."

"Yes, it was I," she admitted, and once again Shiloh noticed her cultured grammar. "Perhaps it was unwise of me to attend. I knew, of course, that his sisters and Mrs. Grider would be there. But I just had to go, to say good-bye, and I thought no one would see me. I didn't think I would weep, but I couldn't help it. I'm so sorry he died."

"He must have been very different with you," Shiloh said thoughtfully. "He didn't seem to be the kind of man to inspire such devotion."

"He *was* different with me," she said, not in a defiant or regretful way, just sad. "He caught me stealing books from his library, of all things. He was angry at first, and I'm afraid I was impertinent to him and answered back to him. Once he got over the shock, he started laughing, and then I laughed too . . . and that was how it began. Over books, because I loved them and had no one to teach me, and because he loved them and had no one to share them with." Her blue eyes, innocent in spite of what she had done, went to her mother, then to her father. "It was so wrong, so very wrong. Once again, Mother, Father, I ask you to forgive me."

"We forgive you. We haven't always been able to look at you with honest true forgiveness, Daughter, you know that. But now, with God's charity in our hearts, we can truly forgive you forever," Jerome said in a deep voice.

"Oh, thank the Lord. Thank the Lord, finally," Dolores said, bowing her head. She looked up again at Shiloh. "This is very difficult, Mr. Irons-Winslow, because I have to say some things that are never ever discussed between people who aren't family or . . . or . . . close friends, but my parents do trust you implicitly, so I hope, sir, that you will take these confidences as they are meant, as finally letting the truth be known as it pertains to Louis's death."

"I see," Shiloh said thoughtfully. "You do understand that my wife was appointed coroner for the postmortem examination of Mr. Grider, and I assisted her. In that capacity we have some obligation to the provost marshals as far as investigating Mr. Grider's death."

"You mean, if we say anything that may have to do with his death, you'll have to tell," Flo said.

"Yes, ma'am, I will," Shiloh answered firmly.

"We understand that," Jerome said. "But our decision, as a family, was to tell you what we need to tell you and to abide by what you advise us to do. We're sticking to that." He looked at his wife and daughter, and they both nodded.

"Then I'll finish my story and Timmy's," Dolores said in a clear voice.

"The Griders first moved here in the summer of 1859—Louis and his first wife, Penelope, and Louis's three sisters. By the spring of 1860 Louis and I were having an affair. At the time I was the parlormaid of Sangria House, my mother was the housekeeper and cook, and my father was the stableman and coachman."

She stopped, swallowed hard, and then continued, "Louis . . . was different then. I mean, I haven't seen him since 1863, but my parents have told me what he's been like. Back then he wasn't so severe, so mean-spirited, so inclined to give in to minor ailments. He was strong and healthy, most of the time, and he worked hard and, I suppose, was a hard taskmaster, but he was not cruel, and he was not miserly. Anyway, I found out I was expecting in March of 1863. I told Louis—" she choked a little and then went on in a shaky voice—"and he was very, very angry. He . . . he made me leave and forbade me to ever be seen at the Big House. He made my parents tell his . . . his wife, and his sisters, that I had taken a job in Jacksonville and had moved there.

"But I refused to leave, because I had to stay close to my parents. So he did give me a small cottage in Comales—Sangria Plantation holds all the papers on all the houses there—and he promised to pay me a monthly allowance for the child. I don't wish to go on and on about it, Mr. Irons-Winslow, but I was in pretty sad shape during my confinement and after Timothy was born. Father Manuel Escalante watched over me and prayed for me and with me, and his housekeeper, Señora Oliveros, took care of me. Not long after Timmy was born I prayed and asked the Lord to forgive me for my sins and asked Him to save me. And then I started reading and studying every book I could find, and that Father Escalante could find for me, and I opened a school in Comales. I've been the schoolteacher there ever since," she finished with modest pride.

Shiloh studied her gravely. "Do you know what was in Mr. Grider's will, Miss Espy?"

"Yes, we have a copy of the will," she answered. "Judge Allard said it would be all right for Father Escalante to give us a copy. But, Mr. Irons-Winslow, we aren't thinking about all of that yet. Right now my parents and I are much more concerned with getting our own lives straightened out and making sure that we do everything we can to make amends for our own sins and mistakes."

"But you do understand the terms and conditions of Mr. Grider's will?" Shiloh asked intently.

Dolores cut her blue eyes toward her mother, who sat next to her, head down. "We understand that Mr. Grider suspected someone of trying to kill him, Mr. Irons-Winslow. And my parents realize that they are suspects. But please believe me when I tell you that it was his death, not his will, that made my parents want to live a Christian life and walk in the paths that the Lord sets for them."

He studied her for a few moments. She met his critical gaze squarely, unblinking. Shiloh reflected that, under the circumstances, it was fortunate for the Espys that their daughter was still with them and could speak for them, as she was so articulate, so intelligent, and so obviously honest. Florence and Jerome Espy could never hope to represent themselves, their thoughts and motives, half so well. "I believe you," he finally said.

Florence Espy's head snapped up. "Thank the Lord," she muttered. "We been at odds with the world for so long now, it's a blessing to hear someone thinks we're trying to be honest and true.

"But I ain't always been, Mr. Shiloh. I've been, and done, some bad things. And the Lord's showed me that I've got to confess some things and make some amends. So here goes.

"After Dolores went to Comales, whiles she was still in the family way, Old Grider—I mean, Mr. Grider—got meanlike and angry. He paid Dolores ten dollars for April and May, but then he didn't pay nothing in June or July." Florence glanced at her daughter. "By August I'd about had it, so I shoved my way into the library with him before he could lock hisself in there and hide, like he took to doing after Dolores left. Well, he cut me off short and told me never to say nothing about Dolores or her 'situation' again. He did give me twenty dollars to pay for them two months. And he sent Dolores money in September, and October. But November went by, and he got sick for the first two weeks. He was all right by the end of the month and in December, but he didn't send Dolores any money. Timothy was born on December 20. He ain't never said a word or asked about Delores or sent her a dime.

"Back then," Florence continued, "Mr. Grider give his sisters more money than he did later. For the holidays Mrs. Raymond had gone to Boston to visit her and Mr. Grider's mother's people. Miss Muriel and Miss Phillipa had gone to visit their mother's family, the Carvers, also of Boston. So Mr. and Mrs. Grider and me and Jerome were the onliest people in the house that year, and a sad, pitiful Christmas it was. As I said, Mr. Grider, he'd taken to staying in his library all the time, tending to business and reading. Mrs. Grider—Penelope—she always was quiet and never had much to say to anyone. She was of good family, with old money, I understand, and I guess she never thought much of servants one way or t'other. Sure she never seemed to suspect about Grider and our Dolores. 'Course, her and Mr. Grider had some kind of marriage I don't know much about. They hardly ever saw each other, they kept separate rooms; they were always real polite to each other and talked about their money and the plantation, but they just seemed a lot more like business partners than anything else."

Curiously Shiloh asked, "How long had they been married then, do you know?"

"Twenty years," she answered with a small sad sigh. "That June they'd had a party and invited the Rainsfords and the Ketchums and some others."

Shiloh nodded. "Go on, ma'am."

Flo collected her thoughts for a moment, then continued, "By January it looked like Mr. Grider had just put Dolores and Timmy out of his mind, like she'd never existed and he had nothing to do with any of us. One day—it was January 3, a cold blustery day—Mrs. Grider had gone to call on Ivy Rainsford. I banged on the door and made him let me into the library. I told him about Timmy and that Dolores was in a bad way and she needed money to help with the baby."

Her lined, pained face worked, and Shiloh realized she was trying to hold back tears. "See, always before when I had to say something to Mr. Grider, he was kinda . . . kinda took aback, kinda shamefaced, like. But this time was different. I don't know why. I don't know what had changed him, but this time he stood up and started shouting at me. He said he didn't owe anybody anything, much less Dolores or us. He said the boy couldn't be his anyway; he'd never been able to have children. Somebody else must be the father, and that was Dolores's problem, not his. He said—he said awful things, Mr. Shiloh. Awful things about me and specially about Dolores and Timmy." The tears overflowed, and she bent her head and sobbed.

Dolores leaned over, hugged her, and said softly, "Mum, it's all over now. All the guilt, all the hate, all the bitterness. Believe me, I know how much better you'll feel when you just confess it all and ask forgiveness."

"I don't know if I can forgive that man," she cried. "I don't know if I'll ever be able to forgive him."

"You won't be able to forgive yourself until you forgive him, Mum,"

Dolores said. "And you have to forgive yourself. You have to put all of this behind you. Here and now."

Florence Espy nodded, wiped her eyes and nose, and continued in a shaky voice. "Well, this shouting back and forth and . . . and calling each other horrible things—I lost my temper and shouted back at him, I can tell you—went on and on, it seemed like for hours. But finally he just shouted, 'Get out, you old hag!' So I just ran out.

"But when I got out into the hall, I saw Miss Penelope standing there, her face as white as death and her eyes stretched wide with . . . with horror, I guess you'd say. She'd likely never heard such language and such shouting in all her life. She just stood there and stared at me right in the hall so's I couldn't get past unless I pushed her, and at least I hadn't forgot myself as much as that. But the way she looked at me . . . like I was . . . dirty, or something," Flo sobbed, a dry choking sound. "I sort of broke, like, and couldn't stop myself. I shouted at her. I said, 'I don't know why you'd be looking at me like that, ma'am, down your nose, since your husband managed to get my daughter with child while for all your blue blood you haven't given him a child!' So she just staggered back a little, and I ran past her and out the house and went and hid myself in the cottage. A while later I just packed a little bag and went to Comales and stayed with Dolores for a week."

She stopped, took a shuddering breath, and dropped her eyes to her hands, lying in her lap, palms up, fingers lax. They were reddened with hard work and already showing some of the signs of rheumatism in the swollen joints.

Jerome Espy, seated across from Shiloh in another shabby armchair, shifted and the chair rustled, the wooden feet creaked. "As I'm guessing you might catch on to, Mr. Shiloh, my confession is that my wife and daughter had to confess. You'll have noted that I wasn't anywhere in this story, and that's my sin, and that's what I've vowed to my wife and daughter that I'll amend, the Good Lord willing. So Flo, you've confessed your sins and your fault, and what happened from here wasn't no more your fault than it was Dolores's or Timmy's or mine or even Mr. Grider's. We all of us have to answer to God for our own selves. Miss Penelope same as us, God rest her poor soul."

He turned to Shiloh then, set his face, and said in a hard ringing voice, "Flo came back in a week, and no one in the house said anything. We all acted just like nothing had happened, and we all were walking around in our own private darkness, I guess you'd say.

"Come January 12 of eighteen hundred and sixty-four, it was a Monday, it was cold, too cold for this place, and sleeting, a sharp sleet that felt like it was cutting your skin when it hit you. And the wind, screaming like banshees. I went out to the stables and started my chores, and Mr. Grider come to get me. He looked like death, pure death, with his face white and his eyes staring and red. We went to the front of the house, and Miss Penelope was in the fountain pool. She was dead."

A sharp indrawn breath from Shiloh made Jerome Espy pause, but only for a moment. Jerome Espy said, "She were—" His voice cracked, so he stopped. His face worked, he swallowed hard, and then he went on in the same brittle tone as before. "She were wearing her dress, the same dress as from the day before. I thought she must have been there all night, maybe. Mr. Grider made me get in and get her out and carry her into the parlor. I did, and I laid her on a sofa, a gold damask one they'd had for years. I 'member her dress. It was brown, and it dripped-dripped-dripped on the carpet. Her eyes were open, and she looked . . . lost. Like she was looking around, trying to think where she was. Anyways, Mr. Grider's hands was shaking, but he shut her eyes and took my arm and hauled me out of the room into the vestibule and said, 'I'm going to fetch the coroner. We found her in the river, do you understand? She must have gone for a walk, and she fell in, and because of the cold she couldn't get out. *Do you understand me?*'"

It was silent in the room.

"'Yes, sir,' I said," Mr. Espy whispered.

Florence Espy spoke, her voice heavy with pain. "This house was never the same after that. When the sisters came back, and they didn't know except what Mr. Grider told, even they changed, after a while. Miss Phillipa grew sad and fearful. Miss Muriel was secretive and sly and selfish, and Mrs. Raymond grew bitter and angry. Mr. Grider got sick more and more, and it seemed like he got a lot richer, but he turned into an awful miser.

"About a week after Miss Penelope's funeral Mr. Grider called me and Flo into the library, and that's when he told us that he never wanted to hear Dolores's or Timmy's name ever again. And he said that he'd pay us eighteen cents a day, and if we didn't like it we could leave. But he said if we did, he'd tell everyone in St. Augustine or wherever we went that we had stolen from him."

Flo's voice was muffled. She had dropped her head and put her handkerchief to her mouth. "He said I had stolen from him. I had stolen his wife."

"That's not true," Shiloh said firmly. "Your husband spoke pure plain truth, ma'am. When a person takes his own life, it's only between him and God. No one else can take that responsibility. No one else should try."

Flo gave a ragged, humorless chuckle. "All this time I've thought I killed Miss Penelope. But I didn't, I guess. But now I'm accused of killing Mr. Grider. And I wanted to, plenty of times, but I sure didn't kill that man, Mr. Shiloh. Sometimes—sometimes I hated him so bad I wished he was dead. But I never imagined—I never thought of ways to kill him. I never imagined ways to do it. I never really thought it, being serious."

Shiloh nodded. "I believe you, Mrs. Espy. I can see the truth in you now. But you might still have to answer questions, you know. Probably Major Valentine is going to want to talk to you, and to you too, Mr. Espy."

Jerome's eyes rested on Shiloh, and though he didn't smile—he wasn't the kind of man to smile much—his expression grew warm. "See, Mr. Shiloh, we knew we were going to have to answer questions, hard questions, about Mr. Grider's death. And at first me and Flo thought we just couldn't do it. We just couldn't face it. But then we decided that we were through running. We were gonna confess to the Lord our sins and stop hiding from them. And we decided that the Lord was telling us to confess to you, and so we did. And now, we know that since we've talked to you and prayed with you, we're not afraid anymore. Finally . . . finally, Flo, it's over. We can rest."

CHAPTER TWENTY-ONE

Empty Bottles

MAJOR MICAH VALENTINE was getting to be a regular guest for dinner at Sangria House. This was fine with Richard and Irene Duvall, who had, early on, figured out that the young man missed his parents and found it endearing that he so obviously enjoyed their company, especially Richard's. Shiloh and Cheney, through working with him as he investigated the death of Louis Grider, had come not only to respect him for his hard work and devotion to duty but to enjoy his company, for he was a lively and cheerful companion. Minerva Wilcott was delighted to see Major Valentine anytime, of course, because as time went on her opinion that he was lovely in his uniform was only reinforced; she now thought that his entire person was lovely. And Victoria liked Major Valentine because, quite simply, he was a likable man and an agreeable dinner companion.

It was Friday night, and dinner had been later than usual because they had waited for Major Valentine. They were now down to the nuts and cheeses and fruit and coffee, and it was almost eleven o'clock. The ladies hadn't retired to the parlor and left the gentlemen because this particular group was so congenial that they didn't stand on formalities. Also they had spent the entire dinner updating one another on all of the things that had happened pertaining to the investigation of Mr. Grider's death.

"... and so I didn't really learn much more than I knew after I interviewed the ladies yesterday," Major Valentine was saying ruefully. "If those ladies are telling any lies, they're telling them the same way every time."

"Well, I've gone over and over their interviews in my mind," Richard said, "and I can't think of another thing that might be helpful. What about you, Irene?"

Irene made a graceful "no" shake of her head. "I just can't rule any of them out, based on what I heard. I've tried to puzzle it out, imagine each of them as guilty, each of them as innocent. And I find it just as easy either way."

Minerva—as always, seated by Major Valentine—said, "I suppose I must not have a very good imagination. I still cannot imagine any of those ladies actually poisoning Mr. Grider. Or Mr. or Mrs. Espy either. It's just too bizarre."

"I talked to them too," Major Valentine said, "and everyone else that I could think of who might give me any hint about Mr. Grider and his life, his enemies, his friends. I've heard a lot of things, some facts, some rumors, some stories, and lots of opinion. But I've heard nothing that brings me any closer to arresting anyone for killing Louis Grider."

"My parents tell me that you are a very organized and meticulous investigator, Major Valentine," Cheney said. "Have you kept notes of all the interviews and all the events pertaining to the investigation, such as the visit to the jeweler's?"

"Yes, ma'am, I sure have. In fact, when I get fired as an investigator, I'm thinking I could get a job as some noodle somewhere with a green eyeshade and sleeve garters, making notes and charts that don't really mean anything and that nobody ever reads. Like a lawyer's clerk, maybe," he added dryly. "Nobody ever reads anything they write down."

Cheney smiled. "Nonsense, Major Valentine. I'm sure you're a very good provost marshal and also a very good soldier. Somehow I can't see you as a . . . a . . . law noodle. What I was going to say is that if you think it would help, perhaps we—you and I and Shiloh—could go through your notes and talk things out. I'm no detective, but I can arrange information into organized reports. And Shiloh has insights into people and situations that usually prove to be true and accurate."

Shiloh made a face. "Thanks for the reference, Doc, but this time I'm lost too. I'm with Miss Irene. I can make up stories for any of them to be guilty, and I can see every one of them innocent too."

Major Valentine had brightened at Cheney's suggestion. "No, no, Shiloh, I'd really appreciate it if you—and you too, Dr. Irons-Winslow—would go over my notes with me and discuss a couple of things that I haven't gotten really clear in my head yet. I know, from serving as a staff officer, that even the best generals talk to their officers in order to get a clearer picture of the situation, whatever it is. It would help me, I know, to step back and take another look at everything I've learned."

"Children, you may stay up and play detective as late as you like," Irene said, "but I'm afraid that I must retire. Cheney, dear, you should ask Sketes for whatever you might like—coffee or tea or punch—and then dismiss her and Jauncy."

Richard, Irene, and Victoria all retired, while Minerva said, "May I stay too, Major Valentine? I know I'm not clever like Dr. Cheney and Shiloh, but I am a very good listener, and I shall listen to everything you say, and perhaps that might help. Like the soundboard of a violin, perhaps I may reflect back some sympathetic vibration."

Rising from the table, he held her chair, then took her hand and tucked it in his arm. "Ma'am, you are far too lovely to be any soundboard, although your voice is sweeter than any violin's, and I would be happy to hear that sweet voice, whether you are saying something clever or not."

Minerva's blue eyes widened, and her delicate cheeks blushed a soft rose pink. "You are a very charming gentleman, sir."

"Not at all, ma'am, I'm merely an honest one."

The four of them retired to the parlor. Sketes brought the coffee service with a tray of imported bonbons and nonpareils, and Jauncy brought four candelabra with new candles. Cheney sent Sketes and Jauncy on to bed.

Major Valentine got right down to business. "All right, let's start right at the beginning. Shiloh, you arrived here on Monday, late at night, right? So start from when you set foot on shore. Tell me what happened."

Shiloh began his tale, and when he got to the part when he and the two sailors arrived at Sangria House and went to the gatekeeper's cottage, he said in an unemotional voice, "My cousin Bain was there, and he told me to go to the Espys' cottage. While I was standing at the door, I heard a woman in the room behind Bain. Later I figured out it was Aimee Grider."

Major Valentine cautiously slid his eyes toward Minerva, who was sitting by him on the sofa. Shiloh said, with an affectionate glance at Minerva, "Miss Wilcott is discreet, Major Valentine. I trust her."

Major Valentine looked at Minerva and said warmly, "Then I do too. You do understand, Miss Wilcott, that everything we say tonight is part of a legal investigation into a murder, and that everything, relevant or not, must be kept strictly confidential."

"I understand. I won't say a word, even to Victoria, and she's my best friend," she promised.

Major Valentine turned back to Shiloh. "You know, Shiloh, when I left the other night—what night did I last have dinner here?"

"Wednesday," Minerva answered promptly. "It was a little past eleven when you left."

"Thank you, ma'am. See, I did need you to help me recall some things," Major Valentine said with a gleam in his dark eyes. He turned again to Shiloh. "Her horse was in the stables when I went in to saddle up my horse. The lights were on—well, a candle was burning at the gatekeeper's cottage."

Shiloh nodded. "I'm not surprised, Major. Did you talk to Bain today?"

"Yes, I did. And he wouldn't tell me a blessed thing; wouldn't even admit that Mrs. Grider had ever been in the cottage."

"I'm not surprised," Shiloh said. "The only way I've ever gotten him to talk to me about her is by playing this sort of come-at-it-sideways game and pretend we're talking about some fictional lady with a fictional dead husband."

"That's it," Major Valentine grumbled. "But I will say, Shiloh, even though your cousin was very careful not to say anything . . . indelicate about Mrs. Grider and insisted that he had never had a single conversation with anyone, including any fictional ladies with fictional dead husbands, about killing any husbands, I still got the impression that he has some regrets about possible . . . indiscretions with the lady. That fictional lady, I mean."

"I think that too, Major, but you know I was very careful not to say anything like that to you," Shiloh said firmly. "I didn't want to try to influence you in any way."

"I know, I know," Major Valentine said quickly. "I talked to him with a pretty open mind. Personally I think the man's got a problem now that the lady is unattached, and he would have been the last person to want her to get unattached."

Minerva dropped her head and said in a low unhappy tone, "Men can be very cruel."

Cheney, sitting across from her in one of the big overstuffed armchairs, suddenly got up to sit by the girl and put an arm around her. "Yes, darling, men can be cruel, that's true. But you must remember that women can very foolishly put themselves in situations that cannot possibly end well, and you can't always blame the gentleman for that."

Minerva nodded slightly, but her head still drooped.

Major Valentine said comfortingly, "Miss Wilcott, I can't bear to see you unhappy. Perhaps if I fixed you a cup of very sweet coffee and picked out the best bonbon and the best non . . . non—"

"Nonpareils," she said, lifting her head to look up at him.

"Nonpareils, do you think that would make you feel better?"

"Oh yes, I think that would be very kind of you, Major Valentine, and I would feel much more cheerful," she declared.

Major Valentine fixed the little china cup of coffee, set it on a paper-thin rose-trimmed china saucer with a bonbon and two nonpareils, and funny he did look with his big thick hands delicately setting the fine dishes on the side table by the sofa. When they got Minerva settled down again, Shiloh continued his story of that stormy night and the next few days until he got to Saturday, March 2, the day after the funeral, when he and Cheney had gone back down to the cellar and, with Jauncy's reluctant help, decided that they were probably looking at the scene of a murder.

"You know, Shiloh," Major Valentine said thoughtfully, "I'd like to go down to the cellar again. That mad dash you and I made down there to get the tonic didn't leave any impression on me at all, except that it was dark and chilly. I don't think I'll see anything more than you and Dr. Irons-Winslow have, but I would like to try to re-create what Mr. Grider did that night, and just . . . see what he saw."

"That's a good idea," Shiloh said. "How 'bout it, Doc? Wanna go down into the haunted cellar again?"

"Of course. You don't think I'm going to let you men go crashing around my crime scene without me, do you?" Cheney said.

Minerva said tremulously, "Well, I shall be terrified, but I want to go."

"You don't have to do that, Miss Wilcott," Major Valentine said kindly. "I'll build a fire in here, and I'm sure Sean and Shannon will be good company for you until we get back." The dogs' ears perked up at their names, and Sean's tail thumped twice.

"No, no. I haven't been down to the cellar either, and I have wanted to go to see it, but I would never go down by myself." She gave a little shiver. "But I won't be too frightened with you. All of you, I mean."

They all got up, Shiloh told the dogs to stay, and they took one candelabrum with them down the dark hallway. "We don't lock the door now," Shiloh said. "I got elected to keep the keys, and I don't carry them around. If anyone wants to go down there, we figured that they didn't need me to police them."

"But I would like to do it just as Mr. Grider did," Major Valentine said. Miss Wilcott was hanging on to his arm as if it were a lifeline, but he didn't seem to mind.

"All right. I'll go get the keys, and you can go to the dining room. I'll show you where his plate and things were," Shiloh said.

In just a few moments he returned to the dining room with the keys. He went to the middle of the table and pulled one of the chairs out and placed it just so. "Okay, it was pulled back this way, so you can see why I thought he probably was going toward the hallway. There was a plate with a piece of bread, remnants of a mutton chop, a knife, fork, empty glass, and empty wine bottle."

"Did it have a label?" Major Valentine asked quickly.

"Nope. It was just a long-necked bottle with the cork lying by the plate."

The major nodded. "May I have the keys?" Shiloh handed the large clanging ring to him. "Do you know which one is the cellar key, Shiloh?"

"Yeah, it's—" He took it back, pushed a few of the keys around on the ring, and selected an old iron key. "It's this one. After we went through the locksmith incident, I figured I'd better learn which key was which, just in case."

"Okay, now . . . do you think he tried to take a candelabrum?" Major Valentine asked. "They're kind of inconvenient to carry around."

"No. We've figured out what they did when they went into the cellar," Cheney answered. "Bring the candelabrum. It will go on this table here in the hallway." A small side table, which currently held a vase of flowers, was placed by the door leading out of the dining room into the passage. The four went on down the shadowy passage to the cellar door.

"All right. He would have unlocked it . . ." Major Valentine put the key in, rattled it a little, then took it out and opened the door. "Ah, I see. A lantern and matches, here on the landing. That makes sense, of course. Will everyone come on in?"

Cheney and Shiloh went down a couple of steps, while Minerva stayed close by Major Valentine on the landing. He lit the lantern and then turned around, pulled the door closed, and put the key back in the lock. "Don't worry, I'm not really going to lock it," he said to Shiloh. "I don't relish spending the night down here if something funny happened with this old lock."

"Ooh, it's chilly," Minerva whispered. "And it has an eerie echo. It sounds like people are in the corners whispering about you."

"Are you sure they are human?" Shiloh asked in deep sepulchral tones.

"That's . . . that's not funny, Shiloh," Minerva said, grabbing Major Valentine's arm so tightly he had trouble moving. Finally, in a lock step, they went down the stairs behind Shiloh and Cheney.

Shiloh reached the bottom of the stairs. "He was over there, face-down."

"But remember, Shiloh, he put the lantern up on the shelf," Cheney reminded him.

"You're right, Doc, I had forgotten." He pointed. "Over there is a little shelf. We found the lantern there, dry as dust."

Major Valentine went and put the lantern up on the shelf. It gave enough light to see in a circle around it, but the rest of the room was featureless black. "Okay, Dr. Irons-Winslow, please tell me exactly what you saw."

Cheney told him everything: how they found Mr. Grider's body; the cursory examination she had done while Shiloh went to town to get the coroner; the second time they had come down, with Jauncy playing the corpse; when she and Shiloh had decided to go to Richard and ask his advice.

"And then Colonel Duvall came to me, and regardless of the fact that I still don't know who poisoned this man, I'm very glad he did," Major Valentine said, staring down at the cold damp floor as though Louis Grider's body were still there. "His killer should be brought to justice." He roused, looking around the cavernous room. "I've got the scene down now, I think. Could we get some more light? I'd like to see the whole layout."

"Back behind the wine racks is a worktable with shelves above it," Shiloh said. "Extra lanterns are stored there. I gotta take the lantern, so y'all don't move, okay?" He took the lantern, and like an apparition the light slid around the corner of the wine racks and began to glow at the back of the room.

Their eyes were getting accustomed to the shadows, so the three could still see each other faintly. Minerva, still hanging on to Major Valentine's arm, looked around, up and down, curiously. "So this is a cellar," she mused.

The major looked down at her in astonishment. "You've never been in a cellar?"

"Why, no. Why should I?" she answered with her own puzzlement.

"I don't know, it's just . . ." He hesitated and looked at Cheney. "You know, I thought that Mrs. Grider was lying the other day when she said she had only been down here once. But—I suppose ladies don't go down to their cellars, generally?"

"It depends," Cheney answered, hiding her amusement, "on the lady and the cellar. But you must remember, Major Valentine, that Mr. Grider kept this cellar locked, so even if one of the ladies wanted to come down here, they would have been obliged to ask him to unlock the door. I've been thinking about it, and—Good, here's Shiloh with the extra lanterns. I can show you what I mean." Major Valentine took an extra lantern, and Cheney said, "Please, come over here. You see, this is a good-sized room—completely empty. Now over here, this is what I think normally would be a butler's pantry, to store linens and the silver and cleaning supplies and rags and things like that. You can see it has a worktable, very generous cupboards, and drawers. Empty. Completely empty. Well, we did find a box of silverware in the corner of one of the bottom cupboards, but it had not been polished for so long I doubt that the Griders had ever used it.

"Now, if you'll come over here, on the other side of the cellar, this is the laundry. Well, it was the laundry. It's a nice large room, well equipped with two sinks, a work counter. But it's empty. It's as if it's never used. And there's a reason for that—Mrs. Espy says they never use it. Do you know why?"

Major Valentine was standing in the middle of the laundry room. Since Shiloh had lit more lanterns and the cellar was not so much like a deep cavern, Minerva had loosened her death grip on Major Valentine's arm. She walked over to the outside door and laid her hand on it. "It's because it's so dark," she said softly. "Wouldn't he open this door, though, on washdays?"

"No, he wouldn't," Cheney answered. "He just couldn't stand for a door, any door anywhere in the house, to stand open. And the other rooms were empty for the simple reason that he wouldn't leave the hall door down here unlocked. If anything had been stored down here that the servants needed, they would have been obliged to ask him for the key every time they wanted to come down here. And Mrs. Espy said that even if they had to make two trips down here for some reason, Mr. Grider would lock the door and wait until they returned for the second trip to unlock it again."

"That man definitely had some personal problems," Shiloh muttered. "Anyway, it was easier just to move the washtubs to the kitchen and leave them there. Sketes said she wasn't about to do the washing down in a dark hole, and I can't say I blame her."

They all went back out into the middle of the cellar, where the racks of wine were. "So all that was down here was the wine and Mr. Grider's personal store of wine that he added his concoction to," Major Valentine said.

Cheney went to the first wine rack, the one just a few feet from the bottom of the stairs, where they had found Mr. Grider's body. "Yes, these bottles here, on this row, have no labels. I found them that day we found his body, and I assumed they were his tonic, so that's why I asked you and Shiloh to fetch a couple of bottles and bring them to Duff's so I could test them with the spectroscope. They did contain both esters of sulfur—his self-prescribed tonic—and thallium."

Major Valentine nodded and then wandered over to the far wine racks, holding his lantern high. "There must be hundreds of bottles of wine here," he murmured. "Kind of odd for a family that might drink only a bottle or two in an entire year."

"Grider was a miser," Shiloh said, joining him. "We figure he collected the prime sangria, just as he stashed money. See, the older vintage is back here—hey, what's this?" He had pulled out a bottle at random to show the major the year on the label. Now he shook the bottle, a blank look on his face. "This bottle's empty."

Major Valentine frowned. He reached up and slid out a bottle from the top rack. "This one is too." He tried a third. "This bottle is empty too. What's going on here? Someone came down here and stole the wine but not the bottles?" he joked.

"Maybe the coroner," Shiloh said caustically. "He probably would have thought that was a great idea, just to drink all the wine without having to carry all these heavy bottles."

"Let me see that bottle," Cheney said, and Shiloh handed it over obediently. She easily pulled out the cork and sniffed. "This bottle never had any wine in it, and the cork—" She stopped abruptly. Holding the bottle by the neck, she shook it back and forth. "Do you hear that?

Shiloh, hold the lantern up here." Shiloh positioned the lantern where she had indicated, about a foot from her face. She held the dark green bottle right in front of the bright lantern. "There's some paper rolled up inside this bottle," she said with astonishment. She upended the bottle and tried to shake it out, but it wouldn't come out of the narrow neck.

The four of them stood in a circle around her, spellbound. "Shiloh—Shiloh, my medical bag," she whispered.

Without a word he turned and bounded for the steps, taking them three at a time. He still moved quietly, though, since it was now almost one o'clock in the morning and the household was asleep. Cheney, Major Valentine, and Minerva, no longer afraid of the dark, moved among the wine racks calling out to each other amid the clinks of wine bottles they piled in their arms. "Here's another, another—whoops, this one actually has wine in it, fancy that. This one's empty—did you know you can hear the paper rattling against the side if you put it against your ear? Empty—"

By the time Shiloh came running back with Cheney's medical bag, they had collected over a dozen empty bottles and put them on the work-table in the pantry. He came in, and Cheney took her bag. "I know . . . they're right here . . . here." She pulled out a pair of forceps, like pincers, about eight inches long. Without a word, Shiloh held out the first empty bottle they had found. Cheney put the forceps in it, clamped, and pulled out the rolled-up paper. It was four one-hundred-dollar bills.

CHAPTER TWENTY-TWO

The Key

YAWNING HUGELY, Sketes opened the door to the kitchen and stopped short, mid-yawn and mid-stride. "Save us! What's happened, Mr. Shiloh?" she cried.

"Nothing, nothing—well, actually a lot, but nothing you have to be scared about," Shiloh said, jumping up and coming to the door to take Sketes's plump arm. "We've been working—sorta—all night. A while ago we remembered we were tired, so we're having coffee." He spoke somewhat at random, for the four of them actually were exhausted, though they had reached the stage where they were giddy rather than dull-witted.

They had indeed been working all night, finding empty wine bottles, taking them to the butler's pantry in the cellar, pulling out the money, counting the money, and stacking it by denomination. There had been everything from one-hundred-dollar bills to one-dollar bills. Cheney said there was $238,992; Minerva said there was $239,006. Neither Shiloh nor Major Valentine had wanted to count—again—to settle the difference.

Now that Shiloh was looking at the other three through Sketes's eyes, as it were, he could see why she was alarmed. Their faces and clothing were grimy, and Cheney had a spider web in her hair. Minerva's pale blue dress, with icy net gauze trimming on the sleeves, had a black smudge that completely covered one shoulder and made the trim look like it was colored dingy gray. Major Valentine's splendid uniform was so dusty one could only see daubs of blue instead of daubs of dirt. Quickly Shiloh checked himself; he, like the others, was still wearing his evening clothes, though he had long ago taken off his coat. His black breeches had wet dirty patches at the knees, his dress boots were muddy, the sleeves of his white shirt, rolled up, were filthy, and the white stripes could barely be made out on his black-and-white-striped satin waistcoat. "We look like we've been mugged and left for dead," he quipped as he led Sketes into the room. "Take my word for it, I know what that looks like, 'cause I was once, and that's what we look like."

"Whatever have you all been up to all the night?" Sketes asked suspiciously. Dropping Shiloh's arm she went straight to her stove, checked the hot coffeepot, and opened the bread box. "Mm-hmm, not a muffin left." Sketes usually did have some muffins or sweetbreads prepared for night snacks. Last night there had been four orange spice muffins and half a loaf of lemon pecan bread, and now there were only crumbs in the basket.

"We ate 'em all," Shiloh announced as he popped back onto his stool. "They were good too, Sketes, but we're still starving. Can't we have some real breakfast, please?"

"I would have fixed you some breakfast," Cheney said, chiding him. "You didn't tell me you were still hungry."

"No, no, Doc, you're too tired to cook," Shiloh said quickly.

Cheney stared at him suspiciously but only said, "I suppose you're right. In fact, I think I'm too tired to wait for breakfast too. Isn't it funny that when the sun comes up you're automatically exhausted, no matter how you felt five minutes before sunrise?"

Minerva said blankly, "I'm tired too . . . also. Two of us are tired. Too."

Cheney slid off her stool, went around the table, and put her arm around Minerva's shoulder. "That's it; I must take this child and put her to bed. She's talking nonsense, even for Minerva. Good night, Major Valentine. Tell Major Valentine good night, Minerva."

"But—it's sunrise. You said so, Cheney," Minerva mumbled as she allowed Cheney to lead her out.

"Minerva says good sunrise, Major," Cheney said over her shoulder, with a smile. "Good sunrise, Shiloh. Don't stay up all day. You'll be grumpy tonight."

"Yes, wife," he said good-naturedly.

Sketes, who knew very well how hungry men who had been up working all night could get, fixed eggs with cheese, chops, bacon for Shiloh, ham with redeye gravy, and fried jacket potatoes and squeezed a whole half-gallon of fresh orange juice. Shiloh and Major Valentine ate and drank all the juice, plus a second pot of coffee.

As they were finishing up, Shiloh said, "You know, Mr. Grider really was a smart man. He even gave us a clue about the money."

"He did? Well, like the rest of this investigation, the investigator is the last one to see the clues," Major Valentine said. "What clue?"

"Remember the last quote from *Macbeth* in his will? *'The wine of life is drawn, and the mere lees is left this vault to brag of.'*"

"You're right. He was smart," the major agreed. "So are you. Anyway, let's get back to that vault. I've got one last chore before I drag my tired self back to town." He rose and went to Sketes's side, as she was still standing at the stove, preparing breakfast for the others. "Ma'am, that was the best breakfast I've had since I was at my parents' house, and that would be going on two years now." He took her work-reddened plump hand and bowed over it. "I thank you from the bottom of my heart."

Sketes looked pleased. "I'd be pleased to fix you some breakfast any morning, Major, as you're such a gentleman and so kind."

As they left Shiloh said, "She hits me with the spatula when I come in and ask for breakfast."

"It's the uniform," Major Valentine said, winking at Shiloh. "Ladies really like the uniform. But what am I saying, telling you about the ladies? You must know all about the ladies, Shiloh, since you married one of the loveliest, most intell—" He stopped, gave Shiloh a cautious sidelong glance, and continued in a more subdued tone, "Dr. Irons-Winslow is a fine lady, and I think you're a lucky man."

Shiloh grinned and slapped Major Valentine on the back. It was like hitting an oak board. "It's not luck, Major. It never was. It was a miracle of God, and I thank Him every day for it. How else do you think a mutt like me marries up—like way, *way* up?"

The major grinned back at him, admittedly with relief. He hadn't forgotten Shiloh's black looks when he had unwisely showed a little too much admiration for his wife. But then he sobered and said with a studied carelessness, "I didn't think of it that way, Shiloh, and it seems like Mr. and Mrs. Duvall, and the other ladies don't either. For instance, Miss Wilcott doesn't seem to view you as below her social standing, and she and Mrs. Buchanan are obviously from an old and wealthy family. Of course, I guess Miss Wilcott might think that a soldier, that is, an officer might not be . . . er . . . suitable—"

Mercifully Shiloh cut him off. "Hey, Major, compared to my history you're like the king of Siam. But lemme tell you something about Miss Wilcott's family, which I don't know 'cause I've never met them, but I have met Mrs. Steen, her aunt, Mrs. Buchanan's mother. If you were the king of Siam you still probably wouldn't be good enough for the Wilcotts."

Crestfallen, Major Valentine said, "So I don't have a chance, you think."

"I know you don't," Shiloh said breezily, "with Mrs. Steen or Mrs. Wilcott. Neither did Dr. Buchanan, but he just went right ahead and married Victoria anyway. And I have an idea that Miss Wilcott is like Mrs. Buchanan in that way; I think she pretty well does what she wants."

They went in the back door of the Big House, and both of them automatically wiped their boots. The house was still quiet; evidently no one was up yet, and Cheney and Minerva must have simply fallen into bed and passed out. With his voice lowered, Major Valentine said, "Okay, Shiloh, I want you to lock the cellar door, and I want to seal it. You know it's not because I don't trust anyone in this house—"

"Of course, we all know that," Shiloh said quietly. "It's the right thing to do until we can find out how Judge Allard wants to handle the pile of greenbacks down there."

The morning was cool and the air wet and sticky, as it generally was this close to the sea in the southern climes. They went down the dim passageway, and Shiloh pulled the house key ring out of his pocket. After going through a few keys he picked out the cellar key, an old iron one with a long stem and a decorative head. "Man, we been around the world with this cellar," he said. "That day, with the locksmith, when we—" He stopped talking, froze with the key in the lock, stiffened, and stared blankly into the air.

"What?" Major Valentine asked curiously, watching as Shiloh very slowly took the key out of the lock. "What is it, Shiloh? Something wrong with the key?"

"The key . . ." he repeated. "The key. It's always been the key." He held it up, very close to his eyes. "Can't see . . . no way you could see with the naked eye. Microscope, though . . ."

"Are you speaking English?" Major Valentine asked plaintively.

Shiloh looked up from the key and focused on his face. "Let's ride, Major. We got us what you might call another avenue of investigation."

First they had to go to faithful Mr. Duff's. Major Valentine, happily now that he understood what was at stake, told him to bill whatever he thought was fair to the provost marshal's office for the use of his microscope. This made Mr. Duff very happy.

And when Shiloh found traces of beeswax in the decorative etching on the head of the key, it made Shiloh happy. "I was right. Somebody made a copy of this key."

"I know the only locksmith in town, Alfred Bebley," Major Valentine said eagerly. "He was no friend of Louis Grider's, so he'll tell us if he made copies of his keys for anyone."

Shiloh shook his head. "I don't think it was Bebley, Major, but I think I do know who did make the copy. And I think he'll be able to tell us who the killer was." They were in Mr. Duff's back office, and the two big muscular young men simply overpowered the small cluttered room. Shiloh crossed his arms and looked the major up and down. "And I gotta tell you, Valentine, we're gonna scare people to death if we start ridin' up and collaring them and shouting questions in their face. Especially our little locksmith."

"Well, I don't know if we'd scare them, but we'd probably get them pretty dirty."

Shiloh chuckled. "Right. So how's about we make a plan?"

"Does this plan include a bath? If we're going to catch the killer today, I'd like to be wearing a clean uniform."

Shiloh, seeing that he was actually serious, made himself answer, "Sure, Major, I'd kinda like to get cleaned up myself. Now here's what we'll do . . . ."

At precisely three o'clock that afternoon, Shiloh and Major Valentine, now clean—Shiloh with faded but clean denims and a snowy white shirt, Major Valentine in a crisp fresh uniform—rode into Comales. Originally Ramon de Becerra had started the little settlement by building cottages for the workers in the winery, which was just to the east. But as the plantation had grown, the Becerra family brought over more Spanish workers to work the groves, and the cluster of cabins had grown into a village, with a tiny general store, a blacksmith, a livery, and a Catholic church. Dolores Espy had told them that the school was held in the church, but the first thing she planned to do when she got her inheritance was to build a real school.

All of the streets were dirt, including the path from the river crossing and the main street that went all the way out to King's Road. Shiloh and Major Valentine, riding in from the river, took a left on this main street and rode down to the small shed that was the blacksmith's, for Benito Muñoz was not only the locksmith, he was the blacksmith. He was working, a blacksmith's apron tied around his small but sturdy frame, a red-hot horseshoe on the anvil. They heard the *clang, clang* of hammer against iron that they'd both heard thousands of times in their lives on horses. Muñoz didn't hear them until they had ridden right up to the shed. When he did look up, his eyes met Shiloh's and his face fell.

Without a word he put down his hammer, wiped his hands, and came forward, patting the rear end of the horse in the stall that was waiting for his new shoe as he passed him to take the reins of Shiloh's and Major Valentine's horses. They dismounted.

"*Buenos días, Señor Irons-Winslow,*" he said.

"Hello, Mr. Muñoz," Shiloh said. "I'd like to introduce you to a friend of mine, Major Micah Valentine. Major Valentine, this is Mr. Benito Muñoz, who helped us out with the keys when we first got here."

"I'm glad to make your acquaintance, Mr. Muñoz," Major Valentine said pleasantly. "I'm investigating Mr. Louis Grider's death, and I've got some questions I'd like to ask you."

He nodded. "I have been expecting you, señor. I knew you would come sometime." He smoothed Shiloh's horse's nose in a soft, somehow defeated gesture. "I knew you would come."

"Don't worry, Mr. Muñoz, you're not in any trouble," Shiloh said kindly as he tied up their horses. He and the major leaned up against the hitching post while Muñoz kept petting their horses. It seemed to calm both him and the horses.

Major Valentine, in his usual way, asked the simplest question in the most direct manner. "Mr. Muñoz, did anyone from Sangria House or Plantation ever ask you to make a copy of a key?"

Holding Tocoi's bridle and rhythmically stroking his neck, he answered, "Yes, señor."

The major and Shiloh exchanged triumphant glances.

"Who was this person, Mr. Muñoz?" Major Valentine asked.

Two long strokes of the horse's neck.

Shiloh and Major Valentine waited patiently.

Finally Muñoz said, "It was lady. Eh . . . um . . . *la señora importante, de la Casa Sangría.*"

"Okay," Shiloh said slowly. "But which important lady?"

Benito Muñoz looked up at Shiloh, his face mournful. "I don't know, Señor Irons-Winslow. I have never seen any of them except the one lady. She don't tell me her name. And . . . and she tell me . . . if I say . . . say . . ."

"You mean if you tell?" Shiloh asked.

He nodded.

"Nothing's going to happen to you, Mr. Muñoz."

He ducked his head again, his cheek against the horse's neck. Tocoi whinnied softly. "She said that I would lose my house, that me and Rosario and our little Eladio wouldn't have any place to live, that we would be beggars and starve."

Shiloh stepped up to the man, who seemed very small and defenseless next to Shiloh. He laid his hand on his shoulder and said, "That's not going to happen, Mr. Muñoz. I promise you, and Major Valentine promises you, that no one is going to take your house, and no one is going to harm you or your family in any way."

After a moment Muñoz nodded and looked back up at Shiloh. "But I tell the truth, Señor Irons-Winslow. I only see the lady once. I don't see the ladies at the Big House. None of us do."

Major Valentine frowned. "Can you describe her?"

The locksmith made a helpless gesture. "She is—she's a *gringo,* with white skin. I don't know gringo ladies. I don't look up and talk to them."

Shiloh said, "Okay, Mr. Muñoz, you're going to have to go into town with us to see the ladies from Sangria House."

He sighed, a deep indrawn breath. "I'm afraid of this, Señor Irons-Winslow. But I'll go. Father Escalante told me that when this day come, I would have to stand up and tell the truth. And so I will."

Major Valentine and Shiloh waited while he went into his cottage to clean up and change clothes. The afternoon sun was warm, the village quiet. Down the street they could hear some children laughing and calling, but that was the only sound.

"You sleepy?" Shiloh asked the major.

"No. I should be, but I'm not. I tried to nap a little after I cleaned up, but I couldn't go to sleep," he admitted. "I guess I'm kind of excited about getting this solved."

"I am too. But you know, Major, I think you had the right idea the other day when you took Colonel Duvall and Miss Irene with you to talk to the Grider ladies. Maybe we better stop by Sangria House and see if they could go with you again. Especially Miss Irene."

Major Valentine stared steadily at him. "Like I said before, Shiloh, you're pretty smart. In fact, you and your wife deserve the credit for solving this murder. You sure you wouldn't like to come?"

Shiloh shook his head. "No, Major, there's a time and a season for everything. I don't think it's the time for me and the doc to be there when one of those ladies has to admit to being a murderess. I think that's for you, and Miss Irene, and Colonel Duvall. And it's not about credit. Like the man said, it's about the truth. That's all. It's just got to be about the truth."

Major Valentine got out of the brougham on Aviles Street in front of Fatio House, leaned in and said something to the couple inside, then closed the door. He went into the gracious house and came out several minutes later. Going to the brougham, he signaled Benito Muñoz, who sat up in the driver's bench with Andrew Barentine, and then opened the door. "Mrs. Duvall?" he said, folding down the steps and holding out his hand.

With Irene on his arm, he went back into Fatio House, followed by Richard Duvall and, humbly behind him with head bowed, Benito Muñoz. By now Irene knew the way to Mrs. Fatio's sitting room, so she went on up the stairs without waiting for a maid to announce them. She and Major Valentine stepped into the room, followed by Richard and then the little locksmith.

The ladies were seated as they had been the last time Major Valentine and the Duvalls had been there: Aimee Grider in the far corner of the room, with the three sisters on the sofa by the fireplace. They hadn't been told anything except that Major Valentine was required to speak to them again.

Major Valentine and Richard and Irene couldn't help their curiosity. Without saying a word, they watched the faces of the widow and the sisters. The time seemed to stretch out, longer and longer, the tension in the room heavier and heavier. Slowly Benito Muñoz raised his head and looked at the ladies. He was holding his hat in his hands, nervously smoothing the crown in his fingers, around and around. He studied first Aimee Grider, who looked back at him blankly. He dismissed her, and his dark eyes traveled to Letitia Raymond, on the end of the sofa. She looked at him with disdain as he studied her. She opened her mouth to say something, but just at that moment Phillipa Grider, at the other end of the sofa, let out an explosive sob.

"Oh, God. Oh, God, what have I done? God, forgive me. I can't face it anymore. God, forgive me." She bent, her head buried in her hands, and her shoulders shook convulsively.

Sadly Benito Muñoz said, "She is the lady, Señor Major Valentine. She is the lady with the key."

"Thank you, Mr. Muñoz," Major Valentine said. "Why don't you go on down to the courtyard? Tell Mrs. Fatio that I would like to buy you a bottle of Sangria de Becerra and wait for us there."

"Sí, señor," he said and left.

Aimee Grider was watching her sister-in-law with what appeared to be mild surprise. Letitia Raymond, at the opposite end of the sofa, had leaned forward to look at Phillipa, her blue eyes wide and horrified. Next to Phillipa was her sister Muriel, and Muriel looked as shocked as if she had been struck. She hadn't moved. She only stared down at Phillipa's trembling back.

Irene went forward swiftly, knelt down, and put her arms around Phillipa Grider. "Miss Grider, please try to collect yourself. No one is here to harm you, you know, but you are going to feel better once you tell the truth." She looked up. "Go and ask Mrs. Fatio for some brandy, Richard."

As if she were a puppet whose strings had been jerked, Letitia Raymond jumped up and started pacing, three steps forward, three steps back, three forward, three back. "Phillipa . . . Phillipa . . ." she muttered.

Major Valentine, after looking to Aimee Grider and seeing absolutely nothing there, grimaced and went to Mrs. Raymond, who appeared to be about to work herself into hysterics. "Mrs. Raymond?" he said in his quiet deep voice. "Please sit down, ma'am. I don't want you to get over-excited and too upset. We're going to deal with this calmly, without anyone getting hurt, ma'am." He kept talking to her soothingly, in an even tone, until she sat back down and stared around the room with blank tragic eyes.

Next to her Muriel still had not moved, but big tears, many of them, rolled down her cheeks and dripped off her chin. Major Valentine found his clean handkerchief and offered it to her. "Ma'am?" he said softly, holding it out to her. She took it with one limp hand, but she did tear her gaze away from the heap of her sister to look up at him and thank him in an all but inaudible voice.

Mrs. Fatio, a tall, attractive woman with a gracious, calm demeanor, brought in a tray with a brandy decanter and six snifters. With a glance around the room, she poured four generous drinks and took the first one to Phillipa. Kneeling before her by Irene, she reached out and took one of Phillipa's hands. "Here, my dear," she said in a musical, kind voice. "Drink this. You'll feel better, and you'll feel calmer."

"Th-thank you, Louisa," Phillipa said in a shaking voice. "You've always been s-so kind t-to me."

"Of course, dear." Mrs. Fatio rose and served drinks to the other two sisters and Aimee and then left, closing the door quietly behind her.

Phillipa drank deeply, then made a small deep moan as the hot liquor coursed down her throat. The other ladies sipped; some color came back into Letitia's face, the tears stopped rolling down Muriel's face, and even Aimee's stone features relaxed somewhat. She tossed back the rest of her brandy, then rose, went to the tray that Mrs. Fatio had left on a small console by the door, poured herself another generous drink, and turned. "So, Phillipa. I knew I wasn't guilty, but I was just as sure that it couldn't be you. Why did you do it?"

Phillipa looked up, and she looked like a seventy-year-old woman. "I didn't mean to kill him! I never, never meant to kill him!" She sobbed hard, jerking her whole body.

Irene took her shaking hand, covered it with her own, and held the brandy snifter up. "Miss Grider, sip this and take a deep breath. We just want you to tell us exactly what happened. We want to understand."

It took several minutes for Irene to get the woman calmed down enough to be able to talk, but finally she sat, a small forlorn huddle clutching the brandy snifter as if it were the only thing she had left in the world. Her eyes were glazed and unfocused, but she was coherent as she told the story of how she had poisoned her own brother.

"It all started back in December," she said in a bloodless, almost inhuman voice. "Louis had been sick since December third. It was the same as it always was—first a slight catarrh, then a fever, then the influenza, and finally pneumonia. I nursed him . . . I always nursed him. I took very good care of him. No one could get him well as fast as I could. I just knew how to take care of him. I've been doing it for so very, very long."

She took a sip of brandy, shuddered slightly, and then continued, "And so, by the third week in December, he was well enough to get up and attend to business, at least in the mornings, though he still had to rest in the afternoons. He and Aimee—" she shot a venomous look at Aimee, and the younger woman looked startled—"had started talking about going to England, to Bath, for treatments for Louis. And though I was his nurse, though I was the only person who could help him, neither one of you ever asked me once what I thought about it! Not once! And . . . and . . . it made me feel so . . . useless, so stupid, like I was only good for changing Louis's bed and measuring out his stupid tonic and washing the cloths I held on his head, night after night when he was fevered." She took another sip of brandy. Aimee started to say something, but Major Valentine made a small signal and she closed her mouth.

Phillipa didn't notice this or anything else in the room. Her eyes were staring, but she didn't see the room or the people in it; she was seeing the past, perhaps for the first time since her brother had died. "I was always useless. I never meant anything to Louis anyway," she said dully. "Letitia could handle the business; Aimee he loved like some besotted fool; Muriel could cook and sew. I couldn't even do that. All I was ever good at was taking care of Louis when he was sick. That's the only time he ever asked for me. When he was sick. Even then I knew it wasn't because he loved me so much that I was a comfort to him; it's just that I learned how to be quiet and not to fuss, and to be gentle when I tended to him. He didn't like to be . . . fussed over. He didn't like banging about and busyness. He liked calm and quiet, and sometimes I would sit by his bed for hours, not even reading, just sitting there and changing out the cool cloths on his forehead. He never said thank you, but I thought—I thought—he did appreciate me, even if he never said so.

"And then—then that awful Christmas Eve," she said, and her voice got painfully raw. "He was better, and he went down to the office to work a little. And he said—he came back up to the morning room where we all were, and he said—he said you had stolen money, Letitia. Stolen from his desk while you were tending the plantation business." She turned and stared, with burning eyes, accusingly at Letitia Raymond.

Mrs. Raymond laid a shaking hand on her breast. "I . . . I didn't steal any money from the cashbox, Phillipa! I just did not steal the money, and that's the truth!"

"But you said I did!" Phillipa burst out. "Why did you say that? Why me? Why not Muriel, or even Aimee? Why did you have to say that I took it? You know why, Letitia? Because none of you care about me at all, and you knew Louis didn't care for me at all, and so you all thought, 'Oh, let Phillipa take the blame. She doesn't matter anyway!'"

"That's . . . that's not true, Phillipa," Muriel said weakly. "You're my full sister, and I . . . I do care about you. It's just that I didn't take the money either. So . . . so . . ."

Phillipa nodded, now wearily. "So I must have done it. Just as I said. It doesn't really matter if Phillipa took it. Louis doesn't care about her anyway. It won't change our lives if hers is ruined. Aimee had her husband, Letitia had her brother, Muriel had her Mr. Pendergast. I had nothing. I had no one. And now Louis thought I was a thief and that I had stolen from him. You were all there. You heard what he said. He said I was so ungrateful to steal from him after he had given me a home. He said he ought to let me try to make my own way in this cold uncaring world, then I'd see how long it took to make fifty dollars. He said he might send me back to Boston to see if I could make my own way. He said—he said—he might not take me to England with you." Tears filled her stricken eyes again, and she bent her head and sobbed. Irene, who had taken the chair across from the sofa, hurried to give her a clean handkerchief and to refill her brandy.

In the loaded silence, Major Valentine stated in a hard voice, "I don't believe Miss Phillipa did take that money. So who did?" He was staring hard at Aimee Grider.

She swallowed, then tipped her chin up high in the air. "I did. It wasn't stealing, of course. Louis always gave me whatever I asked for. But he was sick, and I . . . I needed the money for . . . something."

"For what?" Major Valentine demanded in a commanding voice.

"It was a . . . a gold nugget," she said, with the only trace of shame they had ever heard from her. "I had seen them at Cathcart Jewelers early that month, when Louis was still very sick, so I couldn't ask him for the money. Besides, it was for a Christmas gift for him! He had everything. It was so hard to buy gifts for him, and I thought it would be . . . fun, for a paperweight or something. Anyway, I just took fifty dollars from the cashbox in his desk."

Muriel looked at her, horrified. "Aimee, you never gave him a gold nugget for Christmas!"

"I know that!" she snapped. "I decided to keep it after all. Louis would just have thought it was silly."

"But, don't you realize . . . what's happened?" Muriel was so staggered at the awful results of Aimee's uncaring lies and her continued carelessness about it that she finally made an odd little gagging sound and then grew silent.

Letitia seemed not to have understood what had been said, she was so dazed. Now she turned her focus on Aimee. "You have keys to Louis's desk?" she asked, bewildered.

"No," Aimee muttered, dropping her gaze to the amber liquid in the balloon snifter and swirling it in slow circles. "The drawer above it is the one with the stationery in it, so Louis always unlocked that one. If you take it out, right underneath it is the cashbox."

Letitia narrowed her eyes to slits. "Why, you sly little—"

"Oh, be quiet, Letitia. You're only upset because you didn't think of it," Aimee snapped.

Phillipa's tragic gaze went back and forth from Letitia to Aimee. "You mean—you mean you took that money, and you lied and told Louis that I took it? When he wouldn't even have cared if you had knocked him in the head and robbed him?"

Uncomfortably Aimee said, "I . . . Actually, Phillipa, I had forgotten about it by Christmas. To tell the truth I wasn't really paying attention to what Louis was saying that morning. I just dismissed it as more plantation business. If you remember, I didn't say a word, not a word. I didn't say a thing about you."

Phillipa sat back. The shock on her face and in her posture were evident. "No . . . no, now that I think about it, you didn't say a word. My entire life was ruined that morning, in that room . . . and it was all because of a stupid *rock* that you thought you had to have? And you weren't even paying attention?"

"I'm sorry," Aimee said stiffly.

But the inadequacy of it was evident even to her, so she did at least have the grace to drop her head and stare into her brandy again.

Letitia's head swiveled back to Phillipa. The skin seemed stretched too tightly across her high sharp cheekbones, and her eyes burned. "Phillipa, I thought . . . I thought just as you did that it couldn't have been Aimee. She never had to steal from Louis, he was such a fool over her. That's why I thought it must have been you."

"Why not Muriel?" Phillipa asked in a dead voice.

Letitia opened her mouth, closed it, swallowed, and opened it again, but no sound came out. She, too, dropped her head, averting her eyes from Phillipa.

Phillipa looked now at Muriel. "You didn't accuse me, but you didn't take up for me either. You didn't defend me."

"I'm . . . I'm sorry, dear," Muriel whispered and tried to take Phillipa's hand, but Phillipa jerked it back as if Muriel's touch had burned her. "I just didn't realize how hard it was for you."

"No, you didn't, you didn't. Because of everyone in the house, I mattered least. I was the last one considered. I was the last one consulted. And I was the last one that mattered," she said with painful bitterness.

"I'm . . . I truly am sorry, sister dear," Muriel whispered again and started crying softly.

Phillipa sat crumpled up, leaning backward at an awkward angle like a stone, staring blankly into space.

After long moments Major Valentine spoke. "Miss Phillipa, I still don't understand. I have to admit I can see why you might have had a grudge against Mrs. Grider and Mrs. Raymond and maybe even Miss Grider. But your brother was your sole support. Even though he was cruel to you, he did take care of you. Why did you decide to kill him?"

"But I didn't," she cried pitifully. "Don't you see? I didn't want him to die! I just . . . I just wanted him to get sick. Not deathly ill, but just ill enough that he would need me again, that he would remember how much he liked for me to take care of him, that he would remember that when I was taking care of him, he almost liked me. He liked having me around, only me! So I went and got the key to the cellar made, and I took some of the insecticide from the winery. And I just put tiny, tiny bits—just one or two little crumbs—I could barely see it!—in his wine."

"You thought it was arsenic," Richard said quietly. "It doesn't take much arsenic at all to make a person very ill."

"I know, and that's why I made sure I only gave him the tiniest crumb imaginable," she sobbed. "But . . . but he never got sick. So I . . . I put a little more in a few days later. And then he was still not sick, so—I don't know, I kept putting tiny, tiny little bits in his wine, but he never showed any symptoms at all!"

"But he was," Letitia said, horrified. "He became so fearful, so afraid of . . . of nothing, suspicious of all of us, so that he finally sent us all away, half crazed, thinking that we were trying to—"

"Steal from him? That you hated him? Wanted to hurt him?" Phillipa asked with sarcasm dripping from her voice. "And how did that make you feel, Letitia? When the only person standing between you and the gutter suddenly decided he didn't want to have anything to do with you anymore?"

Muriel jerked, her eyes suddenly aware. Even Aimee's shadowed eyes widened a bit, and she swallowed hard. Letitia's mouth actually fell open, and she gaped; then she shut it with an audible snap.

Once again Phillipa seemed to crumple, and all of the fight went out of her. "I didn't want to kill him. When he died I was so horrified, so anguished. I never meant to kill him. I didn't . . . I never . . . wanted him to die . . . I never . . ." She stared blankly and kept mumbling. Her hands grew lax, and quickly Muriel took the brandy snifter out of them, for it was tipping.

Muriel turned to Major Valentine. "She's obviously in shock. Must you take her to prison, or arrest her, tonight?"

Major Valentine, seated across from Aimee, frowned. "I'm not sure, ma'am, but my inclination is to put her under a doctor's care, at least for tonight, and see if she is better tomorrow."

Muriel said, "I will guarantee that she won't try to escape, Major. I will stand for her."

Letitia suddenly jumped up, so naturally the men in the room jumped to their feet. "I will stand for her too, Major Valentine. I will send for Dr. Duff, and I will take care of her tonight, and we will all see you again tomorrow. Then you may do whatever you think is best."

Major Valentine nodded. "All right, ma'am. But don't worry. We'll take our leave now, and I'll send for Dr. Duff."

Irene and Richard walked toward the door. Letitia Raymond, her voice hard but determined, called out, "Colonel and Mrs. Duvall? Thank you for your solicitations. I'm very glad you were here for my . . . for my sister. She needed you, and you helped her."

Irene turned, and there was no mistaking the sweetness in her face. "The Lord be with you, Mrs. Raymond, and with all of you on this night. Richard and I will pray for you, and tomorrow we shall send to see how we might help you with whatever comes. God bless you all and watch over you, and good night."

CHAPTER TWENTY-THREE

Locke's Dream

RAINSFORD HOUSE WAS NOT as opulent as the Rainsford's houses in New York, Cape May, and Boston had been, but the large two-story house had fifteen-foot-high ceilings so that the tropical heat rose, leaving the living areas comfortably cool. Ivy Rainsford had decorated the rooms herself in complete opposition from the stuffy, dark, crowded, gilded rooms of fashionable palaces from America to St. Petersburg. All of the rooms were light, with soft furnishings of pale colors, cleverly woven sea-grass mats, and accessories that added to the graciousness of the rooms rather than merely crowding them into cluttered anonymity.

She also had decided, when they built Rainsford House in the tiny little backwater village of St. Augustine, that she would have a ballroom. Her husband, Samuel, who would have built her the Taj Mahal if she'd wanted it, added a gracious long ballroom on the second floor, with an orchestra box high above the dance floor on one side and a graceful bal-ustraded gallery. On the other side, which overlooked Ivy Rainsford's exquisite rose garden, huge arched windows took up the entire wall, with two sets of double glass doors leading out onto a stone balcony.

On this warm, delightful March night, the box was crowded with a twenty-piece orchestra, and the dance floor was not crowded but was comfortably filled with sixty-four people. Eight quadrille sets of four couples each stood like Greek statues in their squares, waiting for the music to begin. The first strains of the violins playing a Corelli opus began, and the statues miraculously began to move.

One quadrille set consisted of the host and hostess, Samuel and Ivy Rainsford, Colonel and Mrs. Richard Duvall, Shiloh Irons-Winslow, his wife, Dr. Irons-Winslow, and Miss Minerva Wilcott and her escort, Major Micah Valentine. Without speaking they went through the complex first steps, for Major Valentine was not completely comfortable with the old dance. He had only learned that afternoon while calling on Miss Wilcott, as he did every day now, that Mrs. Rainsford was an old-fashioned hostess who always opened her balls with the quadrille. Major Valentine had never seen a quadrille, much less danced one, so although the ball was just opening with this first dance, he and Minerva, with Shiloh and Cheney helping out, had actually been figuring away all afternoon.

Major Valentine, after the first tense minutes, visibly began to relax. The strain on his face lessened considerably, and Shiloh said—in a low tone so the Rainsfords couldn't hear as they passed in the figures—"Hey, Major, you're not doing night maneuvers in enemy territory. Relax. This is what's called having fun."

"Yeah, it's coming back to me now," he growled. "Fun. I remember it, vaguely."

"I can't believe you're doing so well, Major Valentine," Minerva whispered encouragingly. "It took me much longer to learn the quadrille." They were at a place in the steps where they stood together for a few moments.

"It did?" he asked.

"It did. My dancing master practically gave up on me, but my father made him keep on drilling it into me until I learned it," Minerva said, her blue eyes wide. "And he finally quit, but I think it was because my brothers kept putting frogs in his dancing shoes, not because I couldn't learn the quadrille."

"Probably," Major Valentine gravely agreed, "because you dance beautifully, Miss Wilcott."

"Thank you, Major Valentine," she said with delight.

"You're very welcome, ma'am." Then it was time for them to do some figuring again, so they danced.

Shiloh and Cheney, having overheard them, exchanged knowing, amused glances. Major Valentine and Minerva Wilcott were very well suited—at least their personalities were. They were both amiable people, easily pleased and easily entertained. Neither of them was a flaming genius, and they both knew it. Cheney and Shiloh had discussed Cheney and Dev's partner, Dr. Cleve Batson, for he had been escorting Minerva off and on for the last year that she had been living with Victoria and Dev. But Shiloh, who was generally more intuitive about these things than

Cheney, thought that Cleve and Minerva had been more a partnership of convenience and friendship than anything else, and that Cleve likely wouldn't be upset about what was obviously now a courtship. "He's probably found another pretty girl to squire around town while Miss Wilcott's been down here," Shiloh told Cheney. "You know Cleve, Doc; he never gets too exercised about things."

Thinking about it, Cheney had seen the truth in it, and she was glad, because she liked Cleve Batson and would have hated for him to be hurt. The realization meant that she had been having more fun with Minerva and Major Valentine, for in the last two weeks since Miss Phillipa Grider had confessed to poisoning her brother, the two couples had been together quite a bit, picnicking, enjoying the beach, meeting Major Valentine in the courtyard at Fatio's for high tea, and now, at the Rainsfords' Grand Spring Ball, which was always held the evening before Palm Sunday. This year it was March 23.

Cheney, as they went through the slow dignified figures of the dance, watched her parents with happiness. Both of them looked better and stronger than they had in months. Irene glowed in a gleaming wine-colored satin ball gown with black Chantilly lace trim, and Richard, splendidly handsome in black tie and tails, showed no trace of a limp, his eyes sparkling as he watched his elegant wife. Even Dev, who sometimes showed slight impatience with the old slow dances, danced with great dignity and dark grace, and of course Victoria, as always, was like a silver-and-diamond sylph, in white satin with mint green trim and showers of diamonds in her silvery blond hair.

A cotillion, another dignified two-hundred-year-old dance, followed the quadrille, and then, finally to the delight of the younger dancers, the waltz.

After that, they all agreed to take a break, for the next dance was a polka, and they were all thirsty. The Rainsfords excused themselves to go speak to other guests. Irene and Richard went out on the balcony, while Minerva, Victoria, and Cheney took their seats on the side chairs by the doors leading out onto the balcony. A warm breeze, scented with Mrs. Rainsford's old roses, floated in. The gentlemen went to fetch everyone fruit ices. Victoria watched Dev as if she couldn't bear to lose sight of him. Next to her Cheney grumbled, "I can't believe he came down early and took my last weekend. Now Shiloh and I have to go back tomorrow instead of Monday. That's so unlike Dev. He's never impulsive; he's always so dull and dutiful. He must be in love."

Victoria turned to Cheney and smiled as brilliantly as a thousand stars. "Never in my life, Cheney, did I suspect that I would be so happy, that I could love a man like Dev so much, and that he would love me the way he does. I cannot thank the Lord enough. I do thank Him, every day, but I don't think it will ever be enough."

She took Cheney's hand, and though Cheney was not at all a demonstrative woman, she allowed it, smiling affectionately at her friend. "I know. Shiloh and I are such a miracle too. Sometimes when I wake up, just before I open my eyes, I think, was it just a wonderful dream? Is it real? Can I possibly be this blessed? And then, of course, the dogs jump on me and Shiloh grumbles that I've slept late again, and I do know that it is real, that the Lord is good and faithful and true, and that He does bless us mightily."

"He does," Shiloh agreed, appearing to hand Cheney her lime ice. "I assume you're talkin' 'bout me, o'course. Being your biggest blessing and all."

"Actually I was talking about Sean and Shannon," Cheney said brightly. "I do so love those puppies!"

"Yeah, but you love me too." Shiloh turned to Dev, who had taken some ices out to Richard and Irene and now handed Victoria her cherry ice. As he bent over, he whispered something in her ear that made her eyes glow and her cheeks blush a very delicate pink. "Yeah, she loves me," Shiloh muttered to Dev's back. "The doc, she's crazy 'bout me."

Dev straightened, smiling, and his deep dimples flashed on each side of his mustache. Even now, though they had been married for two years, Victoria, watching him, looked like a half-swooning young girl. "You say something to me, Shiloh?" Dev asked.

"Yeah, but that's okay. Nobody cares what I was saying anyway," Shiloh said dryly. "Like, I had plans with my wife down here in this tropical paradise this weekend, but now we gotta go back to town, and did I hear you say it was snowing when you left, Buchanan?"

"It was," he said unrepentantly. "And really cold too. Down in the teens, I heard. I was very glad to leave town."

Cheney sighed. "It seems that I didn't have much of a vacation. It seems, now that I look back on it, that I spent most of my time doing autopsies and peering into microscopes and filling out reports and testifying in court."

"Doc, nobody feels sorry for you," Shiloh said. "Everyone here knows that you would have been bored to kingdom come if you hadn't had a dead body and poison and slides of brain tissue and jars full of kidney pieces to play around with."

"But that's—that's . . . Oh, Shiloh, you had fun too! Admit it! I mean, not of course, that we thought it was fun that poor Mr. Grider got poisoned and was dead and everything, but—well, we did learn a lot and that is fun, isn't it?"

Minerva, sitting by Victoria, rolled her eyes. "Major Valentine, I am so, so glad that I have found a friend who doesn't think squishing your hands around in jars of body bits is fun."

"No, ma'am, I don't," he agreed heartily. "I think waltzes are fun. Would you do me the honor, Miss Wilcott?"

"Of course, sir," she said eagerly, and they whisked away.

Looking after them, Dev grunted, "Well, he seems like a fine gentleman, but he just doesn't know how to have a good time, does he? Cheney, I must say I'm a little envious, since I'm probably not going to have an interesting case such as you had to work on while I'm here."

"I have plenty of things for you to work on while you're here, Dev," Victoria said sweetly.

With surprise he said, "Oh? You said work?"

"Yes. You are going to work on the art of napping in a chaise longue in the afternoon out in the courtyard of Sangria House. You are going to work on sleeping late, and by that you may be sure I mean later than six o'clock. You are going to work on your whist game, because when I can make you concentrate, you are a wonderful player, and your mother and father have beaten me and Minerva so soundly that I'm quite embarrassed for anyone to ever know about the games. And—and—you are going to learn how to swim, because Dart and Solange love it, and Beckett and Carsten are going to teach you, and then we are going to find a private beach and you will teach me, like Shiloh taught Cheney." Breathless, she stopped, her cheeks rosy.

Dev said sternly, "I have already promised you that I will become a libertine, my dear, but I had no idea of the depths of worthlessness you were going to require of me. As you say, I will have to work at it; but I am an intelligent man, and I believe I can become as lazy and decadent as you would like."

"I don't," Cheney declared. "I'm going to make Mother write me, because she'll be an honest witness. I predict that Dev will be his usual hardworking, dedicated, selfless physician self within a matter of days."

"Give the man a chance, Doc," Shiloh said. "Every man has to work to find his own path downward. Check with me later, Buchanan, I got lotsa suggestions that might help you out."

This nonsense went on for a while until Richard and Irene came back in to join the four of them. Irene said, "Shiloh, I must admit I do miss Mr. Winslow. He is a charming and witty dinner companion and such a good dancer. Ivy told me all the young ladies were heartbroken to hear he wouldn't be attending tonight."

Shiloh said, "I invited him to sail back to New York with us on *Locke's Day Dream,* but I guess he wasn't quite ready for that. And I got the impression that he was feeling a bit of . . . pressure, you might say, to . . . leave," he finished lamely, mindful of the ladies.

But Victoria Elizabeth Steen de Lancie Buchanan had long been a lady who spoke her mind, and she said, "You mean that awful Aimee Grider chased him off. Imagine, the woman actually threatened to move to Bequia! I would guess that poor Mr. Winslow was terrified!"

"Doubt that," Shiloh said, grinning in spite of himself. "But Sweet sure was. Bain installed him in the cottage with him to sort of . . . forestall . . . unwanted visitors. But some unwanted visitors would not be forestalled, and so most of the time Sweet was running back to the yacht with his pillow and blanket, hiding from the . . . uh . . . unforestalled lady visitor."

"Poor old Sweet," Cheney said. "Bain does lead him a merry chase. And it is sad that Aimee Grider went back to Boston the day after Bain left. But I did invite our cousin to visit us as soon as he can. I hope he'll be back this summer, when he brings Beckett and Carsten their new yacht."

"Speaking of my disreputable brothers, who is that lady with which Beckett has now danced three times? He knows better than that," Victoria said, spying Beckett waltzing merrily at the other end of the ballroom with a bright-eyed redhead who looked to be in her late twenties. "And she looks older than he."

"I believe that is Mrs. Ewing," Irene said delicately.

"Mrs.? Oh, please, Miss Irene, please tell me she isn't married," Victoria pleaded.

"I'm afraid that is Mr. Ewing over there, speaking with Mr. Rainsford."

Victoria saw a man of about sixty, a dignified balding man with a pince-nez, talking to Samuel Rainsford. "Oh no, no," she moaned. "I am going to pinch Beckett's head! You'd think he and Carsten would have learned their lesson, making fools of themselves as they did dancing attendance on Aimee Grider. But no, they never seem to learn anything. I declare, Dev, they couldn't produce an entire brain between them. I'm so glad Dart won't be like that. You can already tell that he's smarter than those two combined."

"You can, can't you?" Dev proudly agreed.

Irene and Richard exchanged knowing looks. Having raised Dev, who had always been a calm, well-behaved, obedient boy, and Cheney, who was very bright, curious, always into something, always causing trouble, and generally running circles around the entire household, they recognized the kind of boy Dart was. He was certainly nothing like his half brother, Devlin. Already Dart had reminded them of Cheney's childhood like nothing and no one else ever had. But they were the grandparents, and with a mutual glance of relief, their look signaled *Not our problem; we get to give him back when the trouble starts.*

"Actually, Victoria, I don't think there will be a repeat of the difficulties that Beckett and Carsten had with Mrs. Grider," Irene said tactfully. "Mr. Ewing is the president of Samuel's bank here, and Richard and I met him and his wife at Ivy's when we had dinner with them after church last Sunday. The Ewings seem genuinely suited and happy. She is high spirited, and he has a wonderfully sharp wit, and she and Mr. Ewing laugh with each other as if they were still courting."

"Oh, that won't matter to Beckett and Carsten. They're perfectly capable of making fools of themselves, even if no one helps them, as Aimee Grider did." Victoria sighed. "Anyway, at least she's gone. And I haven't mentioned this before, but since you and Cheney are leaving early, Shiloh, I thought I'd let you know that Mr. Henry Pendergast, Esquire, has approached me with a very interesting business proposition."

"Don't you mean Mr. Henry Mortimer *Albert* Pendergast, Esquire?" Cheney corrected her sternly.

"The very same, pardon me. Can you guess whom he represented?" Victoria asked mischievously.

"Gotta be Miss Muriel Grider, his betrothed," Shiloh answered. "But that's too easy. Lemme see . . . Mrs. Letitia Grider Raymond?"

"Yes," Victoria answered. "She is a party to the proposal too—along with Miss Dolores Espy."

"Really?" Cheney exclaimed. "The Grider ladies are making some business arrangements with Miss Espy?"

"Yes, they are, and I must admit it's a bit of a surprise to me,"

Victoria answered. "But everyone in this Shakespearean tragedy is behaving very admirably—now, at least." She made a quick sweep of the dance floor and saw Minerva and Micah Valentine down at the end, having finished the waltz. They were now at the refreshments table, talking to Beckett and Carsten and two giggling young blond debutantes who looked like sisters. Victoria went on in a subdued voice, since the music had not started again, "Major Valentine was very worried about prosecuting Miss Phillipa Grider after he heard her story and, indeed, the way Miss Muriel and Miss Letitia came to her defense. For all of our teasing and making fun of him, I think it is extremely generous and charitable of Mr. Pendergast to offer to take in his sister-in-law when he and Miss Muriel marry. There aren't many citizens of such spotless repute in this town that Judge Allard would have considered releasing a murderess to their recognizance. There are far fewer that would ever take on such a burden."

"It's more than that. It's heroic of him," Irene said firmly. "Ivy and I have discussed it, and we've instructed Samuel to request that Mr. Pendergast send us wedding invitations."

Cheney looked at her mother with surprise that turned to admiration. Muriel Grider, under normal circumstances, would never consider getting married while still in mourning for her brother's death; and Mr. Pendergast was also such a proper gentleman that it likely would have been distasteful to him too.

But Judge Allard, when sentencing Phillipa Grider after she pled guilty to manslaughter, had made an allowance that she might serve her sentence under the recognizance of her sister Muriel and Henry Pendergast after they were married. Until then, Miss Grider was incarcerated in the St. Augustine jail. So it had become known that Muriel Grider and Henry Pendergast were planning their wedding on Tuesday, April 2. The couple had decided to marry hurriedly and to move into Mr. Pendergast's small home until they could make other arrangements. Although Muriel Grider, under the terms of her brother's will, had received a settlement that made her a wealthy woman and so had many other options available to her, she seemed to be genuinely dedicated to taking care of her sister, and so also did Mr. Pendergast. But the furtive courtship, and now the hurried wedding after such a scandal, had definitely smeared their names. But the blessing of Samuel and Ivy Rainsford—and also of Colonel and Mrs. Richard Duvall, Cheney realized—would certainly reestablish the Grider sisters and Henry Pendergast in their proper social standing.

"That is an excellent idea, Miss Irene," Victoria said. "Please ask Mr. Rainsford to also include the Buchanans on the guest list."

"But you said that the business proposition also included Dolores Espy?" Shiloh persisted. "What's that about?"

"It seems that once the estate was settled and Miss Phillipa's fate settled under as favorable circumstances as could be hoped for, apparently Mrs. Raymond and Miss Muriel decided to establish a connection with Miss Espy—and with Timmy," Victoria told them. "He is, after all, their nephew. Mr. Pendergast, while explaining the situation to me in context with the business we were discussing, told me that the Grider family died out with Mr. Louis Grider; there are no more male members of the line. And, in fact, the sisters have no other relatives except distant relatives of their mother's families. Timothy Espy is, in fact, the last connection with their brother. So Mrs. Raymond and Miss Grider met with Miss Espy, and they began to try to make plans for the future so that the sisters wouldn't be utterly cut off from Timothy. They had discovered that they wanted to be a part of his life, and they wanted him to know about his father and not to be ashamed. After all, Mrs. Raymond and Miss Muriel were having to learn not to be ashamed of their own sister, and so they came to the conclusion that perhaps Dolores Espy was not such a bad person after all."

"So some good has come from this tragedy," Dev said quietly. "Illegitimate children can suffer terribly, you know, and I think there are few greater injustices." His half brother, Dart, was illegitimate, and he and Victoria had not tried to make his life a lie, and it had already caused them some pain.

It had caused Irene and Richard Duvall pain too, for they loved Dart as much as if he had been their own blood grandchild. Richard said, "But God is the father of the fatherless, and He is just and true. Shiloh tells me that Dolores Espy is a strong Christian woman, and now Mr. and Mrs. Espy will give Timothy a Christian home too. The Lord will bless him, I know."

"That's true," Victoria said softly. "The Lord will surround him with love, just as He's given us Dart to love." Dev, standing close to her, took her hand, and she smiled up at him. He didn't smile back; Dev was a somber man, generally, but his dark eyes were warm. Victoria turned back to them and said, "Basically, what the Grider sisters would like to do is to buy Sangria Plantation—the groves, the land, the tenant farmers' properties in Comales, and the winery. They don't want the house—

LYNN MORRIS & GILBERT MORRIS

unsurprisingly—so Mr. Pendergast set up a new lease-purchase agreement between me and Miss Espy, who is the new owner of Sangria property, and between her and Letitia Raymond and Miss Phillipa Grider. It's complicated, but basically I could buy Sangria House and grounds and the outbuildings, but the new contract severs all connection to the plantation and winery."

"Are you going to buy it?" Shiloh asked.

"I'm considering it," Victoria answered. "I want to see if Dev likes it. If I could kidnap him down here for a month every winter, it would be well worth it."

"I'm not making any promises until I've learned to swim and the exact procedure for taking naps," Dev said with mock gravity. "All of this fun may be too difficult for me."

"You'll have to try very hard, dear," Victoria said sweetly. "For me."

"So Mrs. Raymond wants Sangria Plantation after all, huh," Shiloh speculated. "Everyone did say she was a good businesswoman. But where is she planning to live?"

"That's where the partnership with Dolores Espy comes in," Victoria answered with a smile. "Evidently Mrs. Raymond and Miss Grider— soon to be Mrs. Pendergast—want to stay here, and they've decided to work on some real estate projects in Comales. Miss Espy had already decided to build a house there for her and her parents, and also a schoolhouse. Now all of Comales is owned by Sangria Plantation, you see. Originally it was just really servants' quarters. So Mrs. Raymond and Mr. Pendergast believe that they might build some housing there, beginning with houses for themselves, and some better houses for the tenant farmers and winery workers. Though Mr. Pendergast and I had originally just discussed my lease-purchase agreement, I grew interested in his plans. He may not be the most dynamic gentleman I've ever met, but he is extremely intelligent and shrewd."

"Not like young people these days," Shiloh said in a credible imitation of Henry Pendergast's dry, precise voice.

"Shiloh, for shame. We said we weren't going to make fun of him anymore," Cheney chided him.

He took her hand and pulled her to her feet. "Come waltz with me, Doc, and I'll tell you how sorry I am." He whirled her away, quite dramatically, for Shiloh was an extremely good dancer, and with his tall, muscular figure and Cheney's vibrant glamorous looks, they commanded the attention of everyone in the room.

But they didn't appear to notice. They only saw each other.

She smiled up at him. "You don't have to tell me how sorry you are. I already know."

"Yeah, but you're crazy 'bout me anyway," he said gravely. "You can't help it."

"No, I can't," she said softly. "I never could."

They waltzed, looking into each other's eyes, circling the floor, whirling in the three-step circles that make everyone who is fortunate enough to waltz with someone they love feel giddy and exhilarated all at once.

Before Cheney realized what was happening, Shiloh had swept her out the double doors onto the balcony, down to the far end where there were no windows into the ballroom. He stopped, pulled her to him, and kissed her. Breathlessly she pressed close to him, clasping her arms as tightly as she could around his neck. His hands encircled her small waist. The kiss was long and sweet. When they separated, they turned toward the moon, a huge half-moon that hung low on the horizon and was covered with a wispy amber haze. The breeze had died, and now only light airs brought them the scent of the roses and, distant and faint, the ever-present smell of the sea. Shiloh, without realizing it, lifted his face and sniffed appreciatively.

Cheney looked up at him. "*Locke's Day Dream* is just over there, Locke, waiting for you."

"For us, Cheney. Always for us," he said in a low voice and bent to kiss her fragrant hair. It smelled of jasmine and was soft on his face. "Do you mind? That I love that ship so?"

"Not at all, my darling," she whispered. "It's one thing that I have come to love about being your wife. Wherever you go, you always keep the sea close. Wherever we are, *Locke's Day Dream* is always there to sail us away, to anywhere we want to go, to anywhere we dream of. Because the sea and the ship are a part of you, Shiloh, they're a part of me. I love them too."

They both looked again at the moon, the gold-veiled moon. "There's a tide at midnight," Shiloh said dreamily.

"Then let's sail away, Locke. Let's just sail away home."

He went down on one knee and raised the hem of her skirt to his lips, just as he had when he had asked her to be his wife. He looked up at her, his face strong and stark in the gauzy moonlight. "Cheney . . . you are my only home."